DEADLINE TO DAMNATION

SONS OF TEMPLAR #7

ANNE MALCOM

To everyone who has been here since Making the Cut. Thank you for making my dreams come true.

CHAPTER ONE

"DO YOU TRUST ME?" he asked, holding out his hand.

I took it without hesitation. Everything I did with Liam was without hesitation.

He grinned, teeth white and straight, smile melting my heart the exact same way it had in the halls of Castle Springs High School two years ago.

He glanced down at the twinkling water below us, then back to me, his eyes carved emeralds. They were brighter when he was happy. They almost glowed now. Especially when they run up and down my swimsuit-clad body.

I blushed under the heat of his gaze. The *knowing*. And he did know my body. Every inch. Since he'd taken my virginity six months ago and treated it like a gift. Treated *me* like a gift. A treasure.

"You want me to go first, wait for you below, or you want to take the leap with me?"

Again, there was no hesitation. "I want to take the leap with you."

Something moved in his eyes, they brightened, with the

mischievous glint that he was known for as a teenage boy. But something else, something that belonged on the face of a man. Which was what he was turning into. His lean muscles were bulking up. His face was getting sharper, more straight edges. And then there was the way he made me feel like a woman. Only a man could do that.

His grip tightened on my hand as he yanked me in, kissing me brutally and beautifully. I melted in his arms.

His eyes were dark when he pulled back, dark with a man's desire. He glanced down to my bikini again. With hunger.

My stomach flipped. And it had nothing to do with the cliff we were about to hurl ourselves off of.

"Ready?" he murmured.

"Always," I whispered back.

Then we jumped.

Together.

"WHY ARE YOU DOING THIS?" I demanded, ripping myself from his arms. Something I'd never done before, his arms were the place I'd live forever if I could.

Where I'd planned to live forever.

Until he told me *his* plans.

Plans that he'd made without telling me. While promising us a future. While we talked about our marriage, made a blueprint for an entire lifetime. He was making those promises to me while making life-changing decisions without me.

Decisions that would take him to a war half a world away, without a promise of return.

"Because it's something I have to do, babe," he said, voice hard. I'd never heard it like that before. "You know that."

"No, I don't know *anything!*" I screamed. I'd never screamed at him before. "I thought I knew you. Knew *us*. And now you want to take yourself away from everything to fight in a war that isn't even yours?"

Those hard edges I'd noticed in the softness of today sharpened even more. Sharp enough to cut. There was no boy from today left. "It *is* my war," he replied. "And yours." He paused, running his hands through his hair as he did when he was frustrated. It was silky, long. I loved to run my fingers through it. It'd be short, gone like the boy of today when the army shaved off his hair and his youth. I took it all in. The hair. The emerald eyes, his handsome, breathtaking face. The one that stole all the girl's hearts at school, but the one who'd only been focused on me.

And he'd never looked at me like this before. With this hardness. With something missing. He was detaching himself from me. Already. The decision was made. Cold terror washed over me. I'd been so confident of the control I had over my life, blissfully happy, wandering around town with a small but heavy diamond on my finger and love in my heart. I'd never had a reason to guard my happiness, I'd grown up in a good family who nurtured me, I hadn't experienced hardship or real tragedy. I saw it, on TV, in other people, so I knew it existed, but I was stupid enough to think it wasn't going to happen to me. I was used to clear blue sky. I forgot that storms existed.

"You knew I was going to enlist," he said finally.

I shook my head rapidly, calling up snatches of conversation where he'd mentioned the army casually, without any commitment. "No, I *knew* that you got into Harvard. Full scholarship. I *knew* you're the smartest person in the room, and that you're going to be somebody. I *knew* we had plans to go to colleges close together, to live together when we were done. Take on the world. I didn't know you were going to throw it all away." I paused, tears prickling the backs of my eyes. "I didn't know you were going to throw *us* away," I choked out.

The naïve happiness of our day was a faint memory and I felt like I'd never be happy again like I had been in that moment. When the future was as cloudless as the sky above us and as clear as the water we'd jumped into.

Together.

Liam crossed the room in two long strides, framing my face with his hands. "I'm *never* going to throw us away," he promised. "You don't throw away a treasure when you find it. And that's what you are." Something moved in his face. Something still soft and kind. I wondered how long it would be there. How long that fleeting hardness would take to become permanent. "Unless you won't wait for me." Uncertainty, vulnerability saturated his tone, his face.

I knew Liam. Better than anyone. He was my best friend. Soulmate. I knew he was smart. He liked to take risks. Like jump off cliffs into water. But only when he knew the water was deep enough. He only jumped when he knew he would surface. I trusted him today. I trusted him yesterday. I had to trust him for tomorrow too.

I glared at him. "I'll wait for you, you ass. Forever if that's what it takes."

It was the truth, that promise. Not made lightly. I was smart too. I knew that what was ahead was going to be hard. That we'd be living lives worlds away, with geography having nothing to do with it. I knew that war would change him. Like it had changed his dad. Harden him. Take away some of the boy I'd fallen in love with. But I loved him. I'd love him for who he was becoming, who he had been yesterday and who he'd have to turn into for tomorrow. It was that simple to me. We'd work because I'd make sure of it.

His face changed. Melted. Then he kissed me, long and hard and almost enough to make me forget about everything.

Almost.

"It won't be forever," he murmured against my lips. "I promise."

Liam might've kept his promises.

But wars didn't.

Sixteen Years Later

Jagger

It was chance that saved his life.

Not fate.

He didn't believe in that bullshit.

Fate was a notion held by people who didn't have the courage to drive their own lives. He may have driven his life right into hell itself, but at least it was his foot on the gas pedal.

So it wasn't fate that saved him. Or even chance.

It was routine.

He was on a run.

On Christmas.

Because Grim, his president, the man who had sent him on these runs every year since he patched, knew that of all the things he could handle, he couldn't handle fucking *Christmas*. He could see a man die in the most horrible and brutal of ways. He could *kill* a man in the most horrible and brutal of ways. He could withstand pain. Torture. He could give out pain. Torture another human being until they screamed, pissed themselves, cried and then passed out.

He could dig a grave, drop a corpse inside it and bury a man he'd killed with his own two hands.

He'd fight until his knuckles bled and until his opponent was on the ground, sometimes breathing, other times not.

The cut on his back made it necessary for him to be able to handle all of these things and more.

But he couldn't handle one fucking day that was created for some false god and hyped up by big business to put people in more debt and give more people the excuse to eat more, work less and just be general assholes.

To be with family.

Jagger didn't have a family.

Not by blood, anyway.

Though he'd shared blood with all the men in his chapter. Considered them brothers.

And they were all dead.

Every single one of them.

His president. The one who was as hard as nails, who killed without hesitation, who had ruled one of the most dangerous chapters in the Sons of Templar for years. Who may have been a hard motherfucker who didn't give mercy to enemies, but he gave Jagger the mercy of sending him away every Christmas.

A mercy that ended up saving his life.

Levi, who'd brought him into the fucking club. The old fuck had seen something in the broken kid with fresh scars and the devil at his heels.

The fresh-eyed prospects who still smiled without stains on their souls. Fuck, even the club bitches. It wasn't like he enjoyed anything meaningful with them, because he wasn't capable of meaningful, but they were good women. In their own way. And they were fucking *dead*.

Apart from Scarlett. She was the one that called him. She was the one that fucking *found* everyone. Voice not even shaking. Bitch was strong. He wasn't surprised she survived. Glad as fuck she did. She was hard. Not an ounce of soft or sweet in her, apart from in the places a woman was soft and sweet. But she was a good person. A survivor.

And Hansen and Macy. They survived.

If his best friend and his fucking *pregnant* wife had been amongst the corpses of his family...he slammed down another shot, hoping the burn might chase that thought away.

It didn't.

Caroline

Five Months Later

I was making my list.

I did it every morning.

My therapist suggested it. Does anyone do anything like write the things that made them happy in a day without some kind of shrink telling them to do it? If you had to write down reasons you were happy, then it was a big sign that you *weren't* happy.

But I did it anyway. It was a visceral and actionable thing to do to control my state of mind. Or at least create the illusion that I could control something as unhinged and damaged as my mind.

"I want you to write a minimum of three," she said. "And there is no maximum. Some days it'll be hard to get three. But others there will be days when you fill up a whole page."

I quirked my brow but didn't say anything. What a load of bullshit, *I thought.*

That was four years ago.

And I'd done it every single day since then.

I have yet to fill up a page.

One day I'd gotten up to the number seven.

Most days I still struggled to get three. No, I *battled* to get three, and that was with the first one on the list being consistently the same since I started the damn thing.

1. *I am inhaling and exhaling.*

YEAH, most people wouldn't consider the mere act of breathing as a reason to be happy. Because it wasn't unique or special. Even people going through the worst shit a human being would ever have to face were still breathing. Inhaling and exhaling didn't denote happiness. But I had to start somewhere. And I also had to remind myself that breathing wasn't something to be taken for granted.

2. *My sister is finally pregnant after trying for two years.*
3. *My paycheck is enough to cover my rent and bills and buy myself a coffee every day for the next month, plus those shoes that are on sale at Nordstrom.*

I CHEWED on the top of my pen.

Three was all I had in me today.

Plus, I had better things to do.

I had a story to write. Well, I had a story to *research*. One that might leave me with more than enough money to buy half price designer sneakers and an overpriced coffee every day.

The roar of motorcycles made me glance up as I watched a

line of them pull into the parking lot of the Sons of Templar compound.

An automatic gate with barbed wire at the top started to close as the bikes disappeared. Security cameras were mounted on the gate and pointed toward the street. I was parked down the road enough not to be caught in them.

Their clubhouse was now a fortress.

Or as close as it could get.

It made sense since a handful of months ago almost every single member of the club was brutally murdered. The police had no leads.

Because they were paid to have no leads.

In a small town in the middle of New Mexico, one-percenter gangs could still pay off the underpaid local cops.

Shit, they could do it anywhere. Money spoke louder than morals. Always.

If I'd learned anything in my years of covering some of the most dangerous stories in the world, it was that. Even embedded in warzones throughout the planet, I saw what a handful of dollars could do. It could change a life. End one. Buy my entry. Buy my exit. Buy my safety. Or buy my pain.

Much more than a handful of money was what bought wars. But they were always paid for in full and in cash, and so much more in pain.

I might've been stateside once more, but I was in the middle of a warzone, no doubt about that. I'd done my research. As much as I could without getting myself on the Sons of Templar's radar. And I knew about their sordid past. The Amber chapter in California was the most notable. Throughout the years they'd had rapes, murders, kidnappings, drive-bys, explosions, all of which somehow involved the women married to some of the most dangerous men in the country.

But I also knew that despite all this, the Amber chapter was relatively legit. Well, as legit as a previous outlaw motorcycle club could be. There were *some* stories there for me.

But not *the* story.

The one that might blow up my career. In ways that my war coverage never could. Yeah, I was somewhat of a household name when people thought of conflict correspondents. But that was likely because I'd stayed alive longer than most of my contemporaries.

And war was now the wallpaper to the newsroom.

It wasn't shocking.

Nor was it even news.

Because it was too common.

Imagine living in a world where mass genocide and crimes against humanity were too *common* for people to care about.

Worse, because we didn't have to imagine that world.

We lived in it.

But I'd lived enough to know I couldn't change it.

I wasn't noble enough to want to do that. People might've been tricked into thinking that because I risked my life to tell stories of suffering, but the truth was I did it to distract myself from my own. To live in outside horror, so I didn't have to inhabit my interior one.

I'd done it for the past twelve years, I'd collected all sorts of different horrors. Unthinkable brutality. Gruesome death. I found myself hungry for more. For something that would shock the American public back into being horrified again.

Selfishly, I wanted *the* story.

And it was inside the clubhouse I was staring at.

Without hesitation, I opened my car door, put my heeled foot on the ground and started my journey toward the belly of the beast.

"YOU'RE NEW," someone slurred.

Someone being a monster of a man in leather with the trademark Sons of Templar cut. He was younger than me. But he towered over me. I guessed he took steroids because there was no way a human got that jacked from the gym.

Then again, most of the men in the room grew biceps from beating up gunrunners, collecting debt sheets from loan sharks, killing rival gangs and eradicating anyone dealing drugs within town limits.

It had taken less than five minutes for me to be approached, despite the fact the room was pulsating with women, in varying degrees of undress and inebriation.

It was exactly what I expected it to be.

So very cliché.

But underneath clichés were usually stories.

Because I noted things in five minutes.

Things that told me someone smart was hiding under a cliché.

The security, for a start. There were cameras covering every single angle of the entrance, and the gate was manned and guarded by a man wearing a cut with no patch and the bottom rocker reading 'Prospect.'

The man in question had given me a long look as I approached. And there was the healthy male hunger that my outfit was designed to awaken. But there was something else. A wary glint that told me he wasn't going to let me in because I was showing off a lot of skin, my makeup was heavy, and my tits were decent.

And he didn't.

He checked my purse.

It was small. Tacky. Cheap. Worn in. It went perfectly with the persona I'd slipped into for the story.

"Pretty as you are, doesn't mean you're not a killer. Pretty will

get you a lot of places, but not into the wrong ones," he drawled, flashing his phone light into my purse.

I hadn't thought they'd be doing this, but I didn't have anything to hide in there.

He picked up my gun with a raised eyebrow.

I didn't carry a gun regularly, but the woman I was pretending to be did.

"Pretty as I am doesn't mean ugly things can't happen to me," I said calmly.

I swallowed the rock that was the truth of that statement.

Maybe he saw something in my eyes before I could hide it. Men like this lived in violence and ugliness, so I guessed it was easier to spot in someone trying to hide it. But then again, I needed to utilize all my ugliness if I was going to get the story.

He put the gun back in my purse. "Gonna let you keep this, because you're not wrong. Ugly things happen to everyone." His eyes went up and down my body that didn't feel sexual, merely inquisitive. "Even the prettiest." He handed me my purse, I took it, but he didn't let go for a beat. "I'll also tell you something different, to paraphrase Sonny Barger 'you treat me good, I'll treat you better. You treat me bad, I'll treat you worse.'" He nodded his head to the clubhouse. "Somethin' to remember in there. Pretty means some, but not everything. And it means nothin' if you mean the club harm."

A cold blade of dread trailed down my spine.

Did he know who I was? Did he know what I was doing? Was he giving me one last warning before I strode into the Gates of Hell?

But I was beyond warnings at this point. Hell wasn't a place. No, it was a feeling.

I didn't hesitate to walk into the building once he stepped aside.

For better or for worse, I was committed to the story.

"Yeah, I just moved here," I said, replying to the slurring man.

'Moved' was a stretch. I was renting the shittiest, cheapest apartment in town. And though the town was small, it was big enough to have a 'good' side and a 'bad' side. I was living in a place with a dried-out pool and paper-thin walls to keep up my backstory and to keep myself afloat financially. I was still paying rent on my apartment in Castle Springs and though I had some good chunks of money coming in from some freelance work I did, I had to make it last. The life of a journalist was not glamorous, and the pay was shit. Even when you're good—which I was—and getting paid more than what most of your colleagues are—which I also was—there was no way to get rich from the job.

I didn't want riches. I just wanted to tell people's stories. Live their pain. For no moral reason other than to use it to insulate me from my own.

"Well, if you're new, then you definitely need someone to take care of you," the man said, getting in my personal space so I could smell the whisky and smoke on his breath.

It wasn't displeasing, nor was the inebriated man. He was relatively good looking, the muscles, menace, and tattoos adding to it all. In a time before this, a life before this, I didn't like men that radiated danger. Scarred by the truths and trials of the world.

Because before all *this*, I had a man. One who was safe, who didn't have hulking muscles, scars, tattoos and that radiating air of menace. And who hurt me worse than any outlaw could.

I smiled a smile that was venom and syrup. "I don't need anyone to take care of me, I can do that for myself." I glanced around pointedly. "And if I was looking for someone to take care of me, do you think that I'd be here?"

The low thump of rock music was loud enough so we almost had to shout, and so the man in front of me had to lean right into my personal space to make himself heard.

But I didn't really have personal space anymore. Life had

ripped away that illusion. I stiffened but made sure to keep my persona, it fit me as well as the tight dress I was wearing.

He grinned, revealing white, slightly crooked teeth. "I'm Claw."

I raised my brow at the name.

He shrugged and it was an oddly boyish gesture for the man wearing a knife strapped to his belt and a Glock on a shoulder holster.

Every single man here was armed.

And somewhat inebriated.

But I didn't think they were the kind to accidentally and drunkenly discharge their weapon. Nor did I think they were too inebriated to spring into action if a threat presented itself.

Claw furrowed his brows, observing me in a way that made me feel more uncomfortable than his previous leer. "Sure you haven't been here before? You look familiar."

I did my best not to react. I had gone to great pains to change my appearance on the off chance the men here regularly watched news coverage. I got recognized, not often, since people were more likely to recognize reality TV stars than conflict reporters. But enough to know it was a risk—a big one—coming in here without changing the face that would make me a target.

Journalists were not welcome here.

For obvious reasons.

So I'd died my blonde hair a dark brown, had my ringlets chemically straightened, put on heavy makeup to hide the freckles I'd gained from hours in unyielding sunlight in the Middle East. My trademark red lipstick was gone, replaced by a bright pink gloss that made my lips full and sexy.

Funny, considering how little clothing I was wearing, it was the absence of that red lipstick that made me feel almost naked.

"Trust me, I'm one of a kind, if I'd been here before, you'd remember me," I replied, winking, shaking off the feeling that he recognized me. He couldn't. And me acting anything but confident would make me a target.

He grinned again.

I exhaled.

I'd dodged a bullet.

And I had a feeling there were plenty more to come.

CHAPTER TWO

Three Weeks Later

IT WAS my third Friday here.

As I sauntered in, now used to the huge heels I wore every time I was here, I was met with chin lifts, ass slaps, and grins.

They knew me now.

Because I made sure they did. I flirted with the right guys, kissed the wrong ones, and slept with none of them.

And that was probably why they knew me here, because if I'd slept with one—or all—of them, they wouldn't go to the trouble of remembering my name.

That didn't mean I wasn't memorable in bed.

I totally was.

But these men lived a hard and dangerous life. They forgot what was easy, women being at the top of that list.

I wasn't easy.

Which was why I was remembered.

Why three different men had tried to haul me onto their laps as I sauntered through the party on platform heels that I knew where tacky and would never wear in the real world.

My real world.

I wasn't even sure about what was real to me. I traded warzones as one would change offices, was only at 'home' long enough to throw out plants I'd killed and buy new ones. I didn't have time to keep and maintain friendships, coffee dates or get addicted to a show on Netflix. My personal style for the past handful of years had been whatever was practical, culturally appropriate and usually topped off with a bulletproof vest for good measure.

This was yet another protective outfit—a leather mini skirt with a bright red cropped top that showed off my ample assets and my flat mid-section. I was wearing far less than I would on any battlefield in the Middle East. But in this current situation, it protected me more than a bulletproof vest would.

My job was to blend in, and if I wore something I was more comfortable in—like jeans and a plaid shirt with discounted Gucci sneakers, I'd stand out. And not in a good way.

So I dressed similar to the other women who were peppered around the room. They did not remember my name. Mainly because there were only a small handful of regulars these past three Fridays—the rest banished from beds in the early hours with a story and maybe an STD.

It had only been a few months since all the club girls had been murdered along with most of the club, so these were new. None of them seeming to be permanent. I wondered if they were scared of being gunned down or if the men were hesitant to have the blood of more women on their hands.

The club girls weren't as friendly as the men, they viewed me as competition, and the ones that didn't only managed to get in a few pleasantries before they were dragged off by a man in a cut.

That all changed with a blonde knockout who I hadn't seen before.

She sauntered up to me with a sober gaze and probing eyes.

Fuck.

This was a woman who saw through bullshit, I could tell that already. If I wasn't careful, it wasn't going to be a man that brought me down.

"Caroline, is it?" she said in greeting, making the prospect on the stool beside me scutter off with nothing but a sharp look.

I raised my brow in appreciation. "It is." Keeping with my real name was a calculated risk. Well, my real first name at least. I hoped that no one got curious enough about me to do a Google image search, and if they did, I hoped my appearance held up.

I'd gone as far as making a fake Instagram for 'Caroline Woods' months ago, peppering a lot of sexy selfies, various quotes and images of life on the road. Cheap motels, cheaper bars, sunsets with stupid quotes attached to them.

"Scarlett," the blonde said, taking a beer from the bartender.

I nodded in response.

She was definitely a Scarlett from her platinum blonde hair to her hourglass body, to her blood red nails.

"I've heard you've been here the last three weeks, and that's all well and good, we throw a good party," she said, sipping on her beer. She paused, probing eyes settling on me. "But you haven't fucked any of the men, you don't have one of your own, because if you did, you wouldn't be going to a biker party alone for three Fridays in a row. And though there are surely a few duds in the mix, none of these men are exactly ugly." She glanced around the room pointedly before moving back to me. "You don't come to a Sons' party to be chaste. What's your deal?"

Her arched brow and lack of polite smile were calmly hostile.

I liked her immediately.

"I like a party," I said, shrugging, downing my own beer.

She was an Old Lady. I knew this because I recognized her from my research. She'd been a 'club girl' for years. Which meant that she was pretty much passed around every member like property. The idea in itself was repulsive, but the woman in front of me told me she was no one's property, and no way had she been some kind of docile victim in her life here. None of the club girls I'd witnessed had.

It wasn't a prison.

It was an alternate lifestyle.

A life beyond the bounds, rules, and laws of society, but somehow still wrapped up in classic patriarchy. Women were only attached to the club if they were wives, girlfriends, or whores.

The beautiful blonde knockout looked me up and down with an expert eye. She had a hardness about her that I had come to recognize on soldiers who'd seen some of the worst things humans could see. Photojournalists forced to document suffering instead of help. Shit, I saw it in the mirror when I really looked, which wasn't often.

"You're not going to find Prince Charming here, darlin'," she continued.

I laughed. I couldn't help it.

"My world isn't driven by the search for Prince Charming, trust me," I said honestly. That tender part of my heart that even war couldn't harden convulsed at a memory. "I'm just here because I like to party. Like to be somewhere that is real. Wrong." I shrugged. "Not pretending to be something it isn't."

I knew I couldn't hang out indefinitely without sleeping with someone. It would make me stand out, and when you were a journalist looking to break a story on one of the most notorious MCs in the country, you didn't want to stand out.

Not if you wanted to live.

I wanted to live.

But I also wanted the story.

So I had a choice to make. As Scarlett had said, it wasn't exactly a hardship to sleep with one—or many—of the muscled, tattooed and menacing bikers. I wasn't a virgin. Nor was I a prude. I learned to separate sex from emotions right after I attached far too many emotions to it.

I used it as a stress reliever.

When you're in the middle of the battle zone, sex is more of a reminder that you're alive than anything else, a base human inter-action that your body craves after seeing, breathing and touching death.

I had a regular thing going with a photojournalist from Sweden.

We both knew the score.

I hadn't heard from him since I'd been back.

He could be dead for all I knew.

It was better not to know.

So using sex for a story wasn't something that was beyond my journalistic morals or ethics. Morals had little place in the real world. And if I wasn't going to use sex, then I'd have to find some-thing more creative and a heck of a lot less legal as a reason to find myself in the clubhouse.

And Scarlett seemed to be my guardian angel in that respect. If angels wore tight red dresses with a neckline that plunged almost to her belly button and hemline barely covering her ass.

"Can you tend a bar?" she asked after a beat, after assessing me with those hard, sharp eyes and coming to some kind of conclusion about me.

I was outwardly calm, forcing myself not to think she'd recog-nized me. Even if the men had seen me on the news, I doubt they'd connect the woman on screen in the bulletproof vest and dirty helmet labeled 'Press' with the brunette who had blowjob lips and half her tits out.

Women, on the other hand, were more observant. More dangerous.

I regarded her for a long second, sipping my beer. "Slinging cocktails put me through college," I said. It was the truth. Because when working with big lies, it was important to tell as many small truths as possible.

She grinned and it made me relax. It wasn't an easy smile, something told me this woman didn't smile easily, it wasn't exactly warm either, but it was genuine. "Can't say this job will be slinging many cocktails, unless Gwen or fuckin' Amy find themselves up here, in that case, you better know how to make a Cosmo. Or at least surrender the bar so they can make them themselves."

"Gwen and Amy?" I repeated, though I knew exactly who they were. Though the club had tried to keep the events of the past few years in Amber quiet, it didn't completely escape notice, considering Amy Abrams was the daughter of a prominent New York family. Both her and Gwen Alexandra—now Fletcher—were regulars on Page Six before they both moved to Amber.

Both of them going through various traumas throughout their courtships with the now president and vice of the Sons of Templar MC.

"Old Ladies," Scarlett continued. "Amber chapter." She paused. "Fuck, I guess *I'm* one of them now too," she muttered as an afterthought. Then her heavily black-rimmed eyes went to a man in the corner who had had his eyes on her since she approached me. I knew this because I knew how to read the room. Especially the danger in it. Especially dangerous men who were hot as anything and bore a striking resemblance to WWE wrestlers.

"Your Old Man, I'm guessing?" I nodded my head in the direction of the man who was staring at Scarlett's ass.

She grinned, turning to give him a heated look. "Yeah, still getting used to that title." She turned back to me. "I'm not exactly in this chapter anymore, but Hansen mentioned the club finally bit the bullet—so to speak—and bought The Rock. Cheaper than paying for damages whenever there are brawls or shootouts every weekend. Need a bartender." She looked me up and down. "You scare easily? Squeamish with blood?"

I thought about the explosions that had rocked me to sleep, about the bodies strewn on the side of the road, rogue limbs after a car bomb. "No and no."

She nodded once. "Didn't think so. Reckon you can handle yourself with this lot too. I'm not gonna say that their bark is worse than their bite, 'cause they don't bite as much as rip your fucking head off if you cross them." She didn't smile as she said this.

Another warning.

That strange feeling hit me again. That certainty that Scarlett knew what I was doing and was giving me another out.

If I said no, then I might be able to walk out of here with a tame story that might sell as a back-page interest story. Or it would become a memory.

I nodded once. "So noted."

"You start tomorrow."

One Week Later

"Caroline, when are you gonna finally realize you're in love with me and get your fine ass on the back of my bike?" Claw asked as I handed him his beer.

I flashed him a genuine smile—him, and many of the men had grown on me in the past week since I'd started at the bar. Now that the club owned it, they were here almost every night.

Which was perfect for me. I'd met every member, even the club's recently patched president, Hansen. He'd been friendly and told me to let him know if anyone gave me any trouble.

It almost made me feel bad about what I was doing.

But there was no room for emotions in stories. I had practice at emotionally distancing myself from humanity when I was writing about it.

"When are you finally gonna realize that just because you haven't slept with me doesn't mean you're in love with me?" I countered, pouring a whisky for Sven, a blond-haired, tanned Norse fricking *god* of a man.

Though I had a feeling he was closer to a demon than a god.

He winked at me as he took it.

Claw glared at him, then me. "Well, then you have to sleep with me to find out."

I rolled my eyes, turning to grab some glasses from the sanitizer. "I don't *have* to do anything, it's a free country, remember?"

Something darkened in his eyes. "Baby, you're in Sons' country, nothin's free here."

A chill settled in the base of my spine at his words. That same foreboding that had come and gone as I got deeper in the lie, deeper in the danger if the truth came out.

"Claw!" Hansen yelled. "Get your ass over here, Jagger's comin' back from his run soon, we've got shit to figure out."

Claw gave me a wink and sauntered off to the table of men.

I watched and considered going over in the guise of clearing empties from the table in order to hear what they were talking about. But it was too obvious, plus the bar was busy. It was still open to the public, public being men who wanted to patch in, or pretend to be tough, or women looking to have a good time or trying to escape a bad one.

I made drinks on autopilot. The bar work was oddly calming

after my 'work' having consisted of something a lot more complicated than pouring beers for over a decade.

I idly wondered about this 'Jagger' character. The men and women had talked about him on and off since I'd been here. He was one of the only two surviving members of the club massacre this past Christmas. Hansen, the new president, was the other.

Scarlett was the only club girl that survived. Which hadn't surprised me. She was someone who I thought might have already survived a lot of horrors that would've killed a lesser woman, or man.

She wasn't the only woman connected to the club that survived. There were old ladies turned widows. Fatherless children. All of whom were 'taken care of' by the club.

The rest of the club were either transplants from other chapters, Nomads or new patches.

It was obvious this was a club that wasn't scarred but still bleeding from an unfathomable loss. But clubs like this didn't stay bleeding for long. Their wounds scabbed over. They drew more blood. And my research had told me that it was someone involved in high profile human trafficking that was responsible for the killing. A retaliation for something this chapter did? A deal gone wrong? Sure, that could've been it, but it didn't seem to me that these were the kind of men to be involved in human trafficking. Though smiles and twinkling eyes could hide a lot. And monsters never seemed like monsters.

So it was possible.

But as I'd done research on not just the club, but those connected to them, I'd seen that Rosie, the biker princess, daughter to a founding member and sister to a president, had disappeared for a year a few years ago. I couldn't locate any more information about that time away, but from what I'd found out about Rosie, I doubted she was sunning herself in St. Tropez. And she wasn't the only one who was involved in things that could ruffle international feathers. Lucy, her best friend and a friend of the Amber club, was a prominent investigative journalist—I'd admired her for many years, broke a story that got her stabbed on the side of the street.

And these weren't even women married to patched members.

It didn't have to be a beef originated in New Mexico. As I'd seen, one chapter was a small part of a whole, which made them strong. But it also made it harder to pinpoint where it all originated, and easier for the enemy in question to strike unexpectedly.

Someone the club was yet to locate.

And this Jagger character was off on some kind of recon mission by the sounds of it. Along with a few notable members of the Amber chapter, where I personally thought this war had originated.

The only reason I was here, and not another, more conventional war zone—or at least what the public was desensitized into thinking was conventional—was not because I'd lost the stomach for it. Because I had grown unable to handle seeing deaths of strangers and friends alike, or because I knew it was only a matter of time before I wouldn't be seeing death, I'd be meeting it.

It was because of my sister.

My family had always supported me. Though all of them had made it very clear how much they hated where I'd chosen to take my job. Or where my job had taken me. Every email from my mother or father had some kind of subtle yet pleading message to come home.

It was selfish of me really, putting them through over a decade of that. Of wondering whether they'd wake up to news of my death, rather than me reporting on others. It was cruel. And I loved my family fiercely, would do anything for them. Anything but that. Other than come home to safety and familiarity.

Because I had to go and stare death in the face. Because it was staring at me no matter where I went anyway.

But my latest trip home was when my sister announced, quietly and with glassy eyes, that she was pregnant for the third time.

After two miscarriages.

And years of trying.

Thousands in IVF.

"I waited this time," she said, smoothing her hand over her shirt, and the now prominent bump visible through the tight cotton. "We've never gotten this far." She paused, eyes glittering with a pain that had settled in those topaz irises since she and James had started trying three years ago. Something shimmered, shook, rippling that sadness. Not quite chasing it away, but battling it just the same.

Hope.

"This time's different," she said, voice firm. "I know it. And I'm not going to bring my baby into a world that has a high chance of you not being in it." She snatched my hand and placed it on the fullness of her belly. It was warm, comforting. Something pulsed in my oh-so-very empty womb. "You're going to meet your niece," she said.

I glared at her, or at least I tried to, through my happiness. "This is emotional blackmail."

She nodded. "I don't care. I'll do anything and everything in my power to get my baby sister out of a war zone."

I gritted my teeth. My mother's tears, pleas, my father's stoic silences with worried eyes and my brother's shouts hadn't swayed me in the past. But the warm roundness of my sister's belly, of my niece growing inside her, it cut through it all.

I snatched my hand back though I ached to leave it there. "You're always a bitch until you get your own way."

She grinned. "So you're staying."

I chased away the panic that came with the reality and nodded once. "I'm staying."

So I stayed.

For my sister.

For my unborn niece.

For my mother.

Father.

Brother.

But not for myself. And not for the love of my life that I buried almost fifteen years ago.

First, I went back home. To Castle Springs, where I had my apartment with the dead plants and lack of personality.

Where I went for a handful of weeks at a time between assignments.

Hometowns were a funny thing.

Thomas Wolfe said you can't go home again.

And that wasn't quite true for me.

I did go home. I could've stayed there. Surrounded by my family, mountains, sunshine. In a town that hadn't realized the world had changed into something dark and scary. A town where people still kept their houses unlocked and children rode their bikes down the street without fear. That's exactly what going home was for me, welcoming a life without fear.

A safe life.

I could still freelance. Write lifestyle pieces. My best friend was an agent in New York, who always got me in front of the right people.

If I'd stayed, I likely would've met a safe, reliable man, with family values and no dreams of leaving the town he grew up in. He'd give me a nice life, because most men were raised right in Castle Springs, Alabama, a town with Southern values as strong as its sweet tea. I'd give him babies, and I'd live in an empty kind of happiness.

But instead of that, instead of empty happiness, I came here, chasing bursting sorrow and pain. Because as much as I loved my sister, my family, the uncomplicated peace of my hometown, I wasn't designed for it. I feared it would kill me quicker than any war zone could. Whatever parts of me were left.

"Caroline!"

The shout jerked me out of my stupor.

I glanced to Henry, the heavyset, tattooed manager of the bar. Not a patched member, but a friend of the club they'd employed to run the place. He was gruff, used fuck as a comma but was reasonable and had a quick dry wit.

We got along well.

"Get your fuckin' ass movin', I told you to get the fuck outta here twenty minutes ago," he continued shouting. "You've been workin' until close all week, I'm commanding you to have a life."

I grinned at him. "You're not a genie, you can't command shit."

He raised a bushy brow. "If I was a genie, think I'd be in this fuckin' shithole? Now go. Before I change my mind and decide to grant one of Claw's wishes."

I rolled my eyes but did as he asked. For appearances more than anything. I didn't have a life outside of this job, because this job, this story, was my life. Apart from daily calls to my sister, and usually my mother, father, or brother.

I spent as much time as I could at the bar for obvious reasons, but to stave off the loneliness too. The quiet. I wasn't used to it. Though you couldn't call hanging out at my crappy apartment 'quiet' since I heard the couple beside me screaming at each other, both when they were fighting and making up. There was always a far-off siren, or a close up one. City noise did little to drown out silent explosions, gunfire, screams, that could be heard nowhere but on the inside of my head.

Despite the fact I was at the bar, with the club for a story, it was giving me something I didn't get in my quiet hometown with my family.

Chaos.

The dangerous kind.

But was there any other?

I winked at Claw, gave a serious looking Hansen a wave and kissed Henry on the cheek. "If you're so convinced you're a genie, then I'll buy you an outfit."

His chuckle was throaty and raspy, showing the pack a day he smoked. "You find one in my size, I'll wear it."

I made a silent promise to myself to scour the internet for just that, Henry was a man of his word.

I got my purse and jacket from the small back office that I was pretty sure was just a converted broom closet. I slung my jacket over my purse as I exited to the back parking lot. I was still getting used to the balmy New Mexico air. Even though it was nearing midnight, the air had a dampness to it, the sun still lingering in the breeze.

The parking lot was oddly silent for the night, though this was the back entrance, so not as busy as the front. I heard some muttered curses and shouts from the front where a lot of men and women lingered by the Harleys smoking, since Henry—despite the fact he was a smoker himself—had a strict no smoking policy. I was glad of it too. I hated smelling of stale cigarette smoke in college, no matter how much I washed my hair.

I didn't feel unsafe as my heels drowned out the rowdiness of the bar. I may have been in a dangerous situation if the Sons found out what I was doing, but for now, I was a fringe part of the club, and that meant I was protected. And more importantly, I didn't really mean enough to hit deep.

"You tell me who was in on the hit, or you die."

The cold promise filtered through the air from the alley to my left.

My keys tumbled to the ground.
Not from the death threat.
From the voice.
The one that came straight from the grave.
My feet moved before my mind did.
To the alley.
Toward the voice of a dead man.

CHAPTER THREE

Jagger

HE KNEW the piece of shit wasn't going to talk.

That's why he'd dragged him from the SUV he'd had him in the trunk of to the alley. Plan was to wait for the new bartender to leave and get this asshole into the bar so the club could interrogate him. They didn't usually do such things in civilian environments, but they owned the bar now and he needed a fucking drink.

He'd heard the new bartender was a piece. He thought idly about hitting that as he pistol-whipped the bloodied and bound man in front of him. He could do with some fresh pussy. A month on the road chasing ghosts and stale leads made him antsy. He'd had no one to kill and no one to fuck. He needed at least one of the two on the regular to keep him even. Or as close as he got these days.

Jagger heaved the man up so he stood. Leaned on one foot really, since he'd already kneecapped him trying to get info. The man was crying now, tears, saliva, and blood mixing together on his swollen and blackening face. Jagger felt no pity. This was one of the men responsible for killing his whole chapter. He hated him even more for the fact he couldn't even handle a beating yet somehow he helped take out some of the most ruthless mother-fuckers he'd ever met.

"I don't know anything," the man sobbed. "I was hired, man. I got paid a lot of money to turn up at the club, Christmas day. Same as all the other guys."

Jagger tightened his grip on his piece. "And where are the other guys?"

"I don't know! None of us knew each other. Everyone hired, same as me. Knew what had to be done, everyone had specific instructions. I was meant to take out the old guy—"

Jagger cut him off with a bullet to the skull.

It was impulsive. He should've waited for more info. Hansen would ride him for that. But his fury, his fucking pain got the better of him. And that thirst, that need for the kill could no longer be held down. In the midst of that, he'd fucked up.

Bad.

Because the man in front of him didn't fall to the ground. He fell on top of the woman who'd been standing directly behind him. Who had been staring at Jagger like she'd seen a ghost.

And a glimpse at those almost amber eyes told him she had.

Him.

Caroline

It didn't happen fast.

When people experienced trauma, and they said 'it happened so fast I can barely remember,' they're usually lying through their teeth. Mostly to themselves. Because if you convince yourself that all those horrible things happened too fast to see, they'd be too hard to remember. You could pretend that they didn't sear into your bones, becoming mangled scar tissue.

I didn't pretend.

So it didn't happen fast.

Not the second I entered the alley and watched a man in a Sons of Templar cut haul a bleeding and bound man to his feet and shoot him in the face.

I didn't know if the man was too focused on the killing to see me until he pulled the trigger or if the shadows afforded me enough concealment that it wasn't until the corpse he created literally knocked me off my feet that I became impossible to ignore.

But I knew he recognized me. *After* I recognized him. Because I recognized him immediately. Even before I saw him. Even with my rational mind telling me that the owner of the voice that brought me to the alley *couldn't* be him. That dead men didn't talk.

It turned out they did.

And they killed too.

Without hesitation.

I saw that in his eyes when time slowed down. Time may stop for no one, but it slowed sufficiently for death.

And he was death. This man with cold, striking eyes. Chiseled jaw. A jagged and ugly scar marring a classically handsome face. The face of a boy I used to know.

A boy I used to love.

The boy I *buried* fourteen years ago.

Though that wasn't even true, we'd buried an empty coffin then and I'd just thought that his real grave was unmarked, covered over by countless other skeletons, flesh decomposed until his bones were nothing but dust.

I'd thought about it a lot over the years, taunted myself with the details, searched for him in every rotting dead body I encountered over my career. I'd known I wouldn't find him in the place he died, wouldn't see him in the face of a decomposing corpse, but never did I expect to find him in a dirty alley wearing a different face and a Sons of Templar cut.

Bile filled my mouth as the body thudded into me with the power of a bullet ripping through its skull.

Funny, how I thought of this person as an *it*, less than a second after the bullet left the gun. There was most likely still brainwave activity, but I was already dehumanizing him in my mind. Because that was the only way to survive seeing death on a regular basis. This wasn't someone's son, someone's brother, someone's father. No, this was an '*it*' with gray matter instead of brains.

Gray matter that hit my face, along with a warm splatter of blood.

I was knocked down more out of shock than anything else.

Not shock at the gunshot, nor the mere proximity of death.

I was used to that.

But it was the proximity of *life*.

The ground came hard and fast, without sympathy for my plight. My teeth cracked together as my head thwacked against the concrete.

The pain was intense, or at least it should have been.

It was exactly three seconds before the body was hauled from me and strong hands settled on my skin.

I was no longer numb.

"Peaches?"

The voice was rough, gravelly, deeper, more tortured than I remembered.

The voice, the single word hit me likely with the same impact of the bullet that had ended a man's life. It didn't open my skull so gray matter spilled out, though. It opened the heart I'd patched up and protected with other people's suffering. It tore that open and my soul poured out, mixing with the blood and brains at his feet.

I was in his arms and up before I thought more on it, before I could respond, but not before I cataloged every inch of this man's face.

Liam's face.

Though there was barely anything of Liam left there. Not just because of the scar that cut through his features, marring his mouth into what looked like a permanent grimace. That was the least of it. It wasn't the lines at the edges of his eyes, the sharpening of his features or bulky muscles, the beard that the terrible scar cut through. Not even the tattoos that covered every inch of skin visible from the neck down.

No, it wasn't any of those changes that stole away Liam.

It was the eyes.

The man in front of me may be alive, but the eyes told me Liam was dead.

It was with that realization that I jerked from my stupor and flailed out of his arms like his touch was acid to my skin. It was. It was acid to my soul.

He didn't loosen his grip with my struggles, his arms only tightened.

"Let me go!" I screamed like a banshee.

It might've been the desperation in my voice, the animal quality to it that made him put me down.

It didn't matter what it was.

All that mattered was that he was no longer touching me, and I was on shaky feet in front of him.

His eyes devoured me with agony. It was so visceral I could taste it. Poison on my tongue. Everything here was acid, even the air, burning away at everything, flaying the skin from my bones.

His hands were shaking.

I doubted it was because of the fact he'd just used them to

pull the trigger on a gun that killed a man. No, I guessed he'd done that enough times to ensure that his hands were steady before, during and after such an act.

He was shaking because of me.

Because I doubted that he expected to be faced with me again.

Of course he didn't.

Because you don't go to the trouble of making everyone who knew and loved you think you were dead if you planned on seeing them again.

Funny thing was, *I* wasn't shaking.

Not one bit.

I'd turned to marble.

I was oddly calm, a cold and awful kind of peace settling around me with the truth staring me in the face.

Liam was alive.

Breathing.

Heart beating.

He was right in front of me.

Like I'd dreamed of, prayed for, for *years*.

There was no elation at this fact. No heartbreaking joy.

Nothing.

He opened his mouth, to say what I couldn't begin to imagine, but the loud and jarring bang of the door to the bar opening and number of motorcycle boots thudding on the concrete snapped his mouth shut.

He'd yanked me around so I was behind him as his brothers rounded the alley, guns drawn.

Interesting, he chose *now* to protect me.

Not fourteen years ago when it might've mattered.

Hansen was the first to lower his gun as he settled his gaze first on the corpse in front of Liam and then me behind him.

"Fuck," he muttered. "This really what it looks like, Jagger?"

Jagger.

Liam was Jagger.

The man that everyone spoke about. That had been with the club for almost...

Thirteen years.

The pain almost brought me to my knees.

"Depends what it looks like," Liam replied, voice saturated with faux laziness. The tension in his coiled body told me he was anything but lazy or relaxed.

Hansen shoved his piece into the back of his jeans. The rest of the men followed suit. "It looks like you killed the man we're meant to interrogate, not only that, you did it in an alley where anyone could see you." His eyes settled on me. "Where anyone *did* see you."

Liam's—*Jagger's*—form stiffened, and I watched his grip tighten on his gun in the flickering streetlight.

I got it then.

I was a witness to a murder. One that implicated the Sons of Templar. I was a loose end.

Liam had positioned himself in front of me because he knew this the second after he recognized me. Because he expected his brothers to...what? Kill me immediately?

"I'll take care of it," Liam said through gritted teeth.

Hansen's face was hard. "No, the club takes care of it."

I stepped out from behind Liam because I wasn't going to let him protect me. And because I honestly was more willing to face whatever the club was going to offer me instead of being faced with the reality of this situation. The reality was the patch on Liam's back, staring at me in grim satisfaction.

Yes, the reaper had taken my fiancé from me.

Just not the conventional one.

He moved to try and grab my hand, I snatched it from his grasp.

"I'm not going to tell anyone," I said to Hansen, my voice even. "If that's what you're worried about."

He eyed me, gaze cold and probing. Gone were the easy smiles from before. This was the president of an outlaw MC gauging a threat and figuring out whether to eliminate it. This was death staring me in the face. I was used to the gaze so I didn't falter.

"It is what I'm worried about," he said finally. "You're a smart woman, so I know you realize I can't take you at your word."

I nodded once. "I expected as much."

Something flickered in his eyes. Surprise, maybe. Respect.

His gaze flickered over me, I followed it.

I hadn't been wearing much, and what I was wearing was covered in the dead man's blood. I failed to have a reaction to this. I'd been covered in the blood of the dead before.

"Claw, take her back to the club, get her showered, checked out."

Claw moved forward, no more flirty smile in his eyes, they were cold, jaw hard.

Liam moved around me once more.

"I've got her," he growled, glaring at Claw.

Hansen raised his brow. I wondered if he was going to question why this Jagger character was facing off against his brothers for a woman he wasn't supposed to know.

I then wondered what Liam's—*Jagger's*—answer might be.

But Hansen didn't ask.

He nodded once, and if I wasn't mistaken, the corner of his mouth turned up in what looked like a knowing smile.

"Claw, you take care of the body. Shot wasn't loud enough to draw the pigs, but let's not take any chances. If they see this, they'll want a fatter envelope than normal and I'd rather use it for bullet money. Get a prospect to clean up the blood." He eyed Liam. "We'll talk once you take Caroline back to the club."

"I'm not going with him," I said, now was when the calm in my voice began to falter.

Hansen's eyes were hard but kind. "Honey, you don't have a choice in the matter."

There was a certainty in his voice.

I recognized it.

I realized it.

I'd just gone from bartender to their prisoner.

I doubted I'd have a choice in a lot of things from here on out, maybe what I'd like for my burial.

Jagger

He expected her to speak after the doors to the SUV closed and he pulled out of the lot. It felt strange being in the cage, after a month on the bike, he'd only been using this to transport the prisoner.

But strange didn't even fucking cut it with who was sitting beside him.

Peaches.

The woman who'd haunted his dreams and soul for almost *fifteen fucking years*. The woman he'd loved with every inch of his soul, for every second since he met her. The woman who he'd resigned himself to bury in his past like the life he'd ended years ago.

But she was here, sitting beside him, covered in blood of a man he'd killed.

She was here, with different hair, with more curves, with more...everything. More beauty than he'd expected possible. And he'd expected a fuck of a lot. Imagined it vividly over the years.

But he never could have imagined her looking like *this*. He wondered why she'd dyed the pure white hair he'd loved so much.

Maybe *because* he'd loved it so much.

His hands tightened on the steering wheel with everything that was different about her. And everything that was the same.

She hadn't spoken.

Not a word.

And they'd been driving for three minutes.

She was staring straight ahead, eyes glassy, stare vacant. He reckoned she was in shock. She'd just watched a man die.

Fuck, he'd just made her *watch a man die*.

Then she'd seen the dead come back to life.

Yeah, she was in fucking shock.

So he'd given her the three minutes. Even though the act of keeping silent was physically painful. Even though every part of him screamed at him to pull the car over and yank her into his arms.

But then he remembered her reaction before. The desperate way she'd flailed under his grip. The fear in her voice.

Yeah, he disgusted her now.

He disgusted himself.

So he didn't pull over.

But he spoke.

Because he couldn't stand the silence for a second more.

Though he had no idea what to fucking say.

"Peaches," he began.

"Don't," she said immediately.

And he flinched at her voice. The deadness in it.

She didn't turn her head, didn't look his way. Her gaze was focused straight ahead.

"Don't...say anything," she continued. Her voice was a plea. A prayer.

It speared through his gut.

He gripped the steering wheel tighter, grinding his teeth together to keep his jaw shut.

Silence reigned again.

But not really.

There was never really silence between them. The years fell away.

"I think we're going to have a wonderful life," she said after turning the radio down, settling her hand on his thigh and grinning.

She did things like that. Made statements seemingly out of nowhere, when he knew she'd been having all sorts of conversations with herself about it in her head.

It was cute as fuck.

He took his hand off the steering wheel and settled it on hers.

"I know we are," he agreed.

She smiled wider. "Only if you promise to always play my favorite songs on the radio, never judge me when I sing the wrong words, or tease me when I cry at movies."

He lifted their intertwined hands and laid his lips on her tiny one.

"I can make you a lot of promises, Peaches, but I can't promise not to tease you when you cry at movies. You're a big softie."

She ripped her hand away and smacked his shoulder. "You ass! My soft heart should be endearing to you."

He sobered and snatched her hand again. "Baby, I promise everything about you is endearing to me. But the softness of your heart is the most precious thing about you. I promise I'll do everything in my power to keep it that way."

Jagger had broken his promise.

That much was apparent as he sat beside the same girl in a different and uglier world than the one in his memories.

She had a hardness about her, something calcified over her eyes that told him she wouldn't cry at movies anymore. He traced a scar on her cheek with his eyes. One that hadn't been there before.

He tortured himself with what that tiny mark could've been from. What sharp edges of this world had cut through his beautiful soft girl.

But did it matter?

She was scar tissue, and nothing could change that.

He didn't know what to expect from her, but the continued silence all the way to the club wasn't that. He expected her to yell. Cry. Demand to know why he wasn't dead. Why he was wearing a cut and a scar that marred half his face. Why he didn't come home to her.

He asked himself those questions daily.

But she didn't utter a single one.

As if the answers didn't matter.

He guessed they didn't.

Caroline

The clubhouse was silent as we walked through the common area I'd only ever seen littered with bodies and pulsating music. Now it was eerily empty, rogue beer bottles scattered around the place.

Someone had obviously called ahead of time to clear it out. I wondered if it was so they could kill me. But they wouldn't have bothered to bring me back here to do that. They would've killed me in that alley, easier to clean up, easier to dump my body in whatever deep grave they were currently digging.

I almost wished for that grave for the seven minutes and thirty-six seconds it took to drive from the bar to the clubhouse. To sit inside an enclosed space with Liam. No worse torture had been invented. I clenched my hands so hard that I cut the insides of my palms with my nails. They were covered in blood now.

What was more blood?

Liam opened a door at the end of a hallway. It was small, clean with an impeccably made bed, military corners and no personal effects.

I walked in silently.

He closed the door behind us.

I held my breath so I wouldn't have to breathe in his scent.

"Pea—Caroline," my name was a plea. It was a prayer. Coming out of a familiar mouth but spoken by a stranger. "Please say something."

I turned, slowly and purposefully to face him. I didn't look at him, though. I focused on a small rip in the wallpaper to the left of his head.

"I'm covered in blood, Liam," I said, my voice a sigh. I couldn't call him Jagger. I wanted to, but I couldn't. "I can't believe I have to say that to you."

I can't believe I'm saying anything *to you*, was what was left unsaid.

"Though it's not the covered in blood part that should come as a surprise, really, this isn't the first time. Likely won't be the last," I added, thinking of the many times I'd stared at dull crimson water draining in the shower as I tried to wash death and reality away.

Liam's face was cold marble, sculpted with fury, sharp edges, not even counting the long scar marring the face of a stranger who'd once known me better than I knew myself. "It's the fucking last," he gritted out.

I smiled at him coldly. "Like you have a say. The fact that you're standing in front of me and *that's* more shocking than being covered in blood means that you don't have a say in my life, ever."

"Babe—"

"I need to shower," I interrupted him. I didn't have the energy to snap at him for calling me that. I knew the term was throwaway for bikers—which was what he was now—it wasn't that for Liam. It was a term of endearment. But there was nothing dear between us now.

He clenched his jaw but nodded once, violently.

Everything that he did now was violent. It wasn't just that jagged scar on his face. It was him. Every moment, every inhale and exhale was fierce. Foreign.

He pulled open drawers to expose neatly folded tees, similar to the one he was wearing now. Simple gray, pressed, with flecks of blood staining it. I wondered if he would go to the trouble of trying to wash the blood out or just throw it in the trash.

The fact that this was his room should've surprised me. Liam had always been disorganized. Messy. Of course, all teenage boys were messy, I guessed. All I knew of him was a boy, long dead. This was a man who made his bed with military corners, had neatly folded tees in an impersonal room at a biker clubhouse, and a man who shot people in the face without hesitation.

He threw some sweats on the bed, along with a tee, eyes moving up and down my body.

I shivered at the intensity of his gaze, as if the air had turned to winter.

He snapped his eyes up. "Change into those." He jerked his head to the bed.

I wanted to argue against putting anything that had been on his body, that smelled like him, on my own. But I couldn't. My clothes, what little there were of them, were ruined. No great loss. But it wasn't like I was free to go home for jeans and a tee.

I wondered when, or if, I'd be free to go home. Home to the shitty apartment that definitely wasn't home. Home to the town that should've felt safe to me but was now filled with emotional landmines with this ugly truth staring me in the face.

"I'll find somethin' from Macy, something your size," he continued.

Ah, so I guessed I wouldn't be leaving anytime soon. I hoped Macy—who I was yet to meet because she'd just given birth—had a more covered sense of style than Scarlett.

"Towels are in the bathroom," Liam continued. His eyes darted sideways, fists clenched. He was obviously struggling. Uneasy.

I couldn't find it in me to care.

"Wait," I said as he turned to leave.

He stopped immediately.

I sucked in a harsh breath.

Fuck, I really didn't want to do this. But there was no other choice. I was covered in blood. I needed to shower. I could've tried to do it the alternative way, but that would've likely had me having a panic attack on the bathroom floor for an hour, I didn't have an hour. And if I was honest with myself, I didn't have the emotional strength to get through it.

"Can you stay?" I asked, trying not to make my voice sound small and pathetic. "In the room, I mean." I pointed to the bed. "While I shower." I paused. "I can't, um, I don't handle it very well...showering in strange places alone."

I held my breath as the words sunk in. Waited for the inevitable question. I was a reporter, so I knew there were always questions. I was used to them. Answering them investigative mode worked so it barely even took my breath away when I explained it like I was reporting from a war zone, where I was more comfortable than the war zone that was my head.

Every part of him changed as my words hit him. He was a man that knew trauma, obviously. And from what I'd seen, he knew pain. In a different way than him, I knew it too. So I knew there were ways to spot it in what people said, the tone of their voice, everything. He was clocking mine, likely running through all the scenarios that would have me needing to make such a request.

I'd thought he was violent before, but as my words ran into the air and over him, he physically changed. Something etched into his body, into his bones. Something that made it impossible to deny that he cared about me.

He clenched his hands into fists at his sides, not taking his eyes off me, not moving.

My breath was fractured, though I kept my façade. I'd kept this even, blank look on my face in front of warlords, so much death I couldn't understand it, bombs, machine gun fire, some of the worst acts of depravity humans have committed and called it war, but keeping my expression blank had never been harder than it was in this moment, with my beautiful, damaged and scarred past staring at me with violence and heartbreak.

I wasn't quite sure I'd survive explaining the truth to him. But no way I could lie.

I didn't have to do either. Because he didn't ask a question. Only nodded once and sat down on the bed.

I exhaled.

"I won't go anywhere," he promised. It sounded like an oath.

But it worked as an omen.

CHAPTER FOUR

I GOT CHANGED in the bathroom after a long and thoughtless shower.

You'd think after being faced with everything I had seen tonight that my mind would be pulsating with pain, with thoughts, panic, anger.

But I had a nifty trick perfected over years of pain, panic, and anger. My job that was nothing but trauma. It was somewhat of a gift. The gift of an empty mind when life became too full.

Too all-consuming.

This situation was all-consuming, to say the least.

So as I washed with soap that smelled of him, in a bathroom with a hint of a scent of bleach, abandoning bloodstained clothes at my feet, I thought of nothing. When I stepped out of the shower and into men's sweats that smelled of him too, I still thought of nothing.

I walked into the bedroom to see him exactly where I'd left him, hands clasped on his knees, eyes on me.

Then there was no such thing as nothing.

I sucked in a harsh breath, pain blindsided me with his simple stare. His simple presence.

I sank my fingernails into my palms once more. It stung, opening up wounds that hadn't even begun to heal. But that's what this was. All of it. An open, festering, wound.

Liam's eyes moved to my hands and he was off the bed in a slow blink. My hands were no longer my own, they were in his grip, in his possession.

He turned them over and let out a curse at the crescent-shaped cuts in my palms. They were bleeding. I was happy about that.

"Peaches," he murmured.

I yanked my hands back. "Don't touch me," I hissed. "And *don't* call me that." I skirted around him so there wasn't a door behind me, so he couldn't back me into a corner. "I need to get out of here. I need you to tell them that I won't talk. That I won't snitch. Then I need to order a taxi, get to my car and go..." I trailed off. Where the fuck was I going to go? I couldn't go home. Not to my true home. Not with the big, ugly rotten truth I'd been exposed to. I couldn't tell a big, ugly rotten lie to Kent and Mary when I saw them. That I still believed their son was dead.

No way could I tell them that he was alive either.

It might kill them.

Not that the son they'd cherished and mourned was *alive*. No, that *he'd made them believe he was dead*.

"So I can leave," I finished, figuring I'd sort it out once this was all in my rear vision mirror.

"Peac—Caroline, I can't let you leave. Not without an explanation."

I stared at him. "There is no explanation," I snapped. "Not one that will do anything. That will excuse *this*. I don't need to hear it. I don't want to. I just want to leave."

My voice had a desperate quality now. Despite the fact I'd moved from the wall, Liam had cornered me. With the truth. With my own pain. I wanted to claw my skin off to escape.

He looked torn. Tortured. Fists clenched at his sides. Tattoos moving with the tenseness of his sculpted muscles. Scar tearing through his face.

I itched to touch it. To know what happened to him that scored through his skin.

But that wasn't my story to know.

This wasn't a man for me to know.

The door was right there, to my right. I could open it. Leave. Run.

Not once in my life, in my career had I run from a story.

Not once had I imagined I might run from Liam.

And I was going to do just that until the door in question slammed open and Claw tore through it, eyes wild, feral and on me.

He had me backed up against the wall before I could fully fathom what was going on.

"Who the fuck are you workin' for, bitch?" he demanded, gripping my throat with a violence I didn't think the man who'd flirted with me over the past month was capable of.

But I knew better than anyone that any man, any human was capable of anything. Or everything, given the right circumstances.

Claw was ripped off me before he could prove my point.

Liam's fist flew into his face, the crunch of bone against flesh echoing through the room.

"You tell me what the fuck is going on before I continue beating the fucking life out of you," he said, voice still. Calm. Cold.

Frightening.

I'd heard some dangerous people speak. I'd interviewed them. It had been disconcerting. But most of the time, I'd been able to discover the human underneath the monster the world saw. Because monsters were all just humans, somewhere.

But in Liam's voice, I didn't hear it.

The human.

Or maybe I was listening for the boy I used to know.

I definitely didn't hear him.

And it frightened me like nothing else had.

Claw's nose was bleeding.

He didn't seem to notice.

"She's a fuckin' *journalist*, man," he hissed, eyes wild on me. "She's been doin' a fuckin' story on us. Wire tapped into her hard drive. She had shit on us. On the club. Notes."

Shit.

I wasn't stupid enough to leave physical notes lying around, in case anyone decided to check out my apartment. My computer was encrypted. I didn't store anything in the cloud because I wasn't an idiot. But I shouldn't have been surprised that the Sons had what I guessed was a world-class hacker.

Liam froze and gaped at me. There was accusation in his stare that he had no right to fling at me, but that hit me just the same.

I jutted my chin up in defiance.

He had no right to say anything about my choice of profession.

He had no right to anything, as far as I was concerned.

Liam shook his head at that head tilt with a familiarity that he wasn't entitled to.

Then he ran his hand through his hair and began pacing. "Fuck," he hissed through his teeth.

"Fuck is right," Claw said, wiping his nose with the back of his hand. He was regarding me with pure hatred.

I was used to such looks. So I didn't waver.

"We thought we had a problem with a civilian witnessing our hit, but now we've got a fucking *rat*," he seethed, spitting the word at me. "Club doesn't need this shit right now. Club can't have this shit right now."

Liam was steel. "Don't think I know that?"

"Well, we need to get rid of the rat."

I was under no illusions about what that meant.

I'd known it could go this way. Half of me had expected it to go this way. I'd always had a strange certainty I'd die for a story. Funny that it would be the past that killed me.

Liam had his hand on his gun the second Claw moved toward me, presumably to kill me. "Unless you want a bullet in your kneecap, you'll stop right there."

Claw blinked some of the hatred from his face, but anger still remained. "You're fuckin' *protecting* her? You know better than anyone what needs to be done for the club. Is this 'cause she's a woman?"

"No," Liam replied. "Because she's my woman."

Both Claw and I jerked in unison at Liam's words. It would've been impressive, the synchronicity of it, were the situation not so dire.

Hansen chose that moment to appear in the open doorway. His eyes flickered between the two men facing off, then to me, then back to Liam. "Church," was all he said before turning on his motorcycle boot and walking off.

I guessed that's how it was when you were president.

The air was wired as Claw stalked off, not keeping his glare from me and Liam not letting go of his gun. I almost wanted Claw to lunge at me, just to see if Liam would really shoot his brother for a girl he used to know.

But he was gone and Liam's hand left his gun. He eyed me. "Let's go."

I raised my brow. "Is this my execution hearing?"

He flinched. "I'd never let anything happen to you, Caroline. I promise."

"Well then I better start digging my own grave, because we both know you don't keep your promises," I shot.

Then I walked to 'church.'

I knew I wouldn't find any god there.

Even the devil had forsaken this place.

"YOU WANT TO START EXPLAINING?" Hansen asked after Liam shut the door behind him.

He was regarding me coldly, clinically, with none of the anger that was present from Claw, the only other patched member in on the meeting.

I was sitting straight in my chair, trying to ignore the fact that Liam was so close to me I could feel the warmth of his body. His gaze was zeroed in on Claw, as if he expected him to launch himself across the table and slit my throat.

His expression didn't do much to help that. Nor the way he was gripping his knife.

"I'm a freelance investigative journalist," I replied. My eyes went to Claw. "Which means I don't work for anyone. No one has hired me to gain intel on you for reasons to hurt or ruin your club from some preexisting rivalry. I found out about the club after Christmas and the small amount of press coverage that followed. I sensed a story. Having just come back from Iraq—"

"Iraq?" Liam demanded, something sounding like panic threading through the single word.

I didn't look at him. "Yes, I was there under contract with Reuters. But that contract ended, and I couldn't obtain a longer visa in the country so I came home. I don't do well not working. So I came here." I gave Hansen a meaningful look. "Under my own volition. No one else knows where I am or what I'm doing. Nor am I feeding information to anyone."

"How the fuck do you expect us to believe that?" Claw demanded.

"I don't expect you to," I replied, glancing to him. "Your entire club was almost wiped out. You've got a powerful heavy-weight in the underworld looking to do whatever damage he can. You'll protect your club at all costs, and I doubt you'll take any chances or take a stranger at her word. I knew that coming in."

Claw blinked twice, some of the fury flickering from his face. I guess he expected me to cry or plead for my life.

It was Liam that spoke. "You knew that coming in?" he repeated, slowly, purposefully.

Still, I didn't look at him. I nodded. "I've known that on every story I've ever covered that there's a chance, a high one, that I won't be alive to write it."

Another flinch. I saw it from the corner of my eye. Then his fist slammed down on the table. Even Claw jumped, not expecting it. I didn't move. Because I was half expecting a gunshot.

Hansen was unflapped too. He was regarding me with furrowed brows. "You've done your research. You see a lot. And no, I cannot take you at your word, because you've proven that you're willing to lie to the club for personal gain."

"It's not for personal gain," I argued.

He raised his brow. "You don't want the fame of having the scoop on the club? Don't want to be the next Hunter S. Thompson?"

I laughed. "No. It's safe to say that I don't want to be known. A good journalist exists only in the footnotes."

"So I'm to believe that your motives are unselfish? You believe you're doing the right thing, exposing criminals?"

"Everyone's a criminal. And there's no such thing as the right thing, so I don't expect you to believe either."

The corner of Hansen's mouth turned up ever so slightly. "You're going to be difficult."

My mouth did not move, I wondered if I'd ever smile again, if I'd have enough time to heal to a point where I was capable of smiling. "I don't have to be. Despite what the past has communicated, I am true to my word. I don't make a habit of becoming a witness. I only bear witness. Silently."

It was as close as I was going to come to pleading for my life. With logic. Because if someone like Hansen had decided to kill me, he wouldn't respond to pleading. He was likely hardened to it. Logic was the only way.

It might've been wishful thinking, but I thought I saw something in Hansen. A precursor to an agreement.

But Liam spoke before his president could grant me a pardon.

"We can't let you go, you understand that, right?"

I gritted my teeth, finally turning my head to regard him. I did my best to empty my expression and hide the reaction to seeing his scarred but beautifully alive face. "I understand that you *can* let me go, but your chosen lifestyle means you *won't*," I said flatly.

A muscle in his jaw ticked. "Why the fuck didn't you tell me you were a journalist?" he asked instead of treating my words with a response.

"Why the fuck didn't you tell me you didn't die in the desert alone?" I screamed, unable to hold onto my composure.

Anger I hadn't let myself feel bubbled up like lava in my throat, suddenly I itched to sink my nails into the skin of Liam's face that wasn't marked and leave scars of my own.

Hansen jerked back, blinking rapidly, as close to a dramatic reaction as he could have. "What the fuck is she talkin' about, bro?"

Liam looked to his president.

"Yes, *Jagger*, do clue Hansen in on what *the fuck* I'm talking about," I said, voice flat.

Liam glared at me, then to Hansen, opened his mouth. Shut it again. There was a cold fury in his features, but there was something else. Guilt. He was saturated with it.

I still couldn't bring myself to care.

Maybe I would've if I didn't see his mother collapse under the weight of the sorrow at his funeral. Watched his father retreat further into himself with the loss of his only son, until he spoke sparingly and went gray at forty-three.

If I hadn't watched his sister develop an alcohol habit that gave her a drunk driving conviction at sixteen because she didn't know how to stomach her pain, so she swallowed cheap vodka instead.

If I hadn't lived with visceral agony every single day up until now.

Then I *might've* felt sorry for the boy I loved more than life in such visible pain.

But this wasn't that boy.

"The cat seems to have snatched *Jagger's* tongue," I said, voice sharp. "No matter. Talking about death comes easy to me, since it's my job." I leaned back in my chair with a faux laziness. "You see, the man you know as Jagger, your *brother*, is also someone I knew as Liam," I said after a beat. "Who has a sister named Antonia, a mother named Mary and a father named Kent."

Liam flinched as I said their names, as if he hadn't heard them in a long time, as if the names were bullets.

I kept speaking. "He went to school in Castle Springs, Alabama, and played football for fun."

Hansen raised his brow ever so slightly. Maybe because Jagger didn't have a hint of a Southern accent, though neither did I, press training ensured that I evened out my accent as much as I could.

"He could've gotten a full ride on that talent alone but he didn't want one," I continued, remembering all those fat envelopes he hadn't seemed excited about. "He also could've walked into any Ivy League college in the country with a scholarship, he was that smart. But he didn't. Instead he enlisted. Became an infantryman in the army. Served exactly sixteen months thirteen days. Then two soldiers came to Mary and Kent's door, with news their son wasn't coming home. I heard Mary scream from my house at the end of the street."

I heard the scream in my mind, tearing at it. I hadn't known humans could scream like that. Now I knew. I'd heard a variation of it all over the world. Not from the dying. But from who the dead left behind.

"I knew it then Liam was dead. I had to be sedated." My voice was even, almost robotic. A tone I employed when talking about stories that touched my heart, but I couldn't get emotional about.

My eyes were dry as I met Liam's shimmering ones.

I hadn't missed the way his body had jerked as I spoke. But I didn't soften in the face of his pain, I couldn't with what I was saying next.

"You see, in addition to being Mary and Kent's son and Antonia's big brother, Liam was also my fiancé," I continued, turning to face a slack-jawed Hansen. "We buried an empty coffin five days later, because they said there wasn't anything to bury." I paused. "And they were right."

I didn't wait for a comment from Hansen or Liam, both of

them wearing granite expressions, Liam had gone a dull gray with my words. As if they had sickened him. I hoped they had. I hoped the poisonous truth was acid to his veins.

Because it was acid to mine.

I turned on my heel and walked calmly out the door.

CHAPTER FIVE

I WAS OBVIOUSLY NOT ALLOWED out the front gates.

Ironically, it was the same prospect that had reservations letting me in that refused to let me out. Silently, with his hand on his gun and a borderline apologetic look on his face.

That's how I knew the news of who I really was hadn't hit yet. There would be no apology in his eyes if he knew he was staring in the face of someone who had betrayed the club. That news was being kept under lock and key, I doubted it was to protect me, likely it was because the club couldn't afford to look weak right now. And letting a woman, of all people, through the club's defenses would definitely do so.

It would get out, though.

Good news didn't travel, fast or otherwise. But bad news traveled with devastating speed.

It was worth more, too.

Good news wasn't worth much at all.

I didn't argue with the prospect. It wasn't worth it, and it wouldn't change anything. He was under orders. And unless I felt like wrestling his gun off him and shooting him, I wasn't getting out of that gate.

Frustration clawed at my throat, but I forced myself to remain outwardly calm, slowly walking to the edge of the parking lot and sitting on the ground, my back up against the outer wall of the clubhouse.

It didn't pay to panic in situations like this.

Ones where you were trapped around a bunch of men with guns who followed orders until death. It wasn't a foreign situation, though it was not one I expected to face on home soil. Or with Liam in the mix.

It was the Liam part that was clawing at my throat.

The rest of it, being potentially labeled as a rat by one of the biggest motorcycle clubs in the country, my fate being held in the steady hands of a man wearing a president's patch and a cold expression, none of it really compared to Liam.

"I'm gonna marry you one day, you know?" he said, drawing lines on the palm of my hand.

"I know," I replied.

He stopped. "You don't seem surprised."

I grinned. "Of course I'm not. I knew from the moment I met you, I'd figure a way to make you fall in love with me."

"You cast a spell on me, Peaches?" he teased.

"A witch never tells."

His chuckle was throaty and deep, more like a man's every day. He continued tracing. "Doesn't matter," he decided. "I'm gonna marry you, spell or no spell."

I expected the man in the cut that settled beside me to be Liam.

Though I knew it wasn't the second I watched the figure stroll over.

I remembered Liam's walk.

It hadn't changed.

Funny how everything about a person could change, but the way they walked stayed the same.

Hansen settled on the ground beside me.

He didn't speak for the longest time.

Neither did I.

As a journalist, I knew the value of silence was almost more than that of questions.

As a human going through unthinkable torment, I didn't have anything to offer the man that might order my death but silence.

"Jagger came to the club fucked up," he said finally. "Fuck, most prospects come to the club fucked up in one way or another. This ain't exactly a mecca for the well-adjusted." He looked at the building as if it were living, staring at him. "But Jagger more than most. I'd served, so I knew the look of a man, one that had seen too much. Done even more. He wore the mark on his face, obvious to anyone, it was fresher then. But that healed. It's scar tissue now. What hasn't healed is whatever brought him here." He paused. "Now I know a little bit of that."

"You mean to tell me you didn't know about what he left behind coming here?" I accused. I found that to be bullshit. Hansen didn't look like a man who only knew half a story. I expected that he helped Liam tie up loose ends.

"Know a lot of what he left behind was death," he said. "Didn't know a thing about the things he'd left livin'."

I gritted my teeth. I knew when people were lying. Hansen wasn't lying.

"He cares about you," he said finally when I didn't respond.

I scoffed. "If he cared so much, or even a little bit, he wouldn't have let me believe he was dead for the past fourteen years."

Hansen gave me a long look. "Or if he cared too much, that's the reason why he let you believe that."

Then he stood.

"Gonna have to get used to this place for a while, sweetheart," he continued. "Though I expect you gathered that already."

I blinked up at him. "So you're not gonna kill me?"

Hansen chuckled. "Got a wife and two kids I love very much. Don't plan on leaving this earth or leaving them, which would be what happens if Jagger even thought he caught a *whiff* of me *considering* doing that. Even without that, no, I wouldn't be killing you. What you did, it doesn't sit well with me. Don't like it. Doesn't mean I don't understand it. Also know you're not a threat to the club. You weren't trying to bring us down."

"And if I was a threat? If I was trying to bring you down?" The question was asked almost instinctively, my reporter's brain still intent on getting more information about the story that had become my prison.

He didn't hesitate. "Then I'm afraid we wouldn't be havin' this conversation. But you already knew that."

Then he walked off, leaving me to contemplate the clubhouse that I'd been staring at one month ago, intent on finding a story. And instead I'd found a ghost.

Instead I'd found my destruction.

I DIDN'T WANT to go back inside.

I really, fricking, didn't want to go inside.

No one had come since Hansen.

Not Liam.

Not even Claw, to kill me when Hansen wasn't looking.

And he was capable of doing that, killing. A woman. Someone he'd become friends with. Because that's the way of the club, they valued it so highly that life became cheap when betrayal was present.

I didn't judge him for it. Not really. Life was cheap everywhere.

But then again, the change after I spoke—after I spewed all those words out at Liam—was palpable. His murderous fury simmered down. He had a human reaction to my story. The sorrow in it. That didn't surprise me either. He was a good man. As good as this world allowed him to be, I guessed.

I didn't know if Liam was a good man now.

Liam was *alive*.

The thought ricocheted through my skull with the speed and damage of a bullet. It hadn't sunk in yet. Though his death had sunk in. Since the second I heard that horrible, animal scream from down the street. There was no adjustment period, no blissed moments in the mornings when I was ignorant of the truth. No, I woke up every single day lucid with the knowledge of what my life was now, constant dark, storm clouds.

"It'll be better tomorrow," my mother whispered, voice no longer strong and sure as I'd come to expect from her in times of crisis.

Because this wasn't a time of crisis.

I didn't even know what this was. There was no word for this kind of ugly, soul-destroying, unfathomable pain.

"I don't want tomorrow," I replied, my voice was soaked with the tears I hadn't shed. It was slow, almost slurred, saturated with medication my childhood doctor had injected into me at some point earlier. "I want yesterday. I would trade every single tomorrow there ever could be for one moment of yesterday. Where he wasn't gone. Where I didn't have a hole punched through my chest."

I rubbed that same spot, feeling that same empty space underneath the skin. It hadn't healed, grown over, with the evidence of what put it there being a lie. Because it wasn't really a lie.

He was still gone.

Even if he was here.

I went inside because I was cold, because my ass was going to sleep, and because I knew I couldn't delay the inevitable.

I wasn't one to delay the most horrible of things. Mostly because my living was made out of staring at the most horrible of things. Making other people stare at them.

It was still quiet when I walked into the clubhouse, the common room illuminated with a dull light that showed a figure slouched at the bar.

No one else was around.

I could tell it was him by the shadows.

Even though his shadow was different. Bigger. Inkier somehow.

He moved the second the door shut behind me. I was surprised that it took that to notice I was in the room. I would've guessed he would've caught on to my presence the second the door opened. When I started walking across the parking lot. Wasn't he meant to be a badass outlaw criminal who could sense danger?

Was I danger to him? Did I mean enough to be dangerous?

But then again, he might be as lost in thought as I was. Sure, he had a lot to think about, how his grand plan of leaving his past behind in the coffin that lay in his cemetery at home was shot to shit now.

"You need to sleep," he said by way of greeting, his husky voice carrying over the room.

Immediately the chill of that voice, of the emptiness prickled against my arms and I rubbed them. "As much as the possibility seems ridiculous under the circumstances, yes," I agreed.

I could fall asleep in all different and dangerous circumstances, it was necessary. You snatched sleep when you could in my line of work, because you couldn't be sure when you'd get it again. It wasn't New York that never slept, it was the story. It was war. Suffering.

I glanced around at the common room and the worn and tattered sofas scattered around the place.

"I'm guessing this is serving as my accommodations for the foreseeable future?" I asked. I'd slept in worse.

"Fuck no," Liam clipped. "You're sleepin' in my room."

My entire body went ramrod straight. "No way in hell is that happening," I hissed. "I'd rather risk getting whatever undiscovered STD lives on these sofas."

He was across the room in a flash, gripping my upper arm firm enough so I couldn't squirm out of his grasp, but not hard enough to hurt.

"You don't have a choice in the matter," he said, pulling me across the room.

I fought him as he did so, but my protests were weak from the upcoming adrenaline crash and the very presence of his touch. My muscles melted and it was all I could do to let him drag me down the hall.

"I'm not sleeping in a room with you, Liam," I said as he walked me into the room I'd showered in.

He regarded me, face hard. "I'm not sleepin' here. I'll crash somewhere else." He looked to the door.

I followed his gaze. There was a padlock on the outside.

I gaped thinking about why that had to be there.

He took my pause as opportunity and began to walk out.

Without a fricking word, he was just going to walk out.

"You're really going to keep me prisoner here?" I asked his back.

He didn't turn. "I have to."

"You don't *have* to do anything," I hissed. "You could walk out of here right now, drive back to the family who've been mourning *your death* for almost fifteen years."

He didn't move, but I watched his large form stiffen. I glared at the grim reaper on his back and it taunted me with its unyielding stare.

"My club is my family now."

And then he walked out.

The click of the lock against the door echoed in my brain.

Not as loud, nor as painful as the words he'd spoken.

I'd been in all sorts of situations as a journalist. I'd even been held prisoner before. By people much worse than this. I'd seen my photographer shot in the face right before my eyes. A piece of his skull cut my cheek.

I still had the scar.

I had been eighty percent sure I wasn't going to make it out alive.

And this time, I didn't think Liam would hurt me. Certainly not kill me.

No, *Liam* would never hurt me.

This Jagger character...I didn't know him. I didn't know what he'd do to me.

Jagger

He didn't sleep. Not a fucking wink.

How the fuck could he sleep when she was there? Right *there*, behind that door he'd been staring at the entire night. After locking her inside the room.

He'd gone to the bar to retrieve a bottle of Jack.

Then he'd sank down to the floor opposite his door and stared at it. He didn't need to do so, he knew that she couldn't escape. His window had bars on it, all of them did now since the attack.

And the lock would hold fast with even Hades putting his

weight on it. Caroline wasn't even a buck fifty soaking wet. He didn't doubt her strength or resilience, but she still wouldn't get out.

He half expected her to try. To scream. As most bitches would when faced with the fact they were imprisoned within a motorcycle club that had discovered they were a rat. Imprisoned with a man they'd once known. Once mourned. He couldn't think of the words she'd spoken in church. Couldn't think of that empty deadness in her voice.

So he thought about her screaming for rescue.

But there was nothing but silence from the other side of the door.

That silence told him a lot of things.

That she was smart. But he already knew that. She would always go on about how smart *he* was, the places he would go with such utter confidence. But she had something about her that was more than intelligence. It didn't surprise him she was a reporter. It fucking enraged him that she was a reporter that did things like risk her life going undercover at a fucking MC. If this was any other MC, even a fucking other chapter, she would've been dead.

He took a long swig on that thought.

The Jack tasted like acid.

She was smart, so that's why she wasn't trying to escape—because she knew she couldn't.

But there was something else. Something about that steely glint in her eye when she spoke with Hansen. The even tenor of her voice.

Her fucking *voice*.

Almost fifteen years he'd gone without it.

He'd imagined her soft whispers every night. Every moment.

There wasn't anything soft about it now.

It was hard. Cold. Controlled. It was the voice of someone

who'd stared death in the face before. Who'd sat at tables with murderers before.

That chilled him.

To the fucking bone.

That's what kept him up all night. Long after the Jack had gone. That's what kept him stone cold sober until Hansen's hand settled on his shoulder.

His president glanced to the empty bottle, to the door and then back to him. "Take it you haven't slept?"

"What the fuck do you think?"

"I think it's time for church," he said in response.

Jagger froze.

He knew what that meant. Hansen was a good friend. Which was why he had let Jagger take Caroline in the alley. Which was why he hadn't killed her immediately when he found out that she was a journalist.

That she was a rat.

Yeah, he did that because he was a good friend and because he sensed what she was to him even before she spouted that rancid truth all over the table.

He was the friend who didn't ask a single fucking question about that truth. The truth he hadn't told him in the twelve years he'd been patched. That they'd been friends.

He imagined bitches would have a lot of fucking questions for their friends, for their families if it came out they weren't who they thought they were.

But this was different. Brothers in the club were different. Everyone had an ugly past. You didn't come to the club if it was all sunshine and rainbows. It was unspoken that that past stayed buried, just like whatever bodies lived there.

Hansen got that.

He also got that Jagger wasn't pretending to be someone else.

He was exactly who they all thought he was. Which was why he was fucking here in the first place.

So yeah, Hansen was a good friend.

He was also a good fucking president.

Jagger knew what church meant.

It meant Hansen wasn't keeping his club in the dark about who Caroline really was. The club, the members, it was fresh, new, built on blood, death. Hansen didn't want lies in the foundation.

He got it.

Respected it.

But it scared the absolute fuck out of him.

Because Hansen was a good friend.

But that didn't mean shit at the table.

That didn't mean shit when the safety of the club was at stake.

And the table would call for blood.

Caroline's.

Jagger took a harsh breath. The air cut his tongue. He swallowed blood.

Not his own.

Caroline's.

But the patch on his back got him up.

And following his president into church.

CURSES ERUPTED around the table after Hansen told the club about last night. About Caroline. Who she was. What it meant for the club. And he hinted at what she meant to Jagger. What she had meant to him in the past.

He didn't tell the full story.

Because in the midst of being a good president, he was being a good friend. Also part of being a president was keeping your brother's secrets.

So he didn't tell the whole ugly truth.

He told part of it.

Which was still ugly.

They had a rat in the club. Months after the club was almost destroyed. In the middle of a war that was only gonna get bloodier before it was over.

This was no time for mercy. It was time for action.

But this was Jagger's woman. He'd declared as much. Hansen reiterated it. But she was also a traitor. It was one of the oldest rules that a member's woman was protected. That if you put a hand on her, you'd not only lose your patch, you'd lose your life.

Another one of their oldest rules was that rats died. Immediately. Despite gender, age or affiliation.

"What do we do here?" Troy asked after a long silence. He was reasonable. Quiet to the point of mute most of the time. Didn't drink much. Didn't fuck bitches for all Jagger could see, and that was not for lack of opportunity. The fucker was a pretty boy. Pale as all fuck. Dark hair. All cheekbones. Strictly black and white tattoos covering his body.

He could have his pick of the bitches.

He didn't.

Jagger had idly wondered if he was gay. It didn't bother him. Who people fucked was none of his business. And though the Sons of Templar weren't known to be particularly inclusive in their history, as younger presidents took over, more progressive ideas came with them. So no one was getting refused a chance to prospect over sexual orientation, race, religion.

Obviously women still couldn't patch in.

They weren't *that* progressive.

But for all the power and strength Jagger had seen from the

Old Ladies, they didn't need a chance at a patch. They already had ones of their own.

It didn't matter who Troy wanted to fuck in that moment.

It mattered that he spoke at all when the entire club was silenced by the reality of what was happening. Which rule did they break? Did they let a rat breathe? Or did they harm a woman of a patched member?

"We do what we need to," Jagger said as Hansen opened his mouth, unable to let the guilt for condemning Caroline to fall on Hansen's shoulders. He'd take that shit on. He'd do what needed to be done. But it'd haunt him. And Jagger was already haunted. It was on him.

"What the fuck does that mean, we do what we need to?" Claw demanded, slamming his hands down on the table. The same hands that had circled around Caroline's throat not twelve hours ago. The same hands that would've kept squeezing, that would've ended her fucking life if he hadn't ripped him off her.

The mere thought of it had Jagger needing to take out his piece and put a bullet in the fucker's brain. His brother's brain. At the table.

That's how turned upside down he was.

What Caroline was doing to him.

And she was obviously doing something to Claw too, if he was ready to protect her, hours after he'd been intent on burying her.

Jagger met his eyes. "You know what the fuck it means," he said.

"You're fucking crazy," Claw hissed.

"He's not fucking crazy," Swiss put in, voice cold. "He's doing right by the club."

"No, he's not," Claw said carefully, accusing Jagger with his eyes.

"You know that what's right for the club sometimes doesn't

line up with what's right in any other way. It's how this club survives. It's how we survive. I'll do it myself," he said, bile filling his mouth as he spoke.

He wasn't sure if it was because he was lying or telling the truth.

How far had he really gone?

Hansen stared at him after his words. The entire table silenced.

He'd never received such a look from his best friend turned president, it was as if Hansen didn't recognize him. Or maybe he was just recognizing him for the man he was tired of pretending he wasn't.

"She's your…"

"Past," he finished for Hansen and tried to convince himself.

Hansen gave him a hard look. "While she's here in the present, she's the club's problem now. We can't let this stand. I won't. Not with everything going on."

Ugliness hung in the air. Ugliness had hung for a while. Since the clubhouse turned into a fucking crypt for almost the entire chapter.

Ordinarily, a case like this would've been clear cut. The club took care of it with a single bullet and a deep unmarked grave.

They weren't pausing because she was a woman.

Men didn't like it, fuck, most of the club abhorred violence against women. Innocent women. They treated women the same as men when they became their enemies. Women could be just as dangerous as men.

More so.

"I won't let it stand, either," Hansen said. "Nor will I handle this how we would with a rat. Because this situation is unique. And I don't have a problem killing a woman who's guilty in our eyes, but I don't think she is guilty of trying to damage the club."

Swiss slammed his hand down on the table. "She's a fuckin'

reporter," he hissed. "That's one step down from a pig."

Hansen regarded him coolly. "And I'm your president, and I'm saying that we're not killing her. Because I don't think she deserves to die. Anyone want to challenge me on that?" He looked around the table before he locked eyes with Jagger.

Jagger knew his best friend was doing this for a number of reasons. Because he was telling the truth and he didn't think she was guilty enough to die. He also knew that he was saving Jagger having to take up arms against his brothers who tried to lay a hand on Caroline.

Because Hansen knew him.

He knew the words before were nothing but empty air.

Jagger knew it too. He would kill every last one of his brothers in arms, in everything but blood if they tried to lay a hand on her.

"Obviously we're not gonna kill her," Claw piped in after a long silence. "She's not only too pretty to kill, but a good distraction. So what the fuck are we gonna do with her?"

Hansen looked around the table once more. "She wants a story. We'll give her a story." He paused. "But first, we needa make sure she knows her punishment for *thinkin'* about betraying the club. And maybe she'll think twice about doin' it again. Because no matter who she is, to anyone, we don't give second chances."

Jagger met Hansen's eyes. Waited until he got the nods of approval from the men around the table. Then he stood as soon as the gavel slammed down. Walked out of the room, calmly. Purposefully.

Then he went and vomited in the bathroom.

He was a man that had seen a lot, done even worse. None of it made him sick.

But the fucking thought of Caroline dying at the hands of his club, it was enough to shed the lining from his fuckin' guts.

CHAPTER SIX

Caroline

I WAS STARING at the door.

I'd been awake since just after sunrise, after a long and thankfully dreamless sleep. But reality didn't hesitate to punch me in the face the second I opened my eyes. I was in Liam's room.

Liam was alive.

Three words kept bouncing around my head over and over.

As I got up, made the bed, doing my best to replicate the military corners, as I finger brushed my teeth, splashed water on my face, the words followed me.

I stared at myself in the mirror.

My skin was sallow. I was always pale. Ever since I was a kid.

I blinked, looking no longer at the woman of the present, but the girl of the past. With blonde ringlets and innocent eyes.

Somehow, despite the fact my brother and sister had a scattering of freckles covering their bodies, I didn't have a single one. Not growing up at least. Not when I was with him. That would change. Once the harsh sun, the harsh life brought them out. But when Liam knew me, my skin had always been clear, white, with peachy undertones.

Peaches.

His hands were everywhere. They were fire, alighting my entire body with his touch, awakening something inside me I thought didn't exist outside of romance novels. A hunger clawed at my throat, on the insides of my thighs. For him.

"Liam," I gasped, coming up for air, our mouths still brushing.

His eyes were wild with need. With carnal desire. For me. "Fuck, Caroline. You're so fucking beautiful." He lifted himself up, tracing his eyes up and down my almost naked body.

I wanted to flinch underneath his gaze. He'd seen me in bikinis before. But this was different. My cotton lace trimmed panties and white bra weren't exactly sexy. But then again, I hadn't planned on my parents being away for the night and having my siblings absent so Liam could come over.

I hadn't counted on being so nervous. So terrified that I wouldn't be enough for him.

But his gaze, the pure reverence and worship in it told me I was enough. It filled me up.

His hand traced along the edge of my bra, above my thundering heartbeat. And then down.

I let out a gasp as he brushed my panties.

His eyes met mine. "You're perfection," he growled. "You're peaches and cream."

His hand went inside my panties.

"You're my Peaches."

I hadn't even realized I'd smashed the mirror until the glass shattered around me, falling into the sink, scattering onto the no doubt bleached floor.

I stared down at it emptily, then to the object I'd used to smash the glass. A soap dispenser. At least I hadn't used my fist.

It clattered as I dropped it into the sink.

I walked back into the bedroom. I didn't avoid the broken glass in my bare feet, but it didn't cut me. Maybe I was already cut up, shredded enough, there wasn't any unharmed skin for it to slice.

I stared at the orderly room. I started with the oak set of drawers to my left.

I wanted to rip his carefully ordered life apart. Just like he'd ripped me apart.

I WAS STANDING in the middle of the room when the lock on the outside of the door rattled.

I was standing because there was nowhere to sit. In addition to ripping off all the sheets and pillowcases, I'd done my best to overturn the mattress. The frame was too heavy to move. Though I might not have been physically as strong as the stranger in the cut with the scar and muscles, my hurt found solace in fury, and fury worked well to give me strength.

An empty kind of strength.

Because I might have been able to ruin his bedroom, tear apart his drawers and smash his mirrors, but he could ruin me just by opening the door. My strength waned and disappeared as his eyes locked on mine.

He gazed around the room, eyes empty, gaze flat. No anger, not even surprise. Just...nothing. Could this really be him? Could he really regard me with that flat gaze after what happened? After what we were?

"It help?" he asked finally, nodding his head to the room.

I bit my lip until I tasted blood. Took a breath. Steeled myself from the sudden and almost unbearable need to run across his ruined and foreign possessions and into the familiar embrace of his arms. My blood cried out for it with a desperation I could barely survive.

I needed him.

It didn't matter if he was Jagger. If he was a member of the Sons of Templar MC. That there was ink all over his body I didn't recognize. A scar ripping across his face evidence of a pain I was ignorant of.

It only mattered that somewhere in there, was Liam. And he was alive.

I even lifted my foot in preparation to launch myself off. Then something caught up with me. Sense. Fury. Hurt.

I placed my foot back down. "What do you think, Liam?" I whispered.

His face wasn't empty anymore, confronted with the brokenness of my tone. Of what I guessed my face looked like. Everything hard about him melted. His body physically sagged as if ten thousand pounds had just been dropped on his back.

He lifted his motorcycle boot. "Peaches." The word was a plea.

It unraveled me.

Somehow my backbone kept me together. I folded my arms. "Has the club decided on what you'll do with me? I have a life to get back to. If you're not going to kill me, that is."

Could he kill me?

I couldn't think about that. Because I wasn't sure if I'd survive the answer. The truth.

His expression shifted and the weight left. Or maybe he got better at hiding the fact he carried it around. "You're not getting back to anywhere," he all but growled. He looked around again. "I'll get a prospect in. Clean this shit up."

"You think it's that easy?" I hissed at him.

He clenched his fists at his sides. "Nothing about this shit is easy, Caroline. Nothing about the past fourteen years has been fucking easy."

I scoffed. "Yeah, I bet it's been so fucking *hard* for you. Here drinking whisky, fucking whores, and living outside the law, being free."

He was across the room before I could blink, wood crunching beneath his boots as he crushed parts of his dresser. He didn't touch me. He didn't need to. Every inch of him was pressed into the air, inches from me.

"I've been a lot of fucking things for the past fourteen years, Caroline," he rasped, never taking his eyes from me, stealing the breath from my lungs. "Only thing I haven't been is free."

He let the words hang between us, a dare for me to do more. To ask more. His chest was heavy with exertion, the veins in his neck pulsating as if he were practicing some sort of epic restraint.

My eyes traced the puckered marks of the scar that dominated the face I once used to know so well. Pain lanced down the exact same spot on my own as agony speared through me with the knowledge of something tearing at his skin like that. Of him having to recover from that without me.

But then again, he made me recover from scars worse than that.

You just couldn't see them.

I sucked in a visible breath and stepped back purposefully, as if the mere foot of distance did something to insulate me against him. The grave hadn't insulated me against him.

He rolled his shoulders back, resting his hand on his belt. "I'll arrange for that prospect to come in here, clean it up."

"If the club is going to keep me prisoner here, I'm not staying in this room," I declared, searching for some leverage in this situation, some control. And I couldn't stay in this room. Even though it was devoid of personality, it showed nothing of the boy I used to love. That was the point. Its very emptiness would swallow me whole.

Something flickered in his eyes. "You don't have a choice in the matter."

I sank my fingernails into the skin of my palms. I itched to argue. I sensed it wouldn't help. The man in front of me was likely hardened to arguments, to pleading. I was aware I needed to be thankful for the fact I was alive at all. If that's what this was.

"Then don't send a prospect, I can clean this up myself. I've had practice." It was petty, but I felt petty.

Though there was no victory in his visible flinch.

This war had no victors.

He nodded once. "I'll get you something to eat. Coffee. I assume you take it the same."

I sank my fingertips in harder. There was something intimate about someone knowing the mundane things about you. I wanted it to have changed. But though many things about me had changed, what felt like my entire genetic makeup, the way I took my coffee had not.

"Don't bother," I snapped. "I won't eat or drink anything you give me."

Again, another stupid move. I didn't gain anything from going on some stupid hunger strike. If anything, I needed to keep my physical strength up if the opportunity to escape presented itself.

Not that it would.

There was no escaping this. Even if I did find a way out of this highly secure compound.

Liam's jaw hardened. "You're fuckin' eating," he clipped.

"You're going to force it down my throat?" I challenged.

His eyes seemed black. "If need be. I won't have you fucking with your health over this."

"Your concern is touching."

He flinched again.

There wasn't victory in that one either.

"Just eat the fucking food, Caroline."

I jutted my chin up and didn't reply.

He ran his eyes over me, they softened at the edges, and I was reminded of that reverent way he'd gazed at me the day he'd taken my virginity, and every day after that. And every day before that, for that matter.

It hurt more than anything I'd experienced, that soft gaze from a dead man.

Then it was gone.

He turned around, began to walk away from me, leaving me in the ruins he'd created.

"I need something," I said to his back.

He stopped. Paused. Sighed. And then he turned. "You're not really in a position to make requests."

I folded my arms and narrowed my eyes at him.

He met my gaze long enough for it to get uncomfortable, for the past to fill the room up until we were up to our necks, about to drown in it.

He sighed again.

"What do you want?"

"Red lipstick," I replied, licking my lips. I pretended I didn't notice the way his eyes followed the motion and the way his jaw tightened. "Any one at a pinch, but if you've got...a woman who knows her way around beauty counters at a department store, then Chanel, shade Pirate."

I didn't think this new Liam—no, Jagger—had an emotional range past fury, frustration, and indifference, but I managed to add shock to the list with my request.

He blinked rapidly. "Lipstick?" he repeated.

I nodded once.

His face shut down and his eyes went glacial. "You think you're gonna be able to fuck your way outta here, you're wrong."

My spine straightened. "I'm not planning on *fucking* my way out." I spat the ugly word at him wishing it was a bullet.

All soft and fond thoughts I had for him, for Liam were gone. This wasn't a soft and kind boy. This was a hard and crude man.

"That's how you were plannin' on getting *in*," he countered, venom in his voice. "And unfortunately for you, sweetheart, the only person you're gonna be seeing from now on is me, and I can tell you for sure you're not fucking your way *anywhere*."

Then he stormed out, slamming the door behind him.

Jagger

He was contemplating his empty whisky glass when Macy came in.

He'd sent a prospect to his room with food, coffee, how she liked it, black with four sugars. Four fucking sugars.

He kissed her and she tasted of coffee and Caroline. "Don't get how you drink that shit." He nodded to her pitch-black mug that was sweeter than sin. "Plus, you don't need anything to make you sweeter than you already are." He kissed her again, slipping his tongue inside. She responded instantly, melting against him. His dick hardened. "Fuck," he murmured against her mouth, meeting her lazy and hungry eyes. "Maybe I can get down with the taste of coffee that sweet. Only if I'm tasting it on you at the same time."

Coffee.

He hadn't been able to drink fucking *coffee* for almost fifteen years because it reminded him of her.

Whisky worked better anyway.

"Why didn't you tell me that *Caroline Hargrave* was in the clubhouse?" Macy demanded, hands on her small hips.

It was still amazing to him that she'd had her second baby almost two months ago. Bitches didn't tend to bounce back that quickly. Not that he expected them to. Nine months growing a child was a fucking lot for a body to go through. Women were tougher than men for that alone.

Macy was tougher than she looked, five foot nothing, a buck twenty soaking wet.

She'd been spending a lot of time at home with their newborn, and toddler, not around the club as much. He thought it might've been because the club was one big crypt and Macy couldn't face the death there. It was hard for him to sit in a fucking room where most of his family had been murdered. He didn't blame Macy one bit for staying at their warm home full of memories that weren't stained with blood, with children that gave her hope. Jagger knew Hansen wanted to be right there with her, but this was not a time to play happy families.

It was time to make sure those families had a chance to be happy in the future.

That meant war.

Blood.

He should have expected this.

Macy wasn't one to stay out of the loop.

It would've made him happy in any other circumstance, her waltzing in here in some hippy getup, hand on her hip, some of the old light back in her eyes.

But because happiness was a memory that was never going to be a reality, it didn't.

"I didn't tell you, 'cause no one was meant to know," he said, hoping that would be the end of it.

This was Macy, of course it wasn't the end of it.

"Well I know, and Hansen has informed me not only that we have her in the clubhouse, but we're holding her *against her will*," she said, voice sharp.

"She's a journalist, Macy," Jagger replied, voice hard.

Macy scowled. "Um, yeah, *I know.*"

"You know?" he asked, genuinely surprised. The way she said it made it seem like she didn't know from her husband telling her business that was meant to be strictly club-only, but she knew some other way.

She nodded. "If I'd seen her and not at home attached to a breast pump, a screaming child, and a toddler who needs attention, then I would've recognized her straight away. But I've been sequestered to the land of dirty diapers and milk vomit." She waved her hand. "Oh, and I love my sons and everything, they are the joy and light of my life—though I am grateful that their father is taking care of them today before I started ripping my own hair out."

Jagger wanted to chuckle. He really did. But he didn't have a reason to laugh right now.

Not that he ever had for the past decade and a half.

But he'd gotten pretty good at pretending.

There was no fucking pretending with *her* around.

He just hoped that his president didn't tell Macy anything more about Caroline. Then again, if he had, Macy would not be approaching shit like this.

When she was a club girl, he'd gotten as close to her as he could've with a woman that wasn't Caroline. Liked the bitch a lot. She was kind. Funny as fuck. Almost a distraction.

But it was always Caroline's face he saw when he sunk his dick into anyone.

Macy wasn't different in that respect.

She was different because she stuck around after the fact.

Watched movies with him. Shot the shit. She was warm. He liked that feeling of warmth. Especially when everything else about him was as cold as the fucking grave they'd buried his dog tags in.

Macy didn't know about his past. Not for lack of asking. So he knew that if Hansen had betrayed his trust—which he wouldn't have—then she would not be approaching the conversation the way she was.

He was glad as fuck for that. He was afraid of what he might say to Macy, what he might do if she tried to bring up Caroline. Their history.

"You would've recognized her?" he asked instead of dwelling on that shit.

"You honestly didn't watch any of her broadcasts?" she said, gaping at him. "Seriously? She's one of the most famous conflict journalists around."

"Don't watch the news," he replied, cracking his knuckles. He was doing his best to act like that singular piece of information didn't spear him right to his very core. The *thought* of her being famous for being in danger filled his blood with acid.

Her. The girl who cried and almost fainted when he'd fallen off his dirtbike and cut open his arm. She cried because she couldn't stand the thought of him in pain and almost threw up because blood sickened her.

And she was in the middle of war zones where all they saw was pain and blood.

Jesus.

Macy rolled her eyes, obviously unaware of what was going on inside his head. Unusual, since she was perceptive, but she was on a roll. And even the most perceptive bitch on the planet couldn't guess at their story. "Of course you don't. Men," she muttered. "Well, she is famous for *many* reasons, because she's a top reporter, of course. One of the bravest out there, men *or* women. She goes embedded sometimes, sure. But her top stories have been her risking her life without backup or with a small private security team. Then there's the fact she's a knockout. And there's another little thing." She held her thumb and forefinger inches apart. "No matter where she is in the world, what war torn country, site of famine, disease or disaster, she's always wearing blood red lipstick."

He froze. No, he'd already been frozen before, when Macy started talking about Caroline risking her fucking life being in war zones. Embedded was bad enough. Soldiers couldn't guarantee a reporter's safety as much as they could guarantee their own. He'd seen more than one reporter lying amongst the dead in a bomb blast. War didn't care if you were fighting or witnessing. Everyone died the same. Whether they had a gun or a fucking tape recorder in their hands. Whether they were there to help or harm. Bile scratched at his throat. "Red lipstick?" he repeated.

She nodded rapidly, grinning. "Badass, right? She's never told anyone exactly why, it's a mystery. Could you ask her why?"

"Fuck," he muttered, slamming the last of his whisky before standing up. "You happen to know what the fuck Chanel and the shade Pirate means?"

She grinned wider, looking slightly unhinged. He reckoned the lack of sleep, screaming newborn and pressures of the club had a lot to do with that. And the fact she was Macy. "I fucking *knew* it was Chanel," she said by response. "I've been searching for years. But *of course* it's Chanel. Elegant. Timeless."

"Mace," he clipped.

Her eyes cleared. "Yes, I know what it is," she said, rolling her eyes. "Men," she muttered again. "I'll get you some. Well, not for you. For you to give to her." She gave him a look. "Because I'm guessing I can't go in and give it to her, chat about beauty routines and how her hair stays so shiny wherever she is and how much I admire her bravery and talent?"

Jagger shook his head once.

She sighed dramatically, not worried that her husband was in charge of keeping one of the biggest conflict journalists in the country prisoner. Likely because she knew her husband. Trusted him with her life. And the lives of others. So she trusted that he'd keep Caroline safe.

Jagger thought about the naked pain in her eyes. The fact that his mere presence had turned her into one raw nerve.

He thought about running his eyes over her body, how even with that pain, his hunger, his need for her was almost feral. A hunger he knew he couldn't hold off for long.

So no. Caroline was not safe.

Macy rolled her eyes. "Okay, I'll go get it. And some for myself while I'm at it." She regarded him. "Only if I get to meet her. At some point soon."

He sighed. He knew it wouldn't be as easy as one head shake. "You know that you can't do that, Macy."

"Why? Because you're all pretending that you're actually going to do something to make her disappear? Despite the fact I'd make Hansen disappear if he did anything to one of the most important voices in journalism, and despite the fact you are all badasses willing to do ugly things for the good of the club, I know you're not gonna to do *this* ugly thing. So cut the crap."

He gritted his teeth. He couldn't risk Caroline meeting Macy and letting something slip like she had in church. That speech.

Fuck.

He'd been held captive and tortured by some of the most evil bastards to walk this earth. Pain he didn't even know existed was born for him there.

But that shit, sitting at that table, that trumped all that shit put together.

He couldn't have Macy hearing that.

More importantly, he couldn't have Macy hearing that,

having it hit her kind and soft heart and doing something stupid like help Caroline escape. Because that was exactly something Macy would do.

And despite what his president said, he didn't plan on Caroline going anywhere. Not now. Not ever.

CHAPTER SEVEN

Caroline

A PROSPECT CAME in and delivered me breakfast.

Eggs, bacon—crispy to the point of charred, because that's how I liked it—whole meal toast and peanut butter. Because whoever had put the plate together knew that I like peanut butter and eggs on toast.

He screwed up his face as he watched me bite into the bread.

I chewed and swallowed, grinning. "It's not like I'm eating cockroaches on toast," I teased.

He shook his head. "It's just weird."

I grinned. "I'm weird and proud of it."

He moved to snatch my chin and snatch my attention. As if he didn't already have it. "I'm proud of you. Never stop being weird. You're the most magnificent weirdo I've ever known."

I didn't eat the toast.

But I guzzled the coffee, despite the fact it tasted like my past, and like Liam kissing me with a smile on his face.

I needed caffeine.

The prospect was not the same one who let me in the gate. He was hulking, older, in his thirties at least, and silent.

He didn't say a word about the ruined room.

Or a word in general.

Then again, I wasn't exactly much of a conversationalist either.

He left me alone in the room I'd yet to straighten up. I ate on the floor. I liked being amongst the mess. It felt honest. Much more honest than that stupid order that had masked it all when I came in.

I could tell I was becoming slightly unhinged. Not at the fact I was imprisoned by bikers known for killing their enemies brutally. No, because of Liam.

I knew I needed to get myself together. To hold onto my trademark cool.

It felt lost. I needed that lipstick.

The one that Liam had thought I wanted to *fuck* my way out of the clubhouse.

The accusation burned like acid. That the simple request of lipstick could be translated to that in his mind. That he could think that of me. Granted, that was the kind of persona I created to get myself into the clubhouse.

But this was Liam.

He was supposed to know me.

No.

This was Jagger.

He didn't know me.

I didn't know him.

I WAS LEFT ALONE, pacing in Liam's room for four hours. I

had planned on keeping it as ruined as possible, but sheer boredom got the best of me and I did my best to straighten it up.

I put the mattress back on the bed. Piled the sheets I'd somehow managed to rip into the corner, along with the ruined pillows. The comforter had survived my assault so I placed it neatly atop the bed.

I replaced all of the drawers. Though they didn't fit right anymore and all looked crooked. I liked it better that way. I went through every single one, trying to discover who this Jagger was. Trying to find a hint of Liam.

I found soft overly laundered tees. Underwear. Worn jeans. Belts. Shoulder holsters for weapons. Sweats. Basic male grooming instruments. A couple of loose bullets. The box for an iPhone.

But no personality.

No mementos.

Not until I searched his bedside table. Full of condoms. I swallowed bile at the thought of that. He was a man, and though I'd thought he was, he wasn't dead. I wondered how many women there'd been since me. If they were better. More experienced than I'd been.

Two books on poetry surprised me.

I leafed through them.

Something caught my eye before I put them back.

The poetry books fell to the floor.

My shaking hand lifted a single white feather.

He was packing his bags.

I didn't want to watch him do that.

Packing made it real.

Like it hadn't been real before.

It had been.

That was the problem. Since he'd announced it, it was

inescapably and brutally real. A truth I couldn't escape, couldn't ignore.

He stopped as I walked into the bedroom, as if he sensed my presence. He always did that, like he was somehow hyper aware of me. I wondered if that awareness would cross oceans.

I glanced to the backpack on top of the messy bed. "You know, they're not gonna let you get away with a bed like that in the army."

He rolled his eyes in response. "Yeah, well, it's only for a small amount of time. You bet your perfect ass that I'll be right back to this when we have our home together and you'll have to nag me every day."

I rolled my own eyes. "I don't nag."

He grinned, crossing the room and grasping my hips. "Of course not, my perfect, beautiful, Peaches."

I glared at him.

He kissed my nose.

I closed my eyes at his touch. At his proximity. It was never something I took for granted. Got used to. But it was something I considered a part of me. I was never complete until I was in his arms. I didn't even care if that was lame and anti-feminist of me. It was the truth.

And the truth was that I wouldn't be whole for months, years, depending on how this went and it was staring me in the face in the form of a backpack.

I let out a breath and pulled myself from his arms.

He hesitated before letting me go, as if he too were hesitant to pass up a moment when we were in touching distance.

But he let me go.

He'd eventually have to let me go, so I supposed it was good practice.

I took the object out of my pocket and laid it on top of a tee.

His heat hit my back, chin on top of my head, hands covering mine. Liam fingered the pure white feather. "What's this?"

"The day I met you, I knew that it was an important day. The most important day of my life," I said. "Even though I was too young to properly understand it, or even know what it meant, I just knew you were going to be someone to me." I paused. "Everything to me. So I wanted to have something I could hold onto. Remember the moment with. I wanted to package that feeling into something I could look at later. Even if my thought process wasn't that complex at the time." I stroked the white feather, slightly worn with how many times I'd held it. "So I found this, just lying on the sidewalk next to a crushed up Coke can."

He was silent, though his arms had tightened around me. His lips on my hair.

"I want you to take it. To take the importance of that first day with you. And to bring it back with you."

Liam turned me around. He clutched my face. His eyes shimmered. "I'll carry it everywhere. Through whatever happens. I'll never let go of our past. And I'll bring it back, ready for us to start our future."

It was dull now. Not pure white anymore. As if it sensed that nothing between Liam and I could ever be pure again.

But he had it here.

In a life he'd built without me. A life that he'd seemingly designed to make sure never involved me again.

I wanted to feel hope with that.

But hope was dead here.

BY THE TIME the prospect came in with lunch—a can of Coke, a turkey sandwich, and a candy bar—I had stopped staring at the feather. I'd managed to clean as best as I could. A pile of trash sat in the corner, all the things I'd ruined, including an expensive looking TV I didn't even remember ripping off the wall.

He placed the tray on the bedside table.

Something rolled around beside the Coke.

My heart stopped.

It was a tube of lipstick. Black, with a distinct double C in gold on the top of the cap.

I picked it up with the same shaking hand that had cradled the feather hours ago.

I glanced up to the man who'd been silently staring at me as I gazed at a tube of lipstick.

"Thank you," I said genuinely. Though giving thanks to someone enabling my captivity was kind of stupid. But he was a prospect, even if he had an opinion on keeping a woman hostage, he didn't get a seat at the table. That was the whole point in prospecting for a club like this. To see the way of life, to understand there wasn't a say in whether it happened or not, but to participate in it, no matter how ugly it got.

Something told me that life had already gotten plenty ugly for this man, and delivering meals to a woman locked in a trashed room was nowhere near the worst thing he'd done.

He didn't reply to my thanks.

I didn't expect him to.

He just picked up the barely touched breakfast tray. "You'll get some of your shit later on today," he said, his voice was thickly accented, Scottish if I wasn't mistaken.

That surprised me. Not just the fact he was speaking to me but the fact they were letting me have some of my own things.

To be buried in?

"If I get a say in it, can I request nothing short or tight?" I asked, clenching my hands around the tube of lipstick. "Jeans and tees would be great."

He eyed me. "Doubt you'll get a say in it," he replied.

I grinned. It might've surprised him, but his face displayed nothing. "Can you see if you can get me a pen and paper? I promise I won't try and use it as a weapon or anything."

He didn't reply.

Just walked out.

But another three hours later, he returned with a bag of jeans, tees and a pen and paper.

He didn't reply to my thanks then either.

I DIDN'T STOP what I was doing when he walked into the room.

I didn't react either.

Not outwardly at least.

"What are you doing?" Liam asked after a beat that I imagined he'd been watching me for.

I could ignore him.

Lie.

"I'm writing the things I'm grateful for today," I replied, neither ignoring him or lying.

Another pause.

"Why?"

"Because I do it every day. Despite whatever situation I'm in. No matter how dire."

"You would class this situation as dire?"

I still didn't look up. "I don't think there is a way to class this situation."

He didn't reply.

"Why do you write what you're grateful for every day?" he asked finally when the scratch of the pen on the paper and our past got too loud.

Another question I wasn't under obligation to answer, honestly or otherwise.

"Because it's something my therapist recommended," I replied. "It's a common tool used on patients who've suffered something traumatic."

I didn't mean to add the last part. I really, really didn't. Admitting I had trauma was begging him to ask the one question I didn't know if I could physically answer, honestly or otherwise.

Anyone given such a statement would need the answer. As humans, we're desperate for morbid information.

Liam stayed silent.

It was turning out to be his way, this new person. He asked questions when I didn't expect him to speak, and he stayed quiet when my heart wouldn't allow me to utter a word.

It was like he was tapped into some part of me, and I didn't like that. I didn't like having a connection with a man that I was supposed to hate. I hated the fact that despite the years, the death, the pain, that connection remained unbroken, unchanged though everything else had changed. I hated that I was faced with Liam embodied in a person he never should've been. I hated most of all, that I couldn't hate him. Not one bit.

I finished writing.

I could try and stare at the paper for longer, I guessed, but it was depressing staring at the emotional straws I'd tried to grasp onto.

1. *I'm inhaling and exhaling.*
2. *I have this pen and paper.*
3. *I'm not tied in some basement being tortured.*

NOT BEING TORTURED HAD BECOME something to be grateful for, apparently.

As I lifted my eyes, I knew I needed to cross that last word out. Because this was nothing short of torture.

I wanted to put Liam's presence on the list to be grateful for. The miracle I'd prayed for every day since this all began. Since it all ended.

But I didn't know yet whether this man was someone to be grateful for.

I didn't even know if this man was Liam.

And I didn't think his presence was a miracle.

It was something much darker than that.

Liam's eyes focused on my lips. I'd painted them red, and it had relaxed me some. It had given me something familiar, that constant I held onto for years when everything around me was chaos. I knew it had made me distinctive as a reporter, like it was some kind of 'style.' It was nothing more than survival.

Which was what it was now.

But it wasn't that.

Not when Liam's eyes darkened touching my lips.

"Macy is Hansen's wife," he said oddly.

I knew this. I'd heard of her, since Hansen pretty much left as soon as he could after club business had been wrapped up, never stayed to get blotto at the bar and never even fricking *looked* at any of the scantily clad girls parading around him.

I knew the club doted on Macy and their boys.

I didn't know why Liam was bringing her up now.

"She watches the news," he continued.

"Ah," I said, understanding why he had a change of heart about the lipstick. "Guessing you ran into her."

He nodded. Clenched his fists.

Silence stretched thin over the room like not enough butter on a large piece of bread.

I vowed not to break it, despite the feeling of the feather in my hands. Despite everything.

"You came here to get a story, but you've found yourself in the middle of a war," he said finally.

I didn't waver my gaze, though it was only because of the years an instinctual reaction of fear or intimidation could mean my death. I never thought I'd have to call up a skill I perfected interviewing rebel warlords in front of the boy I used to love.

This wasn't a boy.

It was a scarred and dangerous man I didn't recognize.

"I'm used to wars," I replied, voice cold.

He moved forward, quickly and smoothly so he was inhabiting all the space in front of me, and all the space inside me. "Not this one, Peaches. And not with me. This is a war you won't be walking away from."

CHAPTER EIGHT

I WAS LOCKED in that room for another week.

A whole freaking *week*.

I saw no one but two prospects. One, Elden, was chattier than the other. And by more chatty, I meant when I asked his name, he grunted "Elden."

He was the older one, with soulful demonic shadows behind his eyes.

The other was John. And I only knew that because Elden told me. 'Telling me' consisted of grunting the name and walking out.

John was not chatty.

He was younger.

With some shadows behind his eyes, but not enough to completely ruin him. I guessed he wasn't talking to me because he was taking his prospecting very seriously, he didn't want to ruin his chance for a patch by cavorting with a rat.

Like it was catching.

Things came in their three-time daily meal delivery that I knew didn't come from them.

New sheets.

White. Egyptian Cotton. Bought by a woman.

I wondered if they were from the Macy who watched the news and who I knew I had to thank for my tube of lipstick. I was almost certain of this fact, when the next day, I was given a small bag with breakfast. It had a quote from *Lord of The Rings*, 'I survived Helm's Deep.' That made me smile.

Macy was a total geek.

And, as it turned out, opening the bag, a total sweetheart.

It contained face wash, face and hair masks, nail polish, magazines, tampons, chocolate, slippers, and a bottle of wine. Even a *glass*. A proper, large and classy one too. One that I would've liked to have sitting in a glass cabinet in a home I might've lived in in another life.

Macy obviously knew I was a prisoner and was obviously trying to make captivity more comfortable.

Which she did.

Kind of.

Comfort was a dream.

This was a nightmare.

But chocolate, wine, face masks, and trashy magazines helped a little. And a little meant a lot in times like this.

I got other things.

Things I knew were from Liam.

Books. Ones only he could pick. *The Valley of the Dolls*. *The Bronze Horseman*. *Shantaram*. I had immediately shoved that one in the trash. Then retrieved it moments later, unable to commit that sacrilege.

I hid it under the bed instead.

As if that helped.

There was also more paper.

Packets of gummy bears.

"*You know those things have horse hooves in them?*" he teased, taking the packet from me.

I didn't look up, I had a test to study for. I was well aware that my grades hinged on this test, and if I wanted to get into a university close enough to the Ivy League that Liam would no doubt be admitted to, I need to focus.

I snatched the bag back.

I also needed sugar.

"I don't care. They are the only joy in my life right now."

My chin was grasped in his thumb and forefinger. I met emerald eyes. "The only joy, Peaches? Now you're just breakin' my heart."

I rolled my eyes. "Okay, you and gummy bears are the only two joys in my life. Without them, I'm destitute, damned."

He grinned. "Well, I'm gonna make sure, for the rest of your life, you're well stocked in gummy bears."

I didn't eat them.

But I filled up the notepad with not only my three things daily, but with ideas for the story, things I noticed.

THOUGH I'M A PRISONER HERE, I'm treated with respect. Well, whatever passes for respect in the underworld, which is not getting beaten, raped or starved.

Everyone carries guns. The prospects assigned to me wear them even when playing waitress to me.

There are floodlights on around the perimeter every night. And there are round the clock guards, prospects and patched members alike.

Are they expecting another attack?

The main room of the clubhouse is somehow soundproofed.

The Sons of Templar do not take kindly to those who try to

cross them, but the brutality I expected is absent. Is it because of who I am? Is it because I'm a woman? Or is it still to come?

I WONDERED whether I would still be alive to write the story.

The answer came to me on the eighth day.

When my door unlocked late afternoon and it wasn't a prospect, it was Liam.

A week without seeing him hadn't made me forget he was here. Hadn't tricked me into thinking I'd somehow hallucinated him in the midst of the trauma at seeing someone murdered in front of me then being held captive.

No, every second I knew he was here, somewhere, beyond a locked door. Wearing a cut. Wearing tattoos. A foreign face. A scar I tortured myself with at the dead of night.

A body I tortured myself with in the dead of night.

His eyes ran over me hungrily. But empty.

I was wearing jeans, loose, and a plaid shirt, nothing sexy by any means. But he made me feel exposed, naked.

Liam had a way of doing that. Stripping me down.

But it was good before. Warm. Nice. Because back then, I wasn't afraid of what I was beneath the surface.

There was nothing good about this. Because beneath the surface, I was decaying memories, rotten experiences, and ugly truths.

"Come with me," he ordered.

I wanted to argue, but I was tired. And I was anxious to get my fate in front of me. Instead of my past.

He led me through the common room.

It was empty, apart from a rogue club girl cleaning up some bottles. She glanced up at Liam, giving him a warm smile.

I almost gagged at the familiarity behind it.

Her eyes touched mine, she recognized me. We hadn't

spoken before but exchanged friendly smiles as the club gathered. But as she glanced between Liam and me, there was nothing friendly about her smile.

I wanted to educate her on the truth. That this was not me coming in and laying claim to some man that she obviously wanted. My claim to him had long died.

But Liam had already opened the door to 'church' and I was faced with another kind of truth.

I stepped inside.

The room was relatively small, taken up mostly by a long, carved wooden table.

Every seat was filled except two.

Hansen sat at the head of the table.

The mood wasn't exactly welcoming.

I would go so far as to say the mood was hostile. Openly.

Hansen nodded to the two empty chairs to his left. One, I guessed was for Liam. "Caroline. Thanks for joining us. Please, sit."

Liam pulled it out for me.

I ignored this and the second he let it go, I moved it as far away from his as I could. The screech of the chair against the hardwood floor echoed through the quiet room. Moving the chair had me almost brushing against Claw's shoulder, but I didn't care. I'd take Claw's murderous glare over...whatever was in Liam's eyes.

I wanted to tell myself I'd take anything over having to see Liam, but that was a lie. I was desperate to see him, even though the pain that came with his presence was overwhelming. I was addicted to it. Every glimpse was like a blade to my soul, but I continued to self-harm emotionally. I kept cutting.

I glanced around the table. All eyes were focused on me with varying degrees of contempt. I focused on Hansen. "I'm assuming everyone here is educated on who I am."

He nodded once. "I'm open with my club. We're a democracy. Not a dictatorship."

I regarded him. "And has this *democracy* come to a vote on my fate?"

I already knew it wasn't death, because if they'd decided to kill me, they wouldn't have sat me down for this chat.

Something moved in his eyes. "We have."

He waited. Likely for me to crumble, plead. Ask for mercy.

I knew none of them would help, so I waited too. Silently.

"You can have your story," Hansen said finally.

My raised eyebrow was my only reply. I was shocked, beyond so. Not only were they not going to kill me, nor were they kicking me to the curb with a warning about coming back to the clubhouse and plenty of death threats. No, they were giving me the story that could've got me killed and maybe ruined their club if I'd got the right story. Or the wrong one. And here was the stoic, handsome and deadly president of the Sons of Templar MC *giving* me my story. But I knew that it wouldn't be that simple. That there would be a catch.

There always was.

"You can live amongst the Sons of Templar, find what you came here for, with notable exceptions of course," Hansen continued after a long beat, not taking his eyes from me. "You don't get to go to church. Ever. Even Old Ladies don't get that. And we tell you to back off, you *back the fuck off.* You don't interfere with club business. Don't bother our kids. I would say don't bother our women, but my wife will likely divorce me if she doesn't get to meet you, so I'll request you not put anything about her in there if you want to see the outside of this compound."

I nodded once, still knowing there was more.

"We have to keep in mind that you've already seen something that could damage the club," Hansen said, glancing to Jagger pointedly and then back to me. "Though you've given your word that you won't try to damage the club. Which is a smart choice. Problem is, your word is kind of shot to shit right now, sweetheart. You continue to live at the compound, continue to work at the bar and you will always have a prospect on you, until I'm satisfied that you will stay true to your word. Then you can finish your story wherever you wish." He paused. "It goes without saying, of course, that anything that's published that damages the club will be treated as an act of hostility against the club. And in that case, I'll make sure you know, with us, there's no such thing as retribution, only decimation."

I leaned back in my chair, digesting the words, the iron jaws of the men around the table and the threat at the end of his little speech. "Subtle."

Hansen raised his brow. "We look subtle to you?"

The corner of my mouth twitched as I regarded him and the men in the room. It didn't waver even though most of them were treating me with murderous glares. I could smile in the face of murderous glares. I was used to them. But that mouth twitch disappeared the second I laid eyes on Liam. He'd been watching me the entire time, and I'd been doing my best to ignore him. That was an impossible feat, even when the president of an outlaw MC just threatened to kill me if I betrayed him.

Hansen's offer was a generous one, considering what I knew about the club in general and about how they treated rats and traitors. Had this been any other story, I wouldn't have hesitated, even with the obvious threat to my life, even though half of the men in the room looked like they'd rather resort to more traditional ways of dealing with a rat.

But this wasn't any other story. The scarred man staring at me was evidence that couldn't be ignored.

I wasn't sure if I could survive staying here, living the story and constantly being faced with Liam. Jagger. He was Jagger. Not Liam.

No, I *knew* I wouldn't survive it.

But I couldn't betray this feeling at the table full of men trained to sniff out weakness and then just as promptly snuff it out. And they wanted me to be weak. That's what this was, bringing a helpless woman to a table full of criminals, murderers, dead men, it was a statement, it was intimidation.

It wasn't working. Not in the way they intended, at least.

I swallowed my fear and it scraped against my throat like a half-chewed potato chip.

"What you're saying, is I can write the story *you* want me to write while I'm a prisoner," I said, addressing Hansen. "That's not writing any kind of story at all. And that's not the journalist I am."

His gaze was even. "You can write the story you want to write. No one's stopping you from doing that. I'm just informing you of all the facts. And you're not a prisoner, you're a guest."

I didn't lower my eyes. "A guest that doesn't get a say in when she leaves and is followed by an armed guard is, by definition, a prisoner."

He shrugged. "You know your options."

I did know my options. It was this or death. He was offering me as close to a pardon as I could get.

Why wasn't I happy about that?

My eye's locked with emerald irises once more.

Oh yeah, *that* was why.

Hansen stood, put his palms flat on the table. "I'll leave you to consider, but your next shift at the bar is tomorrow. It's the play you wanna make, Caroline."

I nodded once and stood myself. "And where am I supposed to stay?"

"We've got an empty room at the end of the hall," he said, something in his eyes.

I wondered who that empty room belonged to, a ghost who now resided in Hansen's eyes.

"One that locks from the outside, I presume?" I asked dryly, forcing myself not to feel sympathy for my jailer.

Hansen didn't acknowledge this. His silence was answer enough. It was clear I didn't have a say in this. Fighting it would be wasting air. And I needed it, even though the oxygen was jagged, tainted with Liam.

"Fine," I sighed. "I want my cellphone back. My computer."

Hansen regarded me.

"I'm not stupid enough to call for a rescue," I snapped.

"Didn't think you were," he replied. "You'll get your shit."

It was incredibly arrogant of them to give a prisoner—because that's exactly what I was—access to communication to the outside world.

But they were smart.

Because there was no chance of rescue. Local cops were likely paid off. I could call in State Police, who couldn't be as easily bought off, but that would mean forfeiting the story.

And I guessed that would mean forfeiting my life, because no doubt they had a way of monitoring my calls, I'd be dead before anyone even picked up at the other end.

I sighed. "Show me to my chambers then."

Hansen moved to jerk his head at the prospect at the end of the room, standing. Prospects didn't get seats, interesting.

"You'll be in my room," a rough voice growled.

I looked to Liam, to his hard eyes, scarred face. He had stood too, his hands fisted at his sides, his entire body taut. "Like fuck I will."

His eyes were solid. "I say you got a choice in the matter?"

"Hansen did," I shot back, jerking my head toward the president violently. "That choice being I stay here, or I accept my punishment for being a rat, that being an unmarked grave and a violent death. I'd prefer that than sharing a room with you."

I turned on my heel and walked out. I swear I heard Claw's chuckle as I slammed the door.

———

TO MY UTTER dismay and panic, I was not showed to an empty room. I was shown to the same room that had been my cell and my solace for the past week.

Liam's room.

And when I tried to get my things and move them, John appeared from nowhere, blocking my way, obviously under instruction from Liam.

"Move," I said through gritted teeth.

He didn't.

I was tempted to run at him, fight him, tear my way out of this room. But it would do little good. He was so big and muscled he took up the whole door. I wouldn't win a physical fight with this man.

I knew I wasn't going to win the metaphorical one I was currently engaged in with Liam.

So I surrendered.

On the outside, at least.

Though I knew the battle I was engaged in with Liam was one I'd eventually lose, it didn't mean I was going to stop fighting. No, I had to keep fighting, battling. There was no other choice.

John sensed that he had won the standoff, turning on his motorcycle boot and walking away, and the door was left open. So I was no longer confined to Liam's room. I was obviously free to walk around the clubhouse. But no matter how desperate I had been for the past week, how intent I was to get out of the room that housed too many memories and one single white feather, I couldn't bring myself to cross the threshold and explore.

Never in my career as a journalist had I let fear stop me from going to cover my story. Not when covering prison conditions in Lagos with a shitty security team, nor when I snuck into Syria to cover the refugee crisis, or in any other deadly situation that was necessary to navigate in order to get my story.

But that door frame was harder to cross than a border to a war-torn and dangerous country.

It was impossible to go, but it was unbearable to stay.

But I stayed. Like a coward, the minutes in Liam's room cutting through me like blades.

John returned with my phone.

I raised my brow when he handed it to me. "Not worried I'm going to call the police?" I had obviously already had this conversation with Hansen, but I was interested in how much the prospects knew. How much they were entitled to know.

He regarded me with an empty gaze. "You can try. We own the police here. And I think Hansen educated you on what happens here if he finds you can't keep your word."

Ah, so John couldn't carry on a normal conversation, but he seemed very capable to regurgitate his president's death threats.

After they gave me back my phone, it took an hour to get through all my voice messages, texts, and emails. A few were from my family, checking in, though they were obviously worried about the lack of response since they were used to such things when I was on a story. They were used to months of silence and the only way they could find out whether I was alive or not was to watch me reporting the news.

So they were lulled into a false sense of safety thinking I was covering some benign story in Arizona. When in reality, I was likely in more danger, or at least comparable danger, here as I was in a war zone.

I texted them all back, choosing not to inform them that I was being held hostage by a biker club and the man they'd welcomed into their family and expected to marry their daughter. A man they'd mourned like he was their own. I know they mourned for a daughter that was their own too. Because I'd died. Not all of me. But a big part. An important part.

I lingered on a photo my sister sent me, she was smiling with her hand over her large rounded stomach. She'd be due in two months.

Where would I be in two months?

Would I be alive?

Would I be able to face my family, my home, with the knowledge I had now?

Would I be able to face myself?

The appearance of a new message shook me from that morbid contemplation. It was Emily. She was my contact for the story, and I'd been calling her nightly to update her on what I had. She was beyond interested in the story and already had big plans for it.

Unlike my family, she knew how much danger I was putting myself in. Hence why most of the calls and messages were from her.

THE LATEST READ:

IF I DON'T HEAR **from you today, I'm calling the police. I don't care if it blows your story. No matter what you think to the contrary, you are more important than your story.**

I SIGHED and dialed her number.

"Holy *fuck!*" she screamed through the phone after barely one ring. "I thought you were *dead*. That the bikers found you out as a rat and that you were swimming with the fishes."

I smiled. The familiarity of the voice was welcome. It was a comfort in a place where nothing was comfortable. Familiar. "We're in New Mexico, Emily," I said, trying to keep the tears out of my voice. "Not many places for me to swim with any fishes, and that's more of a mafia thing. This isn't the mafia."

"It's almost the same thing," she scoffed.

I rolled my eyes.

It wasn't almost the same thing. If I had been found out to be trying to infiltrate the mafia, there would be no conversation, I'd have had a bullet in the back of my skull without so much as a conversation.

The Sons of Templar at least gave their enemies somewhat of a conversation before putting a bullet in their brains.

I thought about the gray matter on the concrete.

Well, half a conversation.

"Okay, since you're not swimming with the fishes, care to tell me where *the fuck* you've been the past week?" Emily asked pleasantly.

Sirens and horns echoed through the phone and I imagined her shouting at her phone while pounding the streets in six-inch heels. She was one of the busiest agents in New York, she was always rushing somewhere, swearing into her phone. "Because I'm on my way to my doctor to get some fresh Botox for the wrinkles *you* caused me worrying about you being buried in a shallow grave."

"I thought it was swimming with the fishes? You've got to stick to your metaphor, Em," I teased.

I only got a growl at the end of the phone.

I smiled again. "You were not worried about me, it's not in your schedule."

Emily was religious about schedules, to the point of OCD. She had bathroom breaks in there. No joke.

"When my best friend makes her living by almost dying daily, I put worrying about you in my schedule, written in blood. Don't worry about that. Right before my morning celery juice and after my morning orgasm."

It wasn't a surprise she even had her orgasms scheduled.

I wondered if this one was from a new girlfriend or a battery-operated device. One thing she didn't have a schedule for was women. She was all about flipping stereotypes and feminism, but she was also acting like the classic toxic male when it came to womanizing. She was afraid of commitment, except when it came to her job. And me.

"Well stop worrying. I'm fine," I lied.

"No, you're not," she shot, calling my bluff immediately and bluntly, as was her way. "For a journalist, you suck at lying."

"Journalists aren't meant to lie, it's kind of the point."

She scoffed again. "And I'm not meant to eat carbs, but I had a bagel for breakfast."

I picked at the comforter of the bed I was sitting on. "Not the same thing," I told Emily.

"Whatever, I'm on a crunch, so fill me in on what the fuck's going on," she demanded.

I didn't have the time, the energy or the creativity to come up with a lie that would satisfy Emily. So I went for the journalistic truth.

Leaving out the part about Liam/Jagger, of course. I wasn't going to bury that lead. I'd obliterate it. She knew all about him. After a night of lemon drops, confessions, and broken hearts. It was the only time I'd ever seen her cry. No, the other being when one of her biggest clients had a meltdown on live TV days before his book launch.

"Shut the fuck up," she said when I finished telling her I was a prisoner here until I was found to be trustworthy enough to be able to leave. Most normal people would express outrage, panic and be calling the police.

Emily was not most normal people.

So I waited.

"You got the president of one of the most notorious organized crime collectives in the fucking country to agree to give you the *inside scoop?*"

There it was.

I couldn't help but smile. "Yeah, with the small detail that I'm a prisoner until I do so."

"Details," she dismissed. "This is big. Like really big. I already had publishers on the line when I pitched the idea of a novel when you were undercover, but now...shit we'll have our pick out of all the fuckers."

I froze. "A novel?"

Traffic honked in the distance. "To begin, but depending on the way this goes, we could get a movie deal. A mini-series. Netflix would love the screenplay for this shit—"

"Emily," I snapped, knowing that she would just keep going. And I needed her to stop. "I didn't ask you to pitch a fucking *novel*. I asked you to put out feelers to the *Times* and the *Tribune* about an *expose*."

I could *hear* her roll her eyes. "With this story plus your talent as a writer, I couldn't physically do something like that. With this exclusive, they're going to triple their advances."

I clenched my fist. "I don't care how much they offer, Emily, I'm not going to do it," I gritted out through my teeth.

"Are you *kidding?*" she demanded. "This is the chance of a lifetime. Let's forget about the money, though that'll be hard to do since there's a lot of it on the table right now. But we'll try. This is every writer's dream. A fucking *book deal*. And not to mention in this climate. *No one* is getting book deals anymore. Especially on *nonfiction*. Especially with an advance like *this*." She spoke quickly, apart from the times she drew out words, long to put focus on them. It was her signature trick, and it worked surprisingly well with everyone but me.

I ran my hand through my hair. "Yeah, I'm sure this book deal is every *writer's* dream, Emily, but I'm a *journalist*, not a writer. I don't want buckets of money so I can sit in my cozy apartment and tell my story. I want to be somewhere that's not cozy, so I can tell the stories of people who aren't offered book deals for their lives. I'm not profiting off the horror I've seen. That's not what I'm here for."

She laughed. "A noble journalist, you may be the last of your kind."

"I'm not noble," I said, the word scraping at my throat. "I've done a lot of morally questionable things to get stories. I've hurt people. Betrayed them." I thought about the man who I'd been in love with once. The one whose eyes had gone dark and who was currently keeping me prisoner here. "I'm not putting all that into a book. I'm going to keep doing my job until I can't, unless I die first."

I hated that it sounded like a premonition.

CHAPTER NINE

THEY CAME for me late that same night.

I had expected as much.

My door wasn't locked anymore, but I didn't venture out into the clubhouse because of the tone in the room earlier today. I knew that a lot of the men weren't happy with their president's decision.

I understood that.

Which was why I wasn't surprised when the man I knew as 'Swiss' came into the room. The nicknames were a mystery to me since this man didn't look Scandinavian, with beautiful midnight chocolate skin, sharp bone structure, and a bald head. But for all I knew, he'd killed a lot of Swiss men.

He'd hit on me on the first night I came to the club. Well, all of the men had. I was a new face, fair game. Likely competition for them as soon as it became apparent I was handing out rejections. He'd almost tempted me, with his smooth voice, his jarring beauty. He had engaging conversation that hadn't started with, "hey baby, wanna fuck?" which had been many of his brother's opening lines, or variations of the same.

But this was not the man from the clubhouse party hitting on a woman. No, I wasn't a woman to him now, I was a traitor.

I wondered if that man was an act, or if this one was. I had a strong feeling it was the former.

I closed my book, standing. "I'm assuming you're not here to ask me to dinner?" I asked dryly.

His jaw clenched. His eye twitched. The hatred for me was painfully obvious. "You wanna see what we do. What we are? For your story?"

He didn't wait for me to speak, he just snatched my arm and dragged me. His grip was tight. Violent. Painful.

I didn't struggle. It wouldn't make a difference.

There was something in his eyes that told me he might like it if I struggled.

So I didn't.

And I *did* want to see who they were. But not for the story.

For my sorry, broken and tortured soul. Because I hadn't put it through enough already, obviously.

We moved through the back end of the clubhouse, past the doors that housed a lot of the members—since most of them were new transplants and didn't have a home in the town yet—we went further than I'd gone. Further than I thought the building had within its walls, it didn't betray this size when looked at from the outside, which I guessed was the point. We stopped at a door at the end of a hallway, separated from anything else.

It had four locks on it.

Something moved in my stomach at the sight of the seemingly innocuous door. Something that slithered up my spine, to the base of my throat.

Swiss stared at me, daring me to say something, anything. His grip tightened on my arm.

"Are you going to show me what you seem intent on showing me, or we just gonna stare longingly into each other's eyes?" I asked, my voice betraying none of the dread or fear that that door awakened inside me.

Something moved around, mingling with the empty cruelty in his eyes. Something more human. But something I was coming to discover with the Sons of Templar was that every man here was a monster, but they were also a human. Not wholly one or the other. Swiss was closer to monster than most but still human.

His grip loosened slightly as if it were a sign of respect.

But it was only to unlock the door, it tightened once again as he opened it and dragged me down.

Down into the bowels of the clubhouse.

The underbelly of the Sons of Templar.

Where the story lay.

Where the humans disappeared, and the monsters came out.

THE BASEMENT STANK.

Of sweet. Blood. Tobacco. Metal. Mold.

It didn't smell of death. I didn't agree with some of the greatest writers and poets of our time. Death didn't have a smell. A sound. Death was silent. It had no odor. No signifier. Only a feeling. A bone-deep *knowing* that every human has. That only comes seconds before you see it, too late for you to run, avert your eyes.

That was the point.

I didn't avert my eyes at the dead body hanging from a hook on the ceiling.

I merely ran them over the man curiously. He was shirtless, wearing only tattered and stained jeans. Though he wore mostly blood.

It pooled underneath him.

Another man sat bound in a chair.

He was alive.

Claw jerked up from where he had been sitting smoking on a small stool to the left of the room. In his other hand, he still held a bloody knife.

"Dude, *what in the fuck* are you doing?" he hissed at Swiss, advancing on us. "You can't bring her in here. This is club business."

Swiss' grip on me tightened as if he were expecting Claw to snatch me away from him. I was nothing but an object right now, to be tugged and bruised. I'd been treated worse for lesser stories, so I didn't protest.

Not just because I wanted the story. Because I needed it. I needed to be sickened by these men, by the life Liam had chosen, in order to be sickened by him, in order to stop wanting him so much.

"Yeah, and she's here to learn about the club business," Swiss said to Claw when it became apparent he wasn't going to tug at my other arm. "She's here to write her story. Hansen gave her permission."

Claw glared. "Yeah, permission to tend the fuckin' bar, watch some idiots get roughed up, watch Blake get too drunk and fall off his bike, see a fuckin' orgy. Not a felony!"

Swiss shrugged, unnerved by the fact a man with a blood-stained knife was glaring at him and yelling at him. "She's already witnessed a felony."

Claw's eyes bulged. "So why don't we add more to the mix? It's not fuckin' Pokémon, you don't catch 'em all."

I couldn't help it, a hysterical giggle erupted from my lips.

Both men looked to me.

I had never lost my composure in the midst of a story. I hadn't cried. Vomited. Screamed. Expressed sympathy. Anger. Disagreement. I certainly hadn't laughed in front of two men, one captive—two if you counted me—and a dead body.

But something about Claw's visceral anger, about the reference to *Pokémon*, of all things made me lose it.

Or I'd already lost it, and this was the straw that broke the camel's back.

"You think this is *funny*?" Claw demanded, directing his fury at me. "Hansen's gonna kill us, and if he doesn't, Jagger sure as fuck will. No way he's okay with you seeing this shit." He jerked his head to the man hanging from the ceiling, the other gagged and bound to a chair next to him.

I finally yanked myself from Swiss' grip. My arm protested, and I knew it'd bruise. What was a bruise, anyway? "I do not live my life according to what *Jagger* defines as 'okay' for me," I snapped. His name was rancid on my tongue. "Swiss brought me here. I can't unsee this." I nodded my head in the direction of the dead man and the live one. "So I'll observe it. Like Hansen said."

Claw gritted his teeth with such force I thought his jaw might shatter. He finally relaxed enough to lift his cigarette up to his mouth and take a pull. His fingers and hands were stained with blood.

"Fuck," he muttered, smoke wafting from his nostrils as he exhaled.

Swiss seemed to take this as agreement, and he walked over to a table littered with well-worn torture instruments. It was like that stupid close up in a horror movie when you're presented with knives, forceps, and pliers to tell you all you need to know about the men who used them.

But this was not a horror movie, as much as it had seemed to start to resemble one.

The instruments on the table only worked to tell me things I already knew about the Sons of Templar. That they were ruthless. Held no mercy for anyone who crossed them. That they weren't' afraid to draw blood.

That cold fear slithered further up my throat with the knowledge I could've been just another stain on a long butcher's knife if things had been different. But then again, every human being in the world was just one choice away from becoming a stain on the pavement. A body in the ground. Just another tragedy.

Claw stubbed out his smoke and walked over to the bound man. He was bleeding from a cut on his forehead, but he looked in much better shape than the man beside him.

"Now you've seen what happens when you don't tell us what we need to hear," Claw said, ripping the man's gag off, jerking his head to the corpse. "It's not pretty. And though it was fun for me, I promise you it wasn't fun for him." His voice had changed. Taken on something not entirely human. There was a lightness to it, that couldn't be human when talking about torture and murder.

The man tied to the chair looked at him with an entirely inhuman look on his face. He was too young for such a look.

But I knew better than anyone that youth was the first casualty of war.

And as Liam had said that first night, this was a war.

Not one I was going to be walking away from unscathed.

But I was going to walk away. I had to.

After.

After I got the story.

From the club.

From Liam.

"Fuck you, biker scum," the man spat.

Claw raised his eyebrow at Swiss. "That's not a very polite way to talk to hosts, is it?"

Swiss shook his head. "Not polite at all, my friend." He shrugged, wiping his blade on his jeans. "Some people aren't brought up right, I guess."

"It's our duty, then, as scumbag bikers to teach him some manners, I'd assume?" Claw asked.

Swiss nodded, eyes darkening as he moved forward, snatching the man's head and yanking it back so he exposed his neck. The flat of the blade laid against it. "Yes, it's time for manners."

He let his head go, and instead of making a cut into a part of his neck as I expected him too, he grabbed the man's hand and sliced off his finger. It was an expert, practiced stroke.

The man screamed as blood poured from the wound.

Swiss regarded the finger for a second, then discarded it, as Claw had with his smoke.

It was the casual brutality that jarred me, not the brutality itself.

But it still wasn't surprising.

Their job was to be outlaws, and torture was just another day at the office.

Both men waited patiently for the screaming to stop.

"Now we've gotten the formalities out of the way, why don't we cut the shit and you start talking before I keep chopping off digits," Swiss said. "Because if you talk now, you might still be able to jerk off with one hand." He held the man's thumb on the opposite hand. "If you don't, you'll be paying whores to do it for the rest of your life, and that shit will add up."

The man glared at him through a haze of pain. "Fuck you," he hissed. "You're gonna kill me anyway."

Swiss nodded. "True. No way I'm letting someone who works for the man responsible for the death of twelve of my brothers just walk outta here. But I might give you a kinder death than you deserve if you decide to start talking." He paused for less than a second, then he cut off the thumb.

More screaming.

More blood.

"If not," Swiss continued, discarding the thumb. "I'll keep

going. And I'm sure you know, there are things you can do to people to make them wish for death."

Swiss glanced at me, I wasn't sure if it was a threat or just curiosity to see if I had fainted or thrown up.

I hadn't done either. My hands were steady.

They shook uncontrolled handling a feather a week ago, but in the face of this...nothing. I didn't know whether it said more about what I was able to handle in the present, or what I was too afraid to revisit in the past.

"What do you think this man knows?" I asked, voice steady, the cold and calm tone I employed while interviewing. It was somewhat of a trademark, along with my red lipstick, that my voice never changed when I was interviewing victims or villains. All villains started as victims, after all.

Claw answered for him. "We don't *think* he knows shit. We *know* he knows enough to help us."

"Help you do what?" I asked.

His eyes narrowed and he opened his mouth, but the bleeding and thumbless man spoke for him.

"I'll never help you. You have my word on that. Do what you wish to me."

Claw grinned, moving his attention away from me. "Oh, I thought you'd never ask."

Then there was more screaming.

A lot more blood.

And as promised, the man didn't talk.

I HAD BECOME STRANGELY REMOVED from the violence both men were taking turns unleashing on their hostage. Because it wasn't merely violence for the sake of it. There was a purpose to it. It was a means to an end.

I wondered how much more this man would endure. There was always a limit to how much pain a human being could withstand. Most men in this world might be able to tolerate unimaginable limits of physical pain. But that wasn't the only instrument of torture. Sleep deprivation, starvation, waterboarding, all effective.

Finding a weakness that didn't exist on the body, but inside the mind was the most certain way to break a person. Whether it be a fear or a psychological trauma. Men usually went straight to rape with women. Because they knew it was almost the surest way to unravel the sense of control, of the sacredness of a woman's body. To tear away the agency she has over her own body.

A lot of men did it because they were evil.

Most of them did it because they were weak themselves.

But in situations like this, with such toxic masculinity cloaking the air, I doubted the ruthless men in front of me would do something like violate another man for information. I hoped they wouldn't do that to a woman. I had heard they had strong opinions on sexual assault. But I wondered how strong those opinions would be when all of their conventional methods of torture failed them with a woman. Would their conviction be strong enough to withstand their thirst for vengeance?

I didn't get to think about it for long—thankfully—because the door smashed open from above us and boots pounded down the stairs.

Liam's eyes found me first.

Then the dead body in front of me.

Then the two men torturing their prisoner to my right.

The energy in the room shifted immediately. I had thought it was violent, deadly before, what with all the violence and death in front of me. But that was nothing, nothing compared to what Liam punctured the air with.

"You're fucking *kidding* me," he hissed at Claw and Swiss.

Claw was smiling.

He had blood on his cheek and forehead, so, along with his grip on a bloodstained knife, it served to make him look maniacal and unhinged.

Then again, from what I'd just witnessed, he *was* maniacal and unhinged.

"What, brother? We're just helping her out with her reporting," Swiss said, voice teasing, taunting.

I had to admire his stupid bravery for provoking Liam like this. The danger in his eyes was physical. It was a hand fastening around my throat. A vice constricting my lungs. More unsettling than anything I'd witnessed in here. Because it was something that I didn't think I'd ever have to witness inside those emerald eyes. Something I didn't even know existed until I buried Liam.

It was a look that told me again that I had buried Liam. This wasn't him.

He strode to me, snatching my hand. "You're getting the fuck outta here."

I tried to snatch it back. He held fast. "They're not done," I said calmly.

His eyes bulged. Then they changed. All fury seeped out. The skin where he was touching me burned, not from heat, but from an icy chill that was coming from his eyes. He let go of my hand. Yanked the gun from his jeans, calmly walked past Swiss and Claw and shot the man in the head.

The gunshot bounced off the damp concrete walls and rang in my ears. But the silence was what roared. There was no silence louder than after a gunshot that ended a life.

Liam put the gun back into his waistband and walked over to me. "They're fuckin' done."

"Dude," Claw whined. "Not fucking cool. We might've got something."

Liam didn't take his eyes off me. "You know you wouldn't have got shit."

This time, when he took hold of my hand, I didn't struggle. I let the man who had just shot a man in cold blood lead me up the stairs and back into civilization. Or whatever it was above us.

I didn't say a word as he walked me back to my room.

He didn't either.

He only let go of my hand when we were standing in the middle of the bedroom.

I blinked rapidly at him, throat still clenched with something like shock.

He still didn't say a word. Didn't try to explain himself. He just turned around and walked out.

The locks clicked after he closed the door.

Jagger

His hand was shaking as he locked the door.

It hadn't been when he pulled out his piece and sprayed the brains of Fernandez's third in command and second cousin all over the floor.

Not even when he touched her, when he fucking touched his *Peaches* with hands he'd used to end a man's life.

It didn't matter that the man in question was involved in one of the most brutal human trafficking rings in the world. Or that he likely had a hand in the massacre of an entire club. That he was likely one of the most vile and soulless human beings to walk this earth.

It didn't matter because Jagger knew that he had just proved he was exactly the same. Just as soulless.

He'd done it on purpose.

He wanted her to be afraid of him.

To be disgusted by him.

So when his resolve failed, and he knew that it would, that she would fight violently against him being anything to her. He needed her to find him a stranger. A monster.

Which was why he locked her inside his room, despite the fact she was no longer a prisoner.

No, that wasn't even why he'd locked her inside.

"Take this." He threw the key at a passing Elden. "Unlock it in the morning."

Elden nodded once and kept walking. No questions. Prospects didn't ask questions.

Jagger thanked fuck for that. He'd given him the key because he didn't trust himself with it. Didn't trust himself not to give in to the urge to storm back in there, rip her clothes off and fuck her senseless. Something about her standing there, in pools of blood, in the ugliest part of their world, calm, collected, not fucking flinching, it disturbed the shit out of him. But it also hardened his cock instantly. Making him wild with need for her.

Not that he wasn't already.

But he'd been able to keep that shit locked down.

Barely.

Mainly because he left as soon as church was over, with instructions to make sure Caroline didn't sleep anywhere but his room.

It was fucked up that he wanted her in there. Especially since it caused her obvious pain being in that room. What kind of sick motherfucker was he? Hadn't he already caused her a lifetime, two fucking lifetimes of agony? Now he wanted to give her more. The boy who won her heart sure as shit wouldn't have made decisions like that. Decisions that hurt her. That boy, no matter how far he was from being a man, would've rather lost a limb than hurt her. That boy was more of a man than he was now.

But he couldn't go back to being him, no matter what, and that was the ultimate cause of Caroline's agony. So maybe that's why he was intent on causing her all these little pains, to distract her from the one huge one that might destroy what was left of the girl he fell in love with.

Or maybe he was a sick son of a bitch who wanted to imprint her smell onto everything of his so he could torture himself for another fourteen years. And then some.

Because he may have been tortured before, knowing he left behind a sweet, innocent, kind girl. But having to let go of this, hardened, bitter, strong and fucking magnificent woman.

Fuck.

Which was why he left the clubhouse after church a week ago.

He wouldn't have left if he hadn't had Hansen's word no harm would come to her. Because his brothers weren't happy. They wouldn't disobey their president, though. So no harm would come from them. But Jagger couldn't be certain that the harm wouldn't come from him.

He came back to the room empty, her nowhere on the property. Only one place she could've been by process of elimination.

He'd damn near ripped the locks off with his bare hands thinking of her in a chair, bleeding after one of his brothers decided to disobey Hansen. He guessed it would've been Swiss. Fucker was cold and lived by a specific code. Just so happened that code aligned with the Sons of Templar. He was not one to bend rules or dole out mercy.

So he imagined Swiss, with his cold eyes and merciless brutality working away the last of Caroline's soft edges.

What he walked in on wasn't worse, or even the same as that, but it was close. Because he saw that she had no soft edges left, confronted with it in that room. The room that some prospects and brothers alike had been unable to handle. That haunted even him.

She was jaded to some of the most brutal acts humans could

commit. Unblinking. That was like seeing her bleeding and bound up in a chair. It was evidence that she'd already been torn apart, vital parts stolen from her in a life he didn't know anything about.

And that's what had him snapping. Had him killing a man right in front of her, adding to the cold brutality they were immersing her in. That he was sure Swiss had been intent on drowning her in. Not knowing that she could swim. Or that she could breathe in that polluted and blood filled water.

Swiss walked down the hall, wiping his hands on his jeans with nonchalance. He eyed Jagger, then the door with a raised brow. "She needed to know what she'd gotten herself into, brother."

That got him. There was only so much of him he could lock down.

His fist flew through his brother's face without hesitation. The crunch of flesh against bone wasn't loud enough to silence his demons.

So he punched him again.

And again.

Caroline

I heard the fight after the click of the locks.

I don't know what was louder.

I wasn't surprised hearing the violence. I shouldn't be. This was Liam's life now. This was *Jagger's* life. He spoke in torture. In pain. Violence.

There were no reasonable, diplomatic conversations. There were thuds of flesh hitting flesh, grunts of pain, muttered curses. Pictures smashed off walls, bodies thumping against the floor.

There were dead bodies strung up in the basement. A man tied to a chair, missing all his fingers with a bullet in his brain.

Peaches.

I miss you.

I'm writing this when I can still see you wavin' at the fuckin' bus. You're not crying.

I am.

Would be embarrassed as all fuck about doing so in front of all these men, were half of them not bawling too.

Not one woman saying goodbye shed a tear.

What does that tell you?

That it should be all of you on this bus instead. You're much tougher.

Though I guess if you were in charge of things to begin with, we might not need to be on this bus.

It's better not to work in maybes.

There is no maybe about the way I feel for you.

That will not change.

I promise you that, Peaches.

Over oceans, battlefields, tears (on my end, obviously), months, years, decades. It's not ever gonna change.

I know you don't understand why I'm doing this. I know you're mad as all hell at me for doing it in the first place. I also know you love me too damn much to do anything but stand beside me. Because that's the kind of woman you are. I know you'll wait for me. For us. I'm a bastard for even asking you to do that. But I'll do it anyway.

I love you.

I MEMORIZED THE LETTER.

I didn't want to remember it, especially not now, with the background noise being all too loud of a reminder of what I'd lost.

But my memories never complied with what I wanted.

So I replayed the letter.

Until there was a painful and violent silence on the other side of the door.

Jagger

Hansen eyed him, unblinking at the blood he guessed was covering his face, his skinned knuckles, ripped shirt. It wasn't exactly an uncommon occurrence for brothers to work out their shit with their fists.

In fact, it was the *only* way brothers worked out their shit. It wasn't like they talked about their fuckin' feelings over bullshit cocktails or something. That's not the way men worked. That sure as shit wasn't the way the Sons of Templar worked at least.

But it was necessary to acknowledge shit that came up between brothers. Sort it immediately. Because rifts could fracture a club. Could fucking ruin it. Especially when you needed to be prepared to die for your brother. Even if you felt like killing him.

It was growing pains too. The club was new. A mix up of nomads, of patched members from other charters willing to relocate to repair New Mexico.

Not everyone was gonna fit.

Not everyone was here for the right reasons.

They'd weeded out most of that at the beginning.

It was ugly.

But Jagger had thought they were getting there. Had warmed to most of them, since he'd known most of them, not counting the prospects. And he thought the prospects had the makings of good brothers.

But Swiss and Hades.

He hadn't warmed to them.

Mostly because they were cold-blooded motherfuckers. Exactly what the club needed at times like this.

But not what fucking *Caroline* needed to see. She didn't need to be breathing their fucking air, let alone watching Swiss *torture* someone.

And Claw. He was as ruthless as them all, but at least there was a bit of human in his monster. He had decided not to kill him for putting his hands on Caroline after seeing his absolute change with her once he heard her story. He knew he had her back. Liked her. Maybe too much. But that worked for him right now. Another man, another brother, to keep an eye on her. He'd deal with that man, that brother, for having that eye too south of her hips and north of her ribs at a later date.

He cracked his bleeding knuckles under his president's stare.

"You feel better?" Hansen asked calmly.

"*Better?*" he hissed. "You think a couple of punches is gonna make up for the shit he pulled? This is a serious fuckin' offense. Showin' our business to a civilian. A journalist at that. My—" he cut himself off before he said 'his woman.' Though that might've been what she was. Always. But not something he could ever say out loud. He didn't deserve to lay claim to her out loud. "There needs to be a full table." He looked around the empty seats. Hansen had brought him in here after three brothers and one prospect managed to tear him off Swiss.

The fucker grinned at him with bloodstained teeth.

Then he'd lunged again.

Jagger had knocked a tooth out. It was embedded in his hand until he'd yanked it out and tossed it at Swiss' boots.

Hansen didn't glance around the table. "She's invited to write her story," he replied.

Jagger gritted his teeth. "Yeah, and I thought it was bullshit about fuckin' parties, club girls. Nothin' *real*. It was nothin' but a farce to make sure she wasn't gonna rat." He paused, understanding washing over him. "This was you," he clipped through his teeth. He had to hold himself still. Very fucking still. He didn't trust himself to even twitch a fucking finger because he might start attacking his president. His best friend. His brother.

His best friend and his brother had ordered to have his woman taken to watch a man be tortured and murdered. He'd ordered Caroline to have more scars on her soul.

Hansen watched him. Waited. As if he expected him to lunge. Hansen read people. He'd known Jagger for all the years he'd been at the club, which mean he knew him. Which was why Jagger was so fucking shocked at the clear knowledge that he was behind this.

"This needed to be done."

He'd always admired Hansen's ability to stay calm in the most volatile of situations. Thought it was what made him a great brother, father, and president.

But right now, he wanted to wring his fucking neck for it.

He slammed his fists down on the table. "Like fuck it did!" he roared. "Caroline did not need to see that shit. That's not shit women should have to fucking see. Not her."

Hansen's eyes softened at the corners. With something resembling pity.

That was worse than his trademark calm.

"Agree with you on that one. Good women should never have to see the ugliness of this world." He paused long and hard, likely thinking of his own woman, what she'd seen. What she'd done. "Unfortunately, it's the best and most undeserving of women that see some of the ugliest shit that would undo even most men. That's what makes them into something more than good women. And I know you've become educated on who Caroline is. Macy showed me her reports. This isn't the worst she's seen, brother. Not by far."

Jagger struggled not to flinch.

"Yeah, it may not have been the worse she's seen," he gritted out. "But that wasn't here. On her home soil. In a club that I'm fuckin' in."

Hansen didn't even blink. "You don't think she knows who you are? *Exactly* what you've become?"

Jagger couldn't hide his flinch. "Yeah." He stood. "That's what I'm afraid of."

Then he walked out, before he punched his best friend, before he broke down in front of his president.

He didn't stop walking until he found himself on his bike.

Then he roared off, seeking the solace the road gave him.

But he found nothing.

Definitely not solace.

He'd locked that in his bedroom at the clubhouse.

CHAPTER TEN

Caroline

"YOU'RE NOT gonna slap me, are you?" I asked, sighing at the person who approached me with a hostile glint in their eye. "It's been a long night."

That was something of an understatement. Working the first night after every patched member of the Sons of Templar found out my true identity was nothing short of miserable. Henry still treated me exactly the same, then again, he wasn't a patched member.

His only comment on it had been a raised brow when I walked in with a prospect behind me. "You've got balls, babe," he commented as I walked behind the bar.

"No, I've got ovaries," I replied.

He grinned. "Well, get those ovaries behind the bar and get to fucking work."

And that had been that.

That was *not* that with the rest of the club.

Claw had *almost* warmed back up to me. But the flirting was definitely gone. I wasn't sure if that was because the thought of hitting on a rat was repulsive to him or if Liam had done or said something to him about it. It was not something to dwell on. So Claw didn't flirt with me when he came up to the bar. Though he still smiled at me when I gave him his beers.

Not like Luther, an older, tattooed and muscled man with mean eyes and shoulder length hair, who not only glared at me but had snatched my outstretched wrist and yanked me so my mid-section pressed painfully against the edge of the bar. "You might have Hansen fooled with your doe eyes, and Jagger because you've obviously got him by the dick. But I'm not softened by doe eyes, and you're a hot piece of ass. Doesn't mean I won't hesitate, won't fuckin' *revel* in taking you down the second I get wind of you goin' behind the club's back."

His breath smelled of smoke, no booze. No one in the Sons had to be drunk to hand out death threats and brutality anyway.

"You don't let her go in the next two seconds, we're gonna have problems," an iron voice informed him.

He snapped his gaze at Liam, who had murder in his eyes. Menace. And horrifying coldness. Something I should've gotten used to by now, but I couldn't. Luther didn't back down, though I guessed that most of the men in this room might've from a look like this, a promise of death. Brother or no brother.

He squeezed my wrist even tighter so I had to sink my teeth into my lip to stop from crying out.

Then he let it go, snatching his beer, giving me one last sneer before he sauntered off.

I yanked my hand back, glaring at Liam. "I don't need your protection," I hissed.

His eyes went to the wrist that was pulsating with red hot pain. "Yes, you do."

"I don't *want* it," I corrected, moving to mix drinks pointedly with my sore hand. It was agony, but it was better than standing there idle with him staring at me.

"Want it or not, you're getting it, Peaches."

"Don't call me that," I snapped.

He didn't reply. Just gave my wrist another glare and walked off.

He watched me the whole night.

Until he left, some kind of cold promise in his eyes as he looked over his shoulder standing at the exit. Different than the one he gave Luther. Different only because it didn't promise violence. But it promised death nonetheless.

Elden still sat in the corner of the room, chain-smoking and nursing his second beer of the night. I guessed captors had to have their wits about them. And he had wits. Spending time with Elden, I put him at least early thirties, with a liberal amount of salt in his pepper hair. It worked for him. Big time. Where every single member of the club, prospects included, boasted some kind of ink, usually it covered their bodies, he had none.

He had muscles.

Plenty of those.

He was one of the largest men in the club. That was saying a lot, considering the men in the club were all six foot or over, and almost pure muscle.

He was a hulk, with a rolling Scottish brogue and emptiness behind his eyes. He barely spoke to me. But he watched. Watched in a way that I knew he wouldn't hesitate to detain me if I tried to run from him. In a way he wouldn't hesitate to dig my grave. I didn't find myself afraid of him. I felt somewhat safe in his presence. There was an honesty in it. He was here because he was ordered to be here. He wouldn't hurt me out of menace. Or pleasure. Only duty.

He'd tensed as the door opened after we were technically closed, and I was gathering dirty glasses. He didn't completely relax when Scarlett walked through the door, eyes narrowed at me.

She somehow managed to look more dangerous in a snake-skin mini dress than most of the men did in a leather cut. Likely why the prospect stayed alert, because he couldn't be sure she wouldn't start clawing my eyes out.

I put the glasses down, straightening, half expecting that too.

She'd got the job for me, after all. Put me in deeper. I'd betrayed her, and the sisterhood that we'd had distantly over the fact we were both here for complicated reasons.

"I'm not gonna slap you," she said in response to my greeting. Her voice was husky, and not at all friendly.

"Shoot me?"

The corner of her mouth ticked. "Wouldn't want the prospect to have to clean up the blood."

I nodded. "Considerate of you."

"I'm known to be considerate if the occasion calls for it."

Silence rang out.

She was utilizing one of my own interview tactics, staring blankly, not asking questions that I knew she was here to ask. Usually I weathered well under such silences as I considered myself the master of them. But this bombshell in platforms and perfect red lipstick at three in the morning was beating me with ease.

"I'm sorry," I said first, breaking the number one rule I lived by as a reporter, never apologize for doing whatever it takes to get the story.

And the other rule I lived by for being a human, as long as I never physically, emotionally or financially hurt someone unde-serving, never apologize for doing what it takes to survive.

It wasn't even like we'd bonded in the weeks since I met her. She was back and forth from the Amber club, her Old Man helping out here by the looks of it, and liaising about whatever was going down.

Scarlett came with him.

We weren't best friends, didn't tell each other secrets. But it was something different with a woman like Scarlett. A woman hardened by the world, who didn't give kindness freely because she'd had to forsake kindness to survive whatever had put the hardness behind her eyes. She saw something in me, likely that same kind of hardness, with a side of hopelessness—I didn't have a man who looked at me the way her biker did—and she'd given me something she didn't have to.

She did it as a rare act of kindness and my using that for my story rubbed me the wrong way.

"I look like I'm asking for an apology?" she asked with a scoff. "I'm someone who's had to do a lot of things to stay alive. Not judging for what you do. Mostly because I've been educated that you weren't out to bring the club down." She raised her brow. "You were, it'd be a different story, and we'd likely be having this conversation in a basement with you tied to a chair."

I had to say I was impressed with her steel, and her knowledge of how the world worked. She was likely in on a lot more than the traditional Old Lady might've been.

"You're gonna have to deal with your share of hate, since I don't think it's escaped you that you're not exactly popular right now," she continued.

"I've noticed," I replied dryly.

"You're not a woman that's gonna let that bother you, though," she said with a chilling certainty. Like she knew me. "No one will hurt you. Not until you give them reason to."

I nodded.

I knew as much, though the purplish bruising on my wrist spoke somewhat of a different story. Though I couldn't worry about bruises in a world of bullet wounds and severed fingers.

"Not gonna be your friend," she continued, walking over to the bar and reaching to snag a bottle of tequila with a wink to Henry. She then snagged two glasses and brought them back over to the table, pouring liberal amounts into them. She sat. Eyed me expectantly.

I did the same, grabbing the glass though I wasn't much of a drinker. If there was ever a night that I needed tequila, it was this night.

Well, it was eight nights before this, but they all merged into one.

"We're not friends, but we can be allies," she said, clinking her glass with mine. "Only if you tell me your story."

I brought the glass to my lips and let the liquid burn at my throat. I put it down. She refilled it. "I'm not usually the one to tell my story. I've made a job out of avoiding my story," I told her honestly.

She set the bottle down. "Babe, we all try to avoid our stories. Till we have to live them. Tequila works as a good accompaniment to tellin' your story. Living it—there's nothing to soften that blow."

I blinked at the philosophical insight coming from a woman in snakeskin at a biker bar after midnight.

"You some kind of expert on life?"

She laughed, it was throaty and attractive. "If there's an exact opposite of an expert on life, that's what I am. No one's an expert. That's the big secret. Even the men in the cuts who try to control life the best they can. We got a brutal reminder on Christmas Day that not even the strongest of us can escape death. Or life, depending on how you look at it."

Her eyes glistened with the same ghosts I'd seen in Hansen's eyes.

She blinked rapidly and downed her drink. She eyed me. "Well, what are you waiting for?"

I took my shot.

Told my story.

THE BOTTLE of tequila was empty.

I was disturbingly sober.

The tequila wasn't there to get me drunk, it was there to use as anesthesia to the emotional surgery I had to undergo in order to tell Scarlett my story.

Our story, I guessed.

Though I didn't think it belonged to either of us anymore.

"Holy shit," Scarlett said when I was done.

Though I wasn't done, was I? The story, the one that wasn't ours, it wasn't finished, it wasn't over.

Or maybe it was.

I didn't know which was worse.

We'd had our happy ending. Ironically the happy ending, the happiest ending under the circumstances, would've been if Liam actually died. If he died without having to become...Jagger. And so I didn't have to see this. Feel this.

But happy endings didn't exist. Happy ever afters were just stories that weren't over yet.

"Yeah," I agreed, trailing my finger around the rim of my empty glass.

I waited for her to curse Liam out, talk about what an asshole he was. She was the kind of woman who didn't hesitate to call a spade a spade or an outlaw and asshole.

But there was only silence.

"That's it?" I asked. "You're not gonna say anything else?"

She shrugged. "No, that's not *it*, but anything I say isn't gonna mean shit since you said it all. And it's not me that has to do any talking. No, it's Jagger, after you tell him the story you told me." She did something I would understand to be very uncharacteristic of her then, reaching over to squeeze my hand. The contact was important not because it wasn't normal for her. But it was a sharing of something. Of a past that she wouldn't share with me, not in words at least. It wasn't sympathy or pity either. It was an acknowledgment of the battles we were both fighting.

"I'm not talking to him," I said after she let go of my hand. "He doesn't deserve my explanation. *I'm* not the one who pretended to be dead. *I'm* the one who had to bury him."

"You didn't bury him, though," she said. "Not really. From what it sounds like, whether he had really died or not, he would've always been alive to you."

Her words hit me to my core because they came from there. She'd sat there and given me truth I was too cowardly or too blind to see.

"Tell me I'm wrong," she challenged after a long silence.

"I can't," I admitted. "But it's not that simple."

"No," she agreed. "It's not."

"What he did..." I trailed off, choking on the truth of it all. "It's unforgivable."

"In love, babe, nothing's unforgivable, that's the ugly truth of it." She paused. "You knew this Liam character...right? Trusted him?"

I nodded. "I did."

"You knew Liam, I know Jagger. He's a lot of things. Some of them bad. Most of them good. On an outlaw scale, at least." She grinned.

The knowledge hit me with that grin. She was a former club girl for this charter. She likely would've slept with Liam. Strangely, the thought wasn't as toxic as it had been thinking of faceless women having his warm body while I had his cold ghost.

No, it was somehow comforting to me.

"I know that he went through something. Something that

follows him around. Something he wears on his face that's more than just torn up skin. It makes sense, seeing you. He was dragging around the guilt of what he did, sure. With pain. If he was really as evil and heartless as you're trying to convince yourself he is, he wouldn't have had that weight. There's no explanation for what he did. Nothing that will make it okay. But there's a reason. One you need to hear. So you can decide whether you're finally going to bury Liam, or accept that he's alive inside another man."

"YOU KNOW, I've been to Scotland," I said, attempting to make conversation with Elden for the hundredth time. At first, I'd been very happy to be surly and silent in a protest to my conditions. I'd been determined to wallow and rot in my own pain.

But there was only so long you could do that.

Only so long I could do that for.

I had some kind of interior self-preservation switch that forced me to alter my behavior to my surroundings, but not my personality.

I wasn't a talker, naturally. I couldn't stand the closeness of friendships, of boyfriends, or even my family. I was terrified to let anyone in, to have to watch them crash out of my life.

That's probably a big reason why I became a reporter. I got the contact I needed, but no commitment. None of that loss. Because I felt for those people I'd interview. The ones who I knew may very well be dead in the next day, the next hour. I'd go in knowing that, and it was almost comforting. Freeing.

It wasn't this way here.

I knew, given the seriousness of this war that any of these men, or women, could die in an hour, a day, a week.

There was no comfort in that.

So I distracted myself with the story.

Or tried to.

Apart from watching one man get tortured and murdered and another shot in the alley, all high-ranking members of the Fernandez cartel, I didn't have much. Well, I had a shitload, but not enough narrative for it all.

Telling the Scottish prospect about the quick holiday I had in Scotland while I had four days free between an assignment in Ukraine and Turkey, wasn't serving my story but I was going crazy in the silence.

"I went to Edinburgh, obviously," I said. "Because I love Harry Potter and the cemetery where JK Rowling got some of the names was so cool. And then I went to Glasgow, it was different. Less magical. Gritty."

"Glasgow's a shithole," he grunted.

I glanced up at him. He didn't make eye contact. "I liked it. It was real. Honest."

Now he looked down at me.

But we didn't get to have that moment because a small person wearing a printed and bell sleeve maxi dress all but tackled me as we made it into the common room, eerily quiet at midafternoon—men only emerged from whatever they were doing toward the later hours.

"Finally!" she snapped, glaring at Elden, then grinning at me and yanking me into her arms before I could do anything, namely stop her.

I was not a hugger.

Unlike every single other member of my family.

They showed affection often and easily. Maybe I used to as well, in the time before, I couldn't exactly remember.

But now, the me I had to painfully remember every day, was not a hugger. Not with friends. Definitely not with strangers. And despite what my research, what word of mouth told me or the sheets and magazines that I got from the woman, Macy was still a stranger.

A stranger who hugged.

Whether I liked it or not.

I tried my best not to flinch away from her touch, she'd done a lot for me without knowing who the heck I was, I could handle a hug. One that told me she had a good but subtle taste in perfume and that she was warm and strong for her small size.

She let me go, kept hold of my shoulders and her gaze ran over me. "You are even more beautiful in person," she declared. "How is that a thing?"

I didn't quite understand where her words were coming from since she was easily one of the most stunning women I'd ever seen. Up close, her dress was even more kick-ass, even to a woman whose fashion sense was limited to jeans, slouchy tees, and red lipstick. My only splurge was hideously expensive sneakers, I thought of the majority of them fondly, back in my small apartment in Castle Springs, almost taking up a whole wall.

There was one LBD dress in my closet. Not for dates. For funerals.

I had tight, sexy and slutty clothes in my closet at the motel. I wondered if they were even still there since I paid weekly, cash—because it wouldn't have done well paying with a credit card registered to me if the Sons looked into me.

Those were not chosen because of an interest in fashion.

Originally, they were chosen for an interest of not getting killed.

Fashionista I wasn't. And Macy was.

Definitely not in the way Scarlett was.

Her dress up close was the most beautiful shade of turquoise with a circular flower pattern, long sleeves, and a plunging neckline. She had about three chunky necklaces slung around her neck, wedged cork mules and her choppy hair was messy in an effortless beautiful kind of way.

Her makeup was light because she was naturally beautiful with soft features that went with her kind smile and warm eyes.

Her warm eyes cooled and narrowed as she glared at my ever-present, hulking, Scottish, roguish shadow.

"Right. You can leave now. We're having girl talk and I'll be sure not to plan an escape with her." Her eyes went back to me, warm again, the transition was flawless and totally adorable. "As a rule, I'm totally against these guys holding women hostage, but I'm secretly kind of happy about you being a hostage and I'm a big fan. Big." She enunciated the word with a wink. Then she transitioned to a glare at Elden. "Run along and torture some infidels," she demanded.

Her voice was light, joking. I wondered if she knew about that door with the padlocks and bloodstains on the concrete.

I couldn't make assumptions based on the fact her eyes were warm, and her smile was easy. Some people went dead behind their eyes at the sight of such things, at the knowledge of such things. Other people went more alive, packed more warmth onto their souls so they could insulate themselves from the horrors of the world.

It was no secret neither I nor Liam went that way.

I glanced to the man Macy was glaring at. He was silent. Folded his arms in a silent challenge.

Macy raised her brow and didn't back down from a stare that most men would've broken.

It lasted a while.

I was impressed when he sighed, muttered something under his breath about "lasses being the death of me" and stomped off.

Macy straightened and smiled at me. "Good. Now we can talk properly without a decidedly hunky but definitely nosy prospect breathing down our necks." She grabbed my hand and dragged me over to the bar.

A stroller was parked there.

It was kind of comical, seeing that sitting amongst everything that was the Sons of Templar clubhouse. But it fit too.

She smiled down at the sleeping baby. "I'm lucky, he takes after his father in regards to his stance on silence, but once he starts talking he'll obviously take after his mother for her quick wit." She winked. "My friend Arianne has the other one. He's walking now, and if I let him loose in the clubhouse...who knows what he'd find."

I looked down at the beautiful, chubby baby.

My womb pulsated with a memory.

"How many kids do you think we should have?" Liam asked conversationally, trailing his finger over my bare and flat belly.

I tensed. "Liam, we're eighteen years old, we still have to sneak into each other's bedrooms and I kind of want a college degree and a few irresponsible decisions under my belt before I even think about children," I said.

Though even as the words came out, I looked into those emerald eyes and saw the man he was becoming. The father he'd be. Saw our family. Saw myself growing big with his baby.

My stomach fluttered.

In a good way.

"Yes, well, I hope you know I'm going to be there for every one of those irresponsible decisions, you know to make some of my own and to keep an eye on you."

I rolled my eyes. Liam was protective. Bordering on too much, but if I was honest, I liked it. I also liked what he was saying. We hadn't decided on colleges yet, our acceptance letters only starting to arrive. I knew that I had no chance at getting the Ivy League Scholarships he was already being offered, and my family couldn't afford an Ivy League tuition. No way was I getting Liam to sacri-

fice his future to come to a state college as he'd suggested in the past.

I was hoping I'd get accepted to Boston University so we could get a place together.

We hadn't even talked about that, now Liam was talking babies?

"Getting me pregnant before marrying me is not an irresponsible decision you'll be making," I told him. "My dad might straight up strangle you."

He grinned. "Your dad loves me like I'm his own." He thought about my currently troublesome brother. "Probably more than his own."

I smiled back. "Yes, but, he loves his little girl most of all, bad enough that you're bedding her under his roof."

He raised his brow. "Did you just say 'bedding?'"

I smacked his shoulder. It was hard, muscled, he was working out a lot more lately.

I dug it.

Even though it meant my hand bruised when I hit him.

"Ah, so my future wife will be abusive," he said, toying with my hand.

I blinked. "What?" I whispered, right about the same time something cold slipped onto the fourth finger on my left hand.

I looked down at the glittering single solitaire diamond staring at me with a future, a promise.

My gaze snapped back up to Liam. He cupped my neck.

A tear trailed down my cheek before he spoke.

He wiped it away with his thumb. "I want to make all the irresponsible decisions with you. I want to do it with my ring on your finger. Then, when we're finished college, I'm gonna marry you. Then, we're going to travel the world, like you want to. Make more irresponsible decisions, take them international." He stroked away *another tear. "And then, when we're ready, we'll get responsible. Have kids. A family. A forever."*

There were too many tears now for Liam to wipe away.

He grinned. "Am I taking the crying as a yes or a soul-crushing rejection?" he joked, though there was vulnerability behind the tone. Fear.

I didn't answer.

I couldn't.

Instead, I kissed him.

He kissed me back.

It tasted like my tears and forever.

A gentle squeeze on my arm jerked me out of yet another memory. I'd spent fifteen years without remembering, now I couldn't stop.

Macy's eyes were tinged with worry. "You okay? You kind of went away with the fairies."

"Away with the fairies?" I repeated.

She nodded. "Yeah, you know, to a world other than this one."

I gaped at her. This woman might've been a little nuts.

She let go of my arm to pick up a mug of what looked like tea. "It's fine," she said after sipping. "I'd totally go to worlds other than this if I could. Like Middle Earth. It's a peaceful place now that Frodo destroyed the ring of power in Mt Doom."

Okay, she was a lot nuts.

I liked her.

"Plus, I could use a little peace right now," she said in a voice far less bright than the one moments ago. This was not a flawless transition. It was full of pain.

Without even thinking about it, I reached out and squeezed her hand.

Me.

I'd witnessed so much pain, sorrow, loss. So many times when

I wanted to offer comfort. And I did. With words. But never with physical touch. That was crossing a barrier that I couldn't move past. Because when I started doing things like that, I got too involved in the story. In the pain. I needed to be detached in order to survive.

So why was I now attaching myself to the Sons of Templar like a fucking barnacle when I knew I had to cut myself off in the end?

Maybe I had a morbid fascination with emotional bleeding. Emotional cutting.

Macy squeezed my hand without words, smiling sadly.

"Now, I need to hear *everything* about your career. The highs, the lows. And most importantly..."

I stiffened, waiting for the question about how I got here, why I wasn't dead, why I was a prisoner in Liam's room.

"What's the deal with the red lipstick?" she finished.

I waited a beat. She was serious.

My body relaxed.

And I smiled.

For the first time since I could remember.

And I did tell her everything.

Even the deal with the red lipstick.

THE NEXT NIGHT at the bar was much the same as the first one. I was treated with very thinly veiled hostility. Apart from Claw's ever-present smile. It seems the guy had a soft spot for tragic stories.

I wondered idly if he'd have that smile if he hadn't heard my story. If he would've continued on squeezing the life out of me that night had Liam not stop him.

It paid not to wonder about such things.

Swiss seemed to have warmed to me again, in his own way. I guess I'd earned his respect after watching him torture a man without having a human reaction.

I guessed I had a little monster in me too.

The first night at the bar, I had been numbly going through the motions, getting used to being back in whatever passed for the real world around here when I'd spent a week thinking I might not ever leave the clubhouse.

But tonight, I had been able to slip back into the skin that had served me so well on the battlefield. I did my job, wearing more clothes than I had before, I was thankful not to have to keep up that persona.

My real job was watching. Looking for the story.

It wasn't going to jump out at me in one fully recognized idea. It was pieces. I had to collect them up, see how to fit them together. And I already had enough for a half decent story. They were looking for retribution for the Christmas Day massacre, and they were doing so by lopping off fingers of men. Men connected to Miguel Fernandez, who I now knew was responsible for the killings, whose men had been killed and tortured in front of me, and who the club was currently at war with.

I'd done my research on him too.

Any worthwhile journalist knew who he was. Or more aptly, *what* he was. He wasn't a man and a monster. He was purely a monster.

He trafficked humans for a living. And he made a good one. Living, that was. He had more politicians in his pocket than all the organized crime syndicates put together. He was little more than untouchable. Many honorable men and women had tried to bring him to justice. Some of my contemporaries included.

All of them had failed. Disappeared as if they hadn't even existed. Nothing for their families. No closure. No knowledge of where their loved one was laid to rest in one of the most brutal ways possible. No, just nightmares of how horrible their last moments were. They died horribly and nastily in the pursuit of an honorable act.

Honorable people couldn't bring him down.

It was becoming apparent that dishonorable people were trying.

The thought filled me with pure panic.

Because Fernandez was international. He had one of the largest mercenary armies in the world. More than a small country. He didn't hesitate to kill his enemies in the most brutal ways possible. He intimated and controlled governments and here was a largely domestic—apart from a handful of small charters outside the US—motorcycle club trying to bring him down.

It wouldn't happen.

And if, by some miracle, it did, it would only happen with a lot more blood being spilled. And there was a very real chance that I'd be burying Liam again.

For real this time.

I'd likely see a lot more people buried before my time here was out.

And maybe my time here would be out by getting hit in the crossfire. I'd dodged enough bullets throughout my career, my name was on one somewhere.

Death was inevitable, even in the best-case scenario.

I wanted to change that. To stop it. But it wasn't my choice to make. Liam had made his choices. Luckily he wasn't at the bar tonight, even though I felt like bleeding around him. Even though I *liked* bleeding around him.

In my break, I texted one of my contacts in the underworld for all information they could call up on Fernandez.

I spent the night collecting pieces of my story while I continued to lose more of the pieces of myself.

CHAPTER ELEVEN

"BYE HENRY!" I called as I walked out the door.

"Don't come back tomorrow covering up so much," he called back. "You got shit for tips the past two nights."

I rolled my eyes. I got shit for tips because the men knew who I was now. Not because my legs and ass were covered by baggy jeans.

I didn't need tips.

I had my life, and in their eyes, that was gratuity enough.

The door slammed shut behind me and I stared at the empty parking lot.

No, not empty.

There was one bike in it.

One man.

"Where's Elden?" I asked, two words working out of my throat with blood attached to them.

Liam stubbed out the smoke that had been illuminating his mouth far too much for my liking.

He still hadn't quit.

Then again, I doubted lung cancer was a prevailing cause of

death in outlaw bikers.

"He's got club business."

I had discovered that 'club business' was kind of a blanket statement for whenever the men in cuts didn't want to explain where they were or what they were doing. And you didn't ask questions.

Or weren't supposed to.

I folded my arms across my chest, because the night was chilly, I was only wearing a tank and my nipples were having a reaction that had nothing to do with the chill in the air. "What kind of club business?"

Liam sighed. The sound carried over the distance between. "Doesn't matter. Matters that from now on, to and from work, you're on the back of my bike."

I froze.

On the back of his bike.

I knew what that term meant too.

Obviously it didn't mean the same thing with us.

But obviously there was no way in earth I could be on Liam's bike, pressed up to his body. Touching him.

No. Fucking. Way.

"That's not happening," I said immediately.

"It's not something you have a say in."

I gritted my teeth if only to distract myself from the pain that came with this foreign man who didn't ask me things, just told me what to do. Who had no care for my comfort or my autonomy.

"I would rather walk to the club. On broken glass, which is the equivalent of what these heels are." I hissed back. I may have been back in my comfortable uniform, but the only footwear available to me was my skank heels. I didn't want to get my Gucci sneakers stained from the floor of the bar. I turned on my heel and began to do just that until a hand circled around my upper arm.

It was painful. Not because the grip was tight. Because the grip was Liam's.

"You think I'm gonna let you walk three miles at one in the mornin', alone?" he growled. His breath was hot, smelled of smoke, Liam and destruction.

I tried to wrench my hand away. Tried being the operative word. He held fast. "You're going to force me into something else, Liam?" I asked quietly. Exhaustion hit me truly and suddenly. Not physical, though I'd been on my feet all night and hadn't had shit for sleep in what felt like years.

It was an exhaustion I'd been avoiding for years. Fifteen years worth of tiredness hit me in an empty parking lot at one in the morning faced with a biker I used to know in another life.

It must have seeped into my voice, that exhaustion, something in it caused Liam to let go of my arm. He let out a sigh. It was heavier than the last one. I battled not to let it sit on my shoulders. Because there was over a decade's worth of tiredness and pain in that sigh.

"Okay," he said finally.

I jerked in surprise. "Okay?" I repeated.

"Let's walk."

I gritted my teeth again. "The purpose of me walking is so I don't have to be in your presence," I said tightly.

Silence dragged on, stretching like half-chewed gum on the bottom of a shoe.

Liam finally spoke. Though his voice was Jagger's. "You're gonna have to be in it, like it or not, I told you I'd protect you."

"Protecting me is leaving me, Liam," I whispered. Why was I still calling him that? He kept giving me all the evidence I needed to bury Liam once and for all.

But I wasn't strong enough.

It was that simple. I was holding onto a dream, a memory, a lie.

I couldn't see his face in the darkness but I imagined it hardening, his features tightening.

"I'm not leaving you, Caroline," he said, voice throaty. He cleared it. "So it's walking or the bike, you decide."

I bit the inside of my lip. Walk three miles in the middle of the night even though my feet were killing me. Or get on a bike with Liam for the two-minute ride.

It wasn't a choice, really.

I started walking.

Motorcycle boots thumped against concrete as Liam fell into step with me.

"What if someone steals your bike?" I asked only so I didn't have to suffer the silence that wasn't really silence between us.

"No one's gonna steal my bike," he replied.

"Because everyone fears the wrath of the Sons of Templar?" I asked sarcastically.

He paused. It was only the thump of his boots for a moment, I thought that might be his only answer. He'd given me enough evidence of the wrath of the Sons of Templar after all. "Sure, some people won't steal it 'cause they fear us, rightfully so. The rest of them won't because they respect us. The club. I know you won't believe this, but the club's not all bad." Another pause. A longer one. "Fuck, maybe we are. No one comes out good in the middle of a war."

"No," I agreed.

The silence continued.

For three miles.

Scarlett's words haunted me with every step. But I didn't have the strength to do anything but put one foot in front of the other.

We reached the clubhouse and it was eerily silent. I watched the building as we approached and it seemed that it watched me back. With the deaths it held inside its walls, I wondered if it was a living thing now.

It felt like it.

Did enough death create life?

The man beside me was the embodiment of that.

Whoever he was.

As we approached the perimeter, floodlights switched on and I squinted with the harshness of the light.

"Jesus, Blake!" Jagger yelled. "It's fuckin' me. Put the weapon down before I shove it up your ass."

I squinted past the offensive light, following Liam's gaze upward to the man perched in a small watchtower structure above us. Sure enough, he was holding an automatic rifle, quickly moving the barrel so it was no longer pointed in our direction.

Blake was one of the youngest patched members. He wasn't even old enough to drink, but he managed to make sure he replaced his blood with alcohol in all the parties I'd seen him at. Though there was youth in his face, there was none of it behind his eyes. Though he was easy to laugh, to joke, it was all empty.

"Jagger? Dude, what the fuck are you walkin' for? Your health?" His voice was scratchy, appealing, like the rest of him. Distracting enough for most of the female population not to notice the danger he wore underneath it all.

"Yeah, for my fuckin' *health,*" Jagger muttered. "You know what's good for yours, kid, you'll open the fuckin' gate, rouse a prospect and get them to get my bike."

I could tell Blake itched to ask a lot of questions. But Liam's voice didn't really broker such questions. So instead, the gate opened.

We walked to the clubhouse in the same silence we'd adopted for three miles. It was the silence between two people who were pretending there was nothing to say between them, two people who knew each other too well to have such a thing as silence.

The common room wasn't empty, a handful of club girls were scattered around, in varying states of undress, tangled up with men, also in different states of undress.

My eyes ran over them without reaction.

Even if this wasn't a nightly occurrence in the place that was my prison, I wouldn't have a reaction. Sex was the least shocking to me out of all the things humans could do with an audience.

We both came to a stop outside Liam's room.

As before, when I'd been too afraid to cross the threshold outside, now I found myself terrified to go inside, to close the door and be suffocated by my loneliness.

Liam didn't say anything. Didn't make a move to leave, just stood across from me, staring at the door.

"I feel like I need to thank you," I said finally, moving to meet his eyes with whatever strength I had left.

He blinked. "Thank me?"

I nodded. "I used to think that having you, us being together, it meant I would never be alone, never be lonely. Even with you halfway across the world, even though I didn't see your face, hear your voice for weeks at a time, I knew you were still there. I knew we were still there. We were okay. I was okay. Never alone."

I paused. For a long time. Long enough for those memories, for that pain to wash over me. Somehow fresh, somehow more powerful than whatever was before that.

As I was learning, there was always more pain with Liam.

"Then you died," I whispered to the door. "But even then, I wasn't *alone*. I was lonely for you. Fuck, was I lonely for you." I tried to conjure up those days, the darkest of my existence.

But even with my newfound capacity to remember, to experience pain and still remain standing, my body wouldn't let me go there. There were some things that your mind didn't let you remember.

"I missed you with parts of me I didn't know existed," I said, still talking to the door. "With a pain I didn't know human beings could conjure up without outside forces. I felt all of that. But not quite alone. You were there. Somewhere. Inside me. Outside me. Watching over me." I shook my head, smiling wistfully.

I didn't know where I found the strength, maybe it wasn't strength, it was tiredness that had me meeting his eyes.

Another wave of pain at those emerald irises.

At the unmissable scar.

At the body, taut, wired, coiled.

"I used to talk to you," I said. "I was convinced you were somewhere. You were with me. It's what people do to survive death. Convince ourselves that it's not just some yawning black hole, that the person who was once everything isn't reduced to nothing but compost." I didn't move my eyes from his. "Though most people don't have their dead ones come back to life. And you wanna know what's funny? I've never felt more alone than when I saw you in that alleyway."

He didn't move.

But he flinched.

Somewhere deep inside that, I knew was the worst and most visceral kind of pain.

The most lasting.

I felt satisfied landing that blow.

Emptily satisfied.

I moved my eyes and my hand went to the doorknob. I waited. For what, I didn't know. For him to stop me. Stop the pain.

He did neither.

So I walked through the door and closed it in his face.

The locks clicked.

On my side this time.

Every story that I worked that made a splash, that was real and good, was not purely a result of good reporting. Sure, I was a good reporter, but those stories were not made purely by my talent. Not by a long shot.

My career and my position in the industry was based largely on luck.

My first assignment in Afghanistan, I was allotted a 'fixer,' Dariush. Every foreign journalist was required to have one. They were designed to take care of our safety, facilitate our stay, help with visas, and transport us. Mostly they were employed by the government to make sure we behaved.

Dariush was different than most. He was intelligent, young, though married with two infants, incredibly sloppily dressed and spoke immaculate English. He also abhorred the state his country was in and went out of his way, while putting his life in danger, to help me. To help my story by putting me in contact with people who would give me the real scoop.

The same happened in every war-torn country I visited. With people who had little more than nothing, but information, and that was everything.

There was Uri in Israel.

Anatoly in Moscow.

Faheem in the Sudan.

Zamir in Iraq.

All men. I didn't know if this was because I was a female, because men were the only one allowed to 'fix' things for reporters, especially female reporters. It didn't much matter.

Each of these men worked constantly for terrible money, worse—read, no—benefits, in beyond dangerous circumstances, risking their lives for a foreigner, with the hope a stranger might help their country with some uncensored news coverage.

Which wasn't the case often enough for my liking.

I wondered who my fixer was here.

If there was ever a chance of 'fixing' this.

Though I knew there wasn't. You couldn't fix what wasn't

broken, but you could break something so badly that there was no possibility of reparation.

That was me.

Beyond reparation.

Beyond redemption.

I WAS UP EARLY.

Because in my real life—or whatever passed for it—I was always up early. Constant sunrise bombings, alternating with calls to prayer didn't exactly promote sleeping till noon.

I had been waking early since I'd become a reluctant resident here, but first I'd been confined to this room, so unable to do my morning routine, which usually consisted of a shitload of coffee, a quick yoga session and a bagel smeared with enough cream cheese to clog my arteries.

I didn't much worry about calories since my life was pretty much lived on the edge of death. Fitting into my jeans never really bothered me. That and I'd seen people starving, actually *starving*, children dying, their malnourished bodies bloated and skinny at the same time. No way was I going to put myself on a diet, starve myself like so many women did. It certainly wasn't helping those who actually starved, but it worked for my guilty conscience.

My routine had been obviously ruined along with whatever was left of my sanity.

It was the morning after walking those miles with Liam and our collective demons that I decided I needed to take control of whatever I could. Which wasn't much. But my morning routine might work.

I dressed in leggings and an oversized tee, yanked my hair into a messy bun and did a quick lot of stretches in the small amount of floor space available to me. No way was I trying it in the common room, not just because of the littering of condom wrappers, empty bottles, unconscious bodies and whatever bacteria resided there—though that was a big contributor. No, because I didn't want to run into Liam, skulking around from wherever he was staying.

I hadn't asked him where he was sleeping, though our exchanges didn't really have space for benign questions such as that. We only had space for those big, yawning, gaping, painful questions. Like *'why did you fake your own death and leave me alone with my broken heart, you miserable bastard?'* kind of questions.

And I wasn't strong enough for the answer just yet.

Me, the person who made her living out of asking some of the hardest questions in the world, did not have enough courage to ask the one question that mattered.

It rang around in my skull as I tried to repair my aching body.

Once finished, my stiff and sore body was loosened somewhat. But no matter how much yoga I did, I wasn't going to stretch away the tension that was coiled in my soul.

I dressed in my last lot of clean clothes, reminding myself to venture around the clubhouse, or at least ask Macy, to find out where to do laundry.

I thought I'd feel more comfortable in my boyfriend jeans, black tank, Gucci sneakers, and red lipstick—not wearing scant and tight clothes and enough makeup to sink a ship.

My hair was slowly returning back to its normal color, though it was a strange in between now. Though that worked, since I felt like I was in between. Halfway from that girl in miniskirts and crop tops, but somehow still miles from the woman who routinely wore bulletproof vests with 'Press' plastered on them in block letters.

As if a collection of five words on the vest would provide me with some other layer of protection. Words protected no one. But I had experience in knowing they could harm just as well as any bullet.

Maybe that was why I was too scared to ask Liam those questions.

Because I didn't have on my emotional bulletproof vest.

I had considered myself and my fragile mind lucky that I encountered no one while thinking these thoughts, pouring my coffee in the thankfully clean kitchen off the common room.

The kitchen was well stocked, with a mixture of extremely healthy food—even fricking kale, which apparently Claw put in his smoothies—and total junk. I veered toward the total junk.

I was halfway through a bagel when my luck ran out.

No, that wasn't quite right, my luck ran out about ten days ago, with a bullet in an alley.

No, that wasn't quite right either.

My luck ran out when I heard a scream down the street and my blood went cold almost fifteen years ago.

Liam didn't look like he was expecting me when he entered the kitchen.

I wasn't expecting him either. Not just in the kitchen, but here, walking the earth at all.

You'd think I would've gotten used to it by now. Not just seeing him when I thought he was dead for fourteen years, but seeing this new, hard, scarred version of him.

You'd think someone as accustomed to trauma as me, to seeing all sorts of horrors, I would've been able to brace for impact.

I couldn't.

There was a handful of seconds, every time I laid eyes on him, when his presence tore through every single shield I'd managed to build. Like knives. But it wasn't the pain that was the worst, I was used to that, it barely went away. No, it was the sheer and primal joy that came from my heart before my brain could catch it up.

Because those few seconds weren't full of ugly truth and reality of what him living, breathing, walking around in a motorcycle cut meant.

No, those seconds were simple. *Liam was alive.*

It was the transition from simple to painfully complicated that was the worst thing. Having to let go of that warm joy and replace it with the cold truth.

I quickly swallowed my half-chewed bagel, the sides of it scraping my throat. For a second, I thought it might lodge itself in my airway, a panic came with the thought of standing there choking in front of Liam, on a fucking *bagel*. But then a strange sense of longing overtook me. I *wanted* to choke in front of him. Give him something tangible to be presented with. Show him what his presence did.

But I swallowed.

"I was just leaving," I said coldly, skirting around him. Or trying to.

He snatched my wrist. The skin burned from contact. I even looked down to see if smoke was arising from where our bodies met.

Nothing but a hand covered in tattoos, tanned, weathered, foreign.

"You're gonna have to face me at some point," he said, voice gravely, still half clutched by sleep.

I glanced down and his wrinkled tee and worn jeans. It looked like laundry day was nearing for him too. Did he have one of the club girls take care of those needs? Like he did others?

I swallowed bile.

"I'm not the one who has anything or *anyone* to face up to," I shot, my voice not full of the venom required to land the shot as I intended. I looked down to where his grip tightened at my words. It was real pain now, not just the stuff conjured up by my ruined heart. I liked it. His touch, no longer tender or reverent. It was a nice reminder of who he was now. Of who I was now.

"Let me go," I said through gritted teeth, forcing the command out through sheer self-preservation.

"You're not giving me a chance to," he said, not letting go. "You're determined to hate me." His eyes shimmered, liquid emeralds that I'd gazed into a lifetime ago and jumped off a cliff with. Because I trusted him to know that I would have a soft landing.

It was torture looking into those same eyes knowing he was never going to give me a soft landing ever again.

I ripped my arm from his grasp, pushing past him and into the common room. I knew he was going to follow me even before the footfalls of his motorcycle boots echoed behind me. That was why I walked into the common room instead of his bedroom. I couldn't have him in there, have us in there in such close proximity to that white feather hidden in his drawer.

I couldn't run.

So I sat at the bar, setting my coffee cup on the surface covered in rings from bottles and glasses. A lemony disinfectant smell mixed with whisky, beer, and cigarette smoke.

It wasn't unpleasant.

Liam situated himself beside me with a sigh.

I sipped my coffee.

He watched me.

I knew he was taking this for what it was, surrender. He was expecting the questions that Scarlett had urged me to ask. There was only so long that we could both tiptoe around this elephant.

But I still wasn't ready. Still wasn't strong enough to face my feelings. Face the answers.

So I did what I did best, I hid behind the story.

"The club runs guns," I said. It wasn't a question, though I expected a denial. Or silence. Or a lie.

No one, especially not reporters, should expect the truth when hard questions are asked. It's figuring out how to find truth from the lies people tell, that's where a good reporter is made.

"Yeah, we do," he replied.

I'd heard a lot of things, was hardened to them. Truth from a criminal shocked me. Should I be shocked? Liam had always been honest with me. About the little things.

Little things like being a part of a club that runs guns.

He just wasn't honest about the big things.

Like the fact he wasn't dead.

"How long has the club run guns for?" I asked.

"Since before I started prospecting," he replied.

I winced inwardly. Since before he came back from a war. Since before he chose not to come home to me.

But I was a journalist, I knew how to recover from hard answers, how to make it seem like they didn't bother me.

"It's rooted in criminal activity then," I mused.

His eyes hardened. "It's rooted in brotherhood."

I regarded the room we were sitting in. The leftover bottles and dirty glasses from yet another party. Signals of disorder everywhere. But there were photos peppering the walls, separated by gun and motorcycle memorabilia. Grainy black and white photos of men with their arms around each other, grinning in front of motorcycles. More, in color, newer, with different men, but the cuts, the smiles, the bikes were ever present.

There were framed mugshots.

Another sign that they were an outlaw club.

Then there were photos of children.

Families.

It was a rich, bloodstained, and violent tapestry, weaving through the outskirts of society and the outskirts of the law.

I straightened, meeting Liam's emerald eyes once more. They hadn't moved from me. His attention was uncomfortable, because it was unyielding. Whenever I was in the room, he never took his eyes off me, as if he were terrified I'd go away and he was trying to make me disappear at the same time.

Or maybe that was just what I was doing with him.

"You haven't had any convictions, despite numerous DEA operations," I continued.

Something moved in his face. "You've done your research."

I nodded. "It's what a good reporter does."

"So that's what this is, you're being a good reporter?" Accusation soaked his tone. Accusation that he was not entitled to. That he was not allowed to hurl at me.

I clenched my fists, sinking my nails into the skin that had only just scabbed over. But that's what it was with Liam, every interaction, was picking at a scab, opening barely healed wounds.

I was always bleeding around him.

"Yes," I gritted out. "I'm being a good reporter. Since you're the only one that will answer my questions honestly, for the sake of the story, I'm putting our...personal history aside."

He glared at me. "We're a lot of things, Peaches, but we're not fucking history."

I couldn't hide my flinch. Not this time. I sank my nails farther into my skin. "I asked you not to call me that." I was ashamed at how weak my voice was.

Instead of answering, Liam looked down at my hands and his glare deepened. He snatched them, forcing my palms open and let out a low hiss at the fresh blood covering them. "Jesus, Peaches, what the fuck are you doin' to yourself?"

I wrenched my hands back, standing. "It's not me doing anything," I yelled. "It's you. You're cutting me open and you don't even *fucking know*. You don't even fucking care, *Jagger*." I spat the word at him before I turned on my heel and stalked off.

CHAPTER TWELVE

Jagger

HE WATCHED her walk away and wondered if he should follow her.

But he wasn't physically capable of following her. He couldn't move. Couldn't take a fucking step, bleeding from the wounds he sustained from the short exchange. From seeing her cut her fucking skin open because she couldn't stand being around him.

He was a sick fuck.

Keeping her here.

In his room.

Forcing her to face his fucked up, scarred face every day. Forcing her to watch as he revealed just what a monster he was. He was doing that to push her away. But he wasn't letting her go.

So what the fuck was he doing?

He stared at the pictures on the walls. The ones he'd stared at a thirteen years ago, looking for somewhere to lose himself. If he was honest, he was looking to die. Or maybe he was hoping for the club to save him enough to figure out a way to go back to her. Marry her. Make good on the promise he'd made to her father before he asked her to marry him.

His palms were sweating as he took the beer Trevor gave him.

He took it with one hand and wiped the other on his jeans.

Trevor settled on the chair beside him on the porch, looking out onto the street that both he and Caroline grew up on. She wasn't the girl next door. But she was the girl six houses down. When they got together, they were at each other's houses so much that their parents knew if one wasn't home, they'd be at the other's.

Both of their families took the intensity of their relationship in their stride. Either because they saw what it was, something more than teenage infatuation. Or because they were just good parents who wanted their children to be happy.

Which was what he was hoping from Trevor.

He was hoping he didn't shoot him with any of the number of guns he kept in the house. This was Alabama, after all.

Trevor, the man who'd snuck him beer since he was sixteen. Though it wasn't really sneaking, since his first beer was given to him by his father at sixteen at a family BBQ. His philosophy was if he let his son have a beer now and then, then he wouldn't have a lot all the time.

The theory worked.

Liam liked a beer, but he had no interest in keggers and getting drunk off his ass.

Mainly because whatever parties he was at, Caroline was there too, and no fucking way was he getting drunk off his ass when he had his girl to take care of.

Which was probably why he got a lot of respect—and beer, though he guessed it was the same thing from the man in question —from Trevor. That and because he treated him like his own.

It seemed as if Trevor could sense what Liam was on the porch for. Not that the act itself was an irregular occurrence, they'd sit out here shooting the shit while Caroline was getting ready or whatever.

But Caroline wasn't home. She was shopping with her mom and sister, then going to a movie.

Her mom was trying to squeeze out all the time she could with her daughter before she moved away to college most likely. Liam knew that because his mom was the same.

It would've been annoying as shit if he didn't love his mom so much.

He didn't care whatever any asshole said, it didn't make you a pussy to admit you loved your mom. It made you a man. Because if you can admit you love your mom, you deserve the love of a woman.

That's what his dad said anyway.

And he tended to agree with him.

The silence between him and Trevor lasted for half a beer. Again, not unusual. They didn't have to talk, unlike his wife and daughters, like his son Will, who only spoke in grunts, Trevor was comfortable in silence. As was Liam.

But he wasn't silent because he was comfortable.

He was silent because he was nervous as fuck.

"You sweat any more bullets I'll be able to arm myself for the next year," Trevor commented.

Liam snapped his head over to him.

"You don't have to be nervous, son, you want my approval, you got it," he continued, taking a pull of his beer.

Liam struggled to recover. "What?"

Trevor rolled his eyes in an almost perfect impression of his daughter. "Know you're here to ask for my blessing to marry Caroline. You've got it. Had it since the day you walked in, looked me in the eye shook my hand and then looked to my little girl like you'd lay down your fucking life for her. You're probably gonna get shit from Aggie about how young you both are. And you are young.

Too young for some things. Maybe this. But I don't think so. 'Cause of the way you looked at Caroline the first day you stepped foot in this house. Not a look of a sixteen-year-old kid. It was the look of a man. A man I know will protect my daughter from hurt."

It wasn't a question, but it was. Liam nodded rapidly. "I'd rather die than see her hurt."

Trevor chuckled. "Well don't go and do that, that's a surefire way to destroy her. But you treat her good, we're not gonna have problems. I already consider you my son."

"I'm gonna treat her good," Liam promised.

"I know," Trevor agreed. He finished his beer. "Now you can relax. Probably gonna be your last chance for a while." Trevor winked.

Liam laughed. And he leaned back. Relaxed. On the porch with a cold beer and the warm evening sun. And the knowledge he had forever with Caroline.

A clap on his shoulder had him pulling out his piece.

Swiss grinned at the Glock pointed at his heart. "Good morning to you too, sunshine." He leaned over and snatched Caroline's coffee, sipping it before he could stop him.

Jagger stiffened, forcing himself to pocket his piece when he really wanted to empty the clip into his brother for sipping on Caroline's fucking coffee cup.

Swiss screwed up his face. "Willy Wonka shit in here? Didn't take you for a sweet tooth. Man with as much bitter as you couldn't possibly imbibe that much sugar and survive," he teased.

Jagger gritted his teeth. He still hadn't forgiven the fucker for what he'd done, taking Caroline to the basement. Even though he was just following orders. Hansen was the one responsible.

But somehow it seemed so much fucking easier to be mad at the soldier than the General.

They were easier to dispatch at least.

Jagger snatched the cup back. It was still warm.

"It's Caroline's," he growled. "You sip from her cup again, I'll take you down to the basement for a trip that will not get you off."

Swiss was fucked in many ways. The main being he got off on torture. Like *got the fuck off*. He didn't hurt women. Not without their permission.

Mommy issues up the ass, that one.

And all the other issues in the world.

Swiss grinned wider. "Ah, makes sense. So what's the deal with you and the rat anyway?"

No one knew about him and Caroline's history but Jagger and Claw. He was surprised that big mouthed fucker hadn't told anyone, especially Swiss. They were tight. Both previously Nomad. Maybe that's why they connected, because they belonged in the Sons of Templar, but nowhere at the same time.

Or maybe it was because they were both depraved mother-fuckers.

"She's not a rat," Jagger gritted out, his piece heavy and hot in his jeans, begging to be used.

Swiss shrugged. "Seems not. Yet at least. I get it. She's got a good stomach for blood."

He said it in a way that a man might comment on a woman's ass or tits. Because that's what it was to Swiss, what he found attractive, a woman's ability to withstand and witness torture, apparently.

"Yeah, she does," Jagger agreed reluctantly, thinking of her blank, jaded face in the basement. His cock hardened in his jeans.

Jesus, he was just as bad as Swiss. He was getting off on torture too.

Swiss clapped him on the shoulder. "This is gonna be a fucking mess, isn't it?"

He wanted to hate the fucker, but there was an acceptance, a support in his words. "You think we're not already in a fucking mess?" he shot back. "At war with a man we can't touch, can't find and most likely can't fucking kill."

Swiss shrugged again. "You can kill anyone. No matter how high up anyone is, or in his case, low down, they all die the same. Bleed the same. We'll get him. It'll be messy, sure." Swiss nodded his head to the hall where Jagger's room was. Where Caroline was. "That's messier." He didn't wait for him to speak. Or shoot him. "Speaking of women who make messes. Rosie's at the warehouse."

"Fuck," Jagger muttered under his breath. Rosie was high up on this thing, mostly because she was the one who fucked with Fernandez in the first place. And as much as all the men in her life had tried to fight this war for her, she was intent on being at least a General.

And she was a good one at that.

But she would likely not be happy to hear they'd killed three men when she'd instructed them not to pull any "violent, cavemen and vapid alpha male killing until I say it's okay to let the beast out."

It wasn't that they weren't down with listening to a woman, it's that they needed blood.

Swiss nodded. "Fuck is right. Not a lot I'm scared of in this world. People barely scare me anymore. But that bitch," he whistled. "Fuck. I'm man enough to say I'm terrified of her."

Jagger glanced at the hall again. "Yeah, women are the most scary motherfuckers of them all," he agreed.

HE WALKED into the warehouse and wasn't surprised to see the two-people engaged in an argument in the middle of countless illegal automatic and semi-automatic weapons.

"Rosie," Jagger greeted right about the time she was calling the tightly-wound man in front an 'overprotective caveman who was getting on her last fucking nerve.'

The woman in question gave her husband one last glare and then treated Jagger to the same one.

"Great, another male who thinks he can alpha his way through everything," she hissed in greeting.

Jagger held up his hands in surrender, as was best to do with Rosie. Her brother might have been president of the founding charter and one bad motherfucker, but Rosie was something different. Sure, she'd mellowed some since becoming a mother, but the fact she still killed rapists in her spare time served as evidence she wasn't exactly becoming June Cleaver any time soon.

"Hello to you too," he said, spotting her piece in a shoulder holster, that looked like she'd fucking accessorized or some shit.

Luke came up on her left, body stiff as it always was in situations such as this. You couldn't blame an ex-cop for being a little uptight around outlaws and a felony, but it wasn't to do with that. Usually it was once a cop always a cop. But it wasn't that case with Luke. It was once Rosie's, always Rosie's.

He was Rosie's before the badge.

And after.

He didn't blink at breaking the laws he used to enforce now he was married to the woman he'd loved all his life.

Not that he had a choice.

No one had a choice with women like Rosie.

Not only was she a fucking hot piece, but she'd cut your balls off before you could ever cup them goodbye.

"You fucking assholes think killing is some kind of fail-safe way to deal with everything?" she shot at him.

Jagger raised his brow. "Hey pot, it's the kettle."

She rolled her eyes, huffed out a breath and then glared at

Luke, likely for the fact his mouth twitched upward at Jagger's words.

"I don't kill people with my dick, I do it with my brain," she hissed. "Which is exactly what you assholes are doing. You can't just go kidnapping and murdering every one of Fernandez's men without him noticing and planning retribution."

Jagger stiffened. "We *meant* for him to notice," he clipped. "He sure as fuck meant for us to notice when he slaughtered our whole charter." His voice was acidic in a tone that he'd never used with Rosie, not even when she threatened to castrate him if he didn't fuck her.

It had been a fucking hard decision at the time, when someone who looked like Rosie tried to seduce you, you didn't say no if you had two balls and two heads. And if someone as nuts as her threatened to cut off two of those balls and one of those heads, you heeded that shit.

But Cade had put out the same threat if anyone touched her. Both siblings were likely to make good on their threat, but Cade would not only take his manhood but his cut too.

He didn't exactly choose the lesser of two evils.

But his dick had stayed attached to his body and his cut stayed on his back.

Rosie's features softened, as she revealed the kind, and bleeding heart she hid underneath her murderous and beautiful exterior.

Her eyes shimmered with unshed tears.

A lot of the men in the club had been her family too. Her and Cade had shit for a mother, their dad died in an old club war, so she grew up amongst it all. She had hundreds of uncles, brothers, cousins.

And she loved them all.

This cut her.

Even deeper because he knew that she blamed herself for

what happened. She was the one that pissed off Fernandez in the first place. Pissed off being she spent almost a year in Venezuela, picking off as many of the human traffickers as she could, trying to shut down one of the biggest and most dangerous flesh peddling cartels in the world.

That was Rosie.

And as she was fearless, she wasn't heartless. No, her big heart was what got her in, and out of trouble. Not one fucking patched member in the entire country blamed her, least of all Jagger.

"I know," she whispered. "I know what you lost. Because of—"

"You're gonna stop right fuckin' there," Luke hissed, snatching her hand in ruthless tenderness. He brought it to his lips, not giving a fuck about what that kind of thing would look like in front of Jagger and half the club.

Jagger had a respect for the man. Because he didn't hesitate to kill now, and because he wasn't trying to get the rest of the club behind bars. And because he wasn't afraid to show his woman affection, no matter who was watching. What they had, shit, a cold-hearted fucker like Jagger could taste it.

Only because he'd had a version of that sweetness on his tongue, no matter how long ago, that shit embedded itself. Like muscle memory. Like a parasite, sucking away at your soul.

And now he had the source of that sweetness locked in his room at the clubhouse. He was rotting quicker than death.

"This is not your fault," Luke hissed at his wife, oblivious to the shit swirling in Jagger's head, oblivious to anyone but the five foot nothing piston wearing a mini skirt and stilettos in a warehouse full of illegal weapons.

"Second that," Jagger cut in, mostly because he meant it but also he couldn't witness their shit. However fucked up it was, it was copasetic, and all he had was fucked up. He wasn't a jealous guy, but for some reason, seeing two people he respected in whatever version of a happy ever after those in this world were afforded made him want to kill someone.

"No way is this your fault," he said, meaning every word. "You know the men in these charters would've done the exact same thing as you, though likely not as effectively."

She scoffed, looking at him but not letting go of her husband's hand. "Of course you wouldn't have been as effective as me." She paused her bravado fading. "I brought this war to the club."

"Said stop," Jagger said roughly. "You are part of this club, your wars are our wars. We'll fight to our last man."

There was a chorus of agreements from behind him. Rosie was beloved, feared and respected in every charter in the country.

She rolled her eyes. "Okay, don't get all *Braveheart* over it." She narrowed her eyes. "And stop kidnapping high-ranking members of his crew and torturing and killing them. Unless you get useful information. Which you didn't. Because you won't. These men are trained to die before they give up information."

"Well they're gonna die regardless, so we were really just being efficient," Claw cut in with a grin.

Rosie grinned back. "Well as much as I appreciate you trying to be *efficient,* efficiency could fuck up our whole operation."

"What operation?" Swiss cut in, not smiling. "We've had nothing since this shit happened."

Rosie didn't react to the obvious hostility in his tone, despite the fact Luke did, glaring at the man in question and going on guard.

Jagger didn't blame him. Swiss was a cold motherfucker. Named that way because he was a fucking Swiss Army knife when it came to killing and torturing. He had a plethora of ways to inflict pain and end a life. He wasn't Army, Navy, or Special Forces. He was a fucking psychopath.

Rosie smiled. "You haven't anything to do since you've been chopping off the digits of high ranking soldiers in the cartel." She tilted her head. "I know probably peanuts considering your...skills, but we'll have the rest soon enough. I know none of you have virtues, but *pretend* you at least have patience, for me?"

Swiss rolled his eyes, but the corner of his mouth quirked up. Rosie could even charm psychopaths. Which made sense, considering Fernandez kidnapped her and she managed to get out of his clutches without a fucking scratch. Probably one of the first women in history who could boast such a thing.

"Cade know you're here?" Jagger asked conversationally.

Rosie scowled. "I'm a grown ass woman, he's not my fucking keeper. He's got enough to brood about over in Amber, like how shiny his hair is or if his grunts are manly enough."

"So that's a no," Jagger deduced. "He won't like you taking point on this."

Understatement of the fucking century. Cade adored his sister, he'd gone through hell with the women in his life and he'd move heaven and more accurately, hell to make sure that happened again. He had a family to protect and Cade was a man who needed to be in control.

Rosie could not be controlled.

"Cade doesn't like the color pink, but that does not stop his entire house being decorated in that shade since his daughter is currently obsessed with it," she shot back. "He is not Oz, All Great and Powerful."

Jagger shook his head.

He knew that Rosie was not in danger. Well, for Rosie.

They were all in danger.

But she had a husband who would die for her. They had a security team back in L.A. full of highly trained motherfuckers. Plus, that bitch had connections all over the country, probably more than the Sons of Templar.

And they needed every single fucking one if they were gonna take down Fernandez and survive.

She glanced around their warehouse. "This is the shipment from the Russians?"

Jagger nodded once.

It was normally an offense punishable by death, talking about this shit with a woman and with an ex fucking cop present. But things were far from normal these days.

And Rosie was somewhat of a permanent exception.

"You're running them out to the clubs tonight?" she asked, walking over to an AK-47, loading a magazine, releasing the charging handle, then emptying the clip in their designated testing area.

Gunshots echoed off the walls for a beat before she put it down and waltzed back over like she was on a fucking catwalk.

And damn did she work it.

Jagger had appreciated this for a long time. Enough to be tempted.

But now, he barely fucking *saw* this.

All he saw was Caroline. Even now. Which was dangerous. His head needed to be in the game.

"Good," she said, as Luke yanked her into his side, death glaring his brothers, who Jagger guessed had been checking her out.

They were only human.

He glanced to an expressionless Swiss.

Well, most of them.

"You're gonna need more."

Only half of this was for personal use. The rest was to sell. The club needed all the money they could get. War was expensive.

Jagger nodded. "The Russians are coming in a few days."

"Great. Good. We've got intel that Fernadez is gonna be

stateside within the next two months. Could be a trap. Almost certainly is. But you know what happens when you try and trap the devil?" She grinned. "All hell breaks loose."

Jagger shook his head again. Almost grinned.

Almost.

"Now, let's talk happier things," she continued. "I hear you've got a woman locked in your room at the clubhouse."

"Jesus Christ," he muttered, not even bothering to wonder how Rosie knew. She was like that Tyrion Lannister on that show Macy made them all watch, she drank and she knew things. And apparently she considered holding a woman captive as good news.

"Just wait until after all this shakes out before the wedding, we don't want a gunfight at the reception." Her eyes glowed. "But that's gonna happen regardless."

Jagger stiffened. "There's not gonna be a wedding," he clipped.

She rolled her eyes. "Of course there is. I thought it might've been Sarah, I tentatively cheered for you, but I knew it wasn't her. Not enough drama. But now a reporter, world famous and kick ass mind you, being held captive by an old flame she thought was...farther south, should we say? Or north, depending on how well someone knows you." She winked.

This time Jagger reacted. Because yeah, he was shocked. Rosie was not acting like this was new information, who he really was. He wondered how long she'd known. Probably longer than he'd like to admit.

"That information doesn't exist," he said through gritted teeth, mindful of his brothers listening. Not that he wanted to keep it a secret out of anything but shame and cowardice.

She shrugged. "Skeletons don't sweep under the rug very well. Nor do they stay in closets very long. I know my way around a closet." She waved her hand at her outfit as if that explained shit.

She gave him those kind eyes again. "Your secret's safe with me. Unless I don't get invited to the wedding, then I'm making a Podcast or something."

He crossed his arms. "It's not like that, Rosie, seriously."

She sighed. "It's always like that."

She kissed Luke. "Tell him, honey," she said sweetly.

Luke held his wife tight and glanced at Jagger. "Not somethin' you can tell, unfortunately, it's something you're gonna have to learn the hard way."

Because Jagger was a coward, he didn't want to learn the hard way, he took a run delivering guns, as if the road could clear Caroline from his veins.

CHAPTER THIRTEEN

Caroline

I DIDN'T SEE him for five days.

I told myself that was welcome, that was a good thing. I didn't need distractions from him or the past he carried around with him.

I needed Hansen to trust me.

I needed the story.

And then I needed to get the fuck out of here.

Even if I was falling into some kind of routine. Even if, in a weird way, I was liking my work at the bar. Liking the way that Blake spoke to me in gruff curses and sexist remarks and soft eyes. Mine and Claw's banter that bore no evidence of the fact he'd been willing to kill me a fortnight ago. The fact that Macy came to have coffee with me every day, bringing her beautiful little sons and all of the *Lord of the Rings* movies for us to get through.

Somewhere between Middle Earth and Mt. Doom, I told her everything.

I had never given so much of myself while on a story.

Or ever.

I didn't have close friends, apart from Emily. And the only reason she knew about my sordid past was because vodka shouldn't be drunk on an empty stomach. I hadn't mentioned a word after.

Neither had she.

I had friends in the industry, most of us didn't get close because we might've been friendly, but we were also competition. We all wanted the story, the scoop. And even those I wasn't in competition with, I needed to detach from, because the possibility of them dying was high.

And there also wasn't much opportunity to get deep and meaningful in the middle of a warzone. In the middle of a story.

And here I was, in the middle of both, and getting deep and meaningful with a woman I only just met, a woman who used to fuck Liam.

Her reaction to the story was not the same as Scarlett's. Though they were both good women, they were very fricking different women.

Scarlett was all hard edges, barely letting anything in, mainly so nothing got let out of all those carefully locked closets full of skeletons. I knew that because that was me too.

Macy was the opposite. She was soft. Warm. She let me in, she let my pain in and made it her own. She was crying about one-minute into the story.

Then she turned dry-eyed after giving me yet another hug. I was beginning to get used to it, like I was used to waking up in a biker compound, not being allowed anywhere but the bar I worked. I was getting used to the violence.

But I was not getting used to Liam's absence. Though I had almost fifteen years of practice.

"Get to know him," Macy said when I finished. "He might

not be the man he was, but he's a good man. You might even like him."

I already knew I liked him. Whoever he was now. That was the problem.

"I can't," I whispered. "Because the more I get to know this man called Jagger, the less he is Liam. And when I know Jagger fully, it's gonna be unavoidable, I'll have to accept that he's not Liam, that Liam's really gone. In a way that is worse than before. What if I can't forgive him?"

I did it. I voiced that great fear from a little voice inside me. Confessed it to a woman I barely knew.

Macy smiled sadly and squeezed my hand. "Human beings are capable of some of the most horrific things," she said. "So I think it stands to reason that human beings are also capable of forgiving some of the most horrific acts."

This time I cried.

And Macy hugged me.

And I let her.

Scarlett texted me every day, now she was back in Amber.

Not saying poignant and soulful things like Macy.

The first day...

UNKNOWN: **Have you boned him yet?**

Me: I'm guessing this is Scarlett.

Me: And no. We've got the complicated issue of him pretending to be dead.

Scarlett: Sex won't uncomplicate it but at least you'll get an orgasm. You both need it.

I'D ROLLED my eyes and smiled. But a smile was a big thing

these days. The rest of the texts were along the same vein, some-times her talking about the other old ladies, just chatting. I got the feeling that Scarlett was not a woman to text someone and just chat.

Neither was I.

But I needed it.

I couldn't admit that I was beginning to like some of the members of the Sons of Templar, and becoming friends with their wives.

I couldn't have that personal connection to them, because that would taint my story. Taint the truth. Though, the truth was always going to be tainted.

My story was going nowhere fast. I was witnessing things people already knew about biker clubs, the scantily clad women, the drinking, the violence—there was a cage fight every Wednesday night that I'd been invited to the week previous—and in the daytime hours, they ran a garage.

But they were doing other things.

Running guns like Jagger had admitted.

Torturing enemies like I'd witnessed.

They were gearing up for retributions toward the man that ordered the massacre of the entire club.

I had heard back from my friend, a source that I would never disclose, and he said the Fernandez had deep pockets and no soul. He owned every government official that could be owned, and his client list had hundreds of international dignitaries, movie stars, everyone you wouldn't expect to participate in human trafficking, really.

I knew all this, or at least a version.

My source did tell me something interesting, latest reports had him in Russia. And the Sons of Templar dealt with the Russians for their guns.

It could be a coincidence...

I snapped my laptop shut as the door opened so hard that it fell off one of its hinges. I jerked off my bed—Liam's bed—immediately, with an instinctive reaction that had become second nature when I'd had to be prepared for my hotel to be bombed while covering a story.

But this wasn't an explosive.

Not in the form of a bomb at least.

It was a bomb in the form of a human.

In the form of Liam.

But I needed to stop looking at him like he was Liam. Because he was *Jagger*. With muscles and ink and scars and a motorcycle cut to remind me of that. I might've been able to convince myself of this fact had it not been for those eyes. Those green eyes shining like carved emeralds from his hard face. Every time I met those eyes, I could never think of this man as Jagger. He was Liam to me, still. Or maybe I was holding onto that shred of naiveté that other people called hope. Hope that I was not in a biker compound with strangers. That *Liam* was here. That *Liam* would protect me if things got bad. And things were going to get bad. There was something in the atmosphere, a thickness I'd felt countless times.

And the bad, it was here.

It was here in the form of Liam—of *Jagger*—breaking down a door with blood covering his hands and death in those emerald eyes.

I rushed forward even when my survival instincts told me to stay back.

"No," he growled, voice guttural as I got close. It was strange, it was somehow, distant, almost removed from his body as he spoke. He glanced down to the hands he'd put up to bar me from coming closer. They were stained crimson.

A quick scan at his body told me it wasn't his.

My body relaxed even though it told me things I shouldn't want to know.

"I need to wash this off," he said, looking down to his hands, speaking mostly to himself.

I nodded once. "Okay."

His eyes moved from his hands to me, running them up my body. I was in leggings and an oversized tee. It was his tee. I hadn't intended to torture myself by wearing it, but my hands had acted of their own accord, reaching into his drawers after my shower, lifting the fabric to my nose.

As soon as I inhaled the scent of Liam, of Jagger, mixed together like some kind of painfully beautiful aftershave, I knew I needed it on my body.

I regretted that now with that look. With what it told Liam.

But he didn't say anything, he only looked for a beat longer then disappeared inside the bathroom.

The sound of running of water trickled out.

I stared at the ruined door, now providing no privacy between my bed—Liam's bed—and the very highly trafficked hallway.

Claw walked past, he stopped when he spotted the damage to the door, and likely me standing in the middle of the room like some kind of tragic statue.

"Jagger's decided to come for a visit," he deduced, looking at the ruined hinges, with seemingly little interest or shock.

I nodded once, looking at the blood covering his white tee.

He grinned. "Have fun." He winked and walked away.

I didn't reply. Didn't move. I should've done that. Taken off Liam's tee. Run my fingers through my wet hair, to detangle it, since I likely looked like a total mess right now. But then again, I wasn't the one covered in blood. Maybe I should've run for my life.

But I didn't.

The door to the bathroom opened.

Liam stepped out.

I held my breath as he made his way over to me.

His hands were clean now. In a manner of speaking.

He stopped inches from me, though he didn't touch me. I was thankful for that. Because his sheer presence was overwhelming. My chest constricted with his nearness, with the truth, staring me in the face with emerald eyes.

"Did someone get hurt?" I whispered.

"A lot of people got hurt," he replied.

I clenched my jaw. "Anyone in the club?" Despite the fact I was still their prisoner, I didn't bear ill will to anyone wearing a cut. In fact, the thought of more harm coming to the club filled me with unease.

The thought of something happening to Liam had me poised for a mental breakdown. I was failing to distance myself the way the story required.

But this was more than a story.

"No one in the club," he replied.

I exhaled.

"Fernandez's men?"

I didn't expect him to answer, I was a civilian and a rat to boot.

But he nodded. "No one that can give us shit, but we still got to dig graves."

My hands shook at the casual way he was speaking about death, about murder. That shouldn't have affected me. I knew better than anyone how cheap life was in war. No, even in times of peace, life was cheap. In times of war life was worth nothing, death was worth only a little more, as markers in a scorebook that no one would be considered a victor in.

"Killing isn't easy," he said, as though he were reading my

mind. Or at least my face. I feared my empty façade was no longer present.

"Killing is hard, even for monsters," he continued.

I frowned at him. "That's what you think you are? A monster?"

His stare burned into me. "Isn't that what I am?"

I looked at his eyes, glassy, bloodshot, pupils not quite pinpricks, but close.

"You're high," I said instead of answering his question.

He blinked. It was a long, slow, absent blink. "Not quite."

I gaped at him, first, he had been a stranger who looked like Liam. Then I thought I was getting to know the stranger, not liking him much, but knowing him. Thought I knew he was a version of Liam. But this was evidence that I didn't know anything about this stranger. Or even anything about Liam.

"You said drugs were the instrument for the weak minded," I accused. I didn't even know where my judgment was coming from. I'd seen addicts, interviewed them, listened to their struggles with illness, and not once did I pass judgment. Everyone was trying to self-medicate to cure the disease called life.

His hands took hold of my shoulders. Tightly. "Look at me," he whispered. "Really fuckin' *look* at me. My mind seem strong to you?" His voice quivered as he spoke. His voice actually shook. His body didn't. The strong, sculpted muscles stayed taut, he stood tall, he exuded physical strength. But the absent hopeless emptiness in his eyes, that quiver in his voice overpowered all of that physical strength.

Over my weeks here, I'd seen glimpses of weakness. Of pure, unobstructed sorrow. A pain so deep that even I couldn't understand it.

Every glimpse was a pinprick. A thousand pinpricks into the exposed nerve that was my heart.

But he recovered from those lapses quickly. He shielded

himself from showing any more than a glimpse. Which was a good thing too, because had I been presented with this, this shell of a man, this broken soul in a biker cut, I might've broken sooner. But he was breaking now, and I had no choice but to break too. To fracture all of my anger, my false hate I'd been harboring toward him.

My hand was shaking when I lifted it to his face to wipe away the single tear that had leaked out of his hollow eyes.

That single tear was equivalent to blood gushing out of a mortal wound.

"All my life has been about since I met you, it's been about protecting you," he said. Another warm tear trailed over my finger. "You are the most precious thing in the world to me. And you're so fucking fragile." He squeezed my shoulders harder, as if to make a point. "So fucking *good*. And this world is not fucking good. Even as a boy who knew shit, I knew that. And when the war turned me into a man, I knew it better. I got a chance..." he trailed off.

I knew what he was doing then. He was trying to explain how it happened. How it all came about, the lie that set us both on a course of destruction.

I waited, cupping his scarred and tear-stained face.

He sucked in a ragged breath. "The club's in a war, Peaches," he said finally, voice rougher than before. Whether he couldn't find the words in his drug addled mind or he lost the courage to give me the explanation that fifteen years coming, I wasn't sure.

I found myself relieved that he didn't give it to me.

Because I sensed once he gave me that explanation I would be forced out of this limbo I'd placed us both in. I'd have to make a decision. There would have to be a finality to it.

To us.

I wasn't ready for the decision yet.

"I know the club's in a war," I said in response.

Something moved in his face, some kind of panic so visceral I thought there was an immediate threat.

His hands moved from his sides to clutch me by the neck as if someone were trying to rip me from him.

"This war is different," he rasped. "This is one that could take you from me. Because of your involvement with me, you could get caught up in this. And you wouldn't just *die.* You'd die in one of the ugliest ways possible, they'd..." He trailed off. More tears streamed down his face. "I couldn't survive the knowledge of what they'd do to you. I couldn't live through knowing what happened. And you'd have to suffer it." His voice had that same edge of panic as his expression, as if intruders were about to break through the ruined door and make truth of his predictions.

"That's not going to happen," I said with a surety that I didn't feel.

He either didn't hear me or believe me.

"You've barely lived your life," he said. "You're young still. You have only lived a wrinkle of your life. There's so much ahead of you. Once you leave me, once you leave all of *this* behind you, you'll live that life the way you're meant to. But you can't leave it behind you, not right now, not while you're in the middle of it. I don't know how to get you out, I don't know how to get you *through.* I know I have to get you through. Unscathed. Because that's my greatest fear, harm coming to you. Coming to you because of me, because of the life I chose to take me away from you."

"Stop," I said, my voice firm even though my soul was breaking. "I'm here, Liam. I'm going to get through. Nothing is going to happen to me. Nothing is going to happen to you either, I promise."

His eyes cleared. "You can't make promises like that." He spoke a truth we both already knew too well.

"I can," I whispered a lie we both needed.

I stepped away from him, his grip tightened for a millisecond before he let me go.

I moved around him, grabbing hold of the edges of his cut, feeling the worn and soft leather, a symbol of the hard life he was living.

I wanted to hate the cut. For what it took from me. For what it did to Liam. But I knew that it wasn't the cut or the club that ruined him, it was another uniform, another symbol. If anything, it was the cut that saved him. Whatever of him was left to save.

He let me slip it off.

I hung it carefully on the back of a chair, staring at the grim reaper on the back for a moment. When I turned, I found emerald eyes, intense and focused like he was scared I'd fall right off the face of the earth if he moved his gaze.

I knew the feeling.

"Sit." I pointed to the bed.

He obeyed.

"Boots." I nodded my head downward to the muddy black motorcycle boots he always wore. I wondered how much of that was mud, and how much was blood.

Did it matter? Dirt and blood was all the same when it met the bottom of motorcycle boots.

Liam complied.

I bit my lip as I regarded him in his jeans and long-sleeved Henley.

A hunger that I'd pretended hadn't been present and ever-growing was no longer easy to ignore.

Whatever had died between us—if anything ever had—the carnal way in which my body responded to his had only grown. I didn't even know I was capable of feeling such an animalistic need. With the small number of men I'd had after him, I was only going through the motions. It was to see if a warm body might be able to chip some of the ice from my soul.

But this wasn't a warm body. It was a soul as cold as my own.

It was Liam.

It was Jagger.

I didn't know which man I was more attracted to.

It didn't much matter.

I swallowed roughly.

Liam watched my throat. The veins in his neck stood out as if he were exerting some kind of great strength other than sitting on the bed.

"Don't look at me like that, Peaches," he begged.

Hunger ravaged his eyes. Pure carnal desire that shook me to the core.

But the pleading in his voice had me clutching onto reason and letting go of need.

"Lie down," I said, my own voice little more than a rasp.

His eyes lingered on my body for a long and uncertain beat before he did as I asked.

He moved against the wall so I could lie beside him.

At first, my body was stiff, holding myself tight so I didn't accidentally brush my skin against his. This was the closest I'd been to him voluntarily. I was in a bed with *Liam*, so close but also farther away than when we'd had an ocean between us. I ached to curl up to him, encase myself in his arms that had been second nature in another life.

But I couldn't trust my instincts. Or I no longer had the right to act on them at least. I had belonged to a man named Liam and he had belonged to me. But in another world. Not in this one.

We lay there for a long while, side by side, not touching but somehow finding what little comfort we could in each other.

Darkness blanketed the room at some point, turning everything into shadows.

"I'm Jagger now," he whispered against the darkness, speaking as though we were in the middle of a conversation, I wasn't sure if it was the drugs or if it was us. "You know that. I've proved that to you."

"No," I said firmly as a response to the hopelessness in his tone. "You'll always be Liam to me. Even if it's only to me."

I couldn't decide whether I was lying or not. And sometime after trying to figure it out, impossibly, I fell asleep.

I EXPECTED him to be gone in the morning when sunlight and sleep heralded away the haze of drugs and whatever else had brought him here.

I *wanted* him to be gone in the morning, so I didn't see him in the sunlight. So I didn't wake up with him. Because even doing that once, I'd create a memory, and if there was one thing in the world that lasted forever, it was a memory. I knew that all too well.

He wasn't gone.

It became painfully apparent when I woke, not curled into the fetal position like had become the norm for all these years.

No, I awoke curled up in a position that my body remembered, one that I'd forced my mind to forget, one that was the reason I cried myself to sleep, falling apart and woke up trying to hold myself together, even in my dreams.

But someone else was holding me together.

At the same time as they were ripping me apart.

I didn't try to rectify this situation as soon as it became apparent that I'd searched for Liam in my sleep and that he'd curled his arms around me, holding me tight to his chest.

I didn't move.

Didn't breathe.

I wanted to force myself back to sleep so I could stay here in oblivion.

But I was awake.

Liam, of course, with his new super badass man senses knew this immediately, since his arms tightened around me.

"What was your trauma?" he asked in a voice that signified he'd been awake a lot longer than I had, it wasn't gravelly and choked with sleep like it had been that morning in the kitchen.

I sucked in a breath. It was the question I'd expected weeks ago. On the night that both of us itched for answers but didn't have the strength to ask the questions. I wondered what gave Liam the strength. Maybe now he'd let some of his weaknesses go, he could find it. Or maybe he needed to feign strength after last night.

I didn't have enough wherewithal to figure that out moments after waking. Nor did I have any self-preservation to deflect the question with one of my own.

Maybe that was his intention, maybe he hadn't asked the question that night because he knew he couldn't get answers unless my guard was down.

Or shattered.

"I dated after you," I said, my voice still thick with sleep. "Not in the first four years. Not once. I didn't even *think* about it. I didn't even *see* men. Not live ones anyway. I only saw you."

His arms tightened around me and I tried to tell myself to move from this position that was far too intimate for this story.

For this life.

But I didn't move.

"If it were up to me, I don't think I ever would've wanted to start with anyone else," I continued. "Mostly because I didn't imagine anyone else could give me what you gave me, and a little because I couldn't survive anyone else taking away from me like you did. But it wasn't up to me. Moreover, it was a decision I made because of my family. They worried. They meddled." I rolled my eyes, making sure to keep them safely focused on the door with the ruined hinges instead of the man who ruined my heart. "You know them." I paused, violently and brutally. "Well, you *knew* them," I muttered.

Liam's arms flexed around me in what I supposed was some kind of flinch.

"So to appease them, I dated," I continued, forcing myself to pretend that after last night I still didn't care about his pain. "Sporadically because of my job. It wasn't as bad as I thought it would be. It was almost kind of...nice. Empty. But nice not to be so fucking lonely all the time." I shrugged, trying to shrug off the truth that right here, right now, imprisoned with the man I'd mourned, who'd let me mourn him, was the least alone I'd felt in a decade.

When I needed that loneliness, when it was vital to survival, it didn't come.

"Nothing was serious," I continued. "Nothing ever could be. Not just because of..." I trailed off. "My job didn't exactly foster relationships," I said, a half-truth to cover up the reality that went unspoken but unavailable. "Men tended to be threatened by me. My job. They don't like women who don't want to be protected from the horrors of the world, women that seek them out. It doesn't bode well for their fragile masculinity. It was whatever."

I did a weird shrug with Liam's arms still around me.

"I didn't need to be tied down," I said to the door. "Marcus was no different than the rest. We were casual. He was nice."

I paused, still focused on the door, sitting at an awkward angle, closed as much as it could be given the damage Liam had done to it. I hadn't even bothered trying to close it last night. I wondered who did it. If Liam had gotten up at some point and done it or a passerby had taken it upon themselves to protect our privacy and my modesty. It was a laughable thought. These were men that fucked women in front of an entire party. They didn't protect privacy or modesty.

I focused back on my story, on Marcus. It was almost easy to talk about it now, to think about it. Well, it would never be easy, but years of therapy had made it bearable at least. "He was nice," I repeated. "Until he wasn't. He got...intense."

I chose not to give Liam the specifics because he'd made it apparent how fragile his temperament was these days and I could already feel the tangible change in the air and the way his body had stiffened even with the prelude to the event.

So no, telling Liam about the broken nose, fractured ribs and sprained wrist would do nobody any good. Though there was no good here anyway.

"I broke it off," I said, not mentioning that me breaking it off consisted of threatening him with the gun my brother bought me, but I never used. I didn't press charges, even though that went against everything I believed as a feminist. About punishing men who believed their right was to hurt and control women. Men made women fear breaking up with them because a heartbroken man could turn into a monster in a moment. Women shouldn't have to take the fears of a man's fragility, turning them into a punching bag.

But this was a world of 'shouldn't have tos.' So women did.

And my reaction to having this kind of violence turned toward me was exactly the opposite of how I thought I'd react. I wasn't sure if it was fear that stopped me from reporting him at first. It was emptiness. It was an exhaustion of carrying around all my inside trauma. Maybe there was a sick part of me that *liked* having the outside trauma to match. Whatever it was didn't make sense. Damaged people rarely make sensible decisions when the world damages them even more.

I continued staring at the door as I carried on with the story. "After I broke it off, I started seeing him everywhere. My coffee shop. Grocery store. Then outside my bedroom window at three in the morning. I got the restraining order then."

Whatever had stopped me from reporting the initial abuse disappeared with his face at my window at three in the morning. I knew then it wasn't going to be over when my bruises faded and my bones healed. It would only be over when Marcus had repaired what he considered I'd done to his masculinity. And men like that healed their sense of self by destroying women in all the ways they could.

The police weren't exactly helpful, but I hadn't expected them to be since I'd waited to report the crime. It was another 'shouldn't' I was faced with in a short amount of time. The men and women that were tasked to protect us shouldn't throw judgment and doubt in the face of a woman looking for help when walking through the doors took more strength than taking the initial beating.

The journalist in me wanted to write a story on it. But the world already knew this kind of thing happened. It was too normal for us all. And I didn't have the strength to tell my own story.

"I should've known better than anyone that a piece of paper did nothing against violence," I said, remembering how light and flimsy the paper felt. "But then again, I felt naively safe in my home, even from him. I had a sense that if anything was going to happen to me, it'd be over *there*, in that horrible and deadly war. Not amongst the mundane."

My mind went to the day where I heard Liam's mother scream from down the street. I'd been hanging out the laundry.

Mundane.

"But horrors happen among the mundane most of all," I whispered. "He broke in. While I was in the shower. So I didn't hear him break the window. My neighbor did. Probably the only reason I'm alive. It was very apparent he'd come to kill me."

The police found what I liked to think of as the 'serial killer starter kit' when they responded to the call.

He had rope, duct tape, a hunting knife and a handgun in a backpack he'd left in my bedroom. Along with latex gloves.

He hadn't been wearing them when he attacked me in the shower, I guess maybe he panicked, or got too excited when it became apparent how helpless, and naked I was.

I shivered, Liam's embrace had suddenly become very cold, the air very still. He hadn't spoken the entire time I relayed the past like it didn't belong to me. But it didn't. It belonged to him, even though I didn't want it to be that way, he claimed my past, my present and whatever was going to make up my future. Regardless of what happened between us, he was a scar on my soul.

I liked that I was cold, though. Because the memories of those moments were scorching hot, with him sweaty, the water scalding, slippery. My body temperature rising with panic and terror.

The promise of rape hit me harder than he did in those moments.

And then, like in the movies, right before the deed was done, the door was knocked down, uniformed men with guns burst in, saving me from the worst of the trauma.

Or I was sure that was what it seemed.

Yes, I was attacked in my own home. Groped. Assaulted. My privacy and safety was ripped apart by a single man.

But I wasn't *raped*.

So I must've been able to recover *easier*.

I was sure it would've been harder, infinitely so if he'd defiled me in that way, but I still *felt* defiled, dirty, broken.

Still couldn't shower in unfamiliar places and it took me two years to stop having only baths.

"I saw a therapist for years after it happened, first because Mom insisted I do so, she'd been insisting for a long while before that, but now she had a more tangible, inescapable reason."

I hadn't been living in Castle Springs at the time, hadn't

called my family when I was first beaten, because I didn't want them to worry, because I was ashamed and I didn't want my father or brother to go to prison for killing Marcus, which was exactly what they would've done if they'd seen my face.

But sitting on my bed, with soaking wet hair, mismatched clothes and strangers in uniforms trampling through my personal space, I called my mother. And for the first and last time since losing Liam, I'd broken down. I could barely speak through my tears. But I didn't need to, my mother didn't need to know the specifics, she only heard my tears and she informed me she'd be there "quicker than a bull could shit."

It was the first time I'd heard my mother curse.

The second was when she arrived at my house three hours later, with my father in tow.

She hadn't left for two months.

"And as much as I hate to say my mother was right, she was," I continued, it was the only way she'd leave. "It helped. Not a lot. Barely a little bit. But any kind of help after something like that is welcome." I shrugged. "I survived, which is more than I could've said if my neighbor hadn't heard the crash, if the police hadn't responded immediately."

I had tortured myself with the what ifs, for a long time. Until I had to stop. What ifs would chip away at a soul, whittle it down to nothing. Mine was a fractured shard as it was.

"I don't have scars or hangups about sex," I continued, though it had taken me another three years to have sex again, and since then it had been casual. "But I do have a thing about showers. It's my mind telling me that horrible thing happened in the shower once so the only time something truly horrible can happen to me is when I'm in strange showers." I paused, looking around the room that had been my prison, my sanctuary and something in between. "Which is stupid, because truly horrible things happen everywhere." I ended on a whisper, my words emptying out like

I'd used up my quota for the day within a handful of minutes of waking up.

Silence blanketed over us, I expected words, curses, death threats from Liam, that was the man I'd come to know, at least. A man that used violence as action, as a response.

But there was no violence to be wreaked upon Marcus. He'd been found to have outstanding warrants out of state for aggravated rape, stalking, and domestic violence.

He'd been sentenced to twenty-five years.

I testified.

As did three more of his victims.

We kept in touch, horror keeping us together when it had ripped pieces of ourselves apart.

Marcus was killed in prison two months into his sentence. It made me angry that he only served two months for what he did. The other women decided that he was serving a lifetime in hell, because that helped them. Just like the idea of heaven helped those who wanted to think of loved ones in a better place, hell helped victims banish monsters to a worse one.

I didn't believe in Hell. I didn't lend myself false comforts.

Just like I didn't believe in Heaven.

For whatever reason, I didn't want to believe Liam had been in a better place. Mainly because I didn't *want* him in a better place. I didn't want him watching over me, I wanted him beside me. So it helped me thinking he was absolutely nowhere than , anywhere else.

Which was funny now, because he hadn't been nowhere. He hadn't been in heaven or hell, he'd been in a biker compound in New Mexico.

So I waited for the man, the biker to respond to what I told him. I already knew it bothered him. Even before, Liam had been protective. Not aggressively so, but enough to make it known that anyone who did anything to me would face him. He wasn't exactly intimidating back then, he wasn't one to get into fights, but he would for me.

Now, it was a different story. Everything about him was intimidating. Violent. The entire persona he'd created was meant to promote violence.

His body stayed taut and his mouth stayed closed while I thought on all of that. If Marcus hadn't already been dead, would Liam have killed him?

Did I want him to want to kill for me?

I moved before I got the answer to that.

Or more accurately, Liam moved *us*.

He was halfway across the bedroom before I actually found it in me to speak, protest. My limbs tried to move, but he'd seemingly anticipated my struggle, through his badass manly powers, no doubt.

"What are you doing? Put me down," I demanded as he walked us into the bathroom and turned on the shower.

He didn't answer, merely stepped us both into the stall, fully clothed.

The hot water was a shock to my cold skin.

I didn't have time to acclimate, Liam's lips were on mine, the water cascading over us.

My first instinct was to fight.

And I did.

He fought too.

So my second instinct was to surrender.

My body melted against his, all the ice settled over my soul shattering with his mouth moving against mine.

"I'm gonna give you new memories of a shower," he growled against my lips as he ripped his tee off me.

Ripped. It. Off.

With his bare hands.

"I'm gonna make sure you never think of anything horrible

next time you step in here," he continued as he yanked down my leggings and ripped off my soaking panties.

I should have fought.

I really fricking should've.

Even if the only reason was because the first time we made love after fourteen years of thinking he was dead should not have been brutal and violent, in the shower after telling the story of how and ex-boyfriend almost raped me.

But this wasn't about what *should've been.*

That was clear.

And this wasn't making love.

This was fucking, pure and simple.

It wasn't Liam and Caroline.

It was Jagger and...whoever the fuck I was now.

He entered me, without priming, ceremony, or pretty words.

I screamed as his cock filled me.

That was until he claimed my mouth, thrusting as he held me against the shower wall, our bodies slipping together with sweat and hot water.

Everything was washed off with that mixture.

The past.

The present.

The future.

The only thing that mattered was the pain around my neck and in my soul. And the pleasure at the base of my spine as he coaxed me into a brutal orgasm.

Not a single word was spoken.

Not even as I toppled off the cliff and came harder than I ever had before. Came harder than I ever had the ability to.

With anyone.

Including Liam.

And the sex with Liam had been good.

Jagger may not have been good at keeping promises, at

treating me gentle, at apologizing, explaining, or not shooting people in the head, but he was good at fucking.

His entire body tightened, and he let out a feral growl from the back of his throat as the pads of his fingers pressed into my hips and he emptied himself inside of me. The pain of it, physical and emotional sent me hurtling to a release even more intense than the last.

My limbs became something other than my own.

My soul became something other than my own.

As if it was anything but Liam's in the first place.

But now it wasn't just Liam's.

It was Jagger's too.

CHAPTER FOURTEEN

IT WAS the song that did it.

I didn't know who put it on in the middle of a fricking biker party, but it didn't matter how it got here, it just mattered that it was here. And so was I. Sick of banishing myself to my room every night and staring at the walls, occasionally staring at words on a page, pretending to read.

I wrote a lot too.

Of what I saw. What I was learning from the inside and the outside.

I was learning that the war was no closer to an end, that men were still going out for five days and coming back covered in blood.

That there were many times Hansen closed himself in 'church.'

I also thought I figured out their gun transportation system. No way they were using bikes, or any vehicle registered to the Sons of Templar. Though they owned the local police, by the looks of their records, federal agencies dropped in with warrants on an annual basis.

But the Sons of Templar got their groceries delivered.

Not something surprising considering the sheer amount of mouths to feed and the fact that they had better things to do like kill and torture enemies.

This grocery delivery truck also collected food for the homeless.

In boxes.

Weekly.

I had been in the kitchen many times and had not seen any extra food lying around.

I'd seen plenty of guns, though.

But it wasn't about the guns or the story right now. It was the song.

The song tasted like sickly sweet pink wine, smelled like a cheap and fruity perfume, felt like a youth that was encased in naïve happiness and unfractured dreams.

I lay back on the lumpy mattress, ignored the sheets that smelled of foreign detergent and closed my eyes. I let myself sink past it all and into the song.

"You know, those things will kill you."

A puff of smoke trailed into the night, the light at the end of the cigarette flared as the smoker took one last drag, in defiance, before he crushed it under his boot.

I knew he was grinning before he turned.

"You know that I'm too in love with you to ever do something fucking stupid like die before I get forever," a husky voice said. It floated into the air like the smoke had, but curled around me and droned out the thumping bass of whatever song Sophie had decided to play over and over again tonight.

He snatched my hips and yanked me flush with his body with enough force to spill the wine that had turned flat and totally unappetizing. Plus, I'd already had almost a whole bottle to myself.

"*You love me?*" I stammered.

He grinned. Easily. "*Of course I love you, Peaches. Have you not been paying attention?*"

The song jerked me out of the memory with ear-splitting rock.

I got up from my bed.

And headed straight to the bar.

I RESTED my chin in the palm of my hand, leaning my elbow on the bar. It was sticky. I didn't mind.

"You're cute," I informed Hades, the man I'd sat down in front of.

Yes, his name was fricking *Hades*.

We'd already had a five-minute discussion about that. Well, *I'd* had the discussion. He'd mostly grunted and gave me looks that the actual Hades might even flinch from. But I didn't flinch because I was anesthetized with around half a bottle of tequila on a half-empty stomach.

Because I couldn't stomach food all day.

Not since the shower.

Not since someone had banged on the newly broken door, moments after Liam had taken himself from inside me.

The knowledge that we hadn't used a condom was unmissable.

Luckily I had the implant, for practical reasons more than anything. Birth control wasn't exactly easy to procure in countries I frequented. Though I always practiced safe sex. I didn't want a kid. I never wanted them. Not in this new life anyway.

As he ran down my leg, I had a fleeting and insane hope that he'd planted a baby in me. That thought was gone as soon as it arrived when I realized he'd more likely planted an STI in me if anything.

"Hate to interrupt, what sounds like epic makeup sex, and I really do, but we've got club business," Claw's voice echoed through the closed bathroom door.

I held my breath and Liam stiffened, hands still around me.

I waited for him to curse at the man for his crudeness, tell him to fuck off, then carry me back to the bedroom, dry me off and say something.

Say anything.

Apologize.

Explain.

Hold me.

Make love to me.

Make promises.

"Two seconds," he growled at the door instead.

I froze.

"If that's how long you take for round two, then I feel even more sorry for Caroline than I already did," Claw chuckled.

Liam's jaw hardened, but he didn't say anything else.

Nothing else.

Not as he kissed my head, slowly and tenderly, in a moment that gave me hope for something beyond what had just happened.

But then the moment cracked at the same time the small fractured piece of my heart did.

He let me go.

Stepped out of the shower, reached for a towel and handed it to me.

I took it wordlessly.

He grabbed another.

Dried himself off.

I did the same, on autopilot.

I wasn't numb. I wished I was. Because the aroma of sex and

shame was suffocating inside my brain. I felt used and cherished at the same time. Loved and tarnished.

Liam's eyes didn't move from mine. He held out his hand to me to get out of the shower.

I stared at it for a long time.

Then I ignored it, getting out of the shower with my own strength, though it took almost all of it.

He let out a quiet sigh, his muscles etched from stone and still damp. More scars and tattoos covered that sculpted torso.

I raked my eyes over them, noticing new cuts in places I didn't even know could get injured. Why did I care about his pain when he continued to cause me agony?

He watched me looking at the ruined skin. Waited.

Just like I waited for him to say something.

Neither of us spoke.

He turned and walked out, leaving me the view of the reaper on his back.

And that ink was the scar that cut me deepest of all.

I heard him dressing in the bedroom.

But I couldn't move from the spot, dripping wet, his cum running down my fucking leg, my entire body bruised with him. From the inside out.

I heard him shrug on his cut. Waited for him to come in here. Say something. Even fricking goodbye.

But he sighed and his boots walked out.

I sank to the bathroom floor.

Another horrific memory in the vicinity of a shower.

"Cute?" Hades repeated, his voice a low baritone, one shocking me out of my emotional self-flagellation. It was a voice you could almost taste. I imagined it would be bitter, musky, addictive. Deadly.

Because this man was deadly. I'd only seen him from afar up until now. He had tattoos covering every inch of his skin, including the corners of his face and his forehead. He had dark features but skin almost as pale as mine. His jet-black hair was inky, silky and brushing his shoulders.

And the muscles.

Don't even get me started.

Muscles were a given around here. Especially since all the older members were murdered and the club consisted of mostly new patches.

But muscles weren't what made him dangerous.

There was something about him that made me steer well clear while sober, even though he did his best to separate himself from civilians, I'd observed that when I caught glimpses of him, glimpses were all I got. There was something about him. Like a snake, the deadliest one that could kill you within seconds.

I nodded. "Yes, I find you very cute," I continued. "In a, 'I'll kill you and your whole family without blinking type of way.'"

He stared at me. His face was empty.

It was chilling.

Or it would've been had tequila not been burning in my belly. And had I not already been chilled by the grave before.

I'd had sex with a dead man earlier today.

And it had made me feel more alive than ever before.

I was craving more of the grave.

Hence the tequila and talking to a man who might've been death himself. Or the Devil's bestie.

I glanced down at his cut. At the patch that read 'Enforcer.' "Ah," I said. "So your *actual job* is to kill people without blinking." I nodded, more to myself than to him. "Makes sense. Snakes kill the best. Effective. Don't notice them until they're sinking their teeth into you. And by then, it's too late."

I tried to shrug, forgetting that my elbow on the bar was the thing holding me up and it slipped into dead air.

I would've taken a header right into Hades' crotch had a firm grip not caught me.

My entire body—drunk or not—reacted. It was the snake. Not sinking its teeth in. But there was no way to touch a snake without being seconds away from fangs sinking into your skin.

My eyes met black irises.

"Careful," Hades murmured. "Fallin' down around here, people don't tend to get up lately."

I stared at him, trying to understand whether it was a threat or a warning. Or just some stupid badass shit these bikers said to make them seem more badass.

I didn't get the opportunity to come to a conclusion. Because another set of hands fastened around my bare shoulders, wrenching me back out of the snake's grasp.

I reacted to those hands too.

Though they didn't belong to a deadly snake, the venom from the contact entered my bloodstream too.

My stool swiveled so I was face to face with Liam. No, *Jagger*. He was mad.

And with that simple eye contact that was so far from simple, I realized that I was mad too.

Furious.

"Do not do it, say it or swear it," I hissed at him.

He blinked once, the only ripple in his fury. "Come again?"

I straightened, my body relaxing when Hades was no longer touching me. No matter how attractive he was, there was no way his grip felt comforting.

"Do not come here with that look, that testosterone and that misplaced sense of authority over me," I snapped. "I'm imagining that you're going to attempt to drag me away, lecture me about getting drunk, talking to snakes and pretty much doing whatever is outside your approved actions for women you *fuck*. Here's a newsflash from Caroline Hargrave, right on the ground...fuck you." I gave him a hand gesture communicating the same message for good measure.

I would've sworn I'd seen Hades smile from my peripheral, but of course that was wrong, snakes couldn't smile.

Liam did not smile.

His face emptied, with a blankness that was chilling.

"I'm not going to *attempt* to drag you anywhere," he said, voice flat.

And then, before I could react, he struck.

Maybe there was more than one snake around here.

The glass I was drinking from toppled to the ground with a smash that made no one in the room jump. Glasses breaking were a soundtrack in the clubhouse just as much as ACDC was.

No one blinked at the fact that I was being dragged across the room, kicking and screaming, by a stone-faced biker capable of murder.

A few of them clapped.

Claw grinned.

Swiss raised his beer.

Most of them barely noticed.

As if men dragged women around the place all the time in these places.

Savages. All of them.

I screamed at the common room in general before Liam thrust me into his bedroom, slamming the newly repaired door. Some prospect had done it earlier today.

"You're drunk," he hissed.

"That's usually the desired effect while drinking tequila," I snapped. My eyes ran over him and I was ashamed at the hunger that prickled the bottom of my stomach, merging with the fury in a cocktail that somehow wasn't displeasing as it should've been.

"You're not drunk," I continued, doing my best to ignore my

body's traitorous reactions. "Or high," I shot it at him because I wanted to hurt him. Shame him. It was cruel.

And it worked.

"No, I'm painfully fuckin' sober." Something moved in his eyes, something from last night, that vulnerability that broke me.

I sucked in a ragged breath. "You're not drunk, therefore you arguably have all of your facilities available to you, which means you should've known that dragging a woman bodily is not *fucking okay*," I continued my voice almost a shrill scream.

Liam advanced with wild eyes.

I scuttled back, even the fearlessness offered by tequila was trumped with a man that was sobriety, a hangover, sex, heartbreak, and death all in one.

"What's not fucking okay is my woman leaning across a bar, breathing the same air as a man without a soul or morals to trouble him," he hissed, his breath hot and minty on my face.

"This whole fucking club has neither a soul nor morals," I threw the words at him even though I didn't believe them. "And distinguishing the damned members from the redeemed isn't something that I'm spending my time doing."

"We're all damned," he replied immediately.

"You ensured that," I spat.

He flinched, but I didn't notice. I was ready to unleash everything that I'd been holding onto. All my anger. I wanted to make it physical and fucking beat him with it.

"You were a coward," I hissed. "Not coming home to us because you were scared. You're a fucking coward now too."

"I know," he agreed.

I blinked, losing a little bit of my fuel.

He continued to advance. "I'm a coward. Not because I was afraid of coming home. But afraid of not having a home after what I'd become. You are my home, Peaches." He stopped just shy of my body, not touching me.

"You were my North Star, my fucking guiding light, every day, every hour, every fucking moment. From the day I left you, 'til that night in the alley."

The words were as effective as a punch to the chest at winding me.

All of those words I'd wanted to fling fell flat.

I stared at him.

I devoured him with my eyes, need pulsating through my core. I itched to rip his clothes off, to fuck all of my pain into him.

"If I were an honorable man, I'd walk out that door," he rasped, hands clenched beside him, staring beyond me to the door.

Silenced pulsated between us, as though it were a living thing. It scratched at my skin, tore at the flesh. My thighs clenched at my carnal response to the pain.

To Liam.

"I'm no longer an honorable man," he finished.

"Thank god," I breathed.

I don't know who moved first. But I know I ran to him, jumped on him.

I know he caught me.

Then he kissed me.

Then he unraveled me.

IT WAS LATE.

I was sober.

Kind of.

Because if I was completely sober, I wouldn't have spoken into the darkness, with Liam's arms around me, his breathing and tight body telling me he wasn't sleeping either.

"I was afraid that I would miss you my entire life," I whispered against his chest. "That I'd always be broken." I traced the lines of ink and scars.

"You won't have to miss me again," he promised. "I'm not going anywhere."

I didn't look at him. "Yes, I'll always miss you, whatever happens here."

"Jesus," he croaked out. "Can you stop talking like that?"

"Like what?" I asked.

"Like I'm..."

"Dead?" I finished for him.

He flinched.

"It's a hard habit to break," I whispered. I stared into the night. "I want to know it all," I continued. "I *need* to know it all."

His entire body tightened.

"But I can't," I finished. "Not now. For whatever reason. Because I'm weak. Because I'm selfish. Because I need to pretend that I have Liam with me in the place I'm being held prisoner."

His hands went to my hair, ran through the curls that were coming back after getting it chemically straightened. He didn't speak for a long time. "I'm selfish too," he said, voice a rasp. "Because I don't want you to be let go. I fuckin' want to be your jailer. Want to make sure you can't leave this. Me. I want it and I convince myself it's for the club."

I froze. "You want me to be a prisoner with you?"

He moved me so I was on top of him, straddling him. I let out a gasp as his cock rubbed against my naked skin. "I want you any way I can have you."

And he did have me.

Every way he could.

CHAPTER FIFTEEN

I THOUGHT I'd escaped successfully. Well, with a reasonably deep gash in my arm from scaling the wall and making an ungraceful plummet to the earth, but in the grand scheme of things, scraping your arm while escaping from an outlaw MC's compound is the absolute best-case scenario.

I should've known better than to hope, in my world at least, there is no such thing as a best-case scenario.

The barrel of the gun pointed at me should've been what stopped me.

It wasn't.

It was *him*.

Carving a figure out of the moonlight, his body a shadow, his soul one too.

I hadn't seen him since I woke up alone in the morning. My body was bruised, so was everything inside me. Sleeping with him had changed everything and at the same time changed nothing.

The fact he was standing here pointing a gun at me as I tried to escape his club proved that.

I gritted my teeth. "You gonna shoot me?"

The gun didn't lower.

"You can't leave. You know fuckin' better than that." His voice was a whisper. But whispers in the moonlight were screams. "You know what happens if you try and leave here without our permission."

I laughed. The sound was cold and ugly. "Without your permission? I'm guessing the only way I leave with your *permission* is in a body bag."

The flinch was tiny. I only caught it because I was staring at him so intently. Eating him up, even though he had nothing to offer me but bitter memories and rancid reality.

"Jesus, Caroline," he gritted out. "Get back inside."

Something in his tone, the danger in it, the death in it, had something visceral inside me almost instinctively obeying. But I held firm. "No," I said.

There was a long pause. "Don't make me throw you over my fuckin' shoulder."

It wasn't a threat.

Another part of me, driven by instinct, a dark carnal instinct craved that. Craved the touch of this familiar stranger. Craved it more than my next breath.

My panties were damp.

My blood was hot.

But I held fast.

"You can drag me back in by my fucking *hair*, I'll just find another way to get out," I told him. And it was the truth. Not just because I wanted him to tug at my hair, hurt me. Like he had last night. Because that pain distracted me from the other, deeper stuff. The stuff that was packed into his midnight stare.

"You got a death wish, Caroline?" he asked. It crawled against my skin, the way he worded that, the promise of death still etched into my presence here, if I put one foot—or more accurately two feet and two arms—out of line, I'd be signing my own death warrant.

I didn't think that the flimsy friendships I'd made with the men here would change that. Or even the more solid friendships with Macy and (kind of) Scarlett.

Women had a lot more sway than the men in the club liked to admit, but they couldn't go so far as to stop the club from punishing rats.

Maybe Hansen might hear me out if anyone but Liam found me, maybe not.

Fuck, I didn't even know if Liam finding me was a good thing. I felt pockets of safety with him, like traveling in a plane with almost constant turbulence. Those fleeting patches of clean air gave you a false sense of safety that you weren't about to plummet to your death.

Everything with Liam was rough air.

The plummet was inevitable.

"No," I ground out the response to his question. Because I didn't have a death wish, not even in my darkest of moments did I wish myself dead. "This is nothing to do with death and everything about life."

Another pause.

There was a question in it.

I may know nothing about Jagger, apart from the fact he was prone to violence, fits of rage, he fucked like the devil, and was a complete stranger.

But I knew *everything* about Liam. And that small pause was Liam.

It had irritated me when we were together. The way he'd never actually ask me questions, he'd just wait, stare at me, will me into answering. That had been where I got my most effective interview tactic.

A lot had changed since then.

Everything, in fact.

Apart from this one small thing.

"Kate is pregnant," I said finally unable to take the silence between us. Unable to breathe around it. I paused, thinking of the phone call I'd gotten while playing poker with Claw. "Well, she's not pregnant *anymore*." I called up the picture in my mind of my wrinkly, tiny nephew, the one I'd looked at after banishing myself to 'my' room. After seeing it, it took me about two seconds to decide to risk my life in order to meet my nephew. "She's a mom now. And I'm an aunt. And he's just under month premature. He's okay. Kate's okay. And for once, unlike with other milestones in my family's life, I'm not on the other side of the world, causing them all worry. I'm not hiding away from their happiness so I have to fake my own." I paused. I knew I'd have to fake a lot of things no matter what. My happiness was to be determined.

I sucked in a breath as if an inhale and exhale could banish reality.

"You can force me back in there." I nodded to the clubhouse. "But I'll just find another way out. I'm *going* to see my family, to be with them. I'm sure you don't understand what that means since you abandoned yours, but mine still mean everything to me."

I was telling myself that was the reason I was risking my life for this escape was for them. For my family, for my sister, so I didn't miss out on another milestone like I had routinely done for the past fifteen years.

Anniversaries, birthdays, new jobs, new boyfriends and girlfriends, weddings. I'd missed most of it because I couldn't stand my family moving on while I couldn't. Or maybe I cared about them too much to show them how little I'd moved on, because then they couldn't at all.

Now I had the chance to make it right.

Or make it a little better.

To hold my nephew.

That's why I was escaping.

I wasn't risking death to escape from Liam and the new truth between us. The new nearness amidst the distance. To escape my need for him.

A grip on my arm jerked me back into a present I could never escape.

"Let go of me," I said through gritted teeth as Liam began to drag me.

"Not a chance."

I didn't fight, though the grip was painful. He wasn't dragging me back into the club, as promised, he was dragging me *out*.

Jagger

He wasn't sure if the decision was made by his cock, his heart or his soul. But he didn't have the latter two, and his cock had been telling him to do exactly what Caroline invited—drag her back into the clubhouse by the hair, fuck her until she passed out and lock her in his room until he figured out how the fuck to control her.

But his head told him that that was crossing the line. Whatever was left of the fucking line. It was making sure that Caroline would never trust him, never stop hating him.

As it was, he knew the chances of her not hating him were slim. Even if she didn't hate him, there was no way she would forgive him.

Some things were unforgivable.

What he'd done was unforgivable.

To her.

And now to his club.

Who he abandoned tonight.

And he'd been dreading this fucking phone call, but he had to answer it, he owed his best friend and his president that.

"Where the fuck are you?" Hansen demanded. "We have the Russians coming. We've got runs to make. Oh, and we're in the middle of a fucking *war* with Miguel Fernandez."

Jagger gritted his teeth, looking up at the motel room he'd rented after he'd stopped at a Walmart to get Caroline and him the shit they'd need for the almost twenty-hour ride. He had to convince her they needed to stop, because he could ride for a long time, but he was fucked. And also, because the closer he got to Castle Springs, the more he felt like he was going to lose it. He was riding back into the town that he promised himself he'd never return to as the man he was now.

It wasn't a question as to whether he was going to enter town limits, have a family reunion. Even thinking about it had him tempted to empty the contents of his stomach onto his boots.

No, that wasn't even an option.

He was doing this for one reason and one reason only.

Caroline.

"I'm in Texas," he said. "Close to the state line in Louisiana."

There was nothing but dead air on the other side of the phone. Hansen's accusation didn't need words. But he spoke them anyway. "Caroline's with you?" he deduced.

"I'm not runnin'," he said. "Nor am I letting her go. Her sister had a baby. Caught her outside the compound last night. She was intent on going no matter what we did. Short of tying her to the fuckin' bed. I didn't have a choice." He ran his hand through his hair, paced the parking lot, ignored the woman sitting outside their room, chain-smoking and checking him and his cut out. "She knows that it's twenty-four hours and then we're back."

"Jesus," Hansen muttered. "I knew when you found yourself a woman, it'd be fucked up. With Sarah, it wasn't it, because it was too fuckin' simple. So *of course* it's this." He sighed. "I'm not sayin' I'm happy about this. I'm pissed the fuck off at you. But I know why you're doin' it. If you're not back here by Sunday, it's your fuckin' patch."

He hung up.

It went better than Jagger expected it to go.

Then again, Hansen was a good friend. He'd been through it with Macy. He knew this shit.

Jagger sucked on his smoke. He was avoiding going up to that room. No, he was fuckin' desperate to go up to that room. But he couldn't because the more he fucked her, the more he felt like the kid he was. And if he was going back to the place that he swore he'd never set foot in again, he couldn't go within even an inch of that kid still inside him. He needed to be Jagger so he could survive that twenty-four hours. So he could leave.

So he stayed there, chain-smoking, watching the window of the motel room until the early hours of the morning when the lights turned off.

Caroline

The smell of coffee woke me.

Then the smell of reality on the sheets. Of Liam.

We'd barely spoken since he'd put me on the back of his bike and driven almost ten hours straight until he forced me into a Walmart to get the essentials, had a silent dinner at a shitty road-side diner and got us a room here.

No, we spoke with him laying down the law in a Walmart parking lot, in the middle of nowhere, Texas.

"I'm betraying my club by doing this," he said, shoving the plastic bags in his saddlebags.

I watched, not looking at him. I couldn't. Because I knew

what he was doing. What I was making him do. Abandon his family in their time of need.

A spiteful part of me was happy about that, because he'd done that already, to his real family. I wanted him to feel the pain of doing that again.

But the rest of me, who'd played poker with Claw, who'd watched movies with Macy, drank tequila with Scarlett, that part felt sickened by what I knew he was doing.

"I didn't ask you to do this," I said, still staring at his bike. It was a good bike.

Harley. Of course.

Matte black.

Also not surprising.

Guns in the saddlebags.

Along with a pair of cotton, unsexy Walmart panties, sweats, toothbrush and toothpaste, and face wash. I hadn't exactly been able to travel with any of them when I was climbing out a window.

And fresh bandages for my arm.

Liam had noticed it on the first stop.

He'd been horrified at the blood at the open flesh, which was surprising, considering his chosen lifestyle. His grip was bruising on my wrist and he looked up at me. "Why the fuck do you keep bleeding around me?"

My stomach dropped. "You tell me."

He didn't.

He went inside to the gas station, got what was an impressive first aid kit for a place in the middle of nowhere and tended to my cut.

The outside one, at least.

He'd checked on it before he spoke.

"You didn't ask me to do this," he repeated quietly. "You didn't give me a fuckin' choice!" he yelled.

"I gave you a choice," I said voice even.

He looked from my arm to me. *"You getting hurt at the hands of my club is not a fucking choice."* He paused. *"Get on the fuckin' bike."*

I glared at him. Then got on the fucking bike.

When we got to the motel, he'd paid, cash of course, carried my bags up and then left saying he had calls to make.

He didn't come back for four hours.

At that point, I'd been unable to battle my heavy eyes. You'd think that I would've been kept awake by the reality of it all, of going back to Castle Springs, where there was a grave for the man whose bike I was sitting on the back of. The man I was fucking. The man I was falling in love with all over again.

But it was the reality of it all that had me chasing oblivion. Or had oblivion chasing me.

By the smell of sheets—cigarettes and Liam—he'd slept some. I remembered a dream of being warm, of hands on me, feeling safe, but I couldn't trust it. Because nothing with Liam was a dream. And nothing was safe.

"Coffee." A tattooed hand placed a takeaway cup on the table beside me. The rich scent beckoned me. I sat up, wincing at my sore muscles as I did so.

Liam had moved himself all the way across the room in the space of time it took me to sit up. Then again, it was a slow process.

He watched my movements. "Ridin' long haul on a bike isn't exactly good for the body. You'll get used to it."

"No, I won't," I shot with venom.

His voice was scratchy. Smoky. He was dressed. Showered. In a fresh black tee he'd gotten yesterday.

People had stared at him in Walmart. At first, I thought it was because of the tattoos, the cut, we were in rural Texas, after all. But the more I watched them, I realized it was his face. They stared at his scar obviously as if he were some kind of attraction. It angered me the second I figured it out. It sickened me. People were fascinated by things that they deemed morbid. And an otherwise beautiful man with a jagged scar cutting through his face was morbid for them. Was cause to stare.

And it was the *adults*.

The children barely gave him a second glance. Children, who didn't know any better didn't have the hunger for the morbid.

But adults who should've known fucking better.

Liam didn't seem to notice. I guess his thoughts had been elsewhere. Maybe back in New Mexico, with the family he'd left behind in their time of need. Or ahead in Castle Springs, with the family who visited his grave every Sunday after church.

I was thinking all about that, sure. But I couldn't let the stares of these people wash over me. So I stared back. I glared back.

Wasn't it polite to look away when someone had evidence of pain they couldn't hide? All these people had secret pain that they got to hide away from prying eyes and I bet they wouldn't like me gazing at it in the middle of a Walmart.

I really considered throat punching one woman who actually stopped, whispered to her fricking kid and made him stare too.

"Does it bother you?" I asked, moving to sip my coffee with an aching arm.

He leaned against the table beside the TV. "That you're in pain because you refuse to ride easy, and now we have no choice but to ride hard because we've got a deadline to get back to the club?" he asked. "Yeah, it fucking bothers me."

I sucked down my too hot coffee, relishing the sugar scalding my throat because that was better to focus on than the comfortable warmth I felt with Liam's words. His gaze.

"Not once in fourteen years has my ride been *easy*," I replied. "I'm used to hard, more comfortable with it." I swallowed and my unintended innuendo and the flare in Liam's eyes. "I'm used to deadlines too." I paused. "I mean, yesterday, in Walmart, the people..." I trailed off.

He laughed. "Staring at the monster?" he finished for me. "No, babe, it doesn't bother me. Not just because I've had years of practice going out in public. Didn't exactly plan on entering any beauty pageants anyway." He shrugged.

On screaming limbs that didn't belong to me, I moved from the bed, put my coffee down and walked over to where Liam was leaning.

He watched my approach. From head to toe.

I was wearing an oversized shirt I'd gotten at Walmart, it went down to the middle of my thighs, but I felt naked.

Liam made me feel naked.

In every way.

His body tightened as I moved inches from his body, lifting my hand to trail my fingers across his face.

It was the first time I'd done it. The skin was ribbons of tissue, evidence of something almost tearing his fucking head off.

I swallowed bile.

He lifted his hand,

He touched his face. "This wasn't as pretty as it is now, people shied away from me, as they should've. I didn't want to be around people. It's how I found myself at the club. Men in the club don't shy away from monsters, from ugly." He stared at me. Into me. "I didn't want to come back to you a monster."

The brokenness of his tone got to me. It really fucking did.

But I couldn't let it get to me all the way.

"You could never have come back to me a monster," I said. "No matter your demons, your scars, inside and out." I paused, tracing the jagged and ruined skin of his face. "The fact you didn't come back at all, *that's* what made you a monster in my eyes."

He didn't speak. Just stared at me.

"We're going back home, you're going to have to face it."

His body turned to stone. His eyes shuttered. "No, *you're* going home," he corrected. "I'm going to a shitty small town in Alabama that used to be something to someone I used to be. Someone you buried."

"You need to stop this," I hissed. "The people out there, they would feel nothing but joy to have you back."

He shook his head. "At first, sure. That joy would trump whatever anger has been fueling you. It would trump whatever disgust they had seeing the scars, the ink, everything that's changed about me." He gestured to his body violently. "But that joy is temporary. It washes off. Eventually their eyes will clear, and they'll realize the man they've been mourning is gone." His eyes emptied. Hardened. "Like you have. And then they'll find themselves wishing I had died, because that would've been easier. And because my family are good people, they'll torture themselves for that ugly but human wish. I'll torture them with that."

He picked up his coffee. "I've already tortured you with it. And I'll live with that because I've got no other choice. But I won't do it to them. Nothing you say, no accusations you sling will change that. Because even you can't hate me more than I hate myself."

I opened my mouth, to say what, I didn't know. To tell him I didn't hate him. But I wasn't sure that was true.

"Get showered," he ordered, voice dead. "We've got a long drive."

He turned and left me standing in the hotel room.

A single tear trailed down my cheek.

Then I showered.

Or I tried to.

Because it wasn't until I was under the spray that I realized this conversation with Liam had distracted me so much that I forgot.

I forgot a fear, a phobia, a trauma, whatever it was, that had followed me for years. Something I'd thought was impossible to forget because of how much it had altered me. Damaged me.

But Liam damaged me more.

So it was not until I was naked, vulnerable and alone that I realized where I was.

CHAPTER SIXTEEN

Jagger

HE WAS HALFWAY through his second smoke when he realized what the fuck he'd done.

He dropped his coffee on the concrete and sprinted to the room, bursting through the door.

The shower was on. The door to the bathroom was closed.

He strode over there, hand pausing at the door. He didn't know what the fuck to do. In his time in the army, after patching into the Sons of Templar, he had always known what to do, because most of the right decisions usually involved violence and death.

But with Caroline, he didn't want to treat her with anything but care. He'd forgotten how to do that.

"Peaches?" he called through the door.

Nothing.

He gripped the handle. "Babe, I'm comin' in."

Still nothing.

He was punched in the gut by what he saw.

"Fuck," he hissed, striding over to the shower, reaching in to turn the water off. He flinched away from the water he expected to be hot.

It was freezing.

Caroline was sitting on the floor, knees pressed to her chest, shivering, lips blue.

"Peaches," he whispered, gathering her in his arms. She was cold to the touch, fucking freezing. He pressed her to his body, wishing he could give her whatever warmth was left inside him, which was precious little.

He took them into the bedroom, sat in the sheets that smelled of them both. Her sweet and his bitter, stale smoky scent.

Caroline was still silent.

And she was still fucking freezing. She hadn't been in there long enough to endanger herself, physically at least.

But mentally...he'd done that.

He'd put her in danger.

He fucking knew it too. He'd just been too angry to remember. To keep his woman safe.

Jagger kissed her head again. Her face was blank. So pale her freckles—the ones that she hadn't had before—were stark against the translucent skin.

"*Fuck*, baby," he murmured, maneuvering her so he could yank off his cut and tee and press his bare skin to hers. He didn't know if it would help. But he needed it.

It was killing him that he couldn't help. That there was nothing he could do but hold her, keep her warm and leave her to get herself out of this.

It took thirty minutes.

He knew the second she came back. Because she felt warm. Not her skin. From somewhere different. Her eyes cleared. She moved slightly, but not out of his arms.

"I need to be cold," she explained, her voice raw. "I need to be cold when I'm in there, it usually helps it not to get bad."

Fuck.

That wasn't *bad.*

Fuck.

He squeezed her in his arms and used everything he had not to break the fuck down. He had to be strong here. Hold Caroline together. He'd been strong for years, never even entertained the idea of breaking down. But he'd already done it once in front of her, after sharing a joint with Swiss in search of numbness. Instead, he couldn't hide from his feelings. His fear. He broke down in front of her then, and she had every right to shut the door in his face, tell him he deserved every inch of his pain.

But she didn't.

She was strong for him.

And fuck if he wouldn't be strong for her now.

"When it happened, I felt so hot, like I was on fire," she continued. "And when I get like that, it feels like my skin is burning." She rubbed her bare arms with a vulnerability that was agonizing and beautiful to witness. He wanted that vulnerability. He wanted to be the one she felt safe enough around to reveal that to. She wasn't revealing it now because she felt safe, but because she had no other fucking choice.

"I need to be cold," she continued, meeting his eyes.

He kissed her head. Inhaled her scent. She was lax in his arms. She wasn't fighting to get out, even after everything. She hadn't tried to escape, not since the beginning. No matter what she'd had to go through, watching men die, watching men come back to life, watching men be tortured, have her life threatened, she stayed through it all. She didn't fight to get out.

Until now.

And it wasn't even for fucking *her.*

It was for her sister.

Kate and Caroline had been close, even though they'd been totally different. Liam didn't like girls like Kate, but he liked Kate. Because she pretended to be vapid and shallow to fit into the life she wanted. But she wasn't. Because she was raised by parents who made sure she was more than she appeared.

He knew Caroline was more than she appeared since the first second he'd laid eyes on her. But he thought he'd discovered all of her depths.

Oh how naïve he was.

She was fucking infinite.

Caroline

I liked the bike.

No, I *loved* it.

Not just because I got to be pressed up against Liam, as close as I could and I didn't have any choice in the matter.

Not just because the road stretched out in front of us and we sped past towns, landscapes, everything. The world was outside, off the bike. It was simpler on the road. You'd think the time spent driving would invite dangerous contemplation, but it did the opposite, it did the thing I'd been trying to figure out how to do for the past decade and a half. I got it.

A little bit of it at least.

But mostly I was loving it because Liam and I couldn't speak. You'd think, by now, with us finally alone, with us driving toward a home he couldn't escape from, it'd be time to talk. To ask a fuck of a lot of questions. To tell him what he'd done to me. In detail. Swear at him.

But I didn't want to do that.

Not after he'd held me in his arms, pressed me to his body, cradled me like I was a baby, kissed my head and whispered nothing and everything in my ear for the half hour it took me to regain myself.

He didn't look at me like I was weak when I finally found it in me to talk. He blamed himself. He tortured himself, I saw that. Not just for leaving me in the motel room, but for leaving me at all. Because he likely blamed himself for the fact I even had this trauma in the first place. I wanted to blame him at the start too. I wanted him to blame himself.

But the more I saw, the less I wanted to blame him and the more I just wanted him.

So I was glad that we couldn't talk. So he couldn't tangle me any more in this web than I already was.

Or was I tangling myself?

I PARKED my rental car in an empty spot in the town's small hospital.

Liam didn't drive me to the hospital.

For obvious reasons.

It wouldn't have been surprising if his parents were at the hospital, visiting. They had stayed close with our family like one of those weird, tragedy anomalies. Because I didn't care what anyone else said, tragedy didn't bring people together, make them appreciate what they did have. It only pushed them farther apart. Look what happened to me. It pushed me across oceans, into hot zones, battlefields, and mass graves.

Anywhere but this town.

This beautiful, picturesque, classic American small town. Without a Starbucks, with a grocery store owned by the same family for years, exorbitant prices and little variety.

The town that had turned into a prison after we got the news.

I'd been home for the summer, seeking solace in a place that gave me comfort, safety, and memories of Liam around every corner.

And then, after the funeral, after all of that countless, horrible death stuff, I went straight back to school. I didn't come back, even for holidays. I'd make up excuses. Take extra classes, anything to keep me away.

Then I got a job as an intern in New York. Worked two other jobs, lived in a studio with three other people, was constantly hungry, worried about money and had no free time. It was the closest to happy I'd ever been.

Because I didn't have time to think about how fucking unhappy I was.

That's when I met Emily. She was also an intern at a PR firm, using the word *fuck* as much as she could, sleeping with anything with tits—including her trying me until I told her I was straight and we decided to become best friends instead. She accepted all of my fucked-up things. Like the fact I never talked about my family, my past, never dated and was never standing still long enough to...feel.

And then we both started moving up, stopped having to work in shitty bars and coffee shops. I got a job at The *New York Times*. Writing shitty copy but enough. And then, they had a shitty assignment that was dangerous, with crap pay and no guarantees of safe return.

I took it without hesitation.

I'd watched war coverage with a different kind of morbid fascination than the masses. I couldn't tear myself away from the faces of the soldiers. I looked for his face in every one. Even though I knew he was dead. But the only way I'd really known was to go over there and see it all for myself. Make sure it was real.

So I accepted. Readied myself as much as anyone could

ready themselves for such a thing. I wasn't scared. What left did I have left to be afraid of?

I discovered I did have things left to be afraid of when I went home to inform my family—the people I'd tried to make strangers and they didn't let that happen—of what I was doing, where I was going.

They'd took it as well as a family who had already had war take precious things from them could.

Not well.

Until it became apparent I wasn't changing my mind.

"The flowers are going to do well this year," Mom said with a forced cheerfulness that is somehow more penetrating than the naked sadness I know is below it.

I looked at the petals she was gesturing to. They had seemed surely dead only a couple of months ago. They were coming back to life, as they did every season.

I hated flowers for that simple reason. Because for them, death was never final.

"They will. You'll beat Agnes Wolf by a mile," I replied with that same forced cheer I was learning to despise.

It had become constant as my flight approached. As had benign conversations about roses, cakes, and neighbors who didn't take care of their yards. Any subject was safe, as long as it wasn't about Afghanistan.

We were taking one last walk through our sprawling garden, that was, apart from us kids, my mother's pride and joy.

She gave up her job as soon as she had my brother. And though the feminist in me bristled slightly at her having to give up her career to have her children, it was clear where her joy lay.

Raising us.

Teaching us good Southern manners.

Making us fresh bread that was still warm when we arrived home from school. Jam too.

Making every single sports game, every parent-teacher conference, being the head of the PTA, and most of all, making our home beautiful, warm and welcoming.

Despite her title as a 'stay at home mom,' she was never idle, as our ever-changing home décor and immaculate garden communicated.

Now that her children were grown, with jobs, finances, and wars to keep them busy, she volunteered as well as did the baking for 'Cups and Cakes' the café on Main Street which won a serious bidding war for her services.

Her cookie recipe was sought after in town.

The secret ingredient? Cayenne pepper.

You didn't hear it from me.

Mom stopped immediately in front of a bunch of hydrangeas.

My favorite.

She clicked her tongue, regarding them for a long moment before springing forward to pluck out ones with the browning petals.

That always made me sad.

I identified with those browning and withering petals most of all.

"Why are you doing this?" she whispered as they fluttered to the ground without ceremony.

Her voice was broken.

Not surprising, since it was the first she'd spoken of it since I'd told her and the rest of my family where I was going and when.

I didn't have an answer for her.

At least not a real one.

I didn't even have an answer for myself.

There was no reason why I was doing this.

Just like there was no reason for me not to. Not even a mother that adored me, that grew hydrangeas because she knew they were my favorite, or a dad that sneaked a joint with me every now and then because he knew oblivion was required when life got too loud. Or even for a sister that slept holding my hand for a month after we got the news. Or a brother that didn't do anything specific, but did everything with his presence and borderline sexist jokes.

No, my loving and concerned family was not a reason to stay.

If anything, they were reasons to leave.

Not that I was going to tell my doting, cookie baking mother this.

I grabbed her hand, it was warm, soft and I knew smelled like lemongrass, a hand cream she'd used since forever.

"I'm going because I need to," I told her. "Because other people need me to. Because I couldn't live with myself if I didn't go."

She eyed me with irises that mirrored my own and a penetrating gaze I couldn't escape from. "No, you can't live with yourself without him, that's why you're going."

I flinched, because up until now, my family had been treating me with kid gloves, like I was a cracked piece of antique glass, ready to shatter if handled incorrectly.

Which was ridiculous of course.

I was already shattered.

No longer fragile.

"You loved him, I know that," Mom said. "Everyone knows it. Everyone saw it. Felt it. What you had was special. And it's a tragedy of God that you lost it before you even got to live it. But that doesn't mean you have to go around chasing more tragedy. It's not gonna change it. It's not gonna make it better."

I let go of her hand. "But it's not gonna make it worse either. And that's what's most important."

Tears fell from my mother's eyes. "You can't let this take you away from us."

I didn't feel those tears, I'd already switched off in a way that did me well for years after this. Funny I got my biggest and most *important instrument in war from one of the safest places in my history.*

"That's what you don't get, Mom, it already has."

Then I walked away.

From my loving mom.

Caring father.

Nurturing sister.

Protective brother.

I walked into the hospital and they were all there.

My loving mom.

My caring father.

Protective brother—with his second wife who may or may not be his last, I liked her, but you could never tell with him.

And my nurturing sister.

Lying in a bed in the middle of the room surrounded by my family. By warmth. Comfort.

Her husband was slightly removed from the chaos, because that was him. He was the man who was wearing a neatly pressed shirt and slacks after the birth of his child. His hair was combed correctly, correctly to him was within an inch of its life. His strong, tanned jaw was clean shaven. All of this made you sure he'd be a pretentious asshole. Which he was. But he was also a good guy. He treated my sister well.

And that was all that mattered.

He saw me first, smiled and nodded his head.

A greeting decidedly mundane compared to what followed.

My mother, screaming, rushing over to me and snatching me into her arms.

My father cursing about how skinny I looked. My mother letting me go to yell at my father for cursing in front of the baby. My father arguing with my mother that the baby still couldn't hear yet so he would swear as much as he damn well pleased.

And then my mother giving him a look that guaranteed he would not do what he damn well pleased.

At this, my father grumbled and then yanked me out of my mom's arms for his own embrace.

He squeezed me tight.

Kissed my head.

My brother ruffled my hair.

I punched his arm.

His wife kissed my cheek.

Questions shot at me.

"How did you get here?" "Is the story over?" "Why does your hair look like that?" (Mom) "When are you gonna use that press pass to get me box seats to a Yankees game?" (Will) "Are you hungry?" (Mom).

"Stop!" I all but screeched at my well-meaning family.

They all stopped.

I sighed. Smiled. "I would like to meet my nephew."

My mom smiled, big and light, a smile I'd never given her because, unlike my sister, I was not light and bright.

They parted to reveal Kate, in her glory. Much like her husband, her hair was styled, she had on light makeup, a tasteful silk nightgown and pearls.

I raised my brow at her. "Pearls, Kate?"

She scowled at me.

But her scowl didn't stay for long because of the bundle in her arms.

I made it to the bed and discovered she held the whole world in her arms.

My hand was shaking when I brushed his tiny head. He had a scattering of inky black hair on his head.

"He's perfect," I whispered.

"I know," Kate whispered back.

She reached for my hand.

I glanced to her.

"I'm so glad you came, Linny," she choked out.

I swallowed the lump in my throat that came from that simple statement. "Me too," I whispered.

And I was.

Despite what it might cost Liam. What it had cost us. What it would cost me. I was glad. Beyond belief.

"Do you want to hold him?" she asked.

I nodded, unable to speak.

Carefully, she handed the bundle to me.

Never had anything been so light and heavy at the same time.

HE WAS SITTING on the concrete outside our room in the shitty motel we were staying in. The shitty motel we *had* to stay in because if we stayed closer to town, where the motels were not shitty, but well-kept and not frequented by adultering husbands and drug dealers, we'd run the risk of encountering someone who would recognize Liam. We definitely couldn't go to my apartment, with all the visitors that would likely come if they knew I was home. Visitors that included his parents.

And we couldn't stay separately because Liam was still technically my captor. Here to make sure I was only here for twenty-four hours before going back inside.

I didn't *want* to go to my place. That was the strange thing. It wasn't a home. And I didn't like the thought of Liam alone at this seedy motel, fighting demons in the sunshine that our hometown offered.

Most people, even people that had known Liam, would not recognize him now. There was no way to connect the scarred, inked biker with the all-American War Hero the town honored every year since his death.

Almost everyone that knew him wouldn't recognize him.

But his parents would.

My parents would.

His sister.

They'd see those eyes and instantly recognized the son, the brother, the friend they'd mourned. Then it would be over.

It'd be over for Jagger.

I wanted to expose him.

Even after everything I'd learned, and I hadn't even learned anything really.

The reasons that maybe made a little sense, but a little sense meant less than nothing in the face of the pain he'd put everyone through.

The journalist in me craved to expose him.

But the human in me, the one that still harbored feelings for this man, whether it be Jagger or Liam, I wasn't sure, the human in me could betray him like that. It wasn't my choice to make. Especially if Liam never intended on coming back here. It was one thing to give a son back, to have Kent and Mary swallow the truth the same way I did, but it was quite another to give him back for a fleeting moment and then make them watch him ride away on a motorcycle to a dangerous and foreign life.

As much as it physically pained me, the deception, the dirty secret he was forcing me to keep, I knew there was no other choice. Not for me at least

It was up to Liam.

Before, I would've been certain Liam would've made the honorable choice. To tell the truth, to free those he loved from suffering.

But this man was not honorable.

This man had a distorted view of suffering, higher than most.

The honorable choice for an outlaw usually masqueraded as the dishonorable choice for most everyone else.

He watched me approach, calm, collected. Outwardly at least.

There was a storm in his eyes.

I sat down beside him, thinking of everything I'd just left at the hospital. I stayed longer than everyone else, trying to soak up as much time with my nephew as I could. I'd lied to my family and said I was on a deadline for the story and needed to leave tomorrow.

They weren't pleased. But they understood. And they had false comfort in another lie about the story I was doing.

Everything was coming too easy now. Deception. Lies.

So I stayed holding the purist and most beautiful thing I might ever hold. I thought my chance at a family was shot to shit, even if I survived what was to come.

But visiting hours stopped, my sister waned, and it was time for me to go.

I cupped her cheek. "You did me proud, Katie."

She smiled lazily. "You did too, Linny. Just in case you didn't know it, just in case we don't say it enough. You've done us all so proud."

I rolled my eyes. "You're proud now I made it home."

She reached for my hand and squeezed it. "No, not about your stories, well that too. But we're most proud that you made it here. Made it through. We're proud of the woman you've become even with everything you've lost. And I know that you have to be a little further away from us to get through, I hate it, but I get it. I might not get you, but I love you. I'm proud of you. And I'm proud that my son has an aunt like you."

Tears rolled down my cheeks.

I squeezed my sister's hand. Brushed the one errant hair that had moved out of place. Then I kissed her head.

"Sleep," I whispered. "It's probably the last time you're gonna be able to do that for the next ten years."

I winked and walked out.

I wanted to go home.

So I found myself in a shitty hotel on the outskirts of town, sitting next to a slightly familiar stranger in a motorcycle cut.

"We would've had it," I whispered. "I can almost see it. Taste it. Touch it." I sucked in a ragged breath, the cracked and stained concrete in front of me flickering until it was replaced by grass so green it could only exist in someone's dreams. Freshly mowed, because that's the kind of person Liam was. He didn't hire anyone. He did it himself. Every morning. After coffee, after waking up and making love to me. There were two cars in the driveway. His truck and my Jeep. I always wanted a Jeep. And this was the life I always wanted, wasn't it? My job was stable, our love was strong. Our grass was green. And it was nothing but a forgotten dream. A dream marred by the truth.

I blinked myself back into reality.

It was harsh, stark and so gray it was a color that couldn't exist in a dream.

"There was a life for us, somewhere." My voice was rougher, throatier, hard so it could weather the harshness of the moment. "In the past." I stood on shaky legs. I brushed off the back of my jeans. Gave myself a handful of seconds to gather my wits before I met his eyes.

They weren't hard. Or dull, lackluster in the reality that surrounded us.

No, they were starker than that grass that was too green to be true, and brimming with the life we'd lost and whatever death had given him.

I bit my tongue so hard that I tasted bitter coppery blood.

"We don't live in the past. Whatever's between us, it was. It was buried in that empty coffin along with whoever you used to be."

Liam stood up too.

He didn't let me say anything else.

Didn't let me retreat.

Didn't let me breathe.

He just snatched my face and yanked my mouth to his.

I didn't even try to fight him. I didn't want to. So I kissed him back. Not like I was kissing the man he used to be. Not tender, playful. No, I kissed him like the man he was now. Hard. Passionate. Painful. Soul destroying.

He lifted me, and my legs wrapped around him without hesitation, I didn't stop kissing him as he walked us into the room. The door slammed shut behind us.

One of his hands stayed on my ass, pressing my core into his cock. I bit his lip as he tore his hands through my hair, yanking it.

"You're changing this back to how it was," he demanded against my mouth.

"Nothing is how it was," I breathed.

He threw me down on the bed.

Not softly.

It only turned me on more.

I lay on my back, while the man with the green eyes, the scar, the tattoos and the cut stared at me with a mixture of reverence and hunger. A mixture of Liam and Jagger.

"No. *Everything* is how it was," he argued, shedding his tee and cut. He leaned down to rip off my sneakers, my jeans. My panties. All without ceremony.

Then he just stood there, staring at my pussy. Eating with his eyes. He leaned down, pressed his face into it. Inhaled.

I wasn't even embarrassed with how intimate this was. There was no room for embarrassment with Liam.

"Everything important is *exactly* how it was," he murmured, breath hot on my core. He spread me as if he were cataloging every inch of my anatomy with his eyes. Then he cataloged it with his tongue.

Then, after an orgasm, he fucked me. Still wearing his jeans. His boots. Then he fucked me again.

In the shower.

And then he put me to bed. In his arms.

We didn't speak.

Because we both knew that at some point, before we left Castle Springs, there would be words, too many of them.

So we were silent.

CHAPTER SEVENTEEN

"ARE you sure you can't stay for just one more dinner?" Mom asked. "Kent and Mary are coming for dinner tonight, they've been on vacation in Florida and I know they'd love to see you."

I steeled myself not to flinch. I couldn't. I had distanced myself from Liam's parents too, the best I could. Though they accepted it, they never let me push them out of their lives. They never made me feel like I'd lost them as well as Liam.

But I couldn't face them.

I could barely face myself.

I hated myself.

Even as I cried out into Liam's neck this morning, clawing at his back in pleasure, in an attempt to tear the reaper from his skin.

I hated myself and I began to love him instead of hate him.

I couldn't let myself love him when I didn't even know the truth.

Which was why I slipped out of the motel room while he was showering. Left a note telling him I'd be back before my deadline.

He'd have to believe me. He was all but prisoner here in this shitty and depressing room. I wanted to find satisfaction in that.

I didn't.

First, I visited Kate and Archie—of course that's what they'd named him—at the hospital. Checked in on my dad at the shop, and finally, when I didn't have any other choice, I came home.

"I can't, Mom, this deadline it's..." I trailed off. "Important."

She smiled. "Of course it is, darling."

There was no venom in the words. It was my mom accepting me. She'd been forced to accept that her younger daughter was not going to marry well, become a housewife, head charities and Sunday at the country club.

I couldn't help it. I walked over to her and hugged her, breathing in her perfume, the one that hadn't changed since forever—because a lady always had a signature perfume—and let myself be comforted by someone that loved me for what I was, and for what I wasn't.

She hugged me back without hesitation, knowing full well such things from me were rare.

Eventually, I let go.

Mom cupped my cheek in her hand regarding me with twinkling, smiling eyes. Despite the fact she was now a grandmother, with gray hair and wrinkles to help cement that fact, she was still incredibly beautiful. There was a timeless elegance etched within her that she'd always had.

I hadn't seen her eyes twinkle like that when she looked at me, not in a long time. They were always clouded with worry, sadness, pain.

I hated that. Despised that my mother couldn't look at me and be happy.

And I got it a little bit, Liam's choice. He couldn't face what would be tattooed into his parent's eyes when they had to witness what he'd become. He'd pretend the best he could, but parents always saw pain in their children, no matter what they tried to hide.

Parents were meant to protect their children, good parents. And we both had good parents, when we were old enough to realize that, we understood we needed to protect them right back.

"You seem different," Mom said. "Better." Some of that old sadness flickered into this new happiness. "I would keep myself up at night worrying about you. That's a mother's job, of course. Especially when something hurts her baby like what happened to you. Especially when I knew there was not a thing on this earth I could do but just watch and hope you recovered." She sucked in a breath. "And I know your heart. I know that it's big, it's special and it is precious. So I knew it wouldn't fully recover. I understood why you chased all that war and violence and ugliness. I hated it, with every fiber of my being. Your father did too. But we understood."

They did. As much as they tried to convince me otherwise, tried the best they could to support me.

"And when you came back, I let out some of my worry," she said. "But I still harbored a lot. Because I could see that you didn't know where you fit when you weren't chasing ugliness and wars. I know you couldn't fit into lives like your sister and brother did. Though I wished for that. Because both of them have beautiful lives." She paused. "Well, your brother would if he'd open his eyes and stop divorcing his wives," she muttered.

I smiled.

"All I want for you is beauty," she whispered. "But life gave you ugly. So you can't fit into beauty the same way. I was worried you'd never fit anywhere, not without Liam. But now, you seem like you're more...at peace."

I wanted to laugh. Almost as badly as I wanted to break down in tears. I wanted to seek solace in my mother. Get her counsel. Tell her the ugly truth that I was dragging around my home.

But I had to protect my mother.

And I had to protect Liam.

But I still wanted to laugh at the fact my mother, who I'd always been sure was a little bit psychic because of her ability to see things in me I never said out loud, said that I was at peace when I was in the middle of a war.

But she was right.

I never fit anywhere. The only places I did feel like I could breathe were warzones. My hometown was too quiet. Too loud.

Cities felt too stifling, busy, asinine.

I could never relate to lifestyles my friends picked.

If I was honest with myself, I had that same fear my mother held. I was terrified I'd be lost my whole life, just pretending to fit. Pretending to be happy. Pretending to be human.

I'd been doing a lot over the past few weeks. But I wasn't pretending to be anything.

BEFORE I LEFT, I went to pick up some more clothes out of my old closet, considering I hadn't exactly packed when I left the compound. And for some reason, I still couldn't face going to the place that was meant to be my home. Most of the clothes in this closet were from summers that only existed in memories, sundresses from the girl before, colors, happiness.

But there were a handful of jeans and tees belonging to the woman I had been too, from when I'd lived here for a scant week before moving into my apartment.

I don't even know what I was digging for when I found it.

I didn't even realize it was still in there, banished at the back of a closet. Did I put it there? Did Mom? With some kind of hope I would recycle a wedding dress like I might be able to recycle my heart after having it thrown back at me with no one for it to belong to anymore.

Or did I put it there? With some kind of hope of Liam coming back from the dead? In a different way than this, obviously. In the romance novel, beautiful kind of way, where he walks down the street wearing his uniform, sun shining at his back, future in his hands. I'd see him, be wearing a yellow sundress and I'd sprint to him, jump into his arms, he'd catch me.

Instead it was sixteen years later, and I saw him murder someone in an alley, uniform long gone, replaced with a leather cut and a motorcycle club.

Anger that I'd toyed with that first night came back with more fury than ever before. A need to destroy, to hurt, to annihilate came over me and a red film covered my vision as I snatched the white dress still covered in the dry cleaner's plastic.

"I KNOW it's bad luck for a fiancé to see the wedding dress," I said, not turning as his motorcycle boots thumped against the concrete. I expected him to come. He wasn't anywhere to be found when I pulled up at the motel. It was getting close to the deadline. "But I figured we'd had all the bad luck in the world, and you've been legally declared dead so you're not my fiancé anymore. But you stopped being that much before the US government recognized your death."

I flicked on the lighter. My fingers smelled of gasoline.

"Caroline," Liam choked out as he likely came to the realization of what I was about to do.

He would've stopped me if I hesitated.

If I hesitated setting fire to the beautiful, perfect dress I'd planned on marrying him in. If I paused before I let flames engulf the symbol of our past, of hope for us to have any kind of future that had happiness which had once been attached to that dress.

I didn't hesitate. I threw it into the trash drum I'd dragged from the side of the property.

Heat hit my face the same time Liam snatched me back from the flames. His arms circled my chest as he yanked my back to his front.

I didn't fight him.

I didn't need to.

He let me go as the dress burned.

I had needed to hurt him. I wanted to turn him to ash like the fire was turning my dress to a blackened and ruined mess. I wanted to punish him for what he'd done to me, to his family.

But the second the flames caught, I lost it all. All that anger, all that need.

I didn't want to punish him.

I needed to understand him.

The flames burned too loud for me to speak. They screamed all the things I'd thought I'd wanted them to say, all the accusations and hurt. They screamed until the fire burned itself out.

We both watched it.

It was only then that I found the nerve to look at him. Tears streamed down his face. Lucid agony.

I felt no victory in that.

He wiped his mouth with the back of his hand. He didn't look at me, even after he tore his eyes away from the charred remains of the dress I'd planned on marrying him in. He half walked, half stumbled to the plastic chair situated outside our motel room.

I followed him, sitting down at the one beside it.

It was sticky.

That didn't much matter.

I wanted to give him a reprieve. A breath. I didn't want to

hurt him anymore, didn't want to face those tears trailing down a face already painted, etched with pain.

But I didn't get a reprieve.

Not in a decade.

And I needed one. I had to have one.

In the form of the truth.

No matter how ugly.

Because the ugly truth was better than all the pretty lies in the world.

"I need to know now," I said, staring at the murky water of the hotel pool. Looking at the faded and rickety sun loungers, looking at the unattractiveness of our present, maybe I could weather the ugly past here. "I need to know how you came to the conclusion that making everyone believe you were dead was the right decision." I didn't look at him. "What was the pitch, the contract?"

He looked me square in the face. "Peaches, the devil doesn't have a contract. And that's what it was, that split-second decision made out of shame, cowardice, a misplaced sense of bravery or love, that was me signing whatever was leftover of my soul to the devil."

I swallowed ash.

It didn't come from the fire.

It came from the pit.

"I don't even really know how it happened," he said, continuing. "Someone fucked up, that much was obvious. But you would not believe the number of fuckups in times of combat." He paused abruptly. "Or maybe you would, maybe you've seen it."

I nodded, though his words weren't exactly a question.

"Early on, I kind of fell into a branch of the army that I never planned on seeing. Had a Commander that either liked me or hated me, still to this day can't decide which one it was for putting me on that team. We were on a mission top secret, total black ops, doing shit we were not meant to be doing, in places we were not meant to be. If we got caught, our commander in chief had plausible deniability. We were told that going in, we knew it. What we were doing would never be sanctioned by the US government. Officially."

I nodded again. Through my years reporting in times of war, I knew there was a lot the public didn't know. It was a lot the public didn't *want* to know. We wanted plausible deniability too.

"Mission went bad. Either we were fed bad intel or we hit bad luck," he continued. "War is just a series of bad luck and near misses." His eyes went glassy, far away. "Everyone died. Everyone apart from me. Still don't know why they decided to take me prisoner. Minds of men are unstable in times like that. Maybe they thought I was worth something, maybe they thought I knew somethin'." He shrugged. "I didn't know shit, and what I did know, I didn't tell them. And I thought I was worth somethin', for the longest time." He looked at me, and I cut my palms with my nails once more. "I thought I was worth something, not because of who I was in the war, it was because of who I was at home. It was because of the promises I made to the girl I loved." His words were knives, bullets, every sharp object that could draw blood.

He didn't stop drawing blood. "But there was only so long I could hold onto that. I was already questioning my worth when they took me. I'd already done things that changed me. That took me further away from the man I wanted to be for you," he said. "But with everything they were doing to me, I still was determined to come home to you. That's what got me out. Because no way in fuck was it strength on my part. I was half starved, fully beaten, nearer to death than I had the right to be without actually dying. But I got out, some way."

His eyes touched the smoking barrel that contained my wedding dress, contained our other life.

"The Devil takes care of his disciples, I guess," he muttered. "Was wandering around the desert when patrols found me. That there was the one bit of good luck I encountered in war." He laughed. "If we can call it that. By the time they got me back to base, airlifted me to a hospital in Germany and woke me out of the coma I was in, I didn't know my own name. The fuckers had taken my dog tags, my face was a mess and I wasn't awake to tell anyone who the fuck I was. I didn't *want* to know who I was. Because I knew whoever I was, I'd done something bad. I'd become something bad. I could just fuckin' feel it. And I couldn't face it. Sure as shit couldn't face myself in a mirror. So I forced myself not to remember. Until I forced myself to."

He paused to reach into his pocket, put a smoke in his mouth and light it. Like he needed the comforting inhale of death to get him through the story.

"By the time I could tell them, uniformed officers had already come to my parents' door tellin' them their son was dead," he said. "And it wasn't a lie. But my superiors were willing to rectify that fuckup. But they gave me another choice, not because of concern for me, but for their image. I was the soldier that had been on a mission that wasn't meant to exist, and woke up someone who didn't."

He inhaled and exhaled twice before he kept going.

"I was a liability. It was only in that split second that I made the decision to stay dead. It was not calculated, planned. It came from the core of me, the core that had turned rotten, ugly. And I made that decision, because of who I was to Uncle Sam, who I wasn't meant to be, they let me. They preferred it that way. They turned a blind eye to me doin' that, like the way they turned blind eyes to a lot of shit."

I knew that too. Because I worked for media that was meant to be all about the truth, but they were owned by people who wanted the truth to be relative. So the media turned blind eyes to a lot of shit too.

"It was easier for them for me to be dead," he rasped, inhaling. "Easier for me too. I wandered around as a dead man for a long time."

I looked down at my hands as he stopped speaking. They were stained black with ash.

"Your face," I whispered. "*They* did that?"

He nodded once. "They got frustrated when I didn't talk. I suppose they considered themselves masters of such things. They hated me. I don't know why they didn't just kill me. But they wanted to destroy me first, I guessed."

His hand went up to his face.

"They made me watch."

I flinched.

I wanted to offer him comfort.

I wanted to show him what my family showed me today. Hope. But I couldn't. Not yet.

"I don't know what broke me more, burying you, or having to come to the realization that I didn't lose you to death, but to abandonment," I admitted, still trying to hurt him, prod at those open wounds he'd just uncovered.

"I didn't abandon you," he hissed, face hardening. "I fucking *saved* you."

"Yeah," I scoffed. "You're the hero of this story."

He didn't look at me.

"Met a guy in Iraq," he said instead of arguing. "He'd been over there much longer than me. He was a badass. Best at what he did. Everyone looked up to him. Not just 'cause of how brutal he was in battle, but how rational he was. Fair. He was generally a good guy to be around. Had a wife and baby. Talked about them every day. Wasn't a day where I didn't see him lookin' in wonder at the photos he carried around in his pocket. He wasn't ashamed of it. He was proud as fuck of those two girls." He ran his gaze over me slowly.

My stomach dipped, even in the midst of this, I wanted him.

"Never seen a man so in love with someone, never seen what I felt for you inside of somethin' else. He went home to see them halfway through my tour. Could not stop talkin' about it."

He finished the smoke and lit up a new one.

"Then he came back. He didn't say a word. Something about the way he looked told me not to ask. Something was gone. Somethin' that made every single guy in my unit afraid of him."

Liam looked to the pool.

"He never looked at the pictures anymore. He was still best at what he did. But became the best at worse and worse things."

He turned back to me. "Wasn't 'til later that I found out he'd choked his wife so bad she'd been in hospital. Did it because she forgot to iron a shirt. A fucking shirt."

He shook his head as if to shake out the memories. The futures he likely imagined when he heard that story.

"I left because it's dangerous to be near me," he said. "Because I didn't trust myself around a world like the one I came from. I had to patch into the Sons, because here, I can feed my beast, hurt the right people. If I came back to you, I would've hurt the wrong ones." He got up and still didn't look at me.

He just walked away.

An hour later, we hit the deadline.

And we road back.

To damnation.

CHAPTER EIGHTEEN

AS MUCH AS I was sure Liam wanted to ride hard and fast to get back, we stopped in Texas again. I wasn't sure if it was out of care for me or because even he, as strong and badass as he was, couldn't ride for twenty hours straight through three states.

So we stopped at a hotel.

Slightly nicer than the other two we stayed at.

We were silent as we checked into the hotel. Well, I stopped being silent right after we got our keys and turned toward the elevator.

There were people in the lobby, waiting to check in. The fact that the hotel was nicer meant that we got looks for Liam's cut, tattoos, and the fact our luggage consisted of two Walmart tote bags.

That didn't bother me.

People who looked down on you were already below you.

No, what bothered me was a woman, well dressed, older, just the type you would expect to get drunk on gin and tonic at four in the afternoon and insult her housekeeper.

She was staring. At first, I thought it was because of the riffraff that I was sure she tagged us as. But it became apparent *exactly what* she was staring at.

Liam didn't seem to notice. Then again, Liam didn't seem anything. He had his scary, cold and dangerous biker mask on. But only I could see it. Everyone else just saw the scar.

And this woman was staring.

I. Was. Done.

I walked up to her and she narrowed her eyes at me as if she were expecting me to rob her in a hotel lobby or something. "Excuse me, how old are you?" I demanded.

She blinked rapidly. "I don't think that's an appropriate question," she snapped, recovering and jutting her chin up in the way asshole rich people did to try and make themselves seem important.

I laughed. "Well, you know what I don't think is appropriate? It's a woman with your advanced years and obvious thoughts of superiority staring at someone like she has the right to. Because I see you think money can buy you a lot, but it obviously doesn't buy you class."

"Well, I—"

I held up my finger. "I'm not done," I interrupted. "You remember that we're staying in this hotel. When you fall asleep, you remember that. And maybe next time you encounter someone that doesn't look exactly like you want them to look, you won't *fucking stare*."

I turned on my heel and walked out.

Liam followed me.

He was no longer wearing his mask.

"WHAT DID YOU WRITE?"

I glanced up. "What?"

Despite the slipping of his mask, Liam and I still hadn't spoken since we arrived in the hotel room. Well, apart from him informing me that he was leaving to get us pizza.

He didn't ask me what I wanted, he already knew what I liked.

What I liked on my pizza, how I took my coffee, that still hadn't changed.

I no longer felt uncomfortable in the intimacy of that.

While he was gone, I decided to write in the journal he was now nodding to, standing in the doorway, holding pizza and a six-pack.

"In your notebook. I can't imagine that you have a lot of things to find yourself grateful for today."

That wasn't true. I'd reached five.

1. *I am inhaling and exhaling.*
2. *Liam is alive.*
3. *I have a nephew.*
4. *I have a happy and healthy family.*
5. *I finally know the truth.*

I HAD no idea why I let him see it. I'd never let anyone see this. Though, I wasn't sure if that meant anything since no one but my therapist knew that I kept this diary.

Liam put the pizza and beer down and took the notebook from me.

He stared at the paper for much longer than it took to read it. Then he put it down.

"You're grateful that I'm alive?" he said, voice almost a whisper. But a man who spoke like Liam didn't whisper, he had a low, thick rasp.

The smallness in his tone hurt me. I didn't hesitate to cross the space between us and cup his face the same way my mother had earlier today. "Yes, Liam. No matter who you came back as, I'm glad you're alive. I tried to lie to myself and say I wasn't. But I'm a journalist. I'm trained to spot lies. And that's the biggest one of all. That even in the middle of this pain and misery, I feel joy that I'm standing in front of you right now." I stroked his scar. "That I'm touching you," I whispered.

He put his hand lightly, hesitantly on my hip. "I didn't use to feel anything about being alive," he said. "I didn't feel anything but shame. I tried to build a life as far away from what I could've had with you so it would be like I really was dead. And it suits me. As much as I fucking hate to say that to you, I couldn't live any other life. I couldn't have come home. There would have been one day you forgot to close the kitchen drawer or got the wrong brand of yogurt and I would've done something so ugly and destroyed the beautiful life I didn't deserve." His hand tightened on my hip. "Destroyed the beautiful woman I didn't deserve."

"I know," I whispered.

I didn't like the truth of what he was saying. But no one really liked the truth. *The truth was a bully we all pretended to like.* Never had I gotten that quote from my favorite book like I did now.

His eyes moved over my face, something working between us. Something weaving through the air, now we had cleared the space with the truth earlier today. Something pivotal.

Because I'd told myself that once Liam told me the truth, I'd be forced to make a decision. I'd imagined the decision itself would be some pivotal, climactic moment, like in the movies with all that sad music, it'd probably be raining and it would become a defining chapter in our story.

But the decision was small, *blink and you miss it* type small. It was me packing up that Walmart bag and getting on the back of Liam's bike. Something about the way he looked at me sitting on it told me if I didn't get on, he'd just drive back, leaving me with only the vision of his cut and I'd never see him again. He was giving me an out.

I didn't hesitate.

I got on.

And he drove off.

No rain.

No climatic moment.

It wasn't a chapter in a story.

It was barely a footnote.

But it would define the way it ended.

And here we were, in a hotel room, one last night of just us before we went back to the club for whatever ending awaited us.

This was the moment.

The pivotal one. Where we made declarations. Promises that would be broken.

But he stepped back.

My hands stayed suspended in the air for a beat.

Liam moved to open the pizza boxes, pass me a beer.

I took it wordlessly, the smell of pepperoni and mushrooms filled the air. Our favorite. The one food that we both liked the same way.

We ate in silence, I forced the pizza down even though my stomach was churning. The beer went down much easier.

"You want to ask me shit now?" he asked, putting the pizza away and giving me the last beer. I was outdrinking him.

"What shit?" For once, I didn't actually have any more questions.

No. That was a lie.

I had a lot of questions.

Like, *do you still love me? Is this going anywhere? Will you give up the club for me?*

But they were not the questions even someone like me asked.

"For your story. You're still writing it, aren't you?"

The words were a blow. A dumping of cold water into my psyche. The story. What brought me here, what drove me for the past decade, I'd all but forgotten about the story because I was too busy thinking about *our* story.

Liam obviously wasn't.

I cleared my throat. "Yeah, sure, of course. I'm still writing it."

Something moved in his eyes. Disappointment?

But I had already transitioned myself into my old skin, the journalist mode that I used to feel so comforted, so insulated in. Now it was just cold. Ill-fitting.

I moved to the Walmart bag, rifling through to find the one thing I'd had on me while I'd been scaling the clubhouse wall. I didn't pack a toothbrush, but a small tape recorder, I'd shoved in my pocket. Maybe I was still a journalist.

"Do you mind if I record you?" I asked.

He shrugged in response, lighting up the smoke that reminded me of yesterday's that didn't matter. It didn't matter that the room was nonsmoking, I guessed. He didn't ask me if I minded the smoke. I wasn't sure it was because he didn't care if I minded or if he knew I'd come to crave it, despite what it did to his health. We were bad for each other's health, no matter what.

I didn't need the recorder.

I had one with me out of habit. Much smaller than the one I started with over ten years ago, green, afraid, heartbroken. Not unlike today. Maybe the only thing that had changed since then was the tape recorder. Maybe that was the horrible truth I'd been trying to ignore.

What if I was exactly the same as the girl with the tape recorder and a broken heart all those years ago?

I had the tape recorder out of habit. I took it—or a much bulkier version—everywhere in the Middle East, Africa, Asia, Europe. Because a lot of my interviews were facilitated by translators, who couldn't always be trusted to give me exact translations. Sometimes it was because they thought they were being helpful, saving time, or saving face from seemingly fatal faux pas. But all of my questions where intended the exact way they came out. Before I left, I made sure to study the culture of the region I was reporting on relentlessly. Even if it meant reading on a turbulent and crowded flight into an airport with a safety rating that would've closed any American contemporary.

I knew what background and manners dictated exchanges wherever I was in the world. Most of the time I respected such things, as all visitors and reporters alike should strive to do. But other times I was required to surpass culture in order to obtain the truth. I had to deliberately subvert social norms in order to get the right answer.

And the right answer almost always came from a place of anger.

But my translators didn't know that.

Mostly they knew I was a Western woman, coming somewhere she didn't belong, asking questions she couldn't possibly understand the answers to.

Other translators had different intentions, whether they be for ill or for good—in their eyes, it was always for survival.

That's why tapes were crucial.

I could listen to them later, attempt to translate them with rudimentary knowledge and a shitty internet connection or send them back home to my trusted experts—a lot of whom replied with translations peppered with opinions. Whether it be humor at the 'balls I had for a woman' or others who berated me for asking questions that could get me killed.

I was under no illusion as to what kind of questions I was asking Liam.

The switching on of my tape recorder had nothing to do with language barriers. Harvard scholars or linguists weren't likely to be fluent in outlaw.

It wasn't for that, no.

I just wanted to hold whatever piece of Liam I could in the small device. So I could carry him around with me when this was nothing more than another yesterday.

I turned the tape recorder on.

Liam looked at me expectantly.

I ran through the questions I should've asked in my head. The questions that would give me the story. The questions that would push Liam and me farther apart, back to our respective corners as reporter and outlaw.

It was the smart thing to do to ask the questions. For my career. For my sanity.

I turned off the recorder.

Liam watched me, saying nothing.

I hated how he watched me.

I hated how he could make the simple human habit of staring seem like a sexual act. Hated that my panties dampened, that my nipples hardened, that every part of me responded. I hated that it was something more than sexual. A lot more.

I hated that I wanted him to stare at me like that for the rest of my life.

"I need to ask you something," I said.

"Thought that's what we were here for," he replied. "Though since you turned off that," he jerked his head to the tape, "I'm guessing it's off the record."

"With us, nothing's ever off the record," I said.

He only nodded once.

Plus, I didn't want to have the opportunity to reply to what I was about to ask him.

"What was...do you...is it," I stammered on my words like a kid out of college in their first interview.

Liam was patient.

Kept staring.

"Breathe, Peaches," he said. "You can ask me anything. I won't protect you from the answers, as much as I want to."

I took a breath. "The other night when you..." I trailed off. *Cried in my arms. Showed me Liam wasn't dead. Started to make me fall in love with you all over again.* "Broke the door," I said lamely. "Was it..." I trailed off again. I should've been asking whose blood he had on his hands. But it didn't matter. Once blood became a stain, it no longer mattered. Blood needed to be fresh for it to matter in the news industry. And there was the fact I didn't care whose blood it was. There was something I cared about a lot more. "The drugs," I said. "Is it something you do often?"

His eyes changed as if I'd caught him off guard. I guessed he expected me to ask about the blood too. About the club, about the silent war that was dead bodies and bloodstains. "Not often," he replied. "Well, not anymore. When I first got here, I smoked because it numbed me. Physical pain from my injury, but more than that too. I was weak at the start. Could handle the physical, not the emotional. Got stronger. Stopped smoking. Stopped doin' shit that would numb me because I realized I deserved to hurt. To feel every inch of that shit for what I did to you. To my family."

A tear trailed down my cheek. "And that night?"

"I was a coward again. I couldn't face your pain. I couldn't even fuckin' *look* at something you had to *live* with for *fourteen years.*"

His words were weapons, even though I knew he wasn't

using them that way. But everything was a weapon with Liam now.

***

THE SLIDING DOOR opened and closed, but I didn't move, didn't falter my gaze from what was in front of us, even if it was just houses and fast food restaurants. This was the last time I'd wake up in a room that wasn't inside a biker clubhouse. The last morning things between Liam and I would even be just the littlest bit simple.

Liam sat down beside me. Didn't touch me, didn't pull me into his arms as he used to do in a life before.

"I used to love being alive," I whispered. "It didn't start with you, though the romantic side of me would love to say that it did. But it didn't. For as long as I could remember, I was just a happy person. I stared at the world in wonder, ordinary things never ceased to amaze and delight me."

I tried to reach for all those moments.

My cloudless skies.

"A sunrise. A sunset," I said. "The way the air smells before rain. An old couple holding hands on a park bench. Every day I fell in love with the world a little deeper." I glanced to my side, where Liam was watching me, in jeans unbuttoned and no shirt.

I swallowed roughly.

There were scratches on his torso from my desperate need for blood last night.

"And then I met you," I said through my desire. "I didn't think I knew a love so deep, it amazed and delighted me more than the whole world could." I gritted my teeth and tore my eyes from him. I couldn't look at him for what I was about to say.

"That day, that moment I found out, I lost it. Brutally and immediately. That love for the world was gone." I squinted at the horizon, yellow, orange, faintly blue. "I didn't even want to die. Because a part of me was already dead. A part of me that loved the world. Maybe, if you had come home, that part would've inevitably died with some other disaster, but I don't think so." I sucked in a rough breath, twisting the fabric of his tee between my fingers. "Because losing you wasn't a disaster. I don't even think there's a word for what that was. And I've tried to find it. A word for it."

As a journalist, I was supposed to know all the words for suffering, to use them creatively, in a way to make the biggest impact on the world. I did that. But I couldn't do it for myself. A word hadn't been invented for what I felt.

"I stopped searching for what made me love life," I whispered. "I hate you for taking that from me. And now, since I've been here, in your ugly, brutal and violent world, I hate you for giving it back to me. It didn't happen immediately. I didn't even notice it. But I love a sunrise again. And that's because of you."

He was staring at me now. In that way that made me want to come out of my skin.

I stood so I could sit in his lap. "I know that you think that you're bad for me. And maybe you are. Maybe I'm bad for you. Maybe we're the worst for each other. But you made me love sunrise again."

His arms flexed around me. Then he kissed me.

CHAPTER NINETEEN

One Week Later

"I'M BUYING TAMPONS, ELDEN," I said looking at the store. "If you want to come with me and know just how heavy my flow is, be my guest."

Never did I think the man in front of me was even capable of a blush or that I'd be able to make him do it. He'd likely seen all kinds of violence and death, yet here he was blushing in the face of *tampons*.

Men. They could handle war but not women's menstruation.

"Be quick," he all but barked, brogue rough to cover up his embarrassment.

I smiled all the way to the feminine hygiene aisle.

All the while going through the week since we'd arrived back. I sensed that Hansen was not pleased with our impromptu field trip, considering I barely saw Liam apart from when he crawled into bed with me late at night. He fucked me in the darkness.

He whispered things to me in the darkness.

We were living a life that neither of us were meant to have.

And it wasn't beautiful.

But I had more than three things on my list for the entire week.

So I was thinking of that simple thing and not the other thousand complicated things that were going to come soon.

Until a man in a cheap suit approached me while I was reaching for the Tampax and trying to dissect the fact that I was disappointed that I had my period. Not because that meant Liam and I couldn't have sex. He showed me just how unafraid he was of blood.

I blushed at the mere thought of it.

And I blushed at nothing. Definitely nothing to do with sex.

But never did I think I would be comfortable having sex at this time of the month. I always thought it would be uncomfortable and messy.

It was messy.

But it sure as shit wasn't uncomfortable.

It turned out that I was not only unafraid of blood but turned on by it.

"Caroline Hargrave," the man in the suit greeted.

I grabbed hold of the box of tampons before I turned to him. He didn't even blanch at the box his eyes touched for a second. Points to him.

"Detective," I replied, taking in his slightly weathered but not unattractive face. He didn't have much in the way of muscle underneath his suit, but he had a gun and authority, which surely made him feel like he could bench four hundred.

He raised his brow. "That obvious, huh?"

I smiled tightly. "I wouldn't be too hard on yourself, I'm more perceptive than most people."

He folded his arms, casually, like he always had conversations with women he somehow knew the name of while she had her biker guard outside the door and holding a box of tampons.

"Ah, yes, most people are not world-renowned journalists," he said.

I didn't act surprised. Because the fact that he approached me, knowing my name, when I was alone told me everything that I needed to know. "I'm not world renowned. You're flattering me, and men don't normally flatter women without an ulterior motive." I regarded him. "Mostly that motive is to sleep with them, but I'm guessing detectives don't approach women in the feminine hygiene aisle, already knowing their name and their job with the purpose of getting a date."

He chuckled. The sound was nice. Easy. Which had me on edge. Maybe I was so used to hard, to ugly that I didn't know how to be around well-adjusted people.

But I had a feeling about this not unattractive—if poorly dressed—detective, who was not put off by tampons and had an easy laugh.

I was usually spot on with my feelings.

"Smart, and not one to mince words," he observed. "I'm not trying to pick you up, but you're making me reconsider that."

The line was smooth, and somehow not creepy.

But it felt wrong.

Just like his smile and light eyes.

I didn't have this instinct regarding the law before all this. I didn't generalize them. In my line of work, I'd seen a lot of shitty cops do shitty things. Abuse their power. But cops were people, and there were a lot of shitty people in the world, it was just statistical that some of them would be given a badge.

I'd also seen cops who didn't start out as shitty people, but a flawed justice system, long hours and seeing the worst of humanity on the daily ground them down to lazy, cynical and jaded people.

There were still good cops.

Just like there were still good people.

We just didn't hear about them as much.

The man in front of me had all the signifiers of a good cop and a good person, but I didn't like him.

Maybe I was inheriting the Sons of Templar's uneasiness toward the law just like I was adopting their lifestyle in a way that a reporter shouldn't.

"I'm not looking for a date," I said in response.

He continued to smile. "I guess not. The Sons of Templar keep you pretty busy, don't they?"

I clenched the flimsy box in my hand. "I don't like what you're implying."

He shrugged. "I'm not implying anything. Just stating a fact."

"A fact that you've got knowledge of because of surveillance," I countered. "Who are you with?"

He reached inside his jacket to show me his badge.

"DEA, Detective Rickens," I said, reading it. "In addition to being a world-renowned reporter, I've got a hell of a memory. For names. Faces. Badge numbers. You know, just in case anything to do with this is untoward."

He put his badge in his jacket. "Nothing untoward here. Just curious as to what a journalist is doing so heavily involved with an outlaw motorcycle gang that does not take kindly to rats," he said.

"Club," I corrected without thinking. "They're a club. Not a gang."

He smiled wider. "Ah, so you're obviously fond of the *club*. The fact they've kept you around shows they're fond of you." He paused. "I wonder if they'll be so fond if they found out that you were writing a story on them."

I narrowed my eyes. Was this guy for freaking real? "What do you want from me, Detective?" I said instead of replying to the open threat.

"I just want you to know, that you can make a statement at

the same time as writing a story." He glanced outside where Elden was leaning against the door of the SUV he drove me in. Liam had made a directive that I was not to be on anyone's bike but his. I didn't fight him on it.

I was done fighting with him.

"I'm not interested in making a statement, that's the whole point of being a journalist, I don't take sides." I tried to move and leave him standing there surrounded by tampons, but he moved to block my way.

"Ah, but it looks to me that you've taken sides," he said, no longer smiling. "What would that do to your stellar reputation as being one of the fairest journalists out there?"

I gritted my teeth. "You're brave," I said instead of replying to that.

"For going after a criminal organization that spans the country and who we suspect to be running weapons illegally throughout the country? That's justice, ma'am."

"No, that's not brave. Nor is it justice, by the looks of the way you're going about it. It's stupidity. What's brave is you walking up to me, seeing what I'm holding in my hand, obviously using your detective skills to deduce what time of the month it is, and with prior knowledge of me facing off with men much more intimidating than you, and with all of that information, you still decide to threaten and accost me. You deserve a medal for that, Detective."

On that, I pushed past him and went to pay for my tampons.

"NO WOMEN IN CHURCH," Claw growled as I flung the door open, somehow skirting the prospect that had tried to stop me doing so. It's not like he had much time to react when I all but jumped out of the moving car and rushed into the clubhouse. I'd intended to go to Liam, but the doors to church were closed. So I did what I always did when men shut themselves in a room to discuss things and tried to bar me from the conversation, I bowled right in.

All of the men stopped whatever they'd been talking about to put their hands on their guns and prepare for a threat. Even though there was no way a threat was just going to waltz through the door with all the security they had.

"Well, since the 19th amendment granted the women the right to vote, we've been in the cabinet since 1933, have been able to serve in the military, allowed autonomy over our own bodies when we got birth control in 1960, we've been in space since Sally Ride went up there in 1983, I think we can say that my vagina isn't stopping me from stepping into any place I want," I shot, raising my eyebrow in challenge at the men in the room.

My gaze touched on Liam, the corner of his mouth turned up in amusement or appreciation, I wasn't sure.

"I was threatened today," I said.

Liam lost all amusement.

He prowled over to me. "What the fuck?" he hissed, glaring at Elden. "Where the fuck were you?" he demanded. He didn't wait for the answer, he snatched my upper arms, searching my body for something.

"I said I was threatened, not assaulted," I clarified.

That didn't make him let me go. "Fernandez?" he hissed.

"Nope," I replied.

He froze. It was bad enough when a threat they were expecting made it through their defense, these guys didn't do well with the unknown.

"This one was on the other side of the law."

The air in the room turned wired.

Liam let me go. He turned to Hansen. "Whose radar are we on?"

Hansen clenched his fists. "No one's."

"If I may?" I interrupted.

Hansen's eyes widened slightly, but he nodded for me to speak.

"I know it's meant to be clandestine and I'm not meant to actually *know* this, but you're currently engaged in a war with one of the biggest human traffickers in the world," I said, stating the obvious. "And you're engaging in this was as any outlaw would, with killing, torture. And surely he'll do the same. Because he's an outlaw too." I paused, looking from Liam to Hansen. "But he's also a monster. One that has connections with other monsters inside the law."

I thought on the intel I'd gotten from my contact. The details that had disturbed me when I thought I couldn't be shocked anymore.

"He's brought down people before," I said. "Using the various tools at his disposal. Some of them disappear. Some appear drugged, naked and for sale. Some get put behind bars for charges real or made up. Some of those people are guilty of crimes. It's easier to frame someone when they're guilty." I shrugged. "It could be coincidence that the long arm of the law has finally gotten hold of you around the same time a man who owns half of the world's leaders has decided to take you down. But I don't think so."

"No, there's no such thing in coincidence in this world," Hansen muttered. "Fuck," he hissed.

I swallowed, the weight of what I was doing finally landing. I wasn't proving myself exactly wrong about what I'd said to the detective—I was no longer an observer, I was taking sides.

Shit.

I looked to Liam.

Then my mind spoke of its own volition. Or maybe my heart.

"I've got sources in the DEA," I said. "I can press them, see if they've actually got an ongoing investigation on the books or if this agent is going rogue."

Hansen looked stunned for about half a minute and then he nodded once. He looked to Liam. "I want you calling Wire, see if he can find out who this piece of shit is—"

"Wire doesn't need to do that," I interrupted. Eyes on me again. "Detective David Rickens—45628, the first five letters of his Agent Number."

Hansen's mouth twitched and he looked to Liam. "Well, get him to look that fucker up, check his finances. See if he's dirty."

Liam nodded once, eyes on me.

Hansen focused on me. "Appreciate this, Caroline," he said, voice genuine. "Club appreciates it."

I nodded once. "Don't mention it." And I really didn't want anyone to. Because it was a reminder of how far I was falling.

Right into the underworld.

LIAM FOUND ME LATER, after he'd presumably called Wire and found out whether the detective was dirty.

Claw and I were playing poker again.

Regular poker, not strip poker like he'd been so intent on.

And I was beating him.

Bad.

"Again," he grumbled as I raked in a stake of ones.

I raised my brow. "Seriously? What are you going to do when you don't have any singles to tuck into thongs later on?"

He scowled.

But he was beaten by another man advancing on me, not just scowling, but glowering.

Liam didn't even speak, he just grabbed my upper arm roughly and yanked me up.

"Hey!" I protested as he didn't seem to be perturbed by the tightness of his grip.

I didn't fight because it was useless, and Liam was obviously determined to yell at me about something.

Liam never yelled before.

Now it was his default.

I folded my arms as he slammed the door shut. "I'll have you know that you just interrupted a really fucking great winning streak, so this better be good."

His features were contorted in fury. "*Good?*" he repeated quietly. "No, I'd say this was not fucking good. You were approached by the law today, fuckin' threatened. Threatened because you were protecting the club. Then you came back here, into church, not only told us everything about this fucker down to his badge number, you went and played fuckin' poker with Claw."

I frowned at him. "How is this something for you to drag me across the room about?" I demanded. "If this is some crazy protective stuff, you're stopping that right now, I'm allowed to play fricking poker with another man, Liam. Macy is busy, I didn't feel like watching a movie and I can't exactly go on a walk."

"It's not about the fucking poker," he hissed. "It's about the fact you protected the club and you lied to the law, you went over the line."

I frowned. "What line?"

"The line that separates you from us," he yelled. "The line that keeps you safe, keeps you out of this fucking shit."

I scowled back at him. "If you hadn't noticed lately, I'm about knee deep in this fucking shit."

"No. You were here for your story. Now—"

"No Liam!" I was yelling now. "It was *never* about the story. Even when it was about the story. You need to stop fucking demonizing yourself and this club. Trying to tell me how bad you all are. I've seen bad. And you're not good, but you're not as bad as you pretend to be either.

"Look at our backs," he hissed. "Look at our fucking *patch*."

I did as he asked because the authority, the danger in his tone overruled any strong rational thought.

"You see wings on those cuts, babe?"

He didn't wait for me to answer.

"No, you see the reaper. We're not fucking angels. We're death. You're so fucking familiar with death, you treat it like some old friend."

"Yeah, I do," I agreed, matching the anger in his tone with my own. "I have to be familiar with death, and it was you that introduced us. I had to stare at it every day, regardless. So I thought, maybe if I learned to look it in the eye the way it was staring at me, maybe it wouldn't be so bad."

"And did it work?"

"What the fuck do you think, Liam?" I hissed.

He didn't answer. Instead he snatched my neck and kissed me.

He ripped off all our clothes.

CHAPTER TWENTY

"CAROLINE," Hansen greeted me with five pale, angular, muscled and very well-dressed men beside him. "We have some important guests here tonight. I assume you'll take care of them?"

I nodded, figuring they were Russian even before they greeted me in heavy accents. I knew it because they spoke Russian before they spoke in English. They talked about how it was a shame I wasn't showing enough tit. Then placed bets on who would be fucking me tonight.

With or without my approval, apparently.

I wasn't overtly worried, mostly because of Liam's murderous gaze from across the room. It was foolish to feel protected by him, but I was making a lot of foolish decisions lately.

The fact he drove me home from the bar every single night and spent the rest of it fucking me into oblivion told me that the Russians weren't going to get their chance.

I smiled and got their drinks, not letting on I understood them.

It wouldn't pay to start a conflict with the men I guessed were responsible for supplying the Sons of Templar with their main source of income.

Plus, I was a witness. I wasn't meant to interfere.

Even though I'd already done that two days ago with the detective. And it turned out I was right, he got a deposit into his account from an overseas company a month ago. The month that he reopened the file on the Sons of Templar, New Mexico.

Fernandez was trying to bring them down from both sides of the law.

It was closing in. I could feel it.

And I didn't think the presence of the Russians that joked about raping me meant anything good.

IT WAS toward the end of the night, when vodka had loosened their tongues that I heard it. Most of their talk was centered around women. That was disturbing.

But not the most disturbing thing.

It took everything in me not to react when I heard it. I continued putting away glasses and pouring vodka like I wasn't hearing them discuss the end of The Sons of Templar.

They moved away when they were done to share a beer with the men they planned on having killed.

It was then that I calmly walked to the bathroom in the back, locked the door and vomited.

After emptying my stomach, I rinsed my mouth and regarded myself in the mirror. I was a journalist. It was not my place to take sides. It was the exact defining quality of my profession. Identity. Objectivity.

But I was lying to myself if my objectivity went out the window since I came face to face with Liam.

I had a decision to make. Let this war play itself out, stand on the sidelines and watch it do so. Record the story.

Or insert myself into it. Step onto the battlefield and choose a side.

LIAM DIDN'T EVEN GIVE me a chance to speak when I got off the bike, the rest of the club had ridden with us, all of them staying till close, which was unusual. Sometimes Claw and Elden stayed with Liam. Blake was usually passed out on the table before he woke up, found a club girl and disappeared. But I guessed the Russians meant business.

No. I knew they did.

Liam took off my helmet, brushing my hair from my face. "We've got church, Peaches," he said softly. "Club business."

I nodded. I didn't speak.

I watched them filter into the room and the door close.

I stood in the middle of the common room for twenty seconds. Fighting with what I'd heard, what that meant I should do. It meant I should do nothing, that I should go back into the bedroom and log it into my laptop, let the story unfold without any more of my meddling.

Then I burst into church.

"They're ripping you off. The Russians." I blurt it before I realized what I was doing. I'm traveling outside of the role that has assured my survival and journalistic integrity for well over a decade.

Hansen held up his hand to whoever is behind me, likely about to drag me from the sacred room. "How do you know that?

"Because they said it plainly, right in front of you all," I replied, not sure if I was impressed or disgusted at the fact they were as brash as to talk about the fact that they were fucking the

Sons of Templar over while they smiled and slapped their backs, sharing beers with them.

"You speak Russian," Hansen surmised.

I nodded once, surprised that they didn't at least speak rudimentary Russian. They'd been working with the Russians for years. But that was men for you. "Not fluent, but close enough to know that those weapons they're supplying you with are faulty and they're getting paid a lot more from a man named Miguel to make sure you sell them to city gangs and use them for personal use. I'm guessing selling faulty guns to street gangs won't make you many friends."

Curses sounded from around the table.

Liam said nothing, did nothing, just stared at me.

"I thought you were only here to bear witness, not get involved," Hansen said instead of swearing or promising murder like the rest of his men had,

He was keeping his cool, nothing but a single twitch of his finger betrayed his fury.

"I thought so too," I replied honestly, unable to give him an answer as to why I hadn't just scribbled the findings down in a notebook, waited for a story to come from them.

No, I knew why. Because whatever story that came from this knowledge would be likely stained in blood. Most stories were stained these days, blood, oil, dirt. But blood would've been certain if the Sons of Templar sold a street gang bad hardware.

Or if they tried to fight the aforementioned street gang with that same hardware.

Smart, exterminating a large chunk of the enemy without lifting a proverbial finger.

Hansen looked to Liam who was still glaring at me. Then his eyes went to Hades. He gave him a single nod.

Then his eyes went to me.

"You're goin' with him."

Liam burst out of his chair. "Like fuck she is," he yelled at Hansen.

To his credit, the president didn't have an outward reaction to this outburst. "She is. She needs to see what happens when she decides to stop bearing witness. She needs to be involved in this."

"This blood is not on her hands," Liam seethed through gritted teeth.

"It is," Hansen replied. "Whether or not you like it."

Hades grabbed my arm and took me out before Liam could do a thing.

Hansen's words followed me all the way down to the basement where he killed five Russian arms dealers.

I WAS SITTING on my bed—our bed, Liam's bed, Jagger's bed —eating a peanut butter sandwich when he burst through the door.

I'd been expecting this.

My peanut butter sandwich was history when he ripped me up from my cross-legged position.

He didn't hesitate to manhandle me brutally. And my body did not hesitate to respond carnally, despite the situation. Despite the fact I'd just seen five men die. And they did not die pretty. But then again, death was never pretty.

"Do you have a fucking death wish?" he asked. He accused. It wasn't the first time he'd asked the question and it wasn't the first time I'd wondered the same thing.

I didn't flinch from his glare, though the anger was as foreign as the scarred face it was worn on. I'd seen him angry plenty. But this was something different than that. More than that.

"No," I replied. "That's the opposite of what put me here. I wasn't chasing death. I was chasing life. I was looking for a way to feel alive when I felt like I'd been buried along with that empty coffin of yours."

He flinched.

I didn't react.

It was spiteful and we were meant to be past that.

"Maybe that's why I was chasing all of it, all the danger. I was looking for a way, looking for something to replicate the way my heart beat when I was near you. When I was yours."

He clutched my face. "Babe. You've always been mine."

I smiled only because it hurt so much to do so. "No, I'm not. Not now. Not ever again."

I pulled myself from his grip and walked out the door.

Or tried to.

He yanked me back. "No," he hissed. "We're not doing that anymore. We're not slinging as many shots as we can get in and then abandoning each other. We're talking about what you did tonight. What you fucking saw." His anger rippled slightly at the end, giving way for sorrow.

I sighed. He was right. It was childish, saying the most hurtful things I could and then running away. Maybe because I wanted him to chase me.

"I'm not some delicate flower, Liam," I said.

I really wanted to call him Jagger, I wanted to show him that he wasn't Liam to me anymore. But I couldn't do that. He would never be anyone but Liam to me, no matter how hard he tried. No matter how hard we both tried. "I've seen things, maybe not as much as you've seen. I've done things too, definitely not as much as you've done, but enough to make sure I'm not shocked by violence or death. Or pain. You can't protect me from that now. Especially since you were the one who exposed me to it first."

"You're mine," he hissed, snatching my neck—not at all gently—and yanking me to him.

"I'm not your fucking property," I snapped back, trying to

struggle out of his grip and ignore the fact my panties dampened at the onset of his violence.

I was not a woman turned on by violence. By ownership. By brutal men with brutal souls.

I wasn't that woman.

Except I was.

"You *are* my property," he said, without letting go, if anything, his grip tightened. "Everyone is someone's property, Peaches, whether they know it or not." He yanked my neck, so I was flush with his body. "And you fucking know it."

I did know it.

In my bones.

In my ruined soul.

Even in the mind I'd been so intent on convincing it wasn't so.

"We both might not want it to be this way, but it is this way. I can't change that. I can't change you bein' in the alley that night, or you making the decision to come into the club. And even if I could, I don't think I would. An honorable man would. But I'm not him. So I wouldn't change it, if that damns me, so be it. I've done a lot of damning things in my life."

I struggled with elation with his words and utter dread. I wanted to belong to him. I already knew I did, but it was stifling, terrifying, when I knew every day he got on his bike he might not come back. I could watch five Russians die ugly, but I couldn't keep watching that.

"I need some time off, a vacation," I whispered.

Liam frowned. "From what?"

"This!" I yelled, gesturing between us before I began pacing.

He stared at me pacing, not moving anything but his eyeballs to follow my jerky movements. "You can't take some time off from being in love."

I stopped. Froze. We hadn't said that's what we were. Hadn't admitted it to each other. But it was the truth. And he was bullying me with it. "You did," I whispered. I wanted the words to come out sharp and barbed, an accusation to cut through his skin. I wanted to wound him. Whether I was physically unable to do so or if I didn't have the energy, I wasn't sure. "You took almost fifteen years off, Liam."

His eyes stopped moving and then his body was across the room and I was in his arms. Harsh. Not comforting. Painful.

That's what his grip was now.

That's what *he* was now.

"No," he rasped, the single word violent and grating. "I took fourteen years off from everything *but* that. There wasn't ten seconds I took off from loving you."

My heart thundered in my chest. My ribs fractured. My panties were soaked. "Prove it," I demanded.

And he did.

I WAS BABYSITTING.

Macy and Hansen hadn't had a night to themselves in what I guessed was a long fricking time, in between the whole club being destroyed, then having to rebuild it, then having a brand-new baby, a toddler, then going to war. It didn't leave much time for date night.

And I found myself wanting the cold, ruthless and fair president to have time with his warm, kind and funny wife. I felt something coming, something bad, though you didn't exactly need to be clairvoyant to see that something bad was coming. They deserved time together, time to do something borderline normal, like go to a movie, out for dinner or just fuck each other's brains out on their kitchen table without worrying about a crying baby.

So I was at their house, holding a baby that most definitely wasn't crying and was the most beautiful little human being I'd ever encountered, second to my nephew. Their toddler was asleep in his little bed, I'd exhausted him by playing cops and robbers all evening, probably not the most appropriate game, but whatever.

I had an escort, of course. I couldn't figure whether it was because Hansen still expected me to run, to rat, because he didn't trust me alone with his children, or because he was worried about someone striking while he wasn't there.

I didn't think about it. Because I was holding a beautiful baby. I was somewhere that wasn't a biker clubhouse. In fact, I was in a beautiful home in the middle of the desert. Cluttered with photos, and odd fantasy paraphernalia and decorated in boho chic. Everything about it was the home that I wished I could have. A place that was warm. A place that had roots. That seeped my personality from the walls.

But I didn't even know what kind of decorating style I had.

I was pretty sure I didn't have one.

None of my previous apartments had much but the rudimentary household items and furniture, as I was never there long enough to waste money on such things.

And then when I moved back home into a condo just outside of town—because I couldn't stand being within town limits, let alone at my parent's house—my mother and sister had taken over the decorating and I didn't have any say in the matter. I didn't want a say. Because seeing them fighting happily over which cushions would go with my sofa again filled me with warmth. I was making them happy, for once, instead of filling them with worry.

So I let them create my home.

And it was warm. It was tasteful. It was both of their personalities—my mom's old school Southern Elegance and my sister's slightly stiff WASP style—meshed together in harmony. There were even photos too, like Macy's, but with fewer men in leather cuts.

But it didn't feel like mine.

It didn't feel like me.

But that made sense, because I didn't feel like me.

My phone rang and I glanced down, smiling, wondering if my sister's ears were burning.

"Linny! I've been calling you all week. I wanted to see if you can make it back for Archie's christening."

"Christening?" I repeated.

Sure, we were raised in a God fearing, church going town, but my parents never really pushed religion on us.

"Why are you saying it like that?" she demanded. "Do you want Archie to be in baby limbo if anything happens to him?"

My stomach lurched at the mere thought. "Don't say things like that," I snapped. "Nothing is going to happen to him."

She tutted. "Of course not. But I'm getting him christened. I've already got the gown."

I rolled my eyes. "Well, if you've already got the gown, you're all but trapped."

The baby made a sound, cried out a little, then settled. But my sister's ears heard everything, and now she was a new mother, she was likely attuned to such things.

"Is that a *baby*?" she demanded.

Shit.

"Yeah." I moved the baby slightly in the crook of my arm. I probably should've put him to bed, but I needed the comfort right now. "I'm babysitting."

"That's better than stealing a child from the hospital," she deadpanned.

I muted the TV, rolling my eyes. "Yes, and if the babysitting gig fell through, that's exactly what I was going to do."

"Whose baby is it?" she demanded.

I bit my lip. I couldn't exactly tell her it was the president of the motorcycle club who were—kind of—holding me captive while I wrote my story on them. Oh, and that the president of that motorcycle club was best friends with a man named Jagger, the boy she knew as Liam. "A friend's," I said.

"A friend's?" she repeated. "You have a friend that you know well enough that they trust you with their *baby*?" There was only a light amount of teasing in her voice and an ample amount of happiness. Hope.

My sister had a lot of friends. She always had. Head cheerleader, prom queen, sorority sister...all that. And now that she was married to a successful banker, she was one of the ladies in the top tier of the social circle. She lunched. Headed charities. She had friends. Some of whom were vapid and superficial, but a lot of whom were kind and genuine. I knew it bothered her that I didn't have the same thing.

"Or they don't know me well enough to trust me with their baby," I joked.

"Seriously, Linny, you have friends there?" she asked, tears leaking into her voice. My sister was also a crier.

I looked around at the photos. Of Macy and Hansen. Of the club, past and present. "Yeah," I whispered.

I heard delicate sobs over the phone. "Oh, Linny, that makes me so happy." She paused. "But does that mean you're settled there? In Arizona? That you're not coming home?"

My stomach sank at the reality my sister was unknowingly thrusting in my face. Me, who lived in reality, who thrust it in other people's face, and did it for a living.

Since we'd come back from Castle Springs, since Liam and I had become...whatever, I didn't think past the next five minutes. I was living just like an outlaw, not looking too far into the future, not beyond my next orgasm at least, and hoping I'd survive.

But there was an end here.

Though some may stretch on for a long time—wars always ended. For better or for worse. Always for worse.

And this was gearing up for something. I wasn't stupid enough not to see the change in things, the way the men all seemed tenser every day. Something was coming.

And not only did that fill me with fear knowing that not everyone—including me—would survive it, I was also terrified at what would happen if I did survive it.

After.

Presumably Hansen would let me go.

I'd more than proved my worth.

What happened when I stopped becoming a captive?

The opening of a door interrupted that thought and I tensed automatically, holding the baby tighter to me. Heavy footfalls had me looking toward the gun that Hansen had left me with.

I knew how to use it.

I was from the South.

I was moments away from holding a baby in one hand and a gun in the other when the owner of the footfalls rounded the corner.

Emerald eyes took me in.

"Hello? Linny?" my sister called.

"I've got to go," I said. "I think I need to change a diaper."

She laughed. "Good luck. Talk soon. Love you."

I watched Liam approach. "Love you too. Kiss my nephew for me."

Liam stood in front of me, staring at me with an unreadable look on his face.

"What are you doing here?" I demanded.

He didn't answer straight away. And when he did, he didn't answer at all. "Suits you," he murmured.

"What? Annoyance?" I snapped.

The corner of his mouth twitched. "No, the baby. You're a natural."

I froze. My womb froze too. And unbidden, visions of a different life assaulted me. A life with the baby in my arms being mine.

Liam's.

I jerked myself out.

No.

That life was gone.

"What are you doing here?" I repeated, unable to even address what he just said.

He folded his arms. "Got back to the clubhouse. You weren't there. You didn't tell me where you were at."

I frowned at the accusation in the words. "I wasn't aware that I had to update you on my whereabouts," I snapped. "I may still be a prisoner, but it was cleared with the warden."

He ran his hand over his mouth. "You're not a prisoner, Peaches."

I raised my brow.

He sighed and sat down beside me, kissing the baby's head, then mine. The warmth that erupted in my stomach was painful at the simple, tender gesture.

"It scared me," he admitted, looking at the muted TV. "Not knowing where you were."

I bit my lip, stopping myself from saying that I didn't know where he was for fifteen years.

"I missed you," he continued.

I swallowed roughly.

I missed him too.

But I couldn't say that.

So instead, I watched the mute news story. A story I might've been covering, had I not been here. I knew the reporter. He was an asshole.

Then, unbidden, an old reel of the same warzone was shown, this time with a different reporter.

I froze.

Jagger's entire form tightened as he watched me on the screen.

"Why did you do that?" he asked, eyes glued to the television, frozen in horror. I wasn't sure why. It wasn't like the newsreel of me was in a particularly shocking situation. It was in the aftermath of a bombing in a small remote town in the mountains of Iraq. Seemingly random. But nothing was random.

So I'd hitched a ride out into territory my security detail refused to go into.

And I got the story.

"Do what?" I asked, laying my lips on the soft head of the baby, inhaling that perfect smell of baby powder and innocence. The scent of a clean slate.

He turned off the television. Stared at me.

I couldn't hide behind the baby anymore.

So I stared back.

"Why did you live like that?" he asked. It was more of a plea than a question. A plead for some kind lie. Some kind of digestible truth to explain this. Nothing between us was digestible. It was all poison.

I added more poison to the mix. The arsenic known as truth.

"I was so broken over you," I said, rubbing the baby's head. "But life goes on, for broken people too. Broken people most of all. In order to carry on, I had to live harder than anyone else."

He stared at me, eyes shimmering. I couldn't look away. I couldn't do anything but hold onto the baby and try not to drown in his gaze.

"Peaches," he murmured.

"You make me wish I didn't love you."

"But you do." It wasn't structured as a question, but it was. It was a prayer coming from a man who I knew had forsaken a higher power long ago.

I sighed. "But I do."

"Wishes don't come true, Peaches. There's a lot of maybes in this life, but that's one thing I know for certain. Wish you don't love me all you like, the fact that you do means everything to me."

I looked down at the baby then back up at Liam. "It means everything to me too."

And it was truth. It was both arsenic and sugar.

CHAPTER TWENTY-ONE

I WOULDN'T SAY we entered into a routine.

Because things were happening at the club that were decidedly *not* routine.

There was the fact that a DEA agent was being paid to investigate them, and they still needed to run their guns, and then there was the fact that they couldn't run their guns because they'd killed five of their suppliers.

I wondered if this was the plan after all, to make the Sons of Templar feel cornered, strike out like any other cornered animal might, with only instinct and no brain.

There was no routine with Liam and me really. He watched as I did my stretches in the morning. Sometimes I almost got all the way through them before he snatched me by the waist and took me back to bed. Or before he slipped off my panties while I was in downward dog and, well, slipped right in.

That was a way to make sure I never thought of yoga the same again.

But I'd never think of anything the same again.

Not having coffee. Because every time I drank the bitter and sweet I'd taste Liam's kiss. I'd smell the lemon disinfectant that was always present and needed in the club kitchen. I'd remember Claw coming in and snatching my bagel before I got a chance to bite it. I'd remember Liam punching Claw for stealing my bagel.

I'd remember Macy coming in and demanding I go shopping for new baby clothes with her and then torturing whatever prospect was assigned to us with hours of baby shopping and girl talk.

I sipped my coffee thinking all that, leaning against the kitchen counter. On cue, Liam looked up from his phone—he was always on it as things got more tense—and took my chin in his hands, kissing me.

The feeling was immediate, intense, and not at all pleasant. My vision blurred, images played in the forefront of my mind, images that overlaid this scene almost perfectly. As if from a memory.

But you couldn't remember something that hadn't even happened yet.

But I remembered it.

This had happened.

Somewhere.

Not in my dreams. Because my dreams didn't conjure up such cruelty.

"What?" Liam demanded, hands steadying me.

I hadn't even realized I'd swayed slightly until Liam's grip yanked me from whatever past or future I was lost in.

I blinked at the concern in his eyes. "Déjà vu," I whispered.

His eyes cleared of concern. Something else lay there.

A memory.

"I have a theory," I said, drawing lines on Liam's chest. It was a good chest. Muscular. Tanned. Not too much chest hair.

My fingers trailed through droplets of water, evidence of the fact we'd come straight from our swim to lay on the hot stones of the shore, not bothering to towel off. The sun was hot enough to dissipate most of the moisture in no time.

His eyes glowed as his hands tightened on my bare hips.

Okay, so the sun wasn't gonna take away all the moisture.

"What's that, Peaches?" he asked, voice warmer than the sun itself.

"That we have a path. Destiny," I said. "Something is laid out for us before we're even born. Or maybe as soon as we're born. As soon as we breathe air in this world. And because of a nifty little thing called free will, and because of our ignorance to this plan, we naturally veer on and off course. Life. Mistakes. Accidents. Whatever. But sometimes we line up perfectly with our course. We start walking on the road destiny had paved for us. And because it was already there, it feels familiar, like we've walked it before. Déjà vu. So, whenever we get that, it means we're walking the right line, that we're exactly where we're meant to be. Following our destiny. And whenever it involves another person, it naturally means they're following their path too" My fingers stopped. "And I've never felt it more than when I'm with you."

Something moved in his eyes, something that took away the teasing of before. But not the warmth. "Well, of course, Peaches," he murmured. "You're my destiny. Makes sense that was decided long ago."

A grip that wasn't soft like it had been in the past brought me back to the present with a jolt. Those eyes were no longer warm like the sun. They were scorching like the fires of hell itself. "So you're living your destiny," he said, voice less than a whisper. "It's a cruel world indeed if the universe decides to give someone as beautiful as you a destiny this ugly."

I flinched. "You actually think that of yourself?" I whispered.

"When I began, I was not a perfect soldier, but I like to think I was a good man. But then...it changed. I changed. I became the perfect soldier. And the better I got at being a soldier, the worse I became at being a man. At being a fucking human being."

Macy's words echoed in my brain.

"Human beings are capable of some of the most horrific things. So I think it stands to reason that human beings are also capable of forgiving some of the most horrific acts."

"I forgive you," I whispered, putting my coffee down.

He froze. "For what?"

"For everything," I said. "I forgive you. For not coming back. For leaving in the first place. I forgive you for surviving the only way you thought you could." I touched my lips to his, leaned back and ran my finger down the scar on his face. "I forgive you, Liam."

His eyes shimmered, his entire face changed, moved back eleven years for a moment. "I love you, Peaches." But then it changed back, turned feral and the gentle words disappeared because his hand tagged the back of my neck and he kissed me fiercely, brutally.

I kissed him back with the same fierceness.

He lifted me onto the counter. The coffee cup smashed to the ground. Neither of us stopped. Liam was too busy yanking at my leggings, lifting me so he could get them down to my ankles. He didn't even take off my panties, he just yanked them to the side, pulled down his sweats and entered me.

I bit into his shoulder as he fucked me, in the middle of the kitchen. Where anyone could walk in.

I would never be able to think about the kitchen counter in the same way ever again.

"YOU FUCKING *BITCH,* I have a right mind to take my daily

worry for you off my schedule," Emily greeted the second I'd picked up the phone.

I'd been avoiding her calls. Sending texts to let her know I was alive but otherwise completely ghosting her.

She'd wanted updates on the story. And I couldn't lie to her, or myself anymore. I wasn't sure if there even *was* a story anymore. Well, that was a lie, of course there was a story, there was always a story. And this was exactly the story I came for—a national motorcycle club involved in a war with an international criminal. But it was the story I hadn't come for, the one I wasn't going to publish, the one I was living.

"I'm sorry," I said, meaning it. Being around these people, getting closer to Macy, it only proved how important relationships, friendships were. Things I'd been pushing away for years.

"Of course you're fucking sorry," she snapped. I heard the click of her heels against the floor. I guessed she was pacing in her office instead of running through New York. "But I don't care, I've not finished with my script."

"Your script?" I repeated, smiling.

"Yes, I was going to say all sorts of things about you being selfish, a bad friend and things, but I can't be bothered now."

I laughed.

There was an audible pause. "You're laughing," she commented. "What's happened? Did the bikers give you a lobotomy? Have you gone native?"

I bit my lip. Had I?

She didn't give me time to answer. "Whatever, you need to tell me how the story is going, and you need to tell me when you're going to get out of there and fly up here."

"I'm not sure," I said.

"You not on a deadline?" she asked. "For the story?"

I was not a planner like Emily. But for my stories, I always had deadlines. Obviously I'd had ones other people decided for me while on contract with news companies, but when I was writing more flexible stories, I always had deadlines. To help my schedule but also to make sure I didn't get too close, too attached to the story.

"Yeah," I replied, my voice more a sigh more than anything else. "Every moment here gets me closer to the deadline. Or damnation. I'm not sure which will come first."

"Oh my god," Emily breathed, not sounds overtly concerned with my melancholy tone. "That's it. That's the perfect title for the book. 'Deadline to Damnation.'"

Nope. Not concerned.

"Emily, I'm not writing a fucking book, that's final," I snapped.

"Sure you're not," she replied with faux agreement.

I rolled my eyes. Then something in me moved. Something I didn't have control over. "I can't write the book. Because this isn't just any story. This is my story."

"What the fuck are you talking about?" Emily demanded. Are you some secret outlaw biker?"

"No, but Liam is," I whispered.

All I got was the distant street sounds of New York coming from her office window.

Emily's version of silence.

And I filled my silence.

With my story.

The fourth time I'd told it.

It didn't get easier.

"So yeah," I said when I was done. She hadn't interrupted once, that's when I knew she was really listening. "That's where I'm at."

More street sounds. I expected Emily to recover quickly, say a lot, even just a string of curse words.

But nothing.

"Emily?"

"I've got to go," she said, voice odd. "I've got a meeting."

I flinched back as if I'd been hit. I'd just told my friend some of the most damaging things that had ever happened and she had a *meeting*?"

"Um, okay I'll—" But there was nothing. She'd hung up.

I stared at the phone for a long time after that.

"CAROLINE?" Blake said sometime later, jerking me out of my stupor. I was meant to be writing. I had other freelance jobs to keep up my income, mostly opinion pieces, columns, some interviews for online blogs.

I had deadlines.

So I was meant to be working on those.

Meant to be doing anything but focusing on the fact that my best friend had all but abandoned me in my time of need. I'd heard nothing from her. Nothing. And it had been almost twelve hours.

"What?" I asked, hoping he really wasn't going to ask me to help a woman who'd gotten a kitchen utensil stuck up her...you know. It happened. I recommend he call a nurse. The longer I stayed here, the more the men forgot what I was. Especially after the Russian fiasco. I was no longer a rat. I was the resident woman who apparently men came to to get help with things stuck up their latest fuck's vagina.

"We've got kind of a situation at the gate, we're gonna need you."

I got up, desperate for the distraction I didn't even ask what it was.

But when I got there, it became obvious why Emily had been radio silent for twelve hours.

She had been on her way here.

"There!" She pointed at me through the fence. "That's my friend. Caroline." She scowled at me. "Can you please tell Mr. Scottish Steroid here that I am not some spy sent to infiltrate the club." She grinned. "That's *you*."

Fuck.

I looked to Elden. "She's okay." He didn't move, nor did his expression. I knew that he was figuring out whether he should trust me or not. Because the men might've forgotten that I was a rat when they needed help with vagina stuff, or opinions on after-shave—Claw—or invitations to torture drug dealers—Swiss—but when it came to the safety of the club hinging on my word, I was still a rat.

I waited, interested to see just how far I'd moved from my position, unsure of what I hoped for. Did I still want to be seen as an outsider? Because then that would make me still a journalist. Still kind of what I was before. Or did I want to be accepted by the club I'd become too comfortable with? Did I want to be recognized as part of the family?

I didn't have time to decide because Elden opened the gate and Emily descended on me.

Well, she didn't actually come and hug me and fuss over me like a regular girlfriend might when she had the knowledge that her friend had recently been held captive by a biker club and had her dead fiancé come back to life and then kill someone in front of her.

No, she handed her suitcase to Blake like he was a hotel porter, looked me up and down, I'm assuming hating my outfit and then making sure I didn't have any limbs missing. She met my eyes.

"We need to get fucking drunk."

"WELL," she said after a tequila shot. Her fifth.

She'd been in the building for as many minutes.

No lemon, no salt. Because she said only 'pussies' did that. She was also allowed to be a feminist and call people pussies because she was claiming the word back from the men that thought they owned it. No way they owned it, they didn't even know their way around it.

Her words, not mine.

And despite 'technically'—also her word—being a lesbian, she'd done enough research to be able to have that opinion. Mostly because Emily liked all the information to go to battle on any subject. And because Emily liked sex.

And she exuded it.

She was all curves, all hair, all attitude. And she dressed impeccably, always elegant and tasteful with a dash of slutty and tacky—her words again.

Today, to travel five hours across the country and to a biker compound, she was wearing high waisted white pants, tailored to perfection, a silk white blouse with a plunging neckline that showed her ample bosom, fine gold necklaces going down her chest. Her strawberry blonde hair was curled into loose waves down her back.

And she had on six-inch heels.

In other words, the opposite to me.

It was safe to say she made an impression walking in.

I was pretty sure every single jaw dropped when she sauntered in, ordering everyone around. To my immense surprise, Blake had acted exactly like a hotel porter, dutifully taking her designer luggage into the clubhouse for her.

"You." She pointed at Claw, who was halfway through undressing her with his eyes. "Stop staring at my tits and get me and Caroline tequila."

"You." She pointed at Swiss who was sitting at the bar,

drinking and likely thinking about depraved things he could to do his next victim. Or sexual partner. "We need those stools, and no dicks within earshot."

Again, I held my breath at the reaction these men would have to a woman they didn't know, wearing six-inch heels and class from head to toe ordering them around like servants and not treating them like sex gods like the club girls did.

But I should've known better.

They reacted exactly how she wanted them to.

Swiss moved.

Claw put two shot glasses and a bottle of tequila down on the bar.

"I think I'm in love," Swiss murmured.

"You like eating pussy?" she asked him, sauntering over to take his seat.

His eyes glowed. "Breakfast lunch and dinner, baby."

She grinned. "Me too."

"Fuck, now *I'm* in love," Claw decided.

I rolled my eyes and moved to sit beside her.

"It took *weeks* for them to decide they didn't want to kill me and now you've got them declaring love after two minutes," I said, pouring the tequila.

"We still haven't decided," Claw said with a wink. "It depends how favoring your depiction is of me in the story."

"Movie," Emily corrected. "Without seeing all of this." She gestured around the room, her eyes moved to the men, despite being a lesbian she had a healthy appreciation for the male form. "And all of that. It's definitely a movie."

"Perfect," Swiss breathed. "Idris Elba will play me."

Claw frowned at him. "Dude, you look nothing like Idris Elba."

Swiss glared back. "Idris Elba is a fucking icon and he can

turn himself into anything and anyone. And yes, I do, I'm tall dark and handsome."

"You got one of those right, and it ain't the last one," Claw muttered.

I grinned at them, they were almost kind of cute. You know, if I hadn't seen them ruthlessly torture all those people.

Emily grinned and turned to face me while they bickered amongst themselves.

"I can't believe you're here," I said.

She grinned. "Of course I'm here. Where else would I be?"

I shrugged. "When I told you everything and you just hung up, I thought—"

"I was a totally thoughtless and callous bitch and you planned on making a voodoo doll out of me?" she asked.

I smiled. "Something like that. But now I look like the bitch for thinking it."

She took a shot and nodded for me to do the same. I did, because I needed it and drinking and talking with a girlfriend was a salve to almost any wound.

"Yes, you do," she agreed. Her eyes went up and down me again, likely cursing my boyfriend jeans and simple white tank. I did have Gucci sneakers on though. I went online shopping. A girl just had to have a little Gucci in order to survive the club. And a bulletproof vest.

None of that worked with Liam.

But now I decided I didn't want it to.

"You look good," she deduced. "Not your outfit, of course, it's a fucking train wreck but you, *you* look good." She did something very rare and out of character and had me scared she was going to declare she had some kind of inoperable tumor. She reached over and squeezed my hand. "But you, you look better. Better than I've ever seen you. Not happy. But like...at peace or something."

I swallowed my tears because I knew she hated it when

women cried. "I'm in the middle of a biker war with my dead fiancé and I'm at peace."

She laughed, letting go of my hand. "Well, of course, did you expect it any other way?"

I swallowed my tequila and the words I was going to say.

I didn't expect it any other way because I didn't expect to find peace at all.

That was the real secret behind why I chased war. So I didn't have to feel the failure of never being at peace.

"COME ON, ONE MORE SONG," Emily pleaded.

Her hair was only slightly messier than perfect, her eyes were glowing, makeup still flawless. Somehow. After three hours, a bottle of tequila and somehow negotiating Claw and Swiss into not only letting us go to a karaoke bar but to come with.

Claw had even sung.

True story.

Journey, "Don't Stop Believing."

"We've done two, and it's late and Liam is back from...whatever and he's pissed that I'm not there and he's on his way."

"Even better!" Emily clapped, ushering me on stage. "He can see you on stage. I can see him from the stage, judge him, punch him when we're done, and it'll all be good."

I paused. "Wait, what? Did you just say you were going to punch him?"

She gave me a 'well, duh' look. "Of course. His story is sad and tragic and he's been through so much but also, *fuck that*. He hurt my friend, he needs to be punched." She then resumed tugging me on stage to a small amount of cheers that came from Claw and Swiss since no one else was in a karaoke bar in a small town on a Thursday after midnight.

I was drunk on tequila, with that kind of buzz you can only get with a truly special friend. The kind where you feel happy, safe and that no bad could possibly be as bad as you thought it was.

I was feeling that when the song started.

I was feeling it all the way up until the shooting started.

CHAPTER TWENTY-TWO

Jagger

HE WAS PISSED.

He was pissed that he had to go and make peace with the fucking Russians, pretend he believed their bullshit about the cousins acting on their own and not emptying a clip into the whole fucking lot of them.

He didn't of course. Because that wouldn't be smart.

Starting a war with the Russian Mob was about the last thing they needed right now. So they'd played nice, took the apology and the free guns—every single one of which were all tested—and then he got the fuck out with the knowledge that they would kill every last one as soon as the shit with Fernandez was over.

But then thinking about the shit with Fernandez being over pissed him off even more.

Because that would mean the threat was gone. Hopefully, the DEA would be off their ass and things would go back to whatever passed for normal.

That would mean Caroline would go.

He could live under all sorts of hopes and fairytales that it would work if she stayed, but it fucking wouldn't. He knew it wouldn't because asking her to stay would be asking her to give up her family. The family she'd risked death for climbing out a window. The family she'd cut herself to the bone for—almost fucking literally—without thinking. She'd have to leave them behind, or at the very least lie to them every day.

He was willing to ask her to do a lot, because he was no longer an honorable man. He would demand she never set foot in a fucking war zone again. He would ask her to live a life of violence, deaths, and being dragged into interrogation rooms by cops trying to bring them down.

He wasn't so noble to give her up if it was just that.

But it wasn't.

He'd never go back to Castle Springs. And she had a whole family there.

So yeah, that pissed him off.

Another ugly truth that was unavoidable.

The truth was a bully. Gregory David Roberts was right about that.

It terrified him. The thought of having to let her go, now he'd had her again. Now he'd had her for the first time—had those parts of her that hadn't existed before. He'd fucking fallen in love with her all over again.

And he would love her till the day he died.

And that would be a long and miserable stretch of time without her.

He arrived back at the club craving her touch, her heat, her fucking smell so he could bury himself in her, away from those truths.

But she wasn't there.

She was at a fucking *karaoke club*.

After midnight. Drunk, by the looks of her text.

While they were in the middle of a war with a man that made it clear he had no problem killing women.

He tasted acid.

And rode hard to the bar.

He arrived just in time to kill one of the men who Claw and Swiss had missed. One of the men that had opened fire on his woman.

Caroline

"Oh my god," Emily chanted, looking down at the blood gushing from her shoulder.

I put my hand on the wound calmly.

"You're going to be okay," I told her.

"I *know* I'm going to be fine," she snapped. "It's just a flesh wound. "That's not what I was talking about. This is *totally* gonna get a movie deal. If it bleeds, it leads, baby."

I stared at her under the harsh fluorescent stage lights. "You're fucking insane, you know that, right?"

She nodded. "Multiple therapists have told me, not in so many words."

"Just so you're aware."

I kept my voice even, calm. It was my battlefield voice.

Inside, I was scared to death.

Not just because we'd just been shot at while singing "C'est La Vie" by B*Witched—I'd been shot at before, but not as...personally as this. It was the fact my best friend was bleeding in front of me and I was staunching the flow. Yes, it was just a flesh wound. But it was a *wound.* On my friend. Because of the club.

And then I was even more terrified because I thought about the entire club being shot up. Everyone. Who else did they get?

Swiss and Claw had gone into full, psychopath badass mode.

They'd killed two men seconds after they started shooting. The third ran out.

Swiss had gone to cover me and Emily.

Until she shooed him away. "Go, chase the bad guy, I'm fucking fine."

He gaped at her. Checked me over. "Seriously, fucking in love," he muttered, jogging back to the bar, gun in one hand, cellphone in another.

I prayed whoever he was calling picked up.

My eyes locked with green ones.

Green, furious and terrified irises.

He ran over.

Pocketed his gun.

Looked down at Emily, then at me.

"Are you hit, Caroline?" he asked, voice cold, robotic.

I guessed I was covered in blood so it was hard to tell. "No," I whispered. "No," I said stronger the second time.

Emily looked between us, must've clocked the way Liam's shoulder's sagged at my words. I wasn't expecting it, therefore she was able to push my hand off her bullet wound, stand up and punch Liam in the face.

He definitely wasn't expecting it either, since he stumbled back and almost fell off the stage.

"Emily," I shouted, standing and bracing her as she stayed standing on wobbly legs. "You can't just punch Liam after you've been shot! What if you hurt yourself?"

I wasn't too worried about Liam, he'd surely been punched before, and he did kind of deserve it.

She shrugged and winced with the movement. "I told you I was gonna do it. I'm a woman of my word."

Liam wiped the blood from his mouth. He was still taut, tense, with that cold fear I had been feeling gripping him. "I like her," he said finally.

WE COULDN'T TAKE EMILY to a hospital, for obvious reasons. I argued this fact, but Emily was the one who fought me on that.

"Let them do it their way," she demanded. "I want to see how the outlaws deal with it."

I rolled my eyes.

Elden's mouth twitched.

The entire club had turned up at the bar.

The entire, unharmed club.

It was a relief.

They took care of the bartender, and the sheriff when he arrived. Luckily somehow our favorite detective hadn't been around.

They dealt with the dead bodies. Hansen tended to Emily with a rudimentary first aid kit since he'd been a medic in the army.

She talked animatedly the entire time, not giving off any stress over what happened.

Liam had all but been glued to my side.

But he didn't touch me.

Now we were back at the club because there was only so long you could stay at the scene of the crime even if you owned the local police force. Oh, and the small fact my best friend had a *bullet wound*.

Hansen had seemed competent with the battlefield treatment, but he said he'd call in a doctor who was in town and a 'friend of the club.' He'd given Liam some look on that, Liam's eyes had flared ever so slightly but then they went back to me.

Claw groaned. "Are you sure you like pussy? Because I swear you were made for me."

Emily winked. "I was made for *everyone*, honey. And I was definitely made to like pussy."

He groaned again.

Although Emily was still charming everyone with her brash New York temperament and sheer volume of curse words, she was getting pale and I was getting worried.

"Where is this doctor?" I demanded.

Something moved in Liam's eyes as he focused on someone behind me.

I turned and relaxed. The doctor had arrived. I only relaxed for a split second because it became apparent that the doctor had come for Emily, but the woman had come for Liam.

She was pretty. I noticed that first off and I hated the stab of jealousy that came with that. Even in the middle of the night, wearing black jeans and a tee, she was pretty.

Beautiful, even.

And she was a doctor.

A friend of the club. Who came and tended to bullet wounds in the middle of the night.

Who smiled at the members like she knew them.

"Hey," she said to me, smiling warmly.

She looked up to Liam. Then at the space between us. Understanding dawned. But she still smiled warmly.

Fuck. She was nice too.

"I'm Sarah," she said, focusing on Emily.

Emily, on the other hand, had been focusing on her since the moment she walked in. Even a fricking bullet wound wasn't stopping her checking out a beautiful woman.

"Emily," she replied, smiling. "Here I was thinking that it was such a shitty thing getting shot, but now it doesn't look so bad."

Sarah put on gloves and then inspected what was under the bloody bandage. "It's not so bad. A flesh wound. Didn't hit anything important."

"That's what I told them," Emily replied, giving me a meaningful look.

———

"OKAY, you'll have to wear a sling for a couple of weeks, take antibiotics in case of infection, see your doctor to get the stitches cut out. As long as you've got someone to see who will do it without...asking questions?" Sarah said, taking off her gloves and beginning to clean up.

I had watched Emily shamelessly flirt with her the entire time she was stitching up her bullet wound. Despite the fact she was obviously straight and in love with my...Liam.

I wanted to hate her for that fact alone. But I didn't. Because I didn't hate women for reasons like that. It was ugly and toxic and went against everything I stood for. Also because, despite the fact it was obvious Liam and I were...together, she treated me with kindness and respect. The same with Emily. And she stitched her up.

So I didn't hate her.

In fact, I felt a little pissed for her, considering her and Liam had obviously been something and he didn't say a fricking *word* to her. Didn't even look at her.

Then, when Hansen had beckoned him and the rest of the club to church, he'd moved, kissed me full on the mouth, right in front of her and said, "I'll be back, Peaches, don't go anywhere that isn't within hearing range."

And he walked off. I gave Sarah and apologetic smile.

She pretended to be focusing on stitching Emily's wound. Or maybe she was actually focusing on stitching Emily's wound. But she was a woman. And a doctor. For the Sons of Templar. I sensed that she could stitch a bullet wound and go through emotional turmoil at seeing the man she loved kiss another woman and act like she didn't exist.

"Honey, I live in New York," Emily said, answering Sarah's earlier question. "Doctors have seen a lot of weirder shit than a stitched-up bullet wound. But I'd be happy to fly you over, for a personal consultation."

I couldn't help but admire Emily's stamina.

Sarah smiled. "I think I've got my hands full with the personal consultations," she replied, giving a meaningful look around the clubhouse. "But you can always call me if you have any concerns."

Emily grinned. "I will."

Sarah looked to me. "I've just given her some pretty heavy painkillers, so it would be a good idea to get her to bed soon."

"Yes, it will be a good idea," Emily piped in.

I glared at her, mouthing 'stop.' She rolled her eyes, but her movements slowed as the drugs kicked in.

Sarah squeezed my arm.

For someone who wasn't big on human contact, I didn't have a bad reaction to Liam's ex squeezing my arm.

"You okay?" she asked. "Things like that get...heavy."

I nodded. "Yeah, I'm kind of used to heavy."

She glanced to the door. "I can see that."

She gave me another squeeze and helped me get Emily up.

"It was nice to meet you," I said, truly meaning it as I started to walk Emily toward the hall.

"It was really nice to meet you too," she said, truly meaning it.

Fuck. She was nice.

"She had nice tits," Emily murmured.

Jagger

"What do we know?" Hansen all but barked at the table.

He was tense.

They all were.

Another hit on this club, on fucking *women*.

It was not going down well, to say the least.

Hansen had three prospects along with Blake and Hades and his place. And his security was a fortress.

He was taking no chances with his wife and children.

Jagger didn't blame him.

Caroline was in the next fucking room and he was coming out of his skin thinking about that small distance. Thinking about how close it had been to *her* bleeding, not staunching the bleeding of her friend.

He wished he could kill them all over again.

Slow.

"No tats, no affiliations on the bodies," Claw cut in. He was pissed. Beyond pissed. This happened under his watch. And Swiss. They would answer for it. When Liam was sure he wouldn't kill them.

"Think they're likely paid guns," Swiss cut in. "Paid to watch, look for opportunity to hurt the club."

"Well you fuckin' gave it to them, didn't you, brother?" Jagger seethed, unable to help himself.

Swiss turned, and Jagger readied himself for the fight. But instead of shooting shit back, instead of raising a fist, he looked him clear in the eye. "I did. I fucked up. Put your woman in danger. I take full fuckin' responsibility." He glanced to Claw. "Three quarters."

"How am I only one-quarter responsible?" Claw demanded.

"You just answered your own fuckin' question," Swiss

muttered. "You have a right for payback. After church. Free rein."

Fucker wasn't kidding.

Jagger cracked his knuckles. "We'll focus on them first. Then I might decide to take it out on you."

Swiss nodded once and he upped himself in Jagger's estimation. He still wanted to kill him for putting Caroline in danger, but he respected him.

They talked more about the men. But there wasn't much to say. Fernandez was being fucking smart. Farming out enemies across the board so they didn't have one to focus on. If they didn't strike hard and quick, he'd pick them off.

Hansen brought down the gavel. "I want double the guard tonight. No one is getting through." He looked to Jagger. "Emily good?"

"She's more than good," Claw answered for him. "She's my soulmate.

"She's gay, man," Swiss said.

"I'm persuasive."

"You got a pussy?" Swiss deadpanned.

Claw sneered. "Of course I don't, I'm eight inches of pure man."

"Well, then you're eight inches outta luck."

Everyone chuckled, brushing off another close call.

Hansen dismissed them, likely anxious to get back to his place.

Jagger went out, intending on finding Caroline, to yell at her or fuck her—he wasn't sure yet.

But then he saw Sarah, leaning at the bar, nursing a beer.

Fuck.

He'd forgotten she was even here.

He was an asshole.

She was a good woman. A great lay. Well, nothing compared

to Caroline, but great. She was funny. Kind. Not dramatic. Handled blood well.

Perfect Old Lady.

In another life.

He'd treated her like shit, he realized that. Not intentionally, he never intended on treating good women bad, but he always seemed to.

He sighed and made his way over to her, even though he needed to see Caroline, touch her, catalog every inch of her skin.

He owed Sarah this conversation.

"Why are you here?" he demanded, he hadn't meant for his voice to sound as harsh as it did, but he didn't have much control over it. Fuck, he couldn't even touch Caroline all night because he was scared of what his hands might do.

Sarah's eyes shimmered and it hit him in the gut. Because he still felt something for her. If Caroline hadn't existed, what he felt for her might've been enough. But Caroline did exist. And he felt everything for her.

"I thought I was coming for a big romantic gesture," she said. "I arrived last night. Was looking for the nerve to come here." She smiled. "She's it, right? The one that got away."

He tensed. Fuck, this was a good woman. And he was hurting her. "Something like that," he said. He owed her a better explanation.

Sarah took that shitty explanation. "I like her," she declared. "I get it. I could even see it. Whatever it is between you." She finished her beer, hoisted her medical bag onto her shoulder. "I knew that when we were together I wasn't getting all of you. I resigned myself to the fact I'd never get all of you, because the parts I got, were pretty great. I thought I was getting enough. But seeing you with her, I realized I didn't even get an inch of you. Not really." Her words weren't bitter, or accusatory.

"She gets all of you," she whispered. "And I like that for you. For her."

"I'm sorry," he croaked, throat raw.

She cupped his face. "Never apologize for finding someone who you look at like that. Even to me. I'm a big girl. I can handle it."

"You're a good woman," he said.

She stepped back from him. "I know." She winked. "Take care of her. Don't let her get shot at again."

"Don't plan on it."

In fact, he'd do everything within his power to make sure that didn't happen. And if it wasn't within his power, he'd figure out a way to make it so.

Sarah nodded. Waved. And walked away.

If Jagger was a better man, he would've watched her walk away, thought about what she gave him, what they had.

But he wasn't a better man, so she'd barely turned before he half ran toward his room.

Toward his Peaches.

Caroline

The door opened abruptly, as I expected it too.

I had got Emily off to sleep in one of the empty rooms. The drugs were strong, but not strong enough to complain about the thread count of the sheets. I'd watched her for a few minutes, made sure she was okay, set the meds and water beside her bed and left.

I already had an alarm set for two hours so I could go and check on her.

Church had run long enough for me to do all that and to slip into one of Liam's tees. I snagged it out of the laundry hamper and put it on, inhaling deeply.

He stood in the doorway as I sat cross-legged on the bed, inhaling his tee.

I didn't even have it in me to be embarrassed.

He closed the door, kicked off his boots and his cut, all silently. Watching me the entire time, as if he were afraid I'd just disappear if he looked away.

I knew the feeling.

I still got it sometimes.

He sat down on the bed beside me. Still not touching me.

"She's pretty," I said finally, unable to stand the silence, and the scenarios my mind was playing for me. "And nice," I continued. "And a doctor. Smart." I thought about the steely glint in her eyes. "Strong too," I commented.

Liam didn't say anything.

Why wasn't he saying anything?

"She was something to you?" I choked the words out.

His eyes were gemstones. Cold. "No," he said. "She might've been able to be something to me. If I had it in me to want that."

"What do you want from me, Liam?" I sighed. That's what my voice was, my existence in this moment, a big sigh. I was too tired to carry my anger around anymore.

"Everything," he growled. "I want to scoop you out, everything you have, take it for myself, own it. And I know that's not what you're meant to say, that's not what love is meant to be. But I don't give a fuck. I'm beyond being honorable. So despite the fuck I have nothing to offer you, I want everything from you."

His words weren't pretty or tender. But they worked. Because they were real. Ugly. And exactly what I needed.

CHAPTER TWENTY-THREE

"WHERE ARE YOU GOING?" I demanded when I walked into the common room to see Emily dressed, in heels and a fucking power suit, complete with sling, her small Louis Vuitton suitcase beside her.

She was tapping on her phone. "Do you not even have Uber in this town? How does anyone get anywhere? Horse and carriage?" she demanded.

At this moment, Swiss chose to come from the kitchen, wearing nothing but low-slung sweats.

It was safe to say he was hot.

And had abs so defined water could run through the ridges like a creek.

But we already knew that.

Emily glanced at him too, with none of the female appreciation I was gazing at him with as he walked past. She clicked her fingers at him. "You, you can give me a ride to the airport." It wasn't a request.

I wasn't sure what surprised me more, that Emily clicked her fingers at a biker who I'd witnessed chop the digits of a man who didn't give him the right answer to a question, or that Swiss stopped, smiled and replied, "Of course darlin'."

"You will not be taking her anywhere," I snapped.

He grinned at me. "Sorry, Claw will be absolutely heartbroken when he wakes up and she's gone. He may even cry. I'm definitely taking her somewhere."

He walked away, presumably to get dressed, or to untie whatever girl he likely had tied and naked in his room. I knew this because he left his door open often.

I directed my glare to Emily. "You cannot leave, you were *shot* last night," I hissed.

She sighed. "It was a flesh wound, Caroline. I have meetings today that I only would've been able to cancel had I been paralyzed. Even then, I would've at least been expected to be on video call."

I blinked at her. "You can't be serious."

She nodded. "It was in my schedule to come here for one night, make sure you were mentally sound, punch Liam and then leave on the ten a.m. flight. I've accomplished everything I needed to. And I'm not going to let something stupid like a little cut disrupt my schedule."

"It's a *bullet wound!*" I screamed. I was not usually this hysterical. The cool, calm and collected reporter was getting further and further away, the longer I stayed here. The longer I let myself really care about people.

Emily moved her gaze from me to something behind me. I knew it was Liam, because he didn't hesitate in moving to yank my back to his front. Not because I was in tune to his presence or I could 'feel' his stare—that was bullshit. We were getting back to that thing from before. That thing whenever I was in touching distance, he touched me. And when I wasn't within touching distance, he moved to make sure I was. Last night was obviously an exception to that rule.

"You need to take her back into that room and give her a good fucking," Emily informed Liam.

Liam didn't miss a beat. "What if I've already done that?"

And to be fair, he had done that. Very good. And very bad.

"Well, you haven't done it good enough because she's getting all hysterical and dramatic," she shot back.

Liam chuckled into my neck. It was a sound I hadn't heard before. It was beautiful. Warm.

But I wasn't feeling beautiful or warm right now.

"It's not dramatic to not want my best friend to get on a flight *hours* after she was fucking *shot*," I hissed. "Tell her, Liam."

I waited for my...whatever he was, to have my back.

Silence.

I craned my head to glare at him. "Tell her," I said through gritted teeth.

He sighed. "Can't do that, babe."

I yanked myself from his grip. "And why the fuck not?"

"Because it's safest for her to be back in New York, you know, where she's not getting shot," he replied, voice tight. Something moved behind his voice. I was too pissed, at both of them, to inspect it.

"For the record, I'm not going because I think I'm going to get shot again, if I had it on the schedule, I'd stay," Emily cut in. "I had fun."

Of course she did.

I looked between the both of them. "Fuck." I pointed to Swiss, who emerged from the hall with a woman who had red welts on her wrists and a dreamy smile on her face. "Do not leave without me," I demanded. I looked to Emily. "I'm coming with you to the airport.

She nodded. "I'll allow it."

I didn't look at Liam as I stomped back into our room to snatch a pair of jeans and a tee.

He followed me.

"I'm not talking to you," I snapped, yanking off my leggings and putting on my jeans.

He watched me dress with hungry eyes and a hard jaw. "Maybe you should think about going with her," he said once I'd gotten my tee on.

"I am," I replied, slipping on my sneakers, thinking wistfully of my collection at my apartment.

"No, not to the airport. To New York."

I froze. Looked up. "You want me to leave?"

He moved to grab my hips. "No, I don't fucking want that. But I don't want you to stay in the middle of all of this."

I tried to jerk out of his grip. He wouldn't let me.

"You want me to run. Leave you," I accused.

He let me go to pace the room. "You were fucking *shot at* last night, Caroline!" he yelled. "You know what I'd have done if one of those bullets had hit you?" He stopped pacing to look at me, cold and calculated. "I would've eaten one myself."

My blood turned to acid. "Don't you dare say that," I hissed, my voice was shaking, either from fury or fear. "Don't you *dare* use that as a weapon against me. That's low, Liam. Even for you."

He realized what he'd done too late. "Peaches."

"No, Liam," I said, turning from him and striding out, forgetting promises we'd made about walking away from each other. Breaking promises was kind of our thing now. I'm sure there would be a lot more to break before this was all over.

"CALL ME WHEN YOU LAND," I demanded.

Emily rolled her eyes. "Sure, because how else would you know I arrived safely, it's not like a major airline crash would be on the news or anything," she shot dryly.

I flipped her the bird. My vision blurred a little. "Thank you for coming, Emily. You're a good friend."

"I know I am," she replied.

I grinned. "And modest."

"I took a bullet for you, sister," she said, waving her sling. "I'll be dining out on this for *years*." Her expression turned serious. "Make sure that's the only bullet aimed in your direction. I can't have a shooting mucking up my schedule again."

I nodded. "I'll do my best."

"Do better," she said, voice almost soft. "I'm very glad Liam has come back from the dead much hotter and deadly and from what I can tell, better in the bedroom. I'm even glad he's in an outlaw motorcycle club because no man with a normal job or life-style would've been able to hold your attention or stop you from getting off to war zones. But I'm also not at all glad that you're not jetting off to a warzone. You're in the middle of one." She paused. "Just don't get shot, okay?"

A lump emerged in my throat. I swallowed roughly. "Okay," I agreed.

"Good." Then she snatched her suitcase and walked away.

Emily didn't do goodbyes.

"FUCK," Swiss muttered as blue lights flashed behind us.

We'd barely left the airport, which was an hour away from the clubhouse, since their town was nowhere near large enough to boast even a small airport.

And this town did not boast a paid off police force.

Not that Swiss was even speeding.

"Don't say anything," he commanded as he pulled over.

I gave him a look. "Really? You think this is the point I'd decide to tell the authorities I'm being held prisoner?"

He scowled in response.

The window opened.

"Fuck," I hissed.

Because Detective Rickens was at the window.

"Can you step out of the vehicle, please?" he asked politely. He smiled at me. "Both of you."

Jagger

"They should've been here hours ago," he hissed, pacing the room. He shouldn't have let fucking Swiss take her, it was under his watch that Caroline got *shot at* last night. But she'd stormed out and he'd been frozen by the pain in her voice at his careless words that he didn't have the wherewithal to fucking chase her. To follow her on his bike.

He couldn't have even done that if he wanted to. Not after last night. There was no more slow, he'd called Rosie to let her know that. She'd agreed. There was a plan to ride out to Amber in the coming weeks, get a battle strategy ready, figure out how the fuck they were going to smoke Fernandez out of whatever compound he was hiding in.

There was talk of sending in a couple of their best, Gage, Bull, Brock, Jagger himself. But that would not be as satisfying. But it would make it over.

It needed to be fucking over.

"We've got prospects, Blake and Claw out on the road, checking," Hansen said, expression blank but his eyes were worried.

Because they both knew that Caroline and Swiss had not stopped for fucking ice cream. Neither of them had answered their phones. At first, Jagger had reasoned that Caroline was rightfully ignoring him. Then it became apparent that it was something else.

"Yeah, we know they're not on the fucking road," Jagger

hissed, unable to get the last conversation they had out of his mind. It made him sick to his stomach. He'd fucking *threatened* her with going through his death again if she got hurt. In a situation he'd fucking forced her into.

What kind of piece of shit was he?

"Wire should be calling us any second with the trace on the cellphones," Hansen said.

"I can't lose her, brother," he admitted, inches away from losing it. "I can't fucking lose her."

Hansen's jaw went hard. "This club is not losing anyone else. She is part of this club."

And she was. He wasn't quite sure when it happened. But she was part of it. And he wasn't sure if that made him happy. She was part of his club and that meant she couldn't go out with her friend without getting shot at. Without getting her friend shot. She couldn't drive to the airport without running into...whatever the fuck she'd run into. How much more was this war going to take from him? Was it really going to take away his second chance with Caroline?

Was he really going to let it?

Hansen's phone rang.

Jagger's head snapped up as he watched him open it. His president betrayed nothing. "Thanks, brother." He hung up. "Got them. They're at the Liesten police department.

Caroline

"This is bullshit," I said as Detective Rickens placed the third shitty cup of coffee in front of me. "I haven't done anything wrong."

"You have been fraternizing with a known criminal organization, that gives me the right to hold you for questioning for up to twenty-four hours," he said, sitting across from me.

"No, you do not have that *right* when you are being paid by a *criminal* to harass people instead of doing your job," I told him flatly. "The second you do that, you lose all of your rights in my eyes, and hopefully soon, the US government's eyes."

His eyes flared at the threat in my tone.

"You didn't think we wouldn't do some investigating of our own, Detective Rickens?" I asked him. "Taking bribes from a man who is responsible for the majority of human trafficking in this world is a lot worse than hanging out with a few bikers."

He had paled, but he seemed to recover quickly, tapping on the iPad he was carrying. He set it down in front of me.

It was a dead body. Full of multiple gunshot wounds. It was unrecognizable. He swiped again. More of the same.

"A few bikers who a responsible for this," he hissed. "These people were killed with AK-47s, guns bought illegally from a criminal enterprise who calls themselves the Sons of Templar. These people were not criminals. These people were gunned down because of money, because of being at the wrong place in the right time."

I leaned back. "Plenty more people are killed daily with guns obtained legally," I replied. "You're not going to get me by appealing to my morals or heartstrings. I know enough about death and suffering to know where the blame and the blood lands."

He leaned forward. "Well, the blood is going to land every-where. That's a promise you keep fraternizing with these men." He stood. "I'll leave you to think about that."

"I'm entitled to a phone call," I told him. Despite the fact I was furious at Liam for what he'd said, I knew the fact we'd been gone for hours with no contact would be playing havoc on those volatile emotions of his. It would be playing havoc with the club. I guessed that was the point.

Detective Rickens smiled. "I'll get right on that."

Then he walked out.

Jagger

He did not know what to expect when he made the hour drive to the police station in thirty minutes.

He definitely did not expect to see Rosie leaning against a black SUV illegally parked outside, grinning and waving at him as he pulled up.

Hansen and the rest of club—save who were back at the clubhouse with Macy, the kids, Linda and all other people at risk—pulled in behind him.

"What are you doing here?" he demanded.

She pushed up her aviators. "Hello to you too. I'm here because I'm awesome, and you'll agree in three, two," she trailed off and glanced at the double doors leading into the police station.

On cue, the door opened and Jagger lost his breath as both Caroline and Swiss walked out, flanked by an asshole in a cheap suit.

Rosie quirked her brow at him. "Ready to announce my awesomeness?" she asked.

He didn't answer because he was taking the stairs two at a time to reach Caroline. He expected her to flinch away from him, he deserved that, but instead she all but jumped into his arms. He exhaled for the first time in four hours. Then he inhaled Caroline.

He wanted to hold her for much longer than the handful of seconds that he did, but he had to do something else.

"You good?" he asked softly, holding her neck and inspecting her face for any signs of distress.

Nothing. Of course. As he was coming to learn, apart from when yelling at her friend for getting on a plane after getting shot, she was calm and collected in most situations. It made him proud.

It also hit him deep. Because to remain calm in these kinds of situations, you have had to not only have experience in chaos but in things much worse.

She nodded. "Oh, I'm fine. I have a lot of new material for the way the DEA laughs in the face of US citizens constitutional rights," she said, glancing to the man in the shitty suit.

Fuck, he loved her.

He faced the man, who was sizing him up, then the entire club staring him down.

He had to hand it to the fucker, he didn't even look worried. Though he should be. He should be very fucking worried.

"You take my woman again without cause, you're answering to me," he informed him calmly.

"You threatening a federal officer?" the man asked with too much smugness.

"You bet your ass I am," Jagger replied, grinning at him, slinging his arm around Caroline's shoulder and walking them away.

Rosie was chatting with Hansen when they approached.

"Ah! The jailbirds!" she greeted Swiss and Caroline. She grinned at Caroline. "I'm Rosie, you haven't had the pleasure. But let me tell you, I'm a big fucking fan. I think you're awesome and my best friend is going to fucking lose it when I tell her that I met Caroline Hargrave. She's a journalist too. Lucy Brooke."

Caroline smiled back. "I've read her stuff. She's talented. I hope I get to meet her one day."

Something about the way she said that hit Jagger. Was she planning on staying? Even in the middle of all this?

"Oh, you will," Rosie reassured her. Rosie said it as if she knew something everyone else didn't. And she knew what everyone else didn't about most shit, but not about this.

"We've got you to thank for getting us out," Caroline continued.

Rosie nodded. "I've got connections. And, as Jagger was just saying, I'm awesome. I'm like Kim Kardashian, serving justice all over the damn place, with a great ass to boot." She looked to Swiss. "Dude, I was so fucking sure you'd have an outstanding warrant in at least five states. But nothing. You disappoint me."

He grinned. "I bury my bodies deep, darlin'."

She rolled her eyes.

"How did you know they were here? And how did you get them out?" Hansen asked.

"I know because I know things. I got them out because I know people. And because from the shit we've been finding, we knew Mr. Crappy Suit was on the payroll. I only came to say hello, meet Caroline." She glanced to her phone. "I didn't exactly tell my husband I was going on a road trip. And he's got the baby so he can't exactly chase me this time. Children come in handy."

She opened her car door, giving Hansen a more serious look. "Shit's gonna get real soon."

He raised his brow. "Shit is already real."

She nodded. "You're not wrong." She eyed Caroline again. "We'll see you soon for a drink, or a car bomb or whatever."

And then she closed the door and drove off.

"I like her," Caroline declared.

Jagger chuckled, someone finding it to be easy and real, tugging her into his shoulder.

"Let's go home," she murmured into his cut.

Home.

Fuck.

CHAPTER TWENTY-FOUR

Jagger

HE KNEW something was wrong when he walked in.

Really fucking wrong.

He'd felt it in the pit of his stomach since Caroline had said she wanted to go 'home' yesterday. He felt joy so strong that it turned to acid. Because he wasn't deserving of that shit. Caroline wasn't. She shouldn't be in the middle of it. She was. She didn't resent him for it. Or for the last fucking fifteen years. She didn't run, or act like she was a captive anymore. She called what he thought was her prison her fucking *home*.

And that soured inside him, even as he rode with her pressed to his back. Even as he fucked her hard all night, held her in his arms as she fell asleep and fucked her again this morning.

He'd left her with coffee and her laptop, she had stories to submit. Not *this* story, they'd stopped talking about that.

Hansen had called him into church.

Just him.

He felt the sour crawl up his throat.

It was time for it all to fall apart, because he'd just gotten everything he wanted back together.

"What?" he demanded, eyes on the way Hansen was holding himself, the way his hand shook ever so slightly as he reached for the bottle of Jack in front of him at the head of the table.

"They hit another club," he said after a long gulp. "Likely while we were distracted trying to get Swiss and Caroline out. Fucking diversion tactic."

Jagger swallowed acid. "Who?"

"Nevada."

He took the bottle his president handed him. Took a long gulp himself. "How many?"

"All of them."

He'd expected as much. But even expecting the death blow, it didn't stop how it killed.

He took another swig.

Handed the bottle back to Hansen.

Neither of them spoke for a long time.

There was nothing to say.

Words were weak and useless in the face of something like this. The only thing that worked were bullets and blood.

"He's trying to send a message. Show us we can't beat him in a war," Jagger said finally.

Hansen nodded once. "That's what he's tryin' to do. But we're gonna prove that we can win any war."

Jagger clenched his fists. "We fight him, we're gonna lose more brothers. Forgone conclusion."

Hansen nodded again.

"We might not walk away from this."

He spoke the truth that was already written all over his brother's face. This life, they knew every time they shrugged on their cut it could be the last time. It was something they accepted, it was the price they paid.

But this was different. It wasn't a question of if a Son was gonna die, it was a question of who. Death didn't discriminate just because you were wearing a cut, a wedding ring, because you had kids at home. That didn't mean shit.

It cooled Jagger's blood, that certainty. Any brother in the ground was a hit. Was a travesty. But the brothers who had finally gotten some kind of taste of sweet after choking down bitter for all these years...they were at risk of dying bitter. Whether that be a grave for themselves or for their families.

Jagger could not let go of the premonition that this wasn't going to end without ripping families apart. Without ripping the club apart.

"We're ridin' out to Amber in the morning," Hansen said by answer.

"Everyone?" He thought of Caroline, where she would fit in this. She was in danger now. Real fucking danger. This was going to get uglier. No one was safe. Wars they'd had with rival MCs had cut them. But other MCs knew the score, knew to keep the death to men who wore cuts, who *chose* this shit.

Fernandez was different. He didn't play by the rules. He looked for the deepest blow. And it was obvious that the deepest blow was the women.

He needed to send her home. Away from this shit. But that didn't guarantee anything.

"Everyone, Caroline included," Hansen said.

"I'll get her a car, get her back to Castle Springs," he said instead.

Hansen shook his head. "You know that can't happen, brother."

Jagger clenched his fists. He did know it couldn't happen for all the reasons that Hansen was thinking of in regards to the club. He also knew it couldn't happen because for all of his honorable intentions, he couldn't let her go. Caroline was under his skin in a different way than she had been when they were kids. He couldn't fucking breathe without knowing she was safe. Without knowing she was at least unsafe with him. She was his. He was turning into a fucking caveman and he couldn't help it.

"Yeah, that can't happen," he agreed.

Cade

"We can settle this like gentlemen, can we not?" the other voice at the end of the phone asked.

Cade clenched his fists. "We both know that neither of us are gentlemen," he growled.

Fernandez laughed on the other end of the phone. "Ah, outlaw honesty, I do so enjoy it. It's refreshing."

"Cut the shit, you asshole," Cade snapped. "We both know this is war. We both know there's only one way this ends. It's not with a truce. It's not with surrender. It's with blood, it's until one of us is left standing."

A pause on the other end of the phone. "I understand that what I thought might be a profitable friendship for us both turned into a minor problem I was content on ignoring, with a warning of course, until your club pushed it, so I have no choice but to take action."

Cade's blood boiled. "You slaughtered men and women. That's not a fucking warning. And everything you are, everything you've done, makes it impossible for you to be nothing more than another unmarked grave."

"Ah, so confident," Fernandez mused. "Arrogant. You don't know what you've gotten yourself into. I don't relish a lot of bloodshed. So I will give you one last chance to enter into a deal."

Cade didn't say shit.

This wasn't a deal with the devil.

He'd already made plenty of those.

"I thought as much," Fernandez said as he took Cade's silence for what it was, 'fuck you' in every language.

"You want this to be over. You fight like a fucking man."

"This isn't the Wild West, Mr. Fletcher," he said, his voice smooth and cultured, as if that made him somehow fucking better. "There are no duels at dawn."

"You gonna take the coward's way out and send more men in to murder my men when they're not expecting them?" he spat. "'Cause that ain't gonna work. We're all expecting you. We're ready."

"I expect you are," Fernandez sighed. "You want your war. You've got it. Be careful what you wish for."

He got dead air.

Slammed his fist down on the table.

He stared at the empty table. At the gavel. It had been brought down many times, and it had continued through all the shit the club had been through. Even the darkest of times.

He'd been so fucking sure that the darkest times were behind him, that maybe even outlaws, even devils deserved sunshine.

The massacre of the New Mexico and Vegas charters were proof that they didn't get sunshine.

And now this fucking phone call.

He. Was. Done.

Brock walked into the room. He clocked his expression immediately.

"Fuck," he hissed.

Cade nodded. "Yeah."

CADE HELD CHURCH. Got all the brothers in, all the brothers

that had been to hell, not all of them coming back. He told them what was happening.

What needed to be done.

"We've got New Mexico arriving tomorrow," Cade said. He looked to Steg. "Evie good makin' arrangements for them? And the other charters who will be here in the next few days?"

Steg nodded. "She's got it sorted. Got rental properties empty. She's buying out the supermarket and liquor stores."

Cade nodded once. "Good." He was about to continue.

"I've got it," Wire said, bursting into the room, holding his laptop, his cut hanging off him and eyes twitching. Cade didn't want to know when the last time he ate or slept was. Or how many of those energy drinks he'd been chugging to stay up.

He had known how long it had been since the fucker showered, considered the smell spoke for itself.

But Wire had been working himself, literally, to the bone looking for intel, anything and everything to give them the upper hand. He was doing more grunt work than the men with guns. The way of the future, even outlaws weren't immune to a war fought primarily with keyboards.

Everyone sat straighter.

"He's coming here."

Cade froze. "In Amber?" He had the sudden urge to sprint into the common room and lay his eyes on his wife, his children, just to make sure they were still there.

Wire shook his head. "Private took off from somewhere in Europe and will be landing at an airstrip on the other side of the country. Couldn't get here for two days, *if* they hauled ass. Which they won't."

"How do you know that?" Cade demanded.

"Because they're planning on meeting us at a warehouse twenty miles outside of Amber, got an encrypted message that said to be there at noon two days from now. A minute late, they'd march into Amber. It was heavily embedded in the deep web."

Cade mused this. "They're testing us."

Wire nodded.

"This is a fucking trap," Bull cut in.

"Of course it is," Cade agreed. "But I think his promise on marching on Amber if we don't show up holds true." He looked to Wire. "He's got a big entourage."

Wire looked grim. "Yeah. A small fuckin' army."

Cade didn't react. He had his own army. The rest of the clubs riding in wouldn't get there in time, even if they hauled ass. They had families to protect, provisions to make. New Mexico would make it though. Two charters. Every one of his men was worth ten of those motherfuckers.

"We've got Southern charters riding in," Brock cut in. "But won't arrive in time," he said, mirroring his thoughts.

Cade nodded. "He knew that. He's been watchin', waiting for this. 'Cause he knows he won't win on US soil. He can't come in like he would in his territory. He couldn't face off the whole of us. So he's plannin' on hitting the home charter. Makin' an example."

"Good thing we're ready," Gage said, cracking his knuckles.

Cade nodded once, even though he wasn't sure how true that was.

Caroline

"What happened?" I rose as soon as Liam walked into the bedroom from church. I knew something was bad the second I saw his face.

He shook his head, taking my hand and dragging me into the bedroom.

The door slammed.

Yeah, it was bad.

I closed my laptop, the pit of my stomach finding a new bottom as I stood, kept my face blank and hoped that it wasn't another death. That it wasn't someone I'd come to like. To think of as family.

"Liam—"

I was cut off when he stalked forward. Something about the way he approached had me scuttling back until I hit the wall.

He didn't hesitate in boxing me in.

Nor did he speak.

He grabbed the bottom of my tee, tore it over my head. I put my arms up to let him, they were shaking, my panties were soaked.

My bra was next.

Then my jeans.

Panties.

Until I stood there in front of him, naked, quivering, terrified and more turned on than I had been in my entire life.

Liam was still fully dressed. He hadn't touched me, apart from to take off my clothes. But I felt his grip all over my body. If a stare could leave bruises, I'd be black and blue.

Slowly, with his eyes glued to mine, he knelt at my feet. I expected him to devour me with more than just his eyes, my body was crying out for it. He hadn't explicitly ordered me to move, but I was frozen nonetheless.

Liam didn't move to lay his mouth on the area that was silently begging for his attention. No, his hands gripped my hips and he rested his head on my stomach. In worship. Like a broken man finding solace.

And that's exactly what he was doing. It was the single most beautiful and terrifying moment he'd shared with me. Counting the time he'd shared all those truths. Because without speaking, with kneeling in front of me, he was setting himself at my feet.

I moved my hands down, ran them through his hair. I didn't speak. I know he didn't need that from me.

He took a deep inhale, kissed the bottom of my stomach, glanced up at me with shimmering eyes and then he moved down. Way down.

And he worshipped me in a different way.

Later, much later, he made love to me in a way that was hello and goodbye at the same time.

"IT'S HAPPENING," he murmured against my chest.

I didn't know what time it was. I knew it was dark. Hours had passed, meal times had gone unnoticed. We were feeding on each other, all of our desperate pain.

I stroked his head. I didn't need to ask what.

"We're going to Amber tomorrow morning."

I stopped stroking. It wasn't a question. And it was more than a road trip. It was riding out to war.

A war that I was well and truly in the middle of. I found myself relieved that we could stop waiting, that this thickness would finally disappear from the air.

But then it hit me. A lot of other things were going to disappear before this was all over. A lot of other people.

I pulled Liam tighter to me. "Okay," I whispered, kissing his head.

DRIVING into Amber was not what I expected. As the hub of a lot of the Sons of Templar publicity and from what I understood, one of the founding chapters, I expected the town to be rugged, lawless, just like the men that ran it.

I did not expect the quaint, seaside town that was like old America, pure, Mom and Pop stores lining the well-presented main street. Houses with yards tended perfectly. Not one chain fast food or coffee shop marred the backdrop of the town. Corporate America seemed to have forgotten to breeze through this place, snatching away everything original and special like it had with others of its kind. It reminded me of Castle Springs.

Locals looked up at the line of motorcycles with faint curiosity, most with some kind of familiarity, none of the contempt I would expect coming from the residents of a small and quiet town being invaded by bikers.

And that's what it was, an invasion. Every single patched member and prospect from the charter were in formation, two vans and another SUV behind with Macy and the kids, and Linda, who I only knew of by reputation. We departed from the town proper and into a more industrial area.

The security around the clubhouse was much the same as in New Mexico. Tighter, if anything.

I found myself nervous riding up.

Never had I felt nervous while covering a story.

But I wasn't covering a story anymore.

I was living it.

I was barely off the bike, Liam pulling my helmet off gently before I heard the thwack of heels against concrete and a throaty voice. "Well look what the surly biker dragged in."

I grinned, turning.

Scarlett was smirking between Liam and me, looking very self-satisfied. Her hair was wild curls, she was wearing a black tube top, high waisted black leather pants and black booties with a six-inch heel. "I would say I'm surprised to see you here, but I'm not." She winked at Liam.

A large man came up behind her, yanking her into his chest and kissing her neck. She melted. The strong, sassy woman *melted*. Which was understandable given the size of the arms around her and the man who was holding her.

He gave me chin lift then looked to Liam. "Church in five, brother."

Liam put an arm around my waist. "Got it."

The man everyone called Dwayne—for good reason—nuzzled Scarlett's neck. "You wanna show me what you can do in five minutes?" he asked her.

She glared at him. "No, you want to show me what you can do in five minutes. Come back to me when you've got at least thirty."

He grinned and kissed her full on the mouth with no mind of who was around. "Deal," he murmured.

Liam squeezed my hip. "You good, babe?"

I nodded. Despite the fact I was in a biker compound which looked to be preparing for war, facing the prospect of losing Liam for a second time, I was good. Kind of.

He gave me a quick kiss, only slightly more appropriate than the one that had happened moments before.

"Take care of her," he ordered Scarlett.

She rolled her eyes. "She can take care of herself. But I'll hang out with her."

We both watched the men walk away from us.

"So, should we get drunk?" Scarlett suggested.

"Definitely."

We both watched a bright red convertible enter the parking lot.

"Perfect timing," she said. "They have arrived."

CHAPTER TWENTY-FIVE

Jagger

"IT'S no secret that this grudge originated in this charter," Cade began, voice as cold as the expression on his face. He looked around the room, brothers from wall to wall, not even standing room left. Everyone listened to him. Everyone respected him. Despite the fact that his was one of the only clubs that had stopped running guns and earned legit.

For the most part.

Just because the Amber chapter didn't earn from outside the law didn't mean that they lived inside it. "You didn't ask for this war, but it was brought to your door." He focused on Hansen for a beat. "In some cases, it broke down your door, hit your clubs, destroyed them. I cannot make up for that. I will not ask you to fight a war that isn't yours."

"It's ours," Swiss cut in. "Anyone who harms a brother, who takes down a club, they're our enemy. It's our war. We're with you."

There was a chorus of agreements. Hansen included in this.

Cade nodded once. "I'm not gonna give you all false promises about glory in this war. War doesn't give glory. Or satisfaction. It only takes. I have faith in my brothers that we'll win this war. I know every single man in this room will die for the cut. For their club. I also know that some of you will die. I can only promise that for every Son that falls, we'll cut them down threefold."

"They say there are no victors in war, but they've never met the Sons of Templar."

A chorus of grunts of agreement sounded from around the table, a handful of men slamming their fists down on the smooth oak, others gripping their weapons with an excited glint like Gage and Hades, two fuckers that knew the dangers of this mission but craved the death they would be able to deal out.

But even Gage, one of the craziest and most soulless men Jagger had seen in the flesh, had something else behind his eyes, like a lot of the men in this room.

Fear.

Not for themselves.

But for the women they loved with something more than most civilians experienced.

The women, that Jagger had seen first-hand, loved the men with the same ferocity.

He wasn't a romantic man in any sense of the word. Romance died with him along with many other things years ago.

But one didn't need to be a romantic to see how these women saved his brothers. See how his brothers fucking worshipped them. And for good reason. They were something extraordinary. Something dirtbags like them surely didn't deserve, so they cherished it more than any civilian man could.

This was a war that threatened their lives—something they could all handle without blinking.

But their lives were no longer their own.

They had wives. Kids.

Families that they'd all thought they'd forsaken the second they'd put on the cut.

And a death was a blow to the women that he knew the men would do anything to protect. But they had to fight for their club. They were in the middle of a war that made them fight for their club and sacrifice their women.

It didn't sit right.

Not with Jagger.

It haunted him, the look in Caroline's eyes. The shadows in her. Because of him. Shadows that would never lighten, not in the best-case scenario. And they were fucking far from the best-case scenario now.

His stomach lurched with the thought of having someone tell her he was dead, properly this time. She'd demand to see his body. He knew that already. She would never accept anyone's word on such things.

His brothers—whatever was left of them—would refuse. Because they would want to protect her.

She would fight them. And she would win.

The sight of his lifeless, likely brutally wounded body would not only cause more shadows, it would banish her soul to oblivion.

She'd never repair.

Recover.

She'd endure, because she was strong.

But he'd put her as close to death as she'd ever come.

And he'd do anything to make sure that never fucking happened.

He envisioned himself calmly walking out of that room, away from his brothers—the men who'd saved his life, who'd become his family, who helped give him a purpose—grabbing Caroline, putting her on the back of his bike and riding. Back to that small town in the middle of nowhere, back to his family, where no one would likely trace him. There might not be anyone left to trace him. Where he'd be able to keep her safe. Where he might be able to repair relationships with his family, stitch together some kind of life that he was meant to have.

He clenched his fists.

Then he envisioned his brothers in a hail of bullets, battling for the club, he watched them fall. Watched wives have to bury their Old Men. Children grow up without fathers. Something that might not happen if he's there, another gun in the fight.

He would do almost anything to make sure Caroline did not have to feel his death again.

But what he wouldn't do was sentence another good woman to the same fate.

He would not forsake his club.

Cade

"Go home to your families," Cade said to the table. Something in Cade told him that whatever kind of piece of shit Fernandez was, he had a depraved and deeply kind of fucked up sense of honor. He was giving the Sons of Templar this one last night on the earth. With their loved ones. Family. He was giving them that because he believed this was the last night they'd have.

Fucker was wrong.

"We meet here tomorrow morning," he said. "This place goes on lockdown. Prospects at every entrance. We'll have the kids down in the basement. Women too."

Though he doubted any of the women would be locked in a panic room, his wife included. The only thing that would keep her in there would be the love for their kids. But that might be the thing to take her out, fight for them. Gwen was a lot of things, all of them wonderful, but the thing that scared the shit out of him was that she wouldn't just sit out a fight. Not for her family.

He looked to Brock. "Keltan and his crew comin' in?"

Brock nodded. "Yep. They'll be here early hours." He paused. Something moved on his best friend's face.

Cade didn't even need to hear him say it.

His fucking *sister*.

"For fuck's sake. Crawford didn't put a stop to this shit? Keep her home, safe?"

Brock grinned. "You even *met* Rosie, brother? You think Crawford's gonna let her sit out on this fight. This is her fight."

Cade clenched his fists. "No, it's ours. Her fight is to be a fuckin' mother to her kid. An aunt to mine." He was glad that his wife wasn't here to hear him say this shit, because he guessed she'd have a lot to say about that statement in regards to feminism.

He fully supported women's rights. Celebrated them, in fact, seeing what his wife had done, he knew women were stronger, smarter and fuck of a lot more capable than men in every way.

Except this way.

It was his job to protect his family. And he was gonna do it.

"Luke's coming earlier, got a meeting with the sheriff to run him down," Brock added, reading his mind.

Despite his wife's opinions on the men of the Sons of Templar and their supernatural abilities, none of them could read minds. If they could, their respective courtships would've gone a fuck of a lot smoother.

But Brock was his brother. Best friend. Second. He'd only been on his right-hand VP seat for a short time, but they'd rode together since they got their first bikes. They knew each other.

"Good," Cade said. "I want a prospect and a patch on Rosie. Lock her down, any means necessary."

Brock raised his brow. "Just two? That's seriously underestimating your sister."

Cade leaned back in his chair. "I'm not underestimating her.

I just need to slow her down." He glanced around the table. "I need volunteers."

Silence.

"Jesus, you would honestly rather walk into a battle blind tomorrow than deal with my fuckin' sister?" he asked.

Nods around the table.

Lucky actually fucking shuddered. "She's scary, man. I'm also attached to my balls. And dick. I've got a wife to fuck. And we all know Rosie's gonna go straight for the crown jewels as soon as she gets savvy to what's happening."

More nods.

"For fuck's sake," Cade muttered.

Gage leaned forward. "Let her fight."

All eyes went to their most depraved brother. It was not a secret him and Rosie had a weird connection. Cade didn't want to think too hard on it, because he knew Gage's demons were fucking deepest level of hell type shit. And if he thought about their connection, he had to entertain the thought that his sister had some of those same demons.

"Say again," Cade challenged.

"She's a better shot than half the men here," Gage said, not heeding the warning in Cade's tone, or at least not giving a shit. Gage never met a warning he didn't plow right through. "And she's got more cause than any to be here."

"She's not fuckin' going anywhere near the fight," Cade gritted out.

Gage eyed him for a long time.

"How would you feel if I gave Lauren a fuckin' gun and sent her into a situation where we don't know what we're up against?" he challenged.

Gage's normally cold face morphed with the mention of his wife's name. The only woman that he turned fully human with. Which was fuckin' funny, considering the bitch looked like a librarian and he looked like—he was—a fucking serial killer. But it made sense.

And it would be a stretch to say that Gage had changed since being married and being a father—he still killed with the same ruthless coldness, but he'd calmed some.

Which wasn't saying much with Gage.

"Lauren's different than Rosie, you fuckin' know that," he hissed. "But if the occasion called, I know my wife would be able to bear arms. That she would protect herself. Our child. This club. But that's not gonna happen. I'll make sure it doesn't."

Cade looked to Gage for a beat longer. "So it's settled. Someone volunteer for Rosie duty before I pick one of you motherfuckers myself."

"I'll do it," Swiss, from the New Mexico charter, piped in. He looked to Hansen. "If that's cool with you, prez?"

Hansen chuckled. "Yeah, it's cool with me. Just don't think you'll be smiling when she cuts your balls off."

There were some chuckles around the table, a breaking of the tension. But it still hung in the air. The eerie promise that the table would never be this full after tomorrow. That after tomorrow, there would be empty seats at this table.

But that didn't matter.

It couldn't matter.

All that mattered was there was a table left, and someone to hold the gavel. Hold whatever remained of his club together. Cade was not a praying man, but he sent one up anyway, that he would be able to hold the gavel in twenty-four hours. More importantly, that he would be able to hold his wife and children in twenty-four hours.

But no one upstairs listened to the prayers of men with the reaper on their backs. And at their heels.

Caroline

"Holy shit," Gwen, the beautiful, fashionable woman declared from across the table.

"Holy *fuck*," Amy, the equally beautiful, red-haired, equally fashionable woman corrected from beside her.

"That's like more dramatic than all of our stories put together," Mia declared. She was slightly older than the rest of the women, but also jaw-droppingly stunning. She was also a total fricking lightweight. And hilarious.

"Too fucking right it is," Bex, the heavily tattooed and sober woman beside her agreed.

"Are you okay?" Lily asked, she was the quietest of them all, Lauren after that, but it was easy to seem quiet with Amy, Mia, and Gwen at the table.

We were in the 'girls room' in the Sons of Templar clubhouse. Apparently it was a new addition since the club had undergone some serious renovations of late. They'd likely been preparing for this exact event, and Gwen had decided that in addition to rooms safe in war they'd get rooms safe from 'men.'

It was so different from the rest of the club it was laughable. It had a small bar, complete with a blender for margaritas—which we were drinking right now—pure white walls, dusty pink sofas on either side of the room, and a long white chic table with multiple chairs the same fabric and color as the sofas. Wedding pictures were framed on the walls.

It was ridiculous and awesome at the same time.

I nodded to Lily's question. "I'm okay for the first time in sixteen years." I paused. "Shit, does that make me an asshole for saying this now?"

Amy reached over and squeezed my hand. "Kind of," she agreed, winking. "But you've got to be at least a little bit of an asshole in order to survive this life."

Would I survive this life?

Would I stay long enough to survive it after the war?

"I still can't believe you got Cade to do this," Macy said, staring around in wonder. "Seriously. I'm getting Hansen to give us one." She eyed me. "We need one, right?"

We.

She was speaking like I was one of them. Like I was going to stay.

I wanted to stay.

I really fricking wanted to stay and be a part of this family. I wanted to help Macy convince the ultra-masculine Hansen to build a fricking girl cave in a motorcycle club. I wanted to yell at Blake for asking me about things stuck up a woman's vagina. I wanted to clear out Claw while playing poker. I wanted to watch Macy's boys grow into mini badasses.

But I did not want to have to watch Liam go out every day, wondering if he would come home. It was one thing trying to imagine the horror of what life would be like without him if he didn't. But I didn't have to imagine that. I'd lived it. For fourteen freaking years. And I'd thought it was hard then. I thought it would destroy me. But it didn't. Not properly. This, *this* would destroy me. I wasn't strong enough for this life.

It was that simple.

But I had to lie for now.

Because I couldn't speak the truth. I could barely think it.

I smiled at Macy. "Yeah, right."

AFTER MULTIPLE MARGARITAS for those of us who didn't have children to look after, each of the women had gone—with an escort of course—home to presumably have one last night of peace.

I was now at the bar that wasn't sleek and full of cocktail making implements. It was old, wooden, scattered with rings, and only had beer or hard liquor. I was okay with that.

The opening of a door caught my eye.

The men filtered out from 'church' with forlorn faces, with masks of soldiers I'd seen countless times. Men preparing for death.

Each of the men split off to find the women that made up their hope.

The women around me moved to go to the men who needed something living before they ventured to find death.

I stayed put.

He found me.

I didn't know if I was Liam's hope. I didn't know what I was to Liam. What I was to Jagger. I was a girl from the past, a foreign woman in the present.

"Please," I said, not even caring that the word came out as a pathetic beg.

Liam didn't look up from where he was sliding two handguns into shoulder holsters. "I've got to go." I didn't even know where he was going right now, because from what I'd gathered, it wasn't happening until tomorrow.

I moved forward, clutching his wrists. "You don't *have* to do anything," I said. "You've got a choice. A choice not to run into another war that you might not come back from. One where death is final."

He sighed. Eyes met mine. They were hard. Resolved. They were Jagger's eyes. I supposed I shouldn't have jerked with such surprise, he was Jagger now. I'd just been experiencing too much Liam. I was living in the past.

"I don't have a choice," he said, voice harder than his eyes. "This is my club."

"And what am I, Liam?" I asked, my voice a whisper. "Am I

not more important than a club? A patch? A war that isn't even fucking yours?"

He moved his hands from my grip. "Men that I considered family, men I laughed with, shared beers with, men who saved my fuckin' life multiple times, men with families, wives, kids, they were killed. Massacred. This war is fuckin' mine. Don't ask me to choose. Because I've already chosen you over the club. But I can't choose you over vengeance. That's not who I am now."

And then, Jagger slipped on his cut and walked away.

He didn't look back.

———

I WAS SITTING at the bar. The clubhouse wasn't empty.

Not by a long shot. Most of the women had gone home for one last night in familiar surroundings, before they were all taken here, locked down as the men went to fight.

Because, despite the stories I'd heard from every woman I'd met, it seemed these men still needed to hold onto the notion that they needed protection. That they could protect them.

There was also a scattering of club girls, for the seemingly dwindling number of patched members who didn't have Old Ladies.

And then there was me.

Sitting at the bar, staring into a chipped glass, for once, not staring into the past, but into the future. One where Liam didn't come back. Where I buried a coffin that wasn't empty. It was full of truth, pain, forgotten promises and a ruined past.

Sometime in my contemplation, the previously empty stool beside me was filled.

I glanced to my side to see a woman, beautiful but hard. Cold. Lines around her heavily made-up eyes told parts of her story. But the eyes themselves told more. I knew that because I'd looked into the mirror for well over a decade and saw the same eyes staring back at me.

She was dressed in a more elegant version of biker chic the club girls wore. Silver around her neck, in multiple holes in her ears. Her hands were bare but for a large diamond on her left ring finger. She was wearing all black. Tight. Lace. A bra peeking out under her sheer mesh top. Long boots tucked into tight leather jeans.

She was the biker queen...of the New Mexico charter at least. Evie, Steg's wife was also around somewhere, barking orders at people. Scaring the absolute shit out of prospects.

This was biker widow, Linda.

I knew it instantly.

I was aware that the last president had been one of the victims of the Christmas day massacre. I thought I'd been aware of all of the victims.

But I'd missed one.

One sitting on the stool beside me.

She lit up a smoke. "Guess you know who I am," she said after taking a long drag.

Her voice was husky, evidence of just how many cigarettes she'd smoked over the years. Interestingly, her skin didn't show that same evidence. Apart from the lines on her face that were natural, her skin was clear. Beautiful.

I nodded in response to her question.

She took another drag. "Figured that. You're smart enough to find your way into the club as a rat, and survive them findin' that out, figures you'll know some shit."

I didn't argue her label. In their eyes, I was a rat. I'd been called worse in the pursuit of a story.

She didn't speak for a long time, just kept smoking beside me. I expected her anger. Her disdain. I got none of that.

"Jagger," she said finally. "Came here a broken man. And

trust me when I say, I've seen a lot of men come into this club, broken, lookin' for somethin' not to heal them, but for somethin' to hurt them worse than what brought them to the reaper." She inhaled. "He had something about him that was beyond that. A hurt that scarred more than anything he wore on his face. Was curious, to say the least." She eyed me. "I see it now. You're made of tough stuff. Gotta be to walk into a Sons compound dressed in lies and lace, ready to take them down. Took balls. Doesn't mean I wouldn't have happily helped bury your body if you had thought you were gonna succeed, but I respect it. Also respect the fact that what you lost put you on a path to do things like that." She stared into space. "We go on living out of habit. Then the pain gets too much that we either have to stop the habit or start up some much more dangerous ones."

Something in her voice disturbed me.

Something in her words disturbed me plenty more.

CHAPTER TWENTY-SIX

Gwen

I WATCHED my husband kiss his daughter, murmur something in her ear that sent her giggle into the air, sweetening it.

That's what I was used to now.

Sweet.

The bitter, acidic memories of what happened when Cade and I first met, nothing but that.

Memories.

Even remembering Ian came better. With less of that soul-destroying pain that had seemed so permanent at the start. I had healed. My daughter had healed me. My son. I blinked at the man in the motorcycle cut laying a kiss on our son's head.

Both children had ice blue eyes like their father.

Their father had saved me most of all.

And I knew it was anti-feminist of me to think that. I should've considered myself the heroine of my own story. And I was.

But there was also a hero in this one.

The one, after two babies and years of marriage, still made my stomach dip and my cheeks flush when he sent a knowing and hungry look my way.

"When will you be back, Daddy?" Belle asked, her voice musical and like cotton candy for the ears.

Her first word was daddy.

Obviously.

Kingston's first word was Nigel. Our cat's name. He loved that sadistic fucker. That was the only reason I hadn't accidentally run it over in the driveway.

"So soon, my princess," Cade murmured, lifting both his children into his arms. It was an easy feat for someone like him, with muscles that had not succumbed to that dreaded dad bod.

Actually, the Sons of Templar had created their own version of a dad bod. And it was good. Well, it was good in regards to my husband being hot as fuck.

Not good in regards to my husband being hot as fuck while I welcomed new stretch marks with every new baby.

Not that Cade showed anything but appreciation for the changes my body had gone through since having kids. He had shown nothing but worship.

But still, a girl feels a little self-conscious when her husband is a biker Adonis and she's trying to figure out how to regain control of her pelvic floor.

Cade did make sure that got a workout too.

Luckily, all the things that hadn't bounced back after my babies, my vagina was not one of them.

Usually it did things to aforementioned vagina when I saw Cade with our children in his arms, kissing them with a naked vulnerability that he only had with us. Usually it did things for my vagina when I saw Cade, period.

This time was different.

This time Cade was kissing our children goodbye without certainty he'd be back to say hello.

My stomach lurched as it had off and on for weeks.

It was constant morning sickness, this war, this feeling in the air that I thought we'd said goodbye to after everything the club had been through.

But the Sons of Templar never said goodbye to chaos.

Or war.

In that moment, I had an almost overwhelming urge to pack my children, my Adonis husband and my shoes into our car, drive to an airport and go home to New Zealand to a little town that knew nothing of wars, human traffickers or motorcycle clubs. The need to protect my family was that strong that I opened my mouth to say it.

To beg Cade.

I didn't know his answer. Not for sure. I knew me and the kids were first for him, no matter how dedicated he was to the club.

But me asking him to abandon them when they needed their strong, cold and calculated president just because my kids wanted their vulnerable, beautiful and loving father to come home every night, was that going too far?

I knew everything about the club. Because from the start I told Cade there was no other way this went. So I knew about running guns. I knew about them stopping with the guns to focus on legitimate business. I knew they still farmed themselves out as muscle and hitmen on occasion. And I knew they'd been at war since a human trafficker kidnapped Rosie.

I knew that they had spent years trying to bring him down. Trying to figure out a way to do that that didn't mean mass graves for those who didn't survive the ugly way.

And now, after the Christmas massacre, the ugly way was all we had left.

I had lived beauty for so long, I'd forgotten about the ugly. And now it was staring me in the face in the form of my husband saying goodbye to his kids maybe for the last time. I selfishly wanted beautiful. Just for me. For my kids. My family.

But the club was my family. They saved me too. Cade's brothers were my own. Their wives were closer than sisters to me. Not just because I didn't have sisters. The love I had for them and their families closed my mouth.

No, it was because of the love I had for Cade that I closed my mouth. Because if I asked him to run, and I asked him with the desperation and fear I felt to my bones, he would most likely say yes.

He'd survive.

But it'd ruin him.

I couldn't ruin the man I loved.

Even if that meant I might ruin my family.

"Go and get your brother ready for bed," Cade instructed Belle, putting them both down and eying me.

He knew me well enough to almost read my mind. In addition to being a sex wizard, Cade was Oz Great and Fucking Powerful in regards to pretty much everything. I couldn't hide anything from him. Not online shopping orders, not when I got Belle's ears pierced and not when I was on the verge of having a total fucking mental breakdown.

"I'm a big girl, I can do that," Belle said seriously, grabbing her brother's arm and all but dragging him toward their rooms. Although she looked beautiful and delicate like a little doll, our daughter was not gentle with her little brother.

But he held his own.

Cade crossed the distance between us, yanking my hips so my body was flush was his. Despite my utter fucking mental breakdown, I responded.

Like a lot.

Fucking sex wizard.

"Don't like seeing that pain behind your eyes," he murmured, moving to stroke the side of my face. "Thought I'd seen the last of it."

"You made me push two children out of my vagina, I'd say you were certain you hadn't seen the last of me when you impregnated me. Twice."

The corner of his mouth twitched. "I seem to recall you having a rather active role in the impregnation process," he murmured, hands squeezing my hips.

I swallowed roughly as my vagina urged me to forget all unimportant things like the club's imminent war with a cartel king and the prospect of impending doom and just jump on my husband.

Cade's mouth twitch disappeared. "I'm comin' back, babe," he promised. He was so certain, so strong. My man could control a lot of things, a motorcycle club, the terrible twos, my vagina. But death he could not.

I had too much experience of a strong man making promises in war that he couldn't keep. My heart constricted at the thought of Ian. At the thought of losing someone else to a war.

"You can't make promises like that," I whispered.

His hand tightened. "Yes, I can. I can do anything. I'm Oz the Great and Fucking Powerful."

I froze. "Nope. You cannot be everything you are and read fucking minds now too. I want a superpower."

His hands run along my stomach. "You have a superpower. More than one." He kissed my jaw. "You gave birth to my daughter, my son." He kissed my neck. "You fought through demons that would ruin most people." He went back up my neck. "You saved me," he whispered against my ear.

"I didn't save you," I protested.

His eyes met mine. "Yes you did, Gwen. I was a man that

only knew bitter. Ugly. A man who was willing to live that because that's what he thought life came to offer. Then you arrived. In those fuckin' shoes, with your boxes, with your sweet. Your beauty." He looked around the house, the one that was no longer a bachelor pad, but a tastefully decorated home with warmth coming from the walls, from the photos, from the memories. His eyes shimmered.

Cade.

My great and powerful hero was being brought to *tears*.

"I'm not just being brought to tears," he murmured. "I'm being brought to my fucking knees," he rasped, landing his lips on mine.

And I kissed him back. With everything I had in me. All my beauty. All my ugly. All my fear.

His hands roved over my body, the body he'd touched so many times before, the body he owned, but somehow, it always felt new, dangerous, exciting.

My hunger for him swarmed my mind, destroying the worries that had plagued me seconds ago. Or maybe those worries were the reason for my hunger being so intense. I needed to feel alive in the most carnal way possible. I wanted Cade's touch bruising my skin.

But a crash and a cry sounded from somewhere in the house.

Cade stopped kissing me with a sigh.

Kids made it kind of hard to have crazy animal sex on the dining room table like I'd been planning on doing a second ago.

He kissed my head. "I got them."

His hand moved down to the waistband of my jeans and then inside my panties.

I let out a low moan.

"Hold that thought," he commanded, kissing me once more before stepping back and going in search of whatever Belle had done to her brother now.

I stared at the patch on Cade's back.

"Wait," I called.

He turned.

There was so much to say. So much that I didn't need to say it.

"Did you actually read my mind?" I demanded.

He chuckled, a real chuckle. The sound filled me up, I tried to hold onto it so I could replay it when things didn't feel as safe as they did now. "Your mind has a way of coming out of your mouth without you realizing it, baby."

Shit. I hated saying what I was thinking without even knowing it.

"I wouldn't do well at a murder trial, then," I muttered.

"No, so leave the murdering to me." He winked and left.

I was left with his words. And a glass of wine. Because, obviously I had wine. I had two kids and a husband who was president of a motorcycle club at war with one of the most powerful and dangerous criminals in the world.

Wine was what got me through.

No, *tequila* was what got me through, but I couldn't exactly slam shots in front of my children.

I sipped my wine and considered his words.

The men took care of the murdering. Or so they liked to think. Many of the women in the club had done their fair share. To protect themselves, obviously. Because as much as these men would protect us with their lives, we still had to protect ourselves too.

But who was going to protect them?

Amy

"You're not allowed to die," I hissed, my hand tight around his throat, riding his cock hard and fast.

My thighs burned with the force at which I was moving, but I considered sex my only form of workout, so it was fine. Plus, the fact I'd already had one orgasm from Brock's mouth on my pussy and was working my way up to a second one was a good way to distract from the pain.

Just not all of it.

Brock's body moved, flipping me onto my back, yanking my hand from around his neck and fastening it on mine instead.

My core clenched.

I was totally into a little bit of erotic asphyxiation.

Brock knew this.

Obviously.

Since he'd known everything about my body since the first time he'd fucked me and he'd done it thousands of times since then.

His eyes glowed with hunger, with intensity that hadn't dimmed with years of marriage, a kid, with the extra couple of pounds I was carrying thanks to that kid. He was seriously lucky he was cute.

"You're telling me not to die while you're tryin' to choke me, Sparky," he rasped, plunging into me hard and slow.

My body shuddered as it built up for another orgasm. His muscles were taut, carved from marble, ink almost jumping from his skin, showing me he was close too. And showing me he liked a bit of erotic asphyxiation too.

Though I knew this.

My throat burned as he squeezed for the perfect amount of pleasure and pain.

"You're not gonna die during sex," I croaked, my voice harsh and breathy. "The orgasm is just too good."

He thrust again. I let out a moan. His lips claimed mine. "No, Sparky, the place I end up leavin' this world on my way to hell is inside heaven."

He thrust again.

I was teetering on the edge of a cliff. My body wired, nerve endings beautifully raw.

"I'm too far gone to talk about how disturbing it would be if you died inside me," I breathed.

He grinned, somehow in-between the tight, pre-orgasm face I liked so much. "Maybe I need to keep you here more often," he murmured, nuzzling my neck as he stopped moving. "Keep you more agreeable."

I squirmed underneath him, needing friction. He weighed me down.

"I'm not agreeable if you withhold an orgasm from me," I hissed.

His hands went to my wrists, forcing them above my head as if he sensed I was about to try and fight my way back on top.

Maybe Gwen was right.

Maybe these men had powers.

Kind of weird to think of my best friend while I was in bed with my husband, seconds away from an orgasm—if he fucking *moved*—but that was us.

I was about to curse at Brock, as I was prone to doing, command him to fuck me, also prone to doing, until something moved in his face. He showed something that was mirrored in my soul and my bones.

"I'm not gonna die, Sparky," he whispered.

"I know," I said, sounding more sure than I wanted to be. Needed to be. "I can't do this without you," I admitted.

He looked between us with a grin.

I rolled my eyes. "I can do *this* without you, though battery operated devices pale in comparison."

His hand squeezed my wrist. "Everything pales in comparison to the way I fuck my Old Lady," he growled.

My stomach flipped, despite the arrogance.

There was a time when him calling me that caused a fight that almost broke us up. When I refused to be a title, a piece of property.

But now I wore that title better than I wore Chanel Haute Couture.

"I can't do this, life," I continued. "I can't be a mom who doesn't drink with breakfast and think about dropping her kid at the nearest fire station if you're not there doing all the shitty parent stuff I don't want to do. I exist in this sickly all American small town without you to make it beautifully bitter." I paused, trying to grab onto the feeling of my husband inside me, on top of me. "I can't breathe without you," I admitted, feeling sick at showing my vulnerability. No matter the fact that Brock had spent years showing me I was safe with him, that I could be honest about my feelings, my weaknesses, it still burned.

Old habits and all that.

He clutched my neck, moving so his forehead pressed against mine, both of us let out ragged breaths as the movement brought us both closer to the edge.

"You're a good mom, even though you've barely changed a diaper in your life," he said. "You're strong and bitter enough to handle whatever sweet this town throws at you." His hand moved to lay atop my chest. "And your ability to breathe through pain is unlike anything I've ever witnessed. So you can do it without me." He kissed me, long and hard. "But you're not going to."

Then he moved.

Then we both went over the edge.

Mia

I found Zane in the garage, after wrangling the hellions I called children into bed, a task usually reserved for him, since he had all the muscles and strength needed to force two small humans hell-bent on staying up all night into going to bed.

As it was, I'd had to tie Rocko to his bed frame.

Not all night.

I'd go in soon and untie him.

But likely he would've already figured a way out by then.

"You owe me big time," I told Zane, from where he was sitting on the sofa in the garage that had once been Lexie's jam space.

Now my daughter was a big rock star getting Grammy's and all that stuff, she didn't exactly need our little garage, but we kept it for her.

Not just because she and the boys had filmed a music video in here a few years ago and I could charge people to take photos, but because it meant something to Lexie. To all of us.

It would always be here. Not as a reminder of where they came from or whatever crap people pulled about keeping humble. I wasn't humble about my daughter being one of the most famous and talented people on the planet. But she was a total weirdo and she would've been humble with or without the garage reminder.

"I'm thinking diamonds," I said, moving toward my totally hunky, broody hubby. He was scary to everyone but me, our children and his grandchildren.

His grandchildren.

Not mine.

No way was I a grandma.

I was too young and beautiful.

"Or a car," I continued, taking him in for all of the things that the outside world saw. The muscles, the cut, the tattoos, the seemingly permanent hot guy death stare that communicated he ate puppies for protein or something.

But as you got closer, metaphorically of course, if you didn't know him and got up real close, he'd not only still look menacing and scary, he'd probably punch you or shoot you or something. Closer, in the metaphorical sense, showed Zane as a damaged, broken, beautiful man with a heart bigger than his biceps.

The love of my life.

And I didn't even care if I sounded like a twat thinking that.

I stopped in front of his motorcycle boots. His eyes were on me, as they had been since I walked into the garage, because my husband was obsessed with me. Even though I was wearing his tee—tied at the back because otherwise it would go to my ankles—and cutoffs, flipflops, and no makeup.

I still looked great for my age and how many kids I popped out, but the way he looked at me was like I was J Lo or something.

It was nice.

Warm.

Beautiful.

Because a soft, reverent gaze from a hard, violent man was pretty much like crack. But more addictive.

"I know," I said as my lady parts responded to his gaze and general nearness and hotness. "A new kitchen."

Something moved in his face. Zane's version of a smile. Way hotter than Colgate's version. "A new kitchen?" he repeated, voice low masculine and delicious. I could eat it by the mouthful, like frosting.

I nodded. "Yes, I already have a lot of design ideas on Pinterest."

"Babe, you don't even use the kitchen."

I scowled at him. "I do so. I store snacks in there."

"You don't cook in there," he countered.

"I do so," I snapped back. "I make coffee."

He put his beer down with a grin and snatched my waist, yanking me into his lap. I immediately curled into his warmth, inhaled him in long and deep.

"Still weird when you smell me like that, baby," he murmured against my head.

"It's not weird," I snapped. "It's adorable."

"It's how a serial killer smells their victims," he replied dryly.

Ugh. I was totally happy about Zane coming back to life, smiling more, yada yada yada, but too many of his jokes were being made at my expense. They needed to be made at other people's expense.

I leaned back, locking eyes with him. "You never know, I could be a serial killer."

To his credit, he didn't laugh. Not with his mouth anyway. "Yes, baby, you could totally be a serial killer," he placated, pushing hair from my face.

I rolled my eyes. "You still owe me."

"Another victim?" he deadpanned.

I smacked his arm.

That only worked to break many small bones in my hand.

Or at least bruise them.

I swear he was like Wolverine, bones made from iron or whatever. I made a mental note to get a metal detector and run it over him while he was sleeping. Just in case.

He took my bruised or broken hand into his own, bringing it to his lips and softly kissing.

The pain disappeared.

"Your sons will be looking for their next victim once they untie themselves from their beds."

He raised his brow in response.

"Well, you weren't here," I said to his nonverbal reply. "I needed to get creative if I wanted any private time with my husband." I waggled my eyebrows suggestively.

"So you tied our children to their beds so you could fuck me?" he deduced.

"No," I argued. "So *you* could fuck *me*."

His eyes turned. "I approve," he growled.

In an instant, I was on my back on the sofa, Zane's tee somehow over top of my head.

He let out a feral hiss as the cold air hit my nipples. "No bra, Wildcat," he growled, moving his head down to fasten his lips over my nipple.

"Zane," I moaned.

Even after all these years, he was building me up to orgasm with just his fricking mouth on my nipple.

His beautiful assault moved to the other before he kissed his way up my neck.

I moved my hands beneath his tee, scratched at his skin with desperation as he kissed me. Despite the frenzied movements prior, despite the erotic danger in his eyes, he kissed me slow, tenderly.

And I knew why.

Because of what tomorrow was.

What I had been trying to avoid thinking about and had been somewhat successful at doing because the demons I'd tied to their beds took up most of my attention, making sure they didn't burn anything else down.

But now, with Zane's loving, reverent kiss, I couldn't avoid it.

He stopped kissing me. Rested his forehead on mine. He saw it all. All the things I didn't say. Even to myself. "I know, baby," he whispered.

And that was all either of us spoke for the rest of the night.

Until our boys found us naked in the garage.

Then there were some words.

But nothing about what tomorrow meant.

Because we didn't need to say anything at all.

I knew Zane would destroy heaven, come back from hell if needed.

I needed to trust him to get us through this. Trust the club I'd once been sure was too violent for me, for us. The club that was a part of us.

Lily

It was nearing two when I pulled my car into the drive.

The light went on immediately and the door opened, a shape filled our doorway.

A shape I knew well.

A shape of the man I called my husband, best friend. My everything.

And even though he was dealing with a baby, with everything that was happening tomorrow, he still waited up for me, still lit up the house for me, still walked over to open my car door like he did every single time I was on the night shift, which wasn't often. My superiors knew I had only just come back from maternity leave and tried their best to be kind, but the life of a nurse wasn't exactly kind.

Apart from being able to put my son to bed, not being able to have dinner with my husband, I loved my job. I felt like I was doing something. I also felt strong, confident in a way I hadn't felt without Asher's help in forever.

It hurt.

A lot.

Seeing people suffering from the same disease that took my mother from me. Watching families decay just like the person in the hospital bed. And I couldn't offer help in these times.

Only comfort.

But then there were the other times. When the disease didn't win the war. And I got to see people walk out of the hospital, with a little more death on their souls than before, but a lot more appreciation for life.

I didn't feel like the Lily who couldn't even breathe when she was presented with a stranger or unfamiliar situation when I was at the hospital. I was Lily, the nurse. That stayed calm in the most chaotic situations. It was odd, really. It was an environment that might've triggered a lot of people to have panic attacks, but it cured mine.

My door opened as I put the car into park.

Asher reached over to unfasten my seatbelt and kiss me. "Flower," he murmured against my mouth.

I sank into my husband's touch, still getting freaking butterflies after all this time.

He was the original cure.

"Hey," I whispered against his mouth. "How's the baby?"

He pulled me out of the car, closing the door behind me and locking it. "He's perfect, of course."

He tucked me into his side and walked us into the house.

Asher was always affectionate. Always touching me, claiming me, whenever I was close enough for that. But this was different.

I knew why.

It had lurked at the back of my mind all shift. Caused me to fumble with IVs, drop needles, beginner stuff. Luckily they were minor.

What wasn't minor was the truth that was cloaked all over Asher's touch.

He closed and locked the door silently. I dropped my purse on the counter by the door.

And I just stood there.

Usually the first thing I did was shower and get out of my scrubs, they so weren't the sexiest thing ever, or at all, but Asher seemed to like using them in a number of role plays.

Asher was always waiting up, either to rip my scrubs off me, or to take a shower with me, or to make me a warm tea and hold me if the night had been bad.

Asher, my lighthouse, my steadfast man.

"I can't believe I was away all night. With tomorrow," I choked out. "I needed to be with you so I could—"

"You don't need to be with me tonight, Flower," he murmured, interrupting me and grabbing me so I was flush with his hard body. "Because you're gonna be with me tomorrow night."

"I'm scared," I admitted.

He stroked my jaw with his thumb. "Me too," he said back, barely a whisper.

My heart pulsated with the rawness of his tone, of his face. Of him. Asher was always real with me. He always shed the cut and the biker persona and was just him.

But this was something different.

This was a chance for me to be his lighthouse, his steadfast woman.

I went up on my tiptoes and brushed my lips against his.

He responded immediately.

I let the kiss go on, lazily, tenderly, like we had all the time in the world, like we had no outside worries. He let me take control.

Or I don't even think he let me. He didn't have the strength to take control anymore. And that was sexier than anything else, a man that wasn't afraid to let me be strong for him. And I was able to do it. He taught me how, after all.

Bex

"It's sexist, you know." I cut through my steak viciously. "All you men going out to fight while the little women are locked down in the clubhouse." I chewed. Swallowed. Glared at my husband. "Again." I cut at my steak with more aggression.

"You know, baby, that cow is already dead," Gabriel commented dryly.

I moved my aggression from my steak. "Yeah, but you're not," I shot.

He grinned and the truth came with his easy smile.

My cutlery clattered onto my plate and I pushed my chair back with a screech.

Gabriel had already turned his in preparation for me climbing onto his lap to straddle him. It was fucking infuriating how well he knew me. It was fucking terrifying. Because the man that knew me this well, who smiled when I threatened to kill him, who waited as I fought my way through my own battles, who adored me despite my many imperfections, he was not fucking dead.

Yet.

"I can't do another lockdown," I admitted, cupping his face, running my hands along his stubbled jaw, down his neck, covered in tattoos. Ink that I knew better than my own. "I can't be stuck inside while you're out there. It's fucking—"

"Misogynistic, sexist, and the definition of patriarchal control over women," Gabriel finished for me before I could. His hands moved from my hips to cup my ass, pulling me closer to him so my pussy pressed right against the flesh of his cock.

We were naked.

Because Gabriel had instituted Naked Wednesdays.

I had not complained.

He moved his head down to fasten his mouth over my nipple. I reveled in the pleasure for a moment before I smacked his head.

He jerked back. "That's spousal abuse, you know."

I rolled my eyes. "That's spousal abuse, but me handcuffing you to our bed making you fight so hard that your wrists bled wasn't?" I asked dryly.

His eyes darkened. "No, because I got an orgasm after that. So you give me a blow job, I'd be willing to reconsider calling the authorities on you."

I smiled. Even though I really fucking didn't want to.

That was Gabriel. He made me happy even when I didn't think I could be. Even when I didn't want to be.

And the night before a war that seemed greater than anything we'd ever faced was a time when I really didn't want to be happy. It was a time when I really want to find an eight ball, a needle and welcome oblivion.

Even being clean for as long as I had been, even being happier than I thought human beings like me were allowed to be, I was always going to be an addict. And when times got hard, dark and fucking scary, my kneejerk reaction was always going to be to think about a fix.

But the problem was, there was no fix for this. Nothing could take me away from this reality, not even heroin.

"Gabriel," I whispered.

His smile left his face and he moved his hand up my back, tracing the ink that he had memorized like I had his. He was there for every single tattoo. It was a rule of his.

"Becky, I promise you that I'm not going to do anything stupid and get myself killed tomorrow."

I raised my brow, though my favorite vein itched with his words. "You? Not do something stupid?"

"All my stupidity is calculated, measured," he said, voice light and gaze heavy. "And all my decisions center around coming back to my wife so she can abuse me."

"I'll abuse you extra well tomorrow if you let me come with you," I said.

"I would," he replied, eyes dancing with demons. "I'd be happy to have my warrior princess on the battlefield. But you'll make the other guys look bad, give them a complex and it'll be a whole *thing*." He kissed my nipple. I shivered as he grazed it with his teeth. "How about you get the next war?"

I glared at him. "There's not going to be a next war."

His face turned serious. "Not like this, babe. It's the end. I promise, Becky."

It was the end.

One way or another.

Lauren

I was painting when he walked in.

Hands settled on my hips and he rested his head on my shoulder, watching the movement of my brush.

You'd think with everything that was going on, I'd be painting something red, angry, violent. That I should be angry for what was happening right now, that I had to go through something else where I had to entertain the thought of losing another person I loved.

Burying Anna was agony.

But Gage shared that agony with me. He didn't try to take it away, didn't make it better. He just shared it. He gave me all different kinds of agony. Beautiful pain. He gave me a beautiful son. A beautiful life. Sometimes, for that beautiful life to stay, it had to become ugly. Agonizing.

So I wasn't angry.

I was scared. Terrified.

But I trusted that my husband would never make a decision that had the possibility to take him away from us. That he would choose the path of least pain. I trusted him with my life.

So I wasn't painting angry. I was painting peace. Soft watercolors. Gentle strokes.

"It's beautiful, baby," Gage murmured.

"It will be," I whispered, putting my brush down and turning so he could press my front to his. "It will be soon. But it's going to get ugly, isn't it?"

Gage's face tightened with fury, his hands flexing to the point of pain on my hip. I watched him fight his demons, the past clawing at his throat. "It's gonna get ugly," he agreed, releasing his grip.

"But we're gonna get through it." I moved my hand to cup his face, saying what he thought he had to say to be strong for me. But screw that. This man had been strong enough for me. Strong enough for himself. And he had to be plenty strong for tomorrow.

A cry sounded from the nursery.

I moved my hand. "I got him."

He snatched my wrist and killed my palm, not taking his eyes off me. "I got him."

I smiled, letting him go and be with his son.

I picked up the paintbrush and painted a little more beautiful.

Then I went to find my family. Nothing I painted could reproduce what I found. Gage, sitting in the rocking chair, our son in his arms, fast asleep. His little hand was holding one of his large, scarred ones.

I walked over, wishing I could freeze this moment, wishing I could protect my strong, scarred man from what was to come. Wishing I could protect myself. My son.

But all I could do was gently lift our baby from Gage's arms.

His eyes opened the second I grabbed him. Of course he wasn't going to let anyone take his child from his arms. After what happened in the life he had before, I understood his crazy protection. Why, for the first few months of David's life, he was wired tighter than he had been when we first met. Once I'd been cleared for sex, he did not go gentle. No, he went hard, brutal, trying to fuck his demons out.

And I let him.

Slowly, he got as calm as he could, easier with David. But he still loved him with an intensity that was born out of a place of fear.

But wasn't all love born out of fear?

Because we found a person that rocked our core, the first thought would always be terror at losing them, at losing the part of ourselves we'd take with them.

So love was fear.

I'd never loved my husband or my son more than I did this night.

Macy

Hansen did not come to bed until late.

He stayed up. Looking at whatever intel they'd accrued, studying it. I didn't interrupt him. Because I knew he needed it. I knew he needed to feel like he had every single piece of information. Every part of the puzzle.

That was him. Regimented. Controlled.

And I knew this was screwing with him. The grief that he pretended not to feel for the entire club. The fear he only showed me while making love to me. I let him feel it. Deal with it in his own way.

Because I knew he had to. I just had to be there. Show him I would be here. That with everything that was changing, that was going to change. I wasn't. We weren't.

I hated that this was part of the club life. I despised it. But this was the life I'd chosen. The only life I wanted to live. So I dealt.

I grieved the family that I'd lost. I felt the pain.

Then I squeezed my sons. Then I curled up to my husband at night. And I reminded myself that this too, shall pass.

We were in one of the houses that Evie had arranged. Xander was asleep in the small room beside ours, I'd held his hand as he fell asleep. I had just put the baby down in the crib that was on the other side of the room. He was a good baby. Quiet, staunch, like his dad. But once I put him down, I couldn't move from my position looking at him, my hand on his chest, moving ever so slightly with his tiny inhales and exhales.

I wanted to keep my sons safe from this. I wanted to protect them. The cold and rancid fear that he would be taken from me in this only grew larger, to the point where it was almost unbearable. But I had to bear it. And I trusted that the club would work this out. That Hansen would come home to us. I couldn't even entertain any other possibilities.

I didn't hear him come in.

His lips at my neck were the indicator of his presence. One of his hands slipped up my nightgown, caressing my thigh, the other stroked the hand that was resting on our son's chest.

"We made some beautiful kids," he murmured.

I sighed against his touch, my entire body melted and simmered with his nearness.

"We did," I agreed.

"Xander's gonna make a great president one day."

There was no question in his voice as to whether our sons would join the violent and dangerous life in which he was being brought up.

And it didn't bother me. I wanted them in this life, because it was a beautiful one.

Even when it was ugly.

"He is," I agreed. "But not for many, many more years. And his little brother will likely be right beside him. You're going to lead the club through this."

He didn't answer for a long time. "I miss them," he whispered against my neck. "I fuckin' go to call Grim, ask him to sign off on something, ask him for advice. I keep expectin' Levi to be at his place at the bar. I keep thinking I see their faces at the table."

My heart bled as his words did. I moved my hand to thread

with his. "I miss them too," I replied. "We're not going to be missing any more people," I lied.

He kissed my hair. "No, we're not," he lied back.

Scarlett

I tilted my head one way, staring at the wall. Then the other.

Frustration and fury built up inside of me to the point I wanted to go and get my gun and empty the clip into the photo frame that I was currently trying to get centered on the wall.

And yes, I was aware that the fury and urge to shoot up the walls of mine and Cain's new home did not originate from not being able to hang a photo. It originated on Christmas day, and every day since then.

It was hard, mingling fury with the happiness I continued to feel. The fury was more familiar. More comfortable.

"Babe, what in the fuck are you doing?" a low voice grumbled as arms yanked me into a strong and naked torso.

Okay, there was one thing more comfortable than fury, it was being nestled into Cain's body, my skin touching his. I responded. Immediately, despite the fact we'd just had sex. Twice. Which meant four orgasms for me. Cain was teaching me a lot of things, and though I'd considered myself an expert in the bedroom, he was showing himself to be somewhat of the orgasm whisperer.

Or maybe that was because I was in love with him.

"I'm trying to hang this photo," I answered, sinking back into his arms, letting him take my weight.

It was something I was getting used to, more metaphorically than anything. Leaning on Cain, letting him in. Trusting him.

"Babe," he murmured in my ear. "It's fucking one in the morning, you get outta my arms to hang a fucking picture?"

"It's our wedding picture," I said.

"Yeah, I know, I was there," he growled.

We'd eloped in Vegas.

Amy had threatened to burn our house down if I didn't let her throw us a wedding party.

I'd agreed because I liked our house. Our home. It was small, right by the ocean, it was nicer than I ever thought I'd have. Not because it was just a cottage in California with an ocean view. Because it was somewhere I was putting down roots. Which was why I needed to hang this picture, because, when I'd been in Cain's arms, thinking of tomorrow, I'd realized our home didn't have pictures. And hanging pictures created a permanence. So I thought if I got up, and hung the photo, then Cain couldn't be taken away from me tomorrow, these roots couldn't be ripped out, even though they had only just begun to grow.

"I couldn't sleep," I said by explanation, because no way I was putting all that on Cain, tonight of all nights. When he was riding out to fucking war in eleven hours.

He turned me so he could cup my face and I could get all girly over how fucking hot he was. "You can't sleep, you wake me up," he commanded. "You can do it with your mouth on my dick if you feel like fucking me back to sleep."

My pussy clenched.

He ran his thumb over my bottom lip, eyes probing. "You feel like talking, you just wake me up. I'm not sleepin' while my woman tosses and turns."

"Okay," I whispered.

Me.

I never whispered or agreed when Cain decided to order me around.

Obviously he tried to order me around because he was an alpha male biker, surrounded by all sorts of other alpha male bikers.

He did not get to order me around.

Except in the bedroom.

And, as it happened, at one in the morning before he and the club went to war with an international criminal.

"I like it here," I said.

He grinned. "I'm glad, since we've bought a home here."

"I like it here, and I've got roots when I thought I was gonna be some kind of nomad forever," I continued. "I'm terrified tomorrow is going to rip those roots out. Rip me to pieces. Because as much as I didn't think I'd fit in with Old Ladies and women who have about ten thousand different products in their skincare routine, and love to talk about it in details, I somehow fit."

His hands tightened. "Of course you fuckin' fit," he growled. "And those roots are only going to grow deeper. Curl around this soil. And we're gonna put more photos up." He looked to the wall. "Well, I'll put the photos up 'cause that's wonky as shit. But we're gonna stay. For the long haul. There isn't any other option."

I nodded, because I was trying to shake the tears from my head. I couldn't cry right now. It was stupidly cliché. And weak.

"I'm done talking," I croaked. My hand found the inside of his boxer shorts. His cock responded immediately. "I want you to fuck me back to sleep."

His eyes darkened. "That, I can do."

And he did.

First, he fucked me against the wall so hard that the picture fell off.

Then he carried me to bed.

Where I slept.

CHAPTER TWENTY-SEVEN

Caroline

EVENTUALLY, when everyone began to party like it was their last night on earth, I retreated to the room we'd been assigned.

I wanted to be angry at Liam for disappearing on this night, when every other member was at home with their wives, soaking up what could be the last moments.

But I couldn't be.

Because I understood.

He didn't want us to be around each other, in this horrible prolonged version of goodbye.

We'd done that already.

And as painful and terrifying as this solitude was, I got it.

I wasn't lonely.

For the first time in a long time.

So I put on his tee, crawled into bed and waited.

I didn't have to wait long, just enough for the sun to set.

He came to me in the darkness.

When I was staring at an unfamiliar ceiling, in yet another unfamiliar clubhouse.

He didn't speak. Neither did I. We fucked.

Hard and fast.

And then, after that, with barely any pause, we made love.

MORNING CAME QUICKLY when you were awake to wait for it. To dread it.

Liam and I hadn't spoken a word. I physically couldn't. So I didn't. Neither did he.

He was dressing.

I was watching. Terrified.

It was like watching him put on that military uniform sixteen years ago, after a sleepless night much like this. But there had been talking then. We'd been young. Stupid. Planning ahead, skipping over the war, like it didn't exist, like it was a foregone conclusion he'd come home.

There were no foregone conclusions here.

He was a part of something I couldn't control, couldn't belong to. That uniform, that cut, was a layer of something that separated us.

"Where does the name Jagger come from?" I asked, surprised at the question even after I'd spoken it.

Hadn't I made a promise to myself not to ask these kinds of questions? Not to find out anything more about his life without me than was most painfully necessary?

Yes.

But promises were little but empty air between us.

Made and broken too easily.

He blinked once. Twice. Regarded my face. The question.

Maybe he wouldn't answer.

I hoped he wouldn't answer.

"Bikers mostly have road names. Usually when you start prospectin', someone calls you somethin'. It usually sticks. Didn't want to get stuck with somethin' fuckin' stupid. What someone else chose for me. I was already living a life someone else chose for me."

"You chose it for yourself," I snapped, unable to stop myself from interrupting, unable to withhold the accusation and anger in my tone.

He nodded. "I guess I did. But it doesn't feel like me that made that decision. Not the me I was before or the me I am now. It was the decision of a man who found himself inside the gates of hell. Didn't quite know how to navigate it. Sure as fuck didn't know I could turn around and walk right back out. So I took the road in. The one paved with good intentions. The journey to hell isn't one that makes a man. It destroys him."

I hated how he was explaining things. Like it was tortured poetry. Because it was beautiful as it was ugly. He had a grasp on what he'd done.

"Felt like I was all sharp edges when I found myself there," he continued. "I *felt* jagged. Looked in the mirror one day." He touched his ruined skin. I itched to press my mouth over it.

I didn't.

"Made sense. I was ripped apart on the outside. Jagged." He shrugged as if to say, 'and the rest was history.'

If only that's what it was.

History.

But history was static. Safely tucked away.

What was between us wasn't safe. Wasn't still.

And it wasn't history.

And I prayed, that after today, it still wouldn't be.

There were no dramatic goodbyes or declarations.

We'd done all that.

I just stood when he'd slipped on a shoulder holster and put his cut on top. I wrapped my arms around him. He did the same. His guns were pressing into me, the leather of his cut scored through his scent. I breathed it in.

He let me go, brushed a hair from my face and stared. I did the same, I was cataloging him, making sure there was no part of his face I didn't memorize.

He kissed my head.

His lips lingered for a long time.

Then he let me go and walked out.

Scarlett came in seconds after I decided I was going to crawl under the covers and never come out again.

She was holding two beers.

She was fully dressed, fully made up, in a battle uniform of her own.

I took the beer.

"You better get dressed," she said, sitting down, obviously happy to watch this happen. "It's going to be a long few hours."

"Yeah," I agreed, draining my beer.

We both looked at each other, pretending we weren't afraid.

Pretending that it was only a few hours and then it would be over.

Which I guess it would.

* * *

ONCE I SHOWERED, had another beer—which Scarlett handed me mid shower, because she stayed, obviously remembering my thing about strange showers, or just not having any boundaries—we both emerged to the common room.

I don't know why I expected it to be like a crypt or something, in preparation for the ghosts that today would inevitably create, but it was the opposite. There were people, and children, everywhere.

Each of the ladies from last night were scattered around, and all of them gave me waves, hugs, arm squeezes or kisses on the cheek. And I didn't mind any of the contact. In fact, it felt comforting right now.

There was no sitting waiting, sitting on our hands or wringing those hands pretty much all morning. No. There were children to be wrangled. Food to be made. And in mine, Scarlett and Amy's cases, wine to be drunk. Amy technically had a child to be wrangled, he was suspiciously well behaved. "I gave him baby cough syrup," she said with a shrug. "His father is fighting a fucking war with an international criminal today, I don't give two fucks what the good mothers of America have to say about me drugging my child, it needs to happen."

I did not disagree with her there. And I also thought her, and every single woman here, were amazing mothers. In their own way, but that's what made it all the more better.

There were prospects and patched members scattered around the highly secure clubhouse. Also members of the Greenstone Security company, famous in L.A. for being the only place celebrities went to. The owner, Keltan Brooke, was roaming around the place, dripping sexiness and talking in a hot as shit accent.

The club was as safe as any place could be.

There was also a huge basement that was not a torture chamber, but a 'safe room' that was fully carpeted, with sofas, bathrooms and a small kitchenette. These guys obviously didn't fuck around.

But when I looked around at the small children, at the women who loved each other like sisters, at the family here, I understood why the men didn't fuck around. Why they didn't hesitate in riding off without guarantee of coming home.

I got it.

I also met another woman, Lizzie, who had more adorable kids, was also beautiful, but older and had been around the club longer than even Gwen. Her and Evie were some of the longest serving Old Ladies. Both of them were calm, serene, faces not unlike those serving in battles I'd been a part of all over the world.

Well, Evie's version of serene was to yell at people for not cleaning up after themselves, but it worked.

The meet was at noon. Liam had not told me this because I didn't have the courage to ask. *Me.* I didn't have the courage to ask the fricking question. Scarlett told me. Because hard as she may be, she sensed softness in others.

Sometime after eleven, the doors opened, and Mia stopped trying to keep her little boys from shaving each other's heads with the disposable razors they'd found. She was not happy at the beautiful woman walking through the door.

I recognized her, despite the fact I shunned most popular culture. It wasn't exactly great for a reporter to be ignorant of the happenings in contemporary society, but I was a conflict journalist, my career didn't hinge on which Kardashian got a new husband this week.

That was all soft news for people that needed to be comforted, who needed a mental binge on the emotional version of mac and cheese.

Whereas I needed the hard stuff, to make sure I was never comfortable, always starving for comfort.

Jesus, I was so fucked up.

But in a biker compound, locked down with all the women I'd met in the past twenty-four hours, I'd say fucked up was a pretty relevant term.

Apparently, in the middle of this biker compound was a rock star.

Lexie Decesare was the lead singer of Unquiet Mind, one of

the only popular bands I actually liked. Because they had real talent. They weren't auto-tuned within an inch of their lives and they looked like real, down to earth people. Apart from Sam Kennedy. He was pretty much your quintessential asshole rock star. But even the way he did it was charming. Honest. And I recognized honesty more than anyone else. Their music meant something.

I didn't listen to it for that exact reason.

Because it called up emotions. It was heartbreak in a melody. In a song that tugged at all those things I thought I'd tied up tight.

But I followed their career with interest.

And now, here was the lead singer, walking into the club-house, a baby perched on her hip and a hot guy to end all hot guys trailing her holding another baby.

I recognized him too. It was her husband, Killian. And the head of her security detail.

Another hot as shit guy who looked at his woman as if he were terrified she might fall off the face of the earth.

"Lexie!" Mia demanded, her voice shrill as she rushed toward her daughter. "What in the flipping heck are you doing here?" she demanded, glaring at the woman who was only more beautiful than she seemed online. Which was an anomaly. Everyone 'famous' never looked better in person.

But she did.

Though looking at her mother, it wasn't a surprise.

"I'm here because this is where I belong," Lexie said calmly, putting an absolutely adorable little girl down who immediately ran into the rest of the gaggle of beautiful children playing in the common room, oblivious to everything around them.

I watched the children with the same empty womb feeling I'd had when I first met Macy's boy. Every single one of them was adorable. And not every kid was adorable. It was just the truth.

But it seems the Sons of Templar and their women bred well. Which wasn't exactly a surprise.

I was overcome with pure and naked worry for these beautiful children. What ugliness would befall them today? Who would they lose?

I thought of my beautiful little nephew miles away, in a warm and lovely and most importantly, uncomplicated and safe home. Neither my sister nor my brother in law were going to get involved in an international war with a human trafficker.

But that didn't guarantee him insulation from pain. My mom was a fricking school teacher and my dad ran a furniture business. Our home was happy. Safe.

And I still ended up here.

"You belong in a fortress in L.A. filled with security personnel and far away from here," Mia snapped, putting her hand on her hip.

Her daughter mirrored the look. Though their styles were completely opposite, they mirrored each other in a way they looked like sisters, not mother and daughter. "I am not hiding in L.A. while my family is in danger."

"That's precisely the point," Mia all but screeched. "You'll be in L.A. the only dangerous thing you'll experience is kale juice and I'll be able to breathe a little easier. Now—"

Mia's rant got cut off as Lexie's eyes focused on me. "You're Caroline Hargrave," she breathed.

I'd been around famous and powerful people before. All of them failed to affect me. People were just people, after all.

But something about Lexie, about the fact that she was exactly like she portrayed herself, and that she fricking recognized me, had me a little star struck.

"Yes! She's a journalist," Mia cut in. "So now your publicist is gonna have to deal with the story of why the heck Lexie Decesare came into the middle of a war in Amber."

Lexie rolled her eyes. "I think her angle will be more about the war and less about me."

"Stop being so humble," Mia commanded. "You know you're more famous than any war. Even one with as many hot guys in it as ours."

She was bordering on hysterical and clinging to humor to get her through this, but Mia was right. Lexie was more newsworthy than even a motorcycle gang going to war with a human trafficking cartel in a small seaside town in California.

So was the world.

Cade

They arrived at the warehouse and they knew something was wrong immediately.

The something wrong being that it was fucking *empty*.

Not a soul, or whatever Fernandez was, anywhere.

The sense of foreboding he'd been carrying around grew larger as men cursed around him.

He looked to Steg for guidance, as he had many times throughout his life. But for once, the weathered man looked just as lost as he fucking felt.

"What the fuck is this?" Jagger demanded.

Cade understood the wildness in Jagger's eyes, the fact he was being robbed of the retribution he so sorely needed.

"It's a trap," Gage cut in, pale as he'd ever seen him. As afraid as he'd ever seen him. "Just not one we expected."

"Fuck," Brock hissed.

Every brother had a piece out. And nowhere to point it. No blood to spill.

His phone vibrated in his pocket.

Cold dread intensified.

"What the fuck is this?" he demanded.

"I'm not an outlaw, I'm a king. I don't play by your rules," Fernandez said. "I hope you said goodbye to your wife and children."

The line was dead before Cade could say anything.

He looked at the men. "We need to get the fuck out of here and back to the club. Now."

For the first time ever, his voice almost shook. His terror over how fatal his lapse in judgment might be had him paralyzed.

For a split second.

Then the vision of his wife and children had him moving.

And the rest of the men.

So that meant some of them got out in time when the remote activated bomb went off.

Others were not so lucky.

Caroline

After Mia had told Lexie she was now doing a tell-all *TMZ* interview airing all her embarrassing habits as punishment for her turning up here, things calmed again.

As it neared midday, the children were ushered down to the basement, and they all seemed to sense the need not to fight it. Even Mia's boys, who I was sure were going to do something like steal two motorcycles and ride off into the sunset, went willingly. It was obvious that the women didn't want to sit in some underground bunker without a bar, so we all planned on taking shifts, with Lauren, Lily and two prospects going first.

Everyone tried to distract themselves with stories of the current pranks Amy was pulling on her mother, the fact that Belle had convinced Cade to let her paint his toenails, Mia tying her sons to the bed so she could have sex with her husband in the garage, the time Lucky tried on a pair of Bex's panties to see what they felt like. Nothing worked.

And then, five minutes till midday, Killian jumped into action.

"Stay here," he demanded, eyeing Lexie.

Naturally, we all followed him.

We got outside to see a black SUV pulling in. Killian turned and glared at Lexie, she shrugged.

I was relaxed because I recognized the license plate number of the car. I guessed that's why Killian's weapon was holstered, and they hadn't open fire yet.

Rosie hopped out of the driver's seat.

Swiss, of all people, limped out of the passenger's.

"You're throwing a party without me," she greeted, scowling at us all. "Now that's just rude."

Gwen ran up and hugged her. "What are you doing here? Cade is going to kill you."

Rosie shrugged. "Someone's always trying to kill me. My brother will be a welcome change of pace." She winked at me. "I'm sorry I'm way past fashionably late, this guy here is actually almost a match for me." She pointed to a wincing Swiss. "But I got here just in time, I see. Cade was working on the belief that Fernandez wouldn't turn a small American town into a war zone. Which is a sane belief. I'm not as sane as my brother. So I hedged my bets on a different outcome. He's so not gonna laugh when I say I told you so." Something moved in her face. Something that didn't match up with the lightness of her tone. Like she wasn't even sure if she'd have a brother to say that to. Or if she'd be able to say it herself.

"So, we've got some good news bad news here," she continued.

"And your version of good news is so not gonna be the same as mine," Amy muttered, eyes tight and worried like the rest of the women. But they were not hysterical. Crying. They all held strong. It was obvious why these men were so attached to these women. I was already forming an unhealthy attachment to them. Though that could be because I might possibly be dying with them soon.

Rosie grinned at Amy. "Well, no. There is not a Barney's opening anywhere in the vicinity. But there is an international warlord on his way here with like a carload of goons ready to kill us."

Everyone paled slightly. "And I'm guessing that's your version of good news?" Bex asked dryly.

"No, of course not. The good news is, you have me, and I have these." She opened the trunk of the SUV that just so happened to be bursting with guns.

"Just once, I want you to open a trunk and have it full of Chanel's entire Boy Bag collection," Gwen whined.

Amy laughed.

Bex leaned in and picked one up, not hesitating.

"You're saying we're meant to be fighting them off?" Mia said, looking to her daughter.

"No, we're just last point of contact," Rosie said. "Ideally, we're just gonna hold them, look cool, maybe take some snaps for the Gram. But worst case, yes we might have to get trigger happy."

Killian's jaw was hard, as was Keltan's along with the rest of the crew who had rolled their eyes at Rosie's arrival. I'm pretty sure I saw a guy called Heath exchange money with another man named Duke. Obviously they had a bet going on Rosie evading Swiss.

"Freckles, I want you inside, fucking now," Killian hissed at his wife.

"I'm not going anywhere," she said, folding her arms.

"Listen to your flipping husband!" Mia screamed. "This is the one and only time I'll say this, because this is hopefully the one and only time Rosie presents us with a trunk full of guns.

Rosie shrugged.

Lexie stood her ground.

Mia glared at Killian. "Drag her in there. You have my permission to manhandle her."

Killian looked like a man torn. As did the rest of the men out here, witnessing this. As they all looked like pretty intense alpha males, I was sure their first instinct was to get the women somewhere they could be safe.

Protected.

But these were not women to play it safe.

Rosie began handing out guns, ignoring the alpha male crisis.

Not a single one of the women, the wives, the mothers, the fucking *rock stars* seemed to blink at this. None of them run back into the clubhouse, hysterical, asking to be saved.

Everyone just leaned in and picked one up, with the confidence that showed me they each knew how to use them. Amy and Bex didn't surprise me.

I did question whether Mia should be allowed one, considering the fact she declared it "went with her outfit."

I took one from Scarlett, who was grinning. "Guess this wasn't what you expected when you lied your way into the clubhouse looking for a story, huh?"

I laughed, feeling the weight of the gun in my hands. "I don't expect anything covering a story," I replied. "But even not expecting anything, I didn't expect this."

Rosie looked down at her phone. "Get ready."

"I don't like the way she said that," Gwen said to Amy.

"Me either. The last time she said that, she'd spiked my drink and I woke up in Mexico, with *bad hair*," Amy replied.

A large boom echoed through the air, coupled with a rumble that vibrated the ground enough to almost topple most of the women over.

I'd been close when a large bomb had been detonated before. So I stayed upright.

Rosie grinned. "See you've got your sea legs!" she yelled over the low beep in the air as our eardrums reacted to the after effects.

Men ran around the parking lot. Keltan was talking into a headset. Killian had one hand on his gun, the other on his wife.

"Did you just set off a bomb in the middle of Amber in broad daylight?" Gwen demanded, rubbing at her ears.

"They did it first!" Rosie yelled back. "And it wasn't in the middle of Amber. It was exactly one block away from here, I'd already cleared the area."

"That's meant to be them, right?" Amy clarified. "Blown to high heaven or lowest hell?" She shook the gun and her hand. "And these can stay as accessories?"

"Yeah, it's meant to. But when you make plans, God laughs, so you know, get ready for that sadistic sense of humor," Rosie replied, eyes on the gates, where the prospects and men staying had recovered from the blast.

We all watched the gates, waiting in that horrible loaded silence that comes both after and before death.

Then the gunshots started.

CHAPTER TWENTY-EIGHT

CAN LOVING the wrong man really determine the course of your life?

I didn't think so.

I think loving the right one could.

Because love warped the right man into something wrong.

Love warped the right woman into something wrong.

And losing that love, that intense, fucked up and life forming love, well that ruined a person.

Experiencing it once was bad enough.

Having to witness it was just as bad.

I stood at the cemetery, tucked into Liam's side, a place I'd been ever since he arrived at the clubhouse and literally sprinted toward me until I was in his arms.

I didn't fight him on that.

Because, if I had use of my legs in that moment, I would've sprinted toward him too.

Over the past few harrowing, horrible, and grief-filled days we had barely been out of touching distance. He had no more 'club business' to attend to now that Fernandez was dead. Now that his brothers were dead.

Now that Linda was dead.

I expected it on some level. Hearing the resignation in her smoky voice. But seeing the woman stride through the gates into the oncoming onslaught, armed with two rifles. She took a lot of them down before she fell.

I didn't let myself think of anything beyond that, beyond the fact Liam was in pain and he needed me. Jagger was in pain and he needed me. Because at some point, maybe since the start, realized he was Jagger and Liam. Mostly Jagger.

And I'd spent my time falling in love with the man named Jagger while trying to hate Liam.

So the man I used to love and the man I fell in love with were one in the same. And they hurt. Sometimes it was as simple as that, to let go of the bullshit.

So we let go. I stopped with my tirades, accusations. I stopped with all of it. I just stood by his side.

As we had when he'd rode up to the gunfight that seemed like seconds ago and centuries ago at the same time.

He was covered in blood, in smoke, in the death of the day. I was relatively unscathed, considering I'd emptied the clip of the gun I'd been handed. Every woman did. I don't know how many men we took down before the club arrived, but it didn't matter. We fought, we protected. Somehow, no one at the compound but Linda lost their lives. She had done it because she was sick of the habit.

I wasn't sure who killed Fernandez in the end. No one knew. They found him, amongst the dead, riddled with bullets. No face off with the villain, no dramatics. He died, just like the rest of them.

But by that point, the Sons of Templar had not been

concerned about how their enemy had died. They'd been too busy trying to figure out how many of their family had lived.

Liam didn't let me go the entire rest of the horrible, bloody day. It was all a blur, except my hand in his.

It was darkly comical, all the lead up to the war for it to be over so quickly. But then again, looking at the tear stained, blood stained men—the ones that were still alive—this war would not be over for a long time.

I tried to help as much as possible.

Liam tried too.

But help came in the form of hearses and ambulances.

There was nothing else we could do.

Nothing else anyone could do.

It was done.

So we slipped off, made brutal, frantic love, still covered in grime and blood.

I lay tucked up tight into his chest as I pretended to sleep. He pretended to sleep too.

And now we were at the cemetery. Burying brothers. Fathers. Husbands.

My eyes touched Lizzie, clutching her two children, she was dry-eyed and pale as she watched her husband, Ranger—who I'd never met—get lowered into the ground.

Luther would be buried in New Mexico.

As would Blake.

Claw wanted his ashes scattered.

Cade was standing, barely, leaning on his wife for support. He only got out of ICU yesterday. But his wife gave him all the support he needed.

Lucky, the man who was known to be the joker of the group, was not smiling whatsoever, on crutches with a severely broken leg. One that he'd somehow managed not only to ride on but stand beside his wife and fight on when it came to it.

Steg, the previous president of the Amber chapter, had lost an eye.

He too, should technically still be in the hospital.

As should at least half of the men standing in the cemetery today.

As gruesome as they looked, looked better than a lot of bomb victims I'd seen. They were lucky.

I looked to Lizzie and the children again.

Thought about the fact I'd never play poker with Claw, or listen to whatever stupid thing Blake had done.

No, this was not luck.

This was truth. As ugly as it could be.

And it was also victory. Sometimes victory was even more devastating than loss.

This was one of those times.

Liam's hand was tight in mine.

But he must've sensed my unease or maybe I squeezed back too hard because he fell out of step with the rest of the club, pulled me aside.

His hand went to my neck, eyes intent on mine, searching for something. "Peaches, you good?"

I knew the question wasn't really 'was I good' overall. Because no one in this situation was good. Despite the fact that they technically won the war. The battle took casualties. Casualties that I mourned, for the first time since...ever.

I sucked in a breath. "This is the first time I've been at a cemetery since..." I trailed off.

He stiffened. "Since my funeral," he finished for me. Pain saturated his voice. And blame. Blame I knew he was pointing toward himself. "Fuck, Peaches." He leaned in and pressed his forehead against mine, whether to convince me he was alive or himself, I wasn't sure.

"I love you," I whispered. I didn't know why I said it. No, I knew exactly why I said it. Because it was the truth I was unable to continue swallowing. Because he was in pain and I bled with him. Because I couldn't go another moment without him knowing.

He jerked like I hit him. Leaned back, let me go.

"What did you just say?"

I glanced around, people were milling around and some were still arriving, so I had time to emotionally strip down before the services began. "I love you," I repeated.

"You loved Liam, not me," he countered, voice cold.

I refused to let him push me away. "I did," I agreed. "I loved Liam. And you're not him anymore. Mostly. You're still a little bit Liam. But you're mostly Jagger. And I love him too. You. With an intensity, a depth I never could've loved Liam with. Because I hated you first. And there was no way a love this deep could have been borne out of anything but hate. Anger." I kissed him. "I had to hate you so I could love you."

He held me tight as if he were making sure I wasn't in one of the coffins we buried today.

Three Days Later

I hadn't wanted to leave Amber.

For a number of reasons.

The women being a huge part. Because a loner like me, someone that pushed away deep, meaningful relationships was forced into something that I didn't want to leave.

But we had to.

So tearful goodbyes were had, with promises made to come back, promises I knew I wouldn't keep but made anyway.

And then, we rode back.

To where it all began.

To where it all had to end.

HANSEN CALLED me into church the next day.

Liam and I didn't mention or even look at the elephant in the room since we'd arrived. We'd done something so mundane it felt extreme. We'd ordered takeout, ate it in bed and watched movies until I fell asleep in his arms.

We didn't even have sex.

And somehow that felt more intimate. I think it was a sign of something, when you felt fulfilled and satisfied from just lying in a man's arms with no sex.

We woke up.

Liam watched me stretch. This time he didn't interrupt me.

I finished, raising my brow at him sitting upright in bed, sheets pooled at his waist. Immediately, a wave of bone-crushing emotion hit me and it was an effort not to flinch. Because this was a moment. Not an extraordinary moment. But a simple one. A glimpse into a forgotten future. Liam, sitting in bed, still shrugging off sleep, with light, but hungry eyes, watching me like he could be content to do it for the rest of his life.

And me looking back at him with that raised brow, ready to tease him was me thinking I could do this for the rest of my life too. Me wanting to do this with a need I couldn't stomach.

Because I knew if I did this, if I stayed, if I took hold of something I'd been yearning for, for years, I'd have to say goodbye to things, to people I couldn't let go of.

"You gonna stand there starin' or you gonna come to bed and suck my cock?" Liam asked.

I jerked myself into the present, smiling at him. "Why is it that I have to get into bed and suck your cock? That doesn't sound like I can get anything out of it."

He grinned wickedly. "Well, you can suck my cock while I'm eating your pussy."

And I did just that.

Hansen called me into church while Liam and I were having coffee.

He looked to Liam. "You're welcome to come too."

Liam tensed immediately and the air between us changed. It was stifling. He nodded once and took my coffee from my hand and set it down on the table.

He nodded forward, a gesture for me to go ahead. He didn't touch me.

With rocks in my stomach, I went.

Hansen sat at the head of the table. Liam sat on his right instead of behind me.

That stung.

I didn't let on.

"I'm just gonna say, what you've done for the club during this time, it's noted. Appreciated," Hansen started.

I nodded once instead of replying.

"I said I'd give you leave to go, write your story where you pleased when you earned my trust." He leaned forward slightly, not looking at Liam. "You've earned my trust."

I still didn't speak.

"That means you're free to go," Hansen clarified. His gaze intensified. "You're also free to stay. If you wish." Still, he didn't look to Liam, but I knew he was talking to him too.

I nodded. "Thank you."

I normally didn't say thank you to people for letting me go after keeping me hostage, but it felt necessary.

"You're a good president," I added. "I've seen a lot of men in charge of armies, militias, street gangs, prisons. Almost all of them turn rotten. The cliché that absolute power corrupts absolutely is a cliché for a reason. Not many men stay good when they're given a title. Power. When they're in charge of life and death. I just think it needs to be acknowledged that you've stayed decent. Through things that would've turned a lot of other men rotten."

Hansen nodded once. "Think your gauge of decent is slightly skewed."

I smiled. "I think the world's slightly skewed. I'm just adjusting."

Something moved in his eyes, but he just nodded again. "If you'll excuse me," he said, standing. "I've got a family to go and spend some time with."

"Say hi to Macy for me," I said, hoping he knew I meant to say goodbye to her for me.

"Will do."

Then he left Liam and I sitting across the table from each other.

"This is almost full circle," I said, with sweating palms. "Well, beyond full circle."

Liam didn't speak. He just stared.

I chewed my lip, waited.

"Just because you're not a prisoner anymore doesn't mean you have to go," he said finally.

My stomach dropped.

"You want me to stay?" I clarified.

He nodded once.

"Stay here, with you?"

"We'll get a place," he said. "A home. Somewhere that isn't a fuckin' dorm room." I thought of that room. One that had been a prison. A sanctuary. A twisted kind of paradise. The room I didn't hate being in one bit.

But it wasn't about a room. Or a home.

"And what about my family?" I asked. "What do I tell them?"

He clenched his jaw. "You tell them you've met a man, you want to live in New Mexico."

"And what happens when they come to New Mexico to meet the man who's made me want to settle down, after over ten years of running away from anything like a romance?" I asked him, throwing the question like a bullet.

He opened his mouth, but I already knew the answer.

"You want me to come into your lie with you," I said. "You want to tangle me up in your despicable deception. And yes, I know your reasoning, you're a monster, you're an outlaw, a murderer. You have scars. I even understand some of them. And you know what? I'm tempted. You've taken me down this dark path of yours. I started as a prisoner. But I haven't ended as one. I did this of my own free will. I liked walking beside you in the darkness. I liked the feeling of this new, brutal and ugly you. Because it's okay for the new ugly me to exist with you." I glanced around church. "I can even get used to the lifestyle that you live. The danger. The death. The knowledge you run guns, that you risk life in prison on the daily, your life as well. I can handle all of that. But the lie. I won't be part of your lie. And it seems that means I won't be part of your life."

I waited for him to contradict me. I waited for him to tell me that he would choose his life with me over his lie. That he'd be that good man, he'd do the right thing for his family, for me, for himself.

I waited for a long time for that good man to come out from his scarred façade.

Too long, probably.

Because he didn't come out.

Liam didn't speak.

No.

Jagger.

This was the point he turned into Jagger.

I nodded, the simple gesture agonizing.

But wasn't everything with him now just varying degrees of agony?

"Goodbye, Jagger," I whispered, my voice broken glass.

I turned and walked away.

Got into my car, that someone—Hansen—had decided to give back to me.

Drove home. For twenty hours. Bathroom and coffee breaks my only stops.

And I didn't shed a single tear.

I cried them all for the death of Liam.

I'd just done it fifteen years too early.

Jagger

Jagger felt odd. Empty. Like he was walking around, hollowed out, with nothing on the inside. And that was different than before, when he was walking around this clubhouse with a prospect patch, fresh scars, fresh pain. He was full then. Fucking bursting. Of anger. Regret. Self-hatred. To name a few.

And then, since that night in the alley, since Caroline had been in his room, even when she was locked in there, he was fuller. With anger. Regret. Self-hatred. And then a bitter kind of joy. A depraved form of longing.

The night he sank back into her, the night he slept in her arms and every night after that more of that bitter joy that turned sweeter. The longing only got more depraved. And love. Fuck if he sounded like a chick even thinking this shit, but he didn't care. He fell in love with the new version of Caroline. The hard version.

He loved her more than who she was before. Because if she'd turned up at the club, exactly how she'd been when he left her, he wouldn't have been able to love her like he did now. He wouldn't have been able to have been around her, tainting her. It was a selfish and ugly thought to know what she'd been through and be glad about it. Glad because it made him able to stomach himself when he was around her. Made him be able to swallow good intentions that would've had him walking away from her. He wasn't able to convince himself that he was gonna break her because she was already broken.

Then there was now. Without her.

Without brothers.

They'd won the war.

He didn't feel victorious.

He glanced up from his whisky cup when he sensed movement. Hansen sat beside him. Poured himself a drink.

Fucker should have a weight off his shoulders now the threat was gone. But he carried more than the weight of a threat. He carried with him coffins and skeletons. It was a job that Jagger did not envy, nor aspire to. Hansen did it well. Because he knew when to turn off. And he had a good woman to go home to. A woman to warm him up when this life got too cold.

Jagger was so cold that he didn't even remember warmth. Hence the whisky.

He expected Hansen to start on him immediately. His behavior hadn't exactly been great, even in outlaw terms. The scabs on his knuckles were evidence of that. He'd beaten two drug dealers nearly to death two days ago for dealing within town limits. Drug dealers who were part of a lower level street gang in the next town over. Could've started a beef.

Had the Sons of Templar not just eradicated one of the most notorious criminals in the world. Not that another wasn't gonna pop up in his place. Another probably had. There was no such thing as destroying evil. It was infinite.

But whoever this new flesh peddler was gonna be wasn't likely to have a beef with the club that put him on top.

So they were back to the regular.

Running guns. Taking on contracts for hits, when the occasion arrived. Collecting debt sheets. Protection.

Just another day at the office.

And that's what it was gonna be until he died.

If she hadn't come, he would've been content with that. Fuck, he might've been able to sort his shit out, get an Old Lady. Have some form of life, only remembering the one he left behind—the ones he left behind—in dark hours and empty bottles.

But now? Fuck no. He'd had a taste of something. He was forced to confront what he'd done. That knowledge would haunt him. Guarantee he'd never have that kind of life.

"Have somewhat of a superpower when it comes to people in general," Hansen said after finishing his first glass. Jagger had downed three in the same space of time.

He glanced to Hansen, who was contemplating his glass. "Can tell if they live by their word. Especially 'cause I'm most often the reason if they die by it, if it's not authentic. Knew the second I heard that woman's story she was true to her word. Knew she was no threat to the club."

Jagger gaped at him. "Why the fuck did you make her stay?"

Hansen shrugged. "Guess I'm a romantic at heart. Guess that story fucked with me. Guess I just wanted my best friend to have a little of what I had." He paused. "I really thought she would've stayed."

Jagger squeezed his glass hard enough for a crack to appear down the side. Then he released it. "Yeah, me too."

CHAPTER TWENTY-NINE

Caroline

I WROTE THE STORY.

Not the one that Emily wanted.

Not the one I had intended on writing going in.

Though none of my stories ever ended up how I intended.

Emily was pissed at the start, until I gave her the piece on Miguel Fernandez I'd written from what I'd heard from club members, from Rosie, from various sources, victims.

And then she was happy.

Yes, Emily was happy to hear about one of the most disgusting human beings to walk the planet, to read about his sins, in detail. Because apparently, that was going to be a better movie.

Not that I was going to write a fucking book about it. But she would figure a way to make it happen.

That was Emily.

Apparently my story got all sorts of praise. Awards. I got job offers and emails every day. Dream jobs. A dream life, presumably.

But I didn't want my dream life.

I wanted my nightmare.

I stared at the screen. At the words.

They're sinners, but they're not devils.
They do good deeds, yet no one would call them angels.
You'd put the Sons of Templar slightly toward the worse end of the
good vs. evil scale if such a scale existed. Which it doesn't, of
course.
We fool ourselves with the notion that there is a good, right way to
live life and a terrible and wrong way to live it. And to the
outsider, the Sons of Templar must look so wrong and terrible.
In my time with them, sure, they did some wrong and terrible
things. But not because of the cuts that serve as a second skin.
Because of the fact they're human beings. Just because you live on
the 'right' side of the picket fence, doesn't make you immune from
making terrible choices or doing 'bad' things.
Humanity is a disease that plagues us all, and the only cure
is death.
So for better or for worse, we're all human.
Which is what the Sons of Templar are.
They love their wives with a ferocity I haven't seen in my life.
They respect women, despite the backward fact that 'club girls' are
treated as property. Because these girls are not without agency.
Their titles, from what I see, are not shackles, but something that
makes them freer to do what they want with their bodies and lives.
Elders are respected.
Children are cherished.
Brotherhood reigns supreme above everything.
Blood is thicker than water. And it's blood and motor oil holding
this chapter together. Because it was torn apart last Christmas.

*With a death toll that sickens the soul. Especially when you
understand what a family the club is.
One that breaks the law, is prone to violence and doesn't shy away
from a gunfight, but a family nonetheless.
This reporter had planned on a story that was glaringly honest,
that stripped the ugly underbelly of organized crime and showed it
to the world. I could do that. In my time with the Sons of Templar,
I witnessed damning acts.
But then, what does damned even mean?
In my time there, I learn we're all damned. In our own ways.
So I'm not going to do my duty as a reporter to tell the unvarnished
truth, no matter who it hurts. I'm instead going to do my duty as a
human being.
And I'm going to shut up.*

I shut my laptop, deciding I was never going to open it again.

A WOMAN ENTERED through the front door that I was sure
had been locked. She stepped inside, her heel crunching on something. A takeout box, or more likely a can of something. Beer, that
I'd got for when my brother came to visit, and I'd used as a last
resort. She looked around, wordlessly, expression blank.

"So how does rock bottom feel?" she asked.

I dropped the bottle I'd fallen asleep cradling. I didn't hear it
hit the floor. She was definitely blurry, I was definitely drunk, but
I was pretty sure I was sober enough to make out the fact that
Scarlett was here, in my living room, in Castle Springs.

I squinted against that terrible light she was bringing into my
dark living room. It illuminated the absolute mess I'd been living
in. It illuminated rock bottom. Bottles of wine. Cans of beer.
Barely eaten takeout.

I saw scenes like this in movies, when someone got their heart broken, got fired, or just had a complete mental break. I watched these scenes with scorn, thinking no such thing happened. People couldn't just check out. I'd seen the worst of things, experienced the worst, and I didn't gorge myself on food and booze and live in filth. No, I kept going.

My arrogance was shattered when I got home from New Mexico. After I'd seen my family, cuddled my nephew, used the last of my strength to put on a front.

And then I came home.

I wrote my stories.

Submitted them.

Fielded calls, offers, went through the motions of actually living life. I saw my family every day because I yearned for their company. Comfort was uneasy, wrong when I was with them. I felt dirty, carrying around the secret of where Liam was now. Who Liam was now. I was good at deceiving them, though. It became what held me together.

But there was only so long that it could last.

It happened at the grocery store. Because pivotal, horrible moments usually happened in the most mundane of places.

I was contemplating Ben and Jerry's in the frozen food section, wondering if I would actually be that cliché.

And someone called my name.

Mary.

I froze for the handful of seconds it took for her to approach me, smiling. I was ice when she hugged me. When she spoke normally, happily, not knowing the son she thought was buried was twenty hours away.

I managed the exchange. Somehow.

She said goodbye, something about a bake sale she needed to prepare for. I wanted to scream at her *'your son is alive, and he is broken and you have no idea, you're baking fucking cakes.'*

But I smiled. Hugged her again. Promised to have lunch.

Then I calmly filled my cart up with as much booze as I could. I didn't give a shit about clichés anymore.

Then I drove home.

Unloaded the car.

Locked my door.

And broke the fuck down.

My phone had long since died.

I wondered if my family had been calling, worried. But they likely just thought I was writing a story, and they knew not to bother me for that.

I wondered if Liam had called.

Of course he hadn't.

Dead men didn't use phones.

Liam was dead.

"How did you get in here?" I blinked at Scarlett as she closed the door and tore open the drapes.

The effect was painful and immediate. I flinched away from the sun like a vampire.

Cool air filtered through the window she opened.

"I picked the locks," she said, like it was obvious.

I blinked at her, making out the tight white jeans, pink platforms and a barely-there pink tube top. Her blonde hair was piled atop her head. Her makeup was flawless, if a little over the top.

I idly wondered what the residents of Castle Springs thought when Scarlett breezed through. Then again, Scarlett wouldn't have been wondering one single bit about what people were thinking.

"How do you know how to pick locks?" I asked, rubbing my pounding head and leaning forward to look for the closest bottle that wasn't empty.

"How do you think I would know?" she countered.

Scarlett moved, not to try and stop me from drinking in the

daylight when I was obviously having some kind of emotional break, but to hand me the half empty bottle of vodka.

No way was it half full.

I took it without thanks.

She sat down on the chair across from me, glanced around my immaculately decorated living room, full of empty bottles, dead plants, and dead souls.

"What are you doing here?" I asked after a swig.

She shrugged. "Have had a lot of free time now I'm not helping my husband prepare for a war."

Something lanced inside me at her words. They were drenched in her own, hard kind of sorrow.

I used more vodka for that pain.

"Can I offer you a drink or something to eat?" I asked, my mother's manners all but embedded into me. "Though the only thing nonalcoholic I have at this point is tap water and snacks that consisted of cold pizza and questionable Chinese."

Scarlett grinned. "This isn't a time for tap water." She reached over to take the bottle from me and took a long swig.

She was silent for a long time after handing it to me.

"Are you here to bring me back to the club?" I asked finally. "Lecture me on what a mistake I made leaving?"

She shook her head. "Not my style."

I took another swig.

Scarlett crossed her legs. "I'm here 'cause I guessed you might need a friend and I needed a road trip."

I raised my brow. "A twenty-four hour road trip?"

She nodded.

I waited for more. There was no more. "I don't want to talk about it," I said finally.

"I didn't ask you to talk about it," she countered. Her eyes ran over me. "I will ask you to take a shower, put on some clothes that aren't covered in stains and maybe run a brush through your hair.

More for my sake than yours. It's just uncomfortable looking at you."

I almost grinned. Scarlett obviously did not do sympathy. Or comfort. Which was exactly what I needed.

So I got up. Showered. Put on clothes that didn't smell as bad as they looked, and I ran a brush through my hair.

Scarlett was in the same place as she was when I walked back in. The bottle was actually empty now.

"Okay, I'm gonna need to know one thing," she said.

My stomach dropped. Here it was. The inevitable morbid human curiosity about how things were destroyed, the uglier, the better.

"Where's the seediest and shittiest bar in this town and how okay are you to drive?" she asked instead.

This time I did grin.

———

"WOULD your husband approve of you being in a seedy bar in a tiny town in Castle Springs, drinking in the middle of the day?" I asked after the third drink.

We barely spoke during the first two.

Scarlett, I discovered, was not a woman to do girl talk over cocktails. And she was not a woman to order a cocktail.

She sipped her vodka, straight up. "My husband does not have the right to disapprove or approve of my actions," she replied. "He knew this when he married me, so he knew things like this are part in parcel of life with a former club whore. Plus, he's busy, hanging photos." She winked, but I sensed some vulnerability there.

I sipped my vodka—on the rocks—and thought on it. "How is he?" I asked finally, unable to stop with the emotional cutting. She knew who I was talking about. He was here, a ghost, more so than he'd ever been when I thought he was really dead.

"Crappy. Obviously," she said, not pulling punches. "Though he's showering and going outside every day so maybe better than you." She paused. "Though he is going outside in order to do things like beat drug dealers half to death, so I guess that makes you almost even."

"He's beating drug dealers half to death?" I repeated.

She nodded. "I know. He's salvageable if he's not actually killing them."

I had forced myself to think about how Liam might be doing. Tried to convince myself not only did I not care but that he deserved to feel as horrible as he could.

I couldn't admit that I had not only understood why he did what he did but forgave it too. I couldn't do that because being angry was so much easier than being heartbroken.

"Are you here to tell me that we need to get back together?" I half hoped she was. I hoped she'd sink her nails into my skin and drag me back to New Mexico. So I could be their captive again.

No way I was going there of my own volition.

Scarlett laughed, throaty and attractive. "Fuck no," she said, motioning to the bartender—who had been drooling at her—for two more.

The bar was all but empty, save for the few resident alcoholics that barely glanced at us when we entered the dingy place that was known to be a home for the hopeless. And even Scarlett, a certified sex kitten didn't get a response from anyone but the bartender. Everyone else was too deep in their own sorrows.

And those suckers must've been deep not to surface and appreciate Scarlett.

"I'm very aware that we don't live in a fairytale world," she said. "And what you and Jagger have, it's never gonna result in a happy ever after, even best-case scenario. I know that like I know my ending is never gonna be any fuckin' thing like Cinderella's. Not just because my prince is anything but charming." She winked. "And he's a king. Just not the kind from Disney."

Our drinks were placed in front of us, empties swiped away.

Scarlett grinned.

"On the house," the bartender winked, who looked to be older than dirt and sounded like a packet of cigarettes a day.

"There are still charming men in the world," she said to him, lifting her drink in a toast. She looked to me. "You won't find them in the Sons of Templar clubhouse, though. They're charming in the way the devil is charming. He'll sweet talk you long enough to claim your soul and never give it back. And what you and Jagger have, it's not healthy. For a number of reasons, but let's least start with how fucked up your history is. Like top level fucked up. And this coming from me, means something. You're not good for each other. You're both too damaged, there's too much wrong. In an ideal world, you'd both find someone marginally more well-adjusted than each of you to balance you out. To make sure that every day of your life isn't a battle." She sipped.

I listened with a bleeding heart.

"But this isn't an ideal world, I think we both know that," she continued. "And in our world, every day of our lives is gonna be a battle, the least we can do is know that at the end of that battle we've got an orgasm, a man that's probably gonna damn our soul even more." She shrugged. "I don't know, depends how enjoyable you find damnation."

I clutched my drink.

I enjoyed damnation to the point of destruction.

That was the problem.

"I'm not here to drag you back," Scarlett said. "I am here to tell you that Jagger's gonna turn up tomorrow morning at his parents' house. Your choice what you do. Shower first, though."

I was frozen.

He was coming here.

To see his parents?

Scarlett was right.

I had a choice to make.

Jagger

He was afraid.

No, he was beyond afraid, terrified or just plain scared.

And he wasn't staring in the face of a mission, the barrel of a gun, a knife about to slice through his face and his soul.

No, he was staring at the door to his childhood home. He was staring at the place that held mostly happy memories. Not all happy, because that wasn't how life worked.

How family worked.

Times were good and times were bad. Struggles in his parents' marriage. Trouble with his sister. Money problems. That was the way of life.

But the good memories overtook all that.

Because his family was a good one.

They made it through those hard times that were barely a blip in his memories.

But he'd given them hard times that would be more than a blip. They were a huge, ugly rancid scar on a life that they'd made sure was mostly good for them. He'd made the decision to ruin his family. He'd known they'd hold it together, because that's what he'd had to tell himself in order to live with himself.

Pathetic.

He couldn't entertain the thought that his parents might divorce because the pain of losing a child might fracture their marriage in a way that pain and loss could distance some people. He didn't imagine his sister struggling with the loss of her brother, the loss of her happy life.

He definitely didn't think about Caroline's grief putting her in danger, tearing at her the way it did. He barely survived the knowledge, the truth of what he'd done to her.

How in the fuck was he meant to do it with his mom, dad, and sister?

He couldn't. That was how.

It was the truth. The ugly, unvarnished and cowardly truth. He didn't have it in him. He could run into a battle knowing that he might not come out. He could kill a man in cold blood. See things other people would seek a bullet to the brain to stop haunting them.

All of that wasn't a product of bravery. It was a product of cowardice. Because seeing that, doing that, it was all so he didn't have to stand here, right fucking here, on the stone walk leading to the two-story restored Victorian with blue window shutters, and a lifetime full of memories.

Memories that had once smelled like fresh baked cookies, his father's cigars—ones he sneaked from his mom while she pretended she didn't know—his sister's perfume that she wore too much of until their mother righted her ways.

All of it had mixed together in his mind, one of the sweetest smells, aside from Caroline.

Memories were nice that way, preserving things not even the way they were, but the way they had to be in your mind.

But now they were rancid, rotted, because he was faced with the truth.

Jagger turned his back, intending on getting on his bike and riding back to the club. Finding someone to kill. Then finding a bottle.

Not coming out for a long time.

If ever.

Because he didn't know if he'd be able to face himself sober with the knowledge of what he'd thrown away because he was a fucking coward.

He turned and faced himself with another memory.

But this one was more beautiful than even his mind could preserve.

And she was scowling at him, arms folded.

"You're not turning your back on them, Liam Hargrave," she snapped, snatching his hand and yanking him back around.

He let himself be led up the walk because her hand was warm in his and her smell chased away whatever bitter scent he'd been so sure he'd be breathing in forever.

As a man known to react to deadly situations faster than most highly trained soldiers, he didn't even find his faculties until they were standing in front of a door.

Blue, to match the shutters.

The paint was vibrant, fresh, because his father touched it up every year. It was nice to know that he kept doing that. That even if everything else had changed, fallen apart, been ruined, his father still made sure the paint on the door was fresh.

It was a simple thing that gave him hope. And unfamiliar emotion.

It wasn't that that gave him strength or bravery. It was the small hand gripping his.

She didn't say anything as he stared at the door. She knew him enough to know he needed the silence. She knew what he needed better than he did.

Because he didn't know who the fuck he was. Who was going to knock on that door? Liam? No. It would be Jagger.

Because whatever he'd done, he'd killed Liam. It wasn't a complete lie to let his parents believe they'd buried their son. They had. The most important parts of him. The parts that would've made his father proud, his mother smile and his sister tease him.

The man who'd been worthy of the woman standing beside him.

Or so he'd thought.

She saw Jagger. Every single ugly and rancid part of the man he'd created out of the ruined skeletons of the man named Liam.

She'd seen it all.

And she was still here, holding his fucking hand. Gripping it so hard that it might even bruise him.

She was still fucking here.

"You can do this," she whispered.

He tore his eyes away from that blue door into the crystal blue eyes of something that hadn't stayed the same over the years. Something that had changed more than he could've imagined. Something magnificent.

"How do you know that?" he asked, his voice breaking at the end. He couldn't even control his fucking voice.

She smiled at him instead of shrinking away from his weakness. His cowardice. She squeezed his hand. "Because if you couldn't, you wouldn't have been standing in front of the house in the first place."

It was so simple. Her voice was so sure.

Strength didn't come from the ability to kill a man, from being able to stomach blood or throw a punch. Or even learning how to take one.

Strength came from people who squeezed your hand when you were weak.

He walked down the path.

Knocked on the door.

And waited to face his past, while he had his future firmly in hand.

Caroline

There are so many beautiful reunion videos floating around the internet, shared many times over, to spread the beautiful version of a hello after a long goodbye.

This was not beautiful.

Mary answered the door.

She first smiled at me warmly, then moved her eyes to Liam. The smile froze on her face. Her eyes went up and down the man in front of her, the color draining from her carefully made-up face. Liam was frozen beside me too, squeezing my hand with enough force to bruise my bones. Despite the trauma that she had to endure, the years had been kind to Mary. Probably because of her religious skin care routine and the fact she didn't drink, didn't sit out in the sun without a wide-brimmed hat and heavy SPF and believed in beauty sleep. So though she had aged over the past decade and a half, her hair graying and covered my tasteful highlights, she looked much the same as she did when Liam left.

Obviously the years had been a lot less kind to Liam.

But that didn't stop her from recognizing him immediately.

She let out a strangled sob lifting a shaking hand upward, stretching out to touch Liam's scarred face, as if she wasn't sure she'd encounter real flesh. When she did, her limbs collapsed from under her.

Liam caught her.

They both sank to the floor, her looking extraordinarily small in his arms when she'd always been such a big and vibrant presence.

I stood, watching, tears streaming down my face as Mary clung to the leather of his cut in a death grip now she was faced with life.

Witnessing the sight wasn't easy, it was a private pain that wasn't meant to be seen, but I had experience with private pain. It was my job to make it public.

Eventually, Liam stood, helped Mary up.

Neither of them had spoken yet.

Mary stared at him with a toxic mix of pain and joy, each fighting the other for control. I knew this because still, it was a battle I waged when looking at Liam. She lifted shaking hands to cup his face. "My boy," she croaked.

"Honey, who's at the door? Is it finally Trevor with that part for the lawnmower he promised he'd give me. He better have a cold one—" Kent was cut off when he reached the door.

His eyes met mine, light and happy, then he moved his gaze to Liam.

He froze too. Not quite like Mary

She moved to face Kent. "He's back," she cried. "Our son is home."

Jagger

"You hate me," he said into the night.

It had been a long day, to say the least.

It had been a fifteen-years packed into a day. He thought going off to war was bad, he thought enduring unthinkable torture was unbearable, that living a separate life and forgetting the one before was tough, losing his brothers was agony, and loving Caroline was torment, but this was all of it mixed into one.

Never had Jagger had to expend so much energy into staying upright, into making sure his hands didn't shake.

Holding his mother in his arms was home. She smelled the same, of flowers and lemon.

He had been terrified of rejection. Of his mother glimpsing his scarred face, his scarred soul and shutting the door in his face. For causing her pain. Or whatever was beyond pain. Because making a parent believe their child was dead was beyond pain. And he was responsible for that. He deserved the door in his face.

He didn't deserve to feel his mother cling to him like he was worth clinging to, have her tears of pain and joy.

He didn't deserve his father's immediate acceptance, some form of understanding gathering on his face when his mother released him so he could face his father. A man who had brought him up tough, yet fair. Who loved him in his own way. Different than the coddling, tender way mothers did.

Jagger didn't know what to do in that moment. "I'm sorry," he croaked, his words cracking at the edges.

His mother let out another sob, she was now in Caroline's arms.

Caroline's presence was the reason he got up from his knees, why he remained standing.

"Oh son," his father rasped. The words were a prayer, a thank you, an 'I forgive you.'

Then his father took two strides and yanked his son into his arms.

His mother joined.

Antonia had not had the same reaction. It was after the tears, after they stood awkwardly, unsure of what to do, what to say. He was a stranger as much as he was their son. He knew that. He knew that they knew that.

Caroline sewed up the tears in the moment artfully. "I'll make us some tea," she said, closing the door. "And pour us some scotch."

His father let out a sound that was between a chuckle and a sob. "Better make mine a double, sweetheart."

She smiled at him through glassy eyes. Moved forward to squeeze Jagger's hand for less than a second. He loved her more than anything in that moment. The simple hand squeeze, the smile, her calm.

She was the glue for the rest of the afternoon. While he explained a very condensed version of the past fourteen years. Leaving out the parts he was most ashamed of. Though, that was hard, since he was ashamed of the entirety of it.

The reasons that had seemed so concrete at the time turned to dust as he sat at the kitchen table, surrounded by memories, in front of two people that raised him. Two good people.

They only took what he was willing to give them, didn't ask questions. His mother held his hand the entire time, as if she were afraid he might turn to dust if she let go. He felt a bit like that.

At some point during the afternoon, the door slammed.

"I'm home!" Antonia called. "I know I said I was going to pick up the chicken for tonight. But I forgot. And Mom, before you—"

Antonia cut off as she entered the dining room. Jagger stood.

Fuck. While the years had only slightly touched his parents around the edges, graying his father, softening his mother, they had completely changed Antonia. He left her when she was a troublesome teenager who got on his nerves for always hogging the bathroom and playing bad music.

She was a woman now.

And she was staring at him with none of the mixture of joy and pain his father and mother had.

This was straight up anger.

"What. The. Fuck," she hissed.

He stepped forward. "Toni."

She moved forward. Fast. And slapped him. He didn't flinch. She slapped him again. He let her. And when it became apparent she was going to keep hitting him, he snatched her wrists. She struggled, choking on tears. He yanked her into his chest, fighting tears of his own. And eventually she calmed.

He let her go, she looked him up and down with a hard gaze.

It became apparent she was not going to accept the explanation like his parents.

"Toni," Caroline said, moving past him and grabbing her hand. Antonia took it like it was a life raft. "How about we go for a walk?" Caroline asked, brushing hair from her face.

She nodded.

Caroline gave him a look before leading his sister out.

He had no idea what Caroline said to her on that walk. He just knew they were gone for an hour and when they came back, Antonia's eyes were red and puffy, and so were Caroline's, but she ran to hug him. He squeezed his sister. "You've turned into a beautiful woman," he whispered against her hair.

"Well, one of us had to be the pretty one," she joked. "Because it's not gonna be you."

His family laughed.

And there, somewhere, he realized it was going to work out. Not perfectly. Or happily. But somehow it would work out.

Caroline's family was different. Her mother didn't have much of a dramatic reaction. She was a staunch and kind woman, and he was scared to death of her. She stared at him a long time after they walked through the front door hand in hand. "I'm going to make us something to eat," she said finally, her voice shaking slightly. "You look like you need a good meal." She moved forward. "You look like you need a good meal. And a break from the day I'm guessing you've had. The fifteen years you've had."

He struggled to contain his tears. "Yeah," he agreed.

Caroline's father took one look at him and stormed out of the room. Caroline went to follow him. He kissed her hand. "I've got it, Peaches."

She chewed her lip. "Well, I don't think he had any firearms in the back garden."

He laughed. "If I haven't been shot yet, I think we're good."

Though he wasn't as sure as he sounded.

Trevor loved his daughters fiercely. He would shoot anyone who hurt them, and he'd happily go to prison for that. Jagger idly wondered how he'd handled what Caroline had been through, not being able to end the fucker who stopped her from being able to have a fucking shower without breaking down.

He was pacing amongst the dozens of flowers that made up the garden.

When he spotted Jagger, he stopped pacing. "You broke a promise to me," he accused. "I'm sure you've got reasons, by the look of you, they're fuckin' good ones, and that's the only reason I came out here and not to my gun safe. That and the fact my daughter finally has something behind her eyes other than fake happiness and ghosts. But you broke your promise."

Jagger clenched his fists at his sides. "I did. And I'll spend as long as it takes making it up to her."

Trevor nodded. "Yeah, you will. And she's already forgiven you. I'll take longer. But I will too. Because you're a son to me. And a parent will always forgive a child, no matter how big their mistakes are. And son, this is a fucking big one." He gave his scar a long and pained looked. Jagger was used to it. It didn't bother him, strangers witnessing his pain, gawking at it—no matter how much it bothered Caroline. But the stare of his family, the way they looked at it as if it were their own scar tissue, that burned more than the wound that created it.

"It's been a hard fifteen years," Trevor said. "For my daughter. But it doesn't seem like it's been much better for you."

Jagger laughed. "You could say that."

"It looks like it's looking up for you, son. Because my daughter is at your side. I trust her." He paused. "She wasn't covering a story in Arizona, was she?"

Jagger shook his head.

"That patch, that gonna bring any danger into her life?" he asked, the first person to openly acknowledge the piece of leather.

Jagger wasn't sure if they simply didn't notice it, or because there was only so much information a family could take in in a day.

"Maybe," Jagger answered honestly. "But Caroline has made it clear she's never going to live a life without danger. But now she's not gonna do it alone. This patch has turned me into a lot of things, not a lot of them good, but it means that I know how to protect her, and I'll go all the way to do that."

Trevor nodded once. "I don't doubt that." He looked inside to where Caroline was standing at the window. Her mother was beside her. Both of them beautiful. Strong. "Liam."

Jagger turned. Trevor walked toward him, raised his hand and didn't punch him as he expected. He clapped his hand on his shoulder. "I'm thinking that patch hasn't turned you into a lot of bad, 'cause it's what brought you back here."

He didn't agree. But he was here.

His father laughed at the question he asked when he finally made it home. His mother was inside with Caroline, doing the dishes, though she found reasons to come out to the porch every five minutes just so she could lay eyes on him. His father's laugh was easy, throaty, just like he remembered. How could it be just like he remembered after what had happened? After everything he'd done?

"Son, no matter what a child does, a parent does not hate them," his father replied. "Trust me, your sister has tested that theory out plenty. Still love that little shit."

Jagger smiled, even though he didn't think he'd smile such a smile again.

"I was afraid," he choked out. "That you'd hate me if I came back. Hate me if I didn't."

His father was silent for a long time. Jagger looked over to see tears glistening in the man's face. It punched him right in the fucking chest.

Then he looked at Jagger, straight in the eye, with all that naked emotion, love that men—especially in the South—were not meant to have, let alone show.

He leaned over to take his son's hand, even though it didn't look like his son's hand. Even though it was covered in ink, in blood.

"Many parents live their whole lives with children that didn't come back to them. We had fifteen years. And that felt like a lifetime. I'll be honest, kid, it was no picnic. But it wasn't a lifetime. And you came back. There's likely some stuff to work out, with Caroline, not with us, because our son is home. Sometimes it's that simple."

He wanted to agree with his father. He was a smart man. A man he looked up to. Whom he idolized. He had been in the army, had an illustrated and distinguished career that he gave up when his wife became pregnant. Worked to own his own business. To teach his son how to treat women, how to pull apart an engine and put it back together. How to be a man.

A weight had been lifted from his shoulders at his family's reaction—it hadn't been to jerk back in shock or horror, to sling accusations. It was simple to them, Liam was home.

"I'm not Liam," he said finally.

His father looked back out onto the yard. "I know, son. But you're still our son." He squeezed his hand. "And it's that simple." He took a pull of his beer. Looked to him. "With us, it's that simple. With Caroline...you've got work to do."

Jagger downed his own beer. "Don't I know it."

"She's worth it."

His father's words weren't a question.

"Yeah. She is."

"You fight for that woman," his father instructed. "She is not the same girl she was. And that's a bad thing and a good thing. But you fight for her. Do not let her go."

"Don't plan to."

But it turned out, he didn't need to fight for her.

Because, to Caroline, turning up at Castle Springs, facing his past, was her definition of fighting, even with all she'd seen.

His mother wanted him at home that night.

He knew it.

He wanted it.

But he needed Caroline. Time without her, mere weeks, had been grueling. He couldn't breathe until he was inside her.

His father must have seen that kind of need, so he murmured to his mother, he made promises to come back for breakfast 'as soon as he woke, no matter how early,' kissed his sister, mother, shook his father's hand, and he took Caroline home on the back of his bike.

They barely made it inside her condo for the first time.

They got as far as the hallway the second.

And the third, finally ended in bed.

"I think that it's time we started trying to be responsible," Caroline whispered into the night. "Or at least the outlaw version of it."

Jagger froze, thinking of a conversation from a lifetime ago. Of slipping a ring onto Caroline's finger. "Are you proposing to me, Peaches?"

She rested her chin on her hand. "Depends, is that a yes, or a soul-crushing no?"

He kissed her in response.

EPILOGUE

Ten Months Later

Caroline

THINGS I'M GRATEFUL FOR:

1. *My husband makes me sweet coffee every morning.*
2. *We finally closed on our holiday home in Castle Springs.*
3. *Macy and I have both managed to convince Hansen to construct us our own room. Construction starts tomorrow.*
4. *I have now discovered I have an interior decorating style.*
5. *I do not go to sleep alone.*
6. *I do not wake up alone.*

7. *The club is repairing itself...and I see Scarlett every month when we ride down there.*
8. *I'm no longer afraid of a shower—because I never do that alone either*
9. *I missed my period this month*
10. *I don't have enough time to complete this list because my husband is walking into the room, with a wicked smile and a promise in his eyes. A promise he will never break.*

THE END...
For now.

ACKNOWLEDGMENTS

The Sons of Templar were what started this whole thing. This whole, crazy, whirlwind.

This dream.

These characters will always hold such a special place in my heart. Whenever I go back to writing about the club, I feel like I'm coming home. That's why I never want to say goodbye to this series. I never want to 'end' it. I'm not sure when the next Sons book will be in your hands. I don't know who is going to get a story next. But I know it's going to happen.

So don't worry. The Sons aren't going anywhere.

Writing this book was hard. I knew exactly what I was going to do with Jagger the first time I wrote his name. I knew his story was going to be rough. I know that it was going to be hard for my readers to forgive him once you figured out who he was. What he'd done.

But I wanted to explore the choices we make when we feel like we're trapped. By love. By pain. Fear. I wanted to try and explain that there is no way to make a 'good' choice from a place of pain. A place of love.

This book is one of my favorites of the entire series. Because it's a mix of my 'old' style of writing and my 'newer' style.

I really hope you enjoyed it.

As always, I would not survive the writing process without the people below.

Mum. You know the drill by this point. You are always here, right at the top. Because I would not be here, typing this, without you. You made me into the woman I am. You always support my good decisions. And you support my bad ones too. I know not everyone is as lucky as I am to have their mum as their best friend, and I count my blessings every day that I've got you.

Dad. You can't read this, but I know you're somewhere, having a beer, watching over me. I miss you always.

Taylor. Thank you for being my best friend. For supporting me. Making me laugh. Dealing with my meltdowns. Feeding me wine and treats when I'm freaking out about books. Thanks for going on this ride otherwise known as life with me. Forever and then some, babe.

Jessica Gadziala. You have been my constant support through so many meltdowns and dark periods of my life. You're my #sisterqueen.

Amo Jones. Bitch. What can I say? You are my everything, ride or die. I would not make it through without you. And I'm never going to be without you. 'Cause you're stuck with me for life.

Michelle Clay. I don't even know what to say about you. You are one of the most special people in my life. You do so much for me and many other people without expecting anything in return. You support me, cheer for me and help me through so much. I am forever grateful that my words brought us together.

Annette Brignac. Another woman who is one of a kind. Thank you for being in my life. Thank you for reading my books.

I am honoured to call you a friend. You are one of the best people I know. My life would not be the same without you. To the moon.

My girls, Polly & Emma. You're a whole world away from me and it breaks my heart. I miss you both every single day but I also know that no amount of time or distance will change our friendship. You two are my soulmates.

My betas, Sarah, Ginny, Amy and Caro. You ladies save me. Seriously. Thank you for reading my books when they are at their most raw. Thank you for helping turn them into what they end up being.

Ellie. Thank you for dealing with me. For editing this book. For not changing my voice. For being fucking amazing.

And you, the reader. Thank you. From the bottom of my heart, I thank you. You are why I'm still here, creating characters, writing stories. You've made my dreams come true.

ALSO BY ANNE MALCOM

The Vein Chronicles

Fatal Harmony

Deathless

Faults in Fate

Eternity's Awakening

Standalones

Birds of Paradise

Doyenne

Printed in Poland
by Amazon Fulfillment
Poland Sp. z o.o., Wrocław